D0035914

Praise for Bridget Collins
and
The Betrayals

"Dizzyingly wonderful. . . . Collins summons a Gormenghast-esque richness of place and people . . . a perfectly constructed work of fiction, with audacious twists that clumsier hands would fumble, and irresistibly moving emotional beats. . . . Nabokov called fiction a 'game of worlds,' and Collins plays her own game here with perfect skill."

—Sarah Ditum, *The Times* (UK)

"A surreal epic."

—POPSUGAR

"Another sumptuous act of imaginative world-building. . . . If you're looking for an absorbing, transporting work of fiction—and why would you not be?—*The Betrayals* is just the thing. . . . Settle in, and enjoy getting lost in this captivating book."

—*The Observer* (UK)

"Ingenious. . . . Collins's story holds everything up its sleeve for as long as possible."

—*The Guardian* (UK)

"Brilliant . . . a captivating, imaginative tale."

—*Woman & Home* (UK)

"A storyteller of rare imagination. . . . Both a disturbing portrait of fascism and a soaring meditation on artistic expression."

—*Mail on Sunday* (UK)

"More lavish magical escapism from the unit-shifting author of *The Binding*."

—*Irish Independent* (Ireland)

"The reader is in for a treat: all these mysteries converge in shocking, suspenseful ways. By the time the novel draws to a close, the weave of the story and the tight net of a powerful rivals-to-lovers romance will have captured the reader in their web."

—*Booklist*

"A unique, unexpected, and beautifully unsettling story . . . gorgeously beguiling and totally addictive."

—Joanna Glen, author of *The Other Half of Augusta Hope*

"She's done it again: this is another triumph from the incomparable imagination of Bridget Collins. *The Betrayals* sinks its teeth into you and won't let you go. It's a mesmerizing, intimate, and ambitious story about art, love, and what it means to be human. If you loved *The Binding*, you'll adore *The Betrayals*."

—Erin Kelly, internationally bestselling author of *He Said/She Said*

"It's just beautiful—written with such elegance and poise. What I love about Bridget's books is her ability to write the most magical worlds of escapism and yet anchor those worlds very much in today."

—Joanna Cannon, internationally bestselling author of *The Trouble with Goats and Sheep*

"*The Betrayals* is a beautiful dystopian romance about coming of age as an artist and the love affair artistic collaboration can be, while also being an acute political novel about the fate of spiritual values in a totalitarian system. A rich delight."

—Sandra Newman, author of *The Heavens* and *The Country of Ice Cream Star*

Praise for
The Binding

"A dark chocolate slice of cake with a surprising, satisfying seam of raspberry running through it. . . . Spellbinding."

— Tracy Chevalier, bestselling author of *Girl with a Pearl Earring*

"Succeeds in creating the magic it proposes."

— Naomi Novik, *New York Times Book Review*, Editors' Choice

"*The Binding* held me captive from the start and refused to set me free. It's a beautifully crafted tale of dark magic and forbidden passion, where unspeakable cruelty is ultimately defeated by enduring love. Breathtaking!"

— Ruth Hogan, author of *The Keeper of Lost Things*

"Everyone keeps calling this novel spellbinding and they are not wrong! A true epic in every sense of the word."

— *Cosmopolitan*

"Spellbinding."

— *USA Today*

THE BETRAYALS

ALSO BY BRIDGET COLLINS

The Binding

YOUNG ADULT FICTION WRITING AS B. R. COLLINS

Love in Revolution

MazeCheat

The Broken Road

Gamerunner

Tyme's End

A Trick of the Dark

The Traitor Game

THE
BETRAYALS

A Novel

WITHDRAWN

BRIDGET COLLINS

WILLIAM MORROW
An Imprint of HarperCollins*Publishers*

This is a work of fiction. Names, characters, places, and incidents are products of the author's imagination or are used fictitiously and are not to be construed as real. Any resemblance to actual events, locales, organizations, or persons, living or dead, is entirely coincidental.

P.S.™ is a trademark of HarperCollins Publishers.

THE BETRAYALS. Copyright © 2021 by Collins Chapterhouse Ltd. All rights reserved. Printed in the United States of America. No part of this book may be used or reproduced in any manner whatsoever without written permission except in the case of brief quotations embodied in critical articles and reviews. For information, address HarperCollins Publishers, 195 Broadway, New York, NY 10007.

HarperCollins books may be purchased for educational, business, or sales promotional use. For information, please email the Special Markets Department at SPsales@harpercollins.com.

Originally published in the United Kingdom in 2020 by The Borough Press.

A hardcover edition of this book was published in 2021 by William Morrow, an imprint of HarperCollins Publishers.

FIRST WILLIAM MORROW PAPERBACK EDITION PUBLISHED 2022.

Designed by Bonni Leon-Berman

Library of Congress Cataloging-in-Publication Data has been applied for.

ISBN 978-0-06-283814-8

22 23 24 25 26   LSC   10 9 8 7 6 5 4 3 2 1

For Sarah Ballard

But that the present order of things was not to be taken for granted, that it presupposed a certain harmony between the world and the guardians of culture, that this harmony could always be disrupted, and that world history taken as a whole by no means furthered what was durable, rational and beautiful in the life of men, but at best only tolerated it as an exception—all this they did not realize.

—*The Glass Bead Game*, Hermann Hesse,
trans. Richard and Clara Winston

THE BETRAYALS

Part One

SEROTINE TERM

1

THE RAT

Tonight the moonlight makes the floor of the Great Hall into a game board. Every high window casts a bright lattice, dividing the hall into black and white, open squares and margins. The ranks of wooden benches face one another on three sides; in the space between them, there is nothing but straight shadows on stone, an abstract in pen and ink. It is as still as a held breath. For once, not even an eddy of wind rattles the windows or hums in the great hearth. No dust dances over the dark-barred floor. The empty benches wait. If ever the hall was ready for the first move of a *grand jeu,* it's now: midnight, silence, this geometry of light. Someone else would know how to play, how to begin.

But tonight there is only the Rat, shivering a little in her thread-bare shirt, her arms tight around her rib cage. She stretches one scrawny foot in and out of the light, thinking, *Dark, pale, dark, pale.* She narrows her eyes at the sheen on her toenails. She is listening for footsteps; but then, she is always listening for footsteps. She is hungry; but then, she's always hungry. She has forgotten to notice those things. She scrunches her toes. The stone is cold. The stone is always cold; even in summer the thin-aired nights are chilly, and the daytime heat doesn't have time to seep through the walls. But to-night she notices it, because she has spent the day just gone under the eaves—sweltering breathless under hot slates, watching threads of gold creep over her sweaty knees as the sun dipped. She presses the ball of her foot down and relishes the chill. Cold stone, cold bone. She would like to pocket it and suck on it through the long days of hiding. But it is late heat this year. This is the end of summer.

Yesterday the gray ones were unlocking doors, opening windows, sweeping grit and dry leaves out of fireplaces. Today they were bustling with their baskets on wheels, making beds, flapping sheets full of the stink of soap and lavender. Tomorrow they will be cleaning on the other side of the courtyard, scrubbing the floors and clanking buckets. They will grumble to one another and smell of sweat. The young ones will slip sideways to blow smoke from windows. The Rat always hides, but soon she will be hiding harder. And then there will be the black ones, the male ones, loud and greedy. There will be more food and more danger. For a few weeks she will move more in the chimneys and less in the corridors. Then as the days dwindle, the fires will be lit and she will use the ledges and roofs and the gaps in the walls, or move only at night to the kitchen and back. She will sleep and shiver through the long snows. This is the way the year turns.

For no reason she steps farther into the hall. Moonlight spills up her ankles. She will not enter the space between the benches, but she stands on the edge of it. There is a line of silver framing the bare rectangle, like a runnel of mercury between the stones. She raises one foot, but she is only testing herself. She already knows she will not cross it. Someone else would; someone else would step forward with an opening gambit ready, bow to the empty benches. But she is the Rat, and she wouldn't know a gambit from a claw mark on the wall. All she knows about this place is that it isn't hers. To the Rat, the silver line is a wire, the space a trap waiting to snap shut on her. It is so alien it makes her scalp crawl. The silence stretches.

There's no wind outside. But suddenly there's a gasp and a whisper in the chimney, a half beat of indistinct noise like fabric tearing. The

Rat whips around, poised to run. Something drops into the hearth, flapping and scratching. A dry fan of feathers, moving. Talons scrape on the stone. The small sounds echo, magnified by the stillness. An inhuman voice calls to her, fierce and plangent. For a moment she stays where she is, frozen. Then she takes a step toward the hearth, so slowly she feels every bone in her foot where it meets the floor.

An eagle owl on the hearthstone. It is small: not a chick but a fledgling, still blurred around the edges with the last of its down. But the savage eyes stare at her, unblinking. Its head bobs and it calls again, a rising hopeless note like a question. The wings open into an awkward lopsided spread of feathers. It hops and folds back into itself. A line of moonlight falls across its back, so bright the Rat can see the ghost of brown and cream in its plumage, the fiery glint in its eye. It tries again to fly: the same painful flutter, the same sharp, flinching defeat. She watches.

It tries again and again. It quavers a long note, louder now. Echoes hum in the walls, on the edge of audibility. She imagines the nest it came from, bare stone at the top of a tower or a buttress, high and out of reach. Somewhere there will be a mother owl. Until now the fledgling has been safe. Until now it has been fed and watched over. It goes on calling, as if someone will help. Every time it tries to stretch its wings, she feels a prickle in her chest.

The clock strikes on the far side of the courtyard, a pure single note.

She crosses to the hearth and the fledgling bates. She pauses until it calms again. She glances at the strong claws as they clutch and clutch on the hearthstone. She waits until she is ready. Then she crouches and reaches out, quick as a blink, and both hands grasp slippery-soft feathers with thin light bones beneath. She adjusts her grip and twists.

There is a snap. The Rat is alone again.

She stands up. She drops the fledgling. Some instinct deeper than logic makes her expect a noise like breaking glass; but whatever sound it makes as it hits the floor is drowned out by the rush of blood in her ears. She doesn't kill things very often. It has made her pulse rise into a drumbeat, a booming stutter in her head that won't slow down. She uncurls her hands. Somehow there is blood on them. A scratch across her knuckles starts to sting. At one end, where it's deepest, a dark bead swells, overflows and runs down her wrist. She puts her hand to her mouth and sucks at the broken skin, tasting iron. Her heartbeat trembles in her bones as if they're hollow.

There are footsteps in the passage. For a fraction of a second the Rat thinks the rhythm of her heart has doubled or tripled. But she is always listening; it takes only that split second to hear the difference between the hot thick thump of her heart and the click of shoes on stone. She scrats a foothold in the side of the hearth and swings herself up into the chimney, bracing herself with her back and feet, muscles taut, deep in the darkest shadow. There is a movement in the doorway, a flick of a pale robe. The Rat closes her eyes, wary of the moonlight reflecting off them. It is too late to climb higher; any movement will make a noise.

The figure walks forward into the room. The footsteps pause. The Rat breathes shallowly, her ribs tight with the effort of silence. Her nose is full of the scent of old ash. A long time—a minute, a second—passes. Then she can't help herself and opens her eyes a slit. She stares through the flickering smudge of her eyelashes. She recognizes the figure in white: the female. All the ones in white are male except this one. The female-male, the odd one out. She is standing where the Rat stood: on the edge of the space, poised behind the silver line. She is looking at the moonlight, too. But whatever she sees, it is not what the Rat saw. The Rat clenches her teeth. Her muscles are aching.

The white one makes a movement. It is a strange cutoff gesture, the beginning of something and its end, both at once. It is like a thread linked to her wrist. She lets her hand drop and is still again.

Then, as if the Rat has made a noise, she looks around. The silence snaps taut. The Rat freezes, pulling deeper into the shadow. Her breath catches. Something tickles the underside of her forearm. A line of wetness is crawling from her wrist toward her elbow, dark on her pale skin. Any moment now it will drip.

The white one frowns. She tilts her head, as if to see a different angle of light and shadows. In the moonlight her face is a vertical half mask. Her mouth opens.

The drop of blood falls. There is an instant when the Rat feels its absence, the infinitesimal lightening of her body. Then it ticks on the floor.

"Who's there?"

The Rat doesn't move. If the white one comes closer, she will claw her way upward, climb frantically until she reaches the narrowing in the chimney where she can brace herself and rest. But every movement will send a rain of old soot and mortar down into the hearth, and then they will know she is here. They will search and peer and drag her out. There will be men with hands, faces with eyes. They will try to make her human and hate her when they fail. She knows enough about the world to know that.

"Is someone there?"

Sometimes the gray ones have seen her. A glimpse, a flash, a half print in the dust. But no one listens to them when they say either there is a girl in the walls or the school is haunted. They would believe this one.

The white one takes another step. The shadows slide over her. She sees the owl in its fractured huddle on the hearthstone. She stops.

The Rat is shaking all over now. Her shoulders burn. Sweat is soaking into her shirt, the hot smell of herself wafting from armpits and scalp. Her hand stings. There is a loose stone beside her head, where a tall man could reach. If she reached for it, she would fall. But she would fall with it in her hand. It is heavy enough, big enough to crack a skull. Her heartbeat accelerates, so loud she is sure the white one will hear. If the white one hears . . .

The Rat's fingers curl against the stone. Grit pushes into the tender space under her nails.

The white one turns away. One moment she is there, staring into the Rat's shadow with a line between her eyebrows: then she is gone, out of the doorway in a whirl of white, moonlit to dark in an instant. Her footsteps fade.

The Rat waits. After a long time she lets herself down. Her bare feet press the floor. She stretches her arms slowly, knowing better than to relax. Even when one danger is past, there is always another. But at least she can breathe freely. She is glad that she didn't have to kill the white one. The thought is like a newly missing tooth: she explores the shape of it. Perhaps she isn't glad. Perhaps she is disappointed.

She shakes herself. Glad, disappointed . . . She is the Rat. Life is simple for rats. She does what she has to, no more or less. More and less are for humans. More and less are this hall, the empty space, the white one's gesture-that-was-not-a-gesture. The Rat has no part in that. She will not be human, no matter what happens. Only tonight the moonlight tempted her in.

Her foot brushes the dead owl. A rat would sniff it and leave it: scarce tricky flesh, bony and unappetizing. It is easier to steal food from the kitchens, and she has no other use for a bundle of bones and feathers. But she picks it up. She crosses the hall with it swinging from her hand. She knocked the setting clot off her hand when she lowered her feet to the floor, and now she feels a fresh tickle of blood rolling down between her fingers. The scratch itself is throbbing. She will steal wine and honey from the kitchen, clean it and wrap it in a rag; even a rat would choose not to lose its paw.

The moon has moved. The rectangles of caged light have swept around and up, folding into the right angle of walls and floor. Now the middle of the floor is dark, and the line of silver is hidden. Soon the mountain will swallow the moon completely, and the hall will be dark, the game board extinguished. There will be no *grand jeu* tonight.

The Rat doesn't give herself time to think; or perhaps it is the new gap in her head—the thought of a stone in her hand—that nudges her over the invisible boundary without hesitating. She crouches and puts the dead fledgling down in the middle of the space. She spreads the wings into a lopsided fan of feathers. The dark lies on it like dust. Blood drips from her hand onto the floor beside her toes. She looks up, but from here she can't see the moon, only the bleached blue-black sky and the hump of the mountain.

She gets to her feet and stares into the darkness as if she is meeting someone's gaze. Another drop of blood falls, but she seems not to notice it. She is listening for something else, something she doesn't understand. Then she steps backward out of the space, opening her arms wide, like an invitation.

2

LÉO

When Léo wakes, there's a theme running through his head. For a second he can't place it. It could be a dream: an elusive melody, a shape that broadens into something abstract, a fragment of poetry with the sting of a half-remembered association. He rolls over, squeezing his eyes shut as if he can retreat into sleep, but it's no good. It echoes in his brain, exasperating, taunting him. Then abruptly he recognizes it. The bloody *Bridges of Königsberg*. It mingles with the noise of a door banging and plates clattering in the kitchen below. That must have been what woke him; otherwise he'd have slept late, drowsing uneasily after a night of near insomnia.

He pulls the bedclothes more tightly around his shoulders, but now that he's awake, he's cold. The blankets are scratchy and thin, and the pillow feels damp to the touch. Last night the proprietor gave him a confidential smile as he said, "The Arnauld Suite, sir. I must say, it is an honor," and the maid looked at him sideways as she showed him the room, expecting him to be impressed by the draperies and the heavy gilt-framed portraits of *grand jeu* masters. But there are clusters of dark spots on the headboard where bedbugs are nesting in the cracks, and the mattress sags in the middle like a hammock. Every time he turned over in the night, it jangled and creaked, and now there's a spring digging into his ribs. At this moment, Chryseïs will be spread-eagled under sheets of Egyptian cotton, taking up the whole of their bed. She'll still be asleep, golden hair tangled, an errant smudge of eye-black smeared across her temple, while the curtains billow at the open French window and the scent of hot dust and traffic fumes mingles with the fragrance of roses on the mantelpiece. Sometimes he feels like summer in the city will choke him, but right now, in this mildewed room, he'd give a year's salary to be there, back in his old life. He drags his hands over his face, trying to wipe away the sticky feeling of not having slept properly, and sits up. The theme of the *Bridges of Königsberg* reasserts itself in his head. It's like a stuck record, the move between the melody and the first development of the Eulerian path, then back to that infuriating tune . . . Out of all the games to get into his head, it has to be one he can't stand. He gets out of bed, pulls on his trousers and shirt, and rings for shaving water. "And coffee," he adds as the maid bobs a curtsy and turns to leave. She swings back to him, so eager she almost stumbles, and he notices without caring that they've sent him the prettiest one. "Coffee first. Make sure it's hot."

"Yes, sir. Of course, sir. Will there be anything else?"

"No. Thank you." He sits down next to the window, his back to her. Churlish, but what does it matter? He's not a politician anymore.

The coffee, when it arrives, is terrible—half chicory, half burnt—but at least it's nearly as hot as he likes it, hot enough to warm his hands through the cup. He sips it slowly, watching the sky change color over the houses opposite. The sun hasn't come up over the mountains yet, and the street outside is still dim, even though it's almost eight o'clock. He should be at home in his study, halfway through his second pot, absorbed in one of Dettler's reports; it gives him an uneasy, itchy sensation, to be sitting here with nothing to do. He was buggered if he was going to trudge up the mountain at dawn, as if he were a student; yesterday he deliberately ordered the car for after lunch, but already he's at a loss, shifting in his musty-smelling chair, wondering whether he's hungry enough to ring for breakfast.

How is he going to pass the hours? He winces; the question makes him think of Chryseïs, standing there on the balcony staring at him, the evening after his meeting with the Chancellor. "What am I going to do?" she said, and he almost laughed at her predictability.

"Have another martini, I imagine," he said.

She hardly blinked. "While you're away," she said. She fished in her glass with a scarlet-lacquered fingernail, drew out the tiny coil of orange peel, and flicked it over her shoulder into the street. "What do you expect me to *do*?"

"I'll still be paying the rent on the flat."

"You think I should stay here alone?"

"At least until you find someone better." It would have been kinder to say *somewhere,* but he wasn't feeling kind. "You'll be all right."

"Oh, thank you. I appreciate your concern." She tilted her head and stared at him, but for once he didn't feel any answering spark, just weariness. "Jesus Christ, Léo! I can't—"

"I've told you not to say that."

"Oh, not that again. I'm hardly saying the rosary, am I? What are you going to do, report me to the Register?" She pushed past him, knocking him with her elbow. She'd had her hair freshly marcelled, and a whiff of chemicals caught the back of his throat. "I can't believe you fucked this up. I thought you were supposed to be the government's golden boy. Didn't the Old Man say you were—"

"Apparently not."

"You bloody fool, how could you? You're a coward, that's what it is—now that the Party's in power, you can't stand the pressure—completely *spineless*." She kicked viciously at the leg of the chaise longue. Liquid slopped out of her martini glass and splashed on her dress. "Shit! This is new."

"I'll buy you another one." He crossed the room to the cocktail cabinet and poured himself a whisky. They'd run out of ice, but he didn't ring for more.

"You'd better. And pay the rest of the bill while you're at it." Her voice cracked. She collapsed on a chair. "Oh, look at me, dressed to the nines . . . I thought he was going to promote you—after Minister for Culture I thought, *Finally he's going to get something important.* I got all ready to *celebrate*."

"So celebrate." They stared at each other. Perhaps if he'd said the right thing, she might have softened; but then, if she had softened, he couldn't have borne it.

She got up. She drank the last of her martini in one go and reached for her wrap. "Have a lovely holiday, Léo," she said, and left.

Now he tries to shrug off the memory. Of all the things he's left behind, Chryseïs is the least of his worries. She's better off than he is, yawning and sitting up in bed, pulling on her negligée and ringing for hot chocolate. She'll be fine. And even if she won't be, would he care that much? He turns away from the thought. A month ago, he'd imagined proposing to her: the breathless articles in society papers, the flash of an extravagant diamond on her left hand, the Old Man's congratulations. Now . . .

There's a tap on the door. It makes him jump; when the door opens, he's on his feet, and the maid flinches. "I'm sorry, sir, I thought I heard you say to come in."

"Of course. Yes. Thank you." He waits until she's gone before he crosses to the washstand and splashes his face, blowing air out through his mouth until his heartbeat settles and water soaks his collar. He's not afraid; there's nothing to be afraid of. But sometimes moments catch him off guard: the unexpected knock, the car going too fast as he crosses the road, the glint of metal as a drunkard sways into his path and reaches languidly for a hip flask. Ever since the meeting with the Chancellor. Ever since the Chancellor looked at him with that expression, weighing up how much he was worth. He can still feel the chill of it—as though halfway through a shooting party, a friend had swung his gun casually to point it into Léo's face. And a split second behind, the humiliation that he'd been such a bloody fool not to see it coming, to think it was all a friendly, civilized game . . . To have walked into the office a little nervous, of course—like being brought up in front of the Magister Scholarium—but sure that the Old Man would come round, only slightly disconcerted when it was the Chancellor and not the Old Man himself who was sitting behind the desk with Léo's letter in front of him. "Ah, Léo," he said. "Thank you for coming. I trust I haven't interrupted anything?"

"I'm sure Dettler can manage without me for an hour."

"Well, we must certainly hope so." He picked up the telephone. "Tea, please. Yes, two cups. Thank you. Sit down, Léo."

He sat. The Chancellor folded his hands and bowed his head as if he was about to say a prayer. "Léo," he said at last, "thank you for your letter. We all admire your passion and your energy, you know that. And it is in a young man's nature to be forthright. So thank you for your honesty."

"As Minister for Culture, I felt it was only right to ask if I could talk things through with the Prime Minister before the bill goes to the vote."

"Naturally. And he was very sorry he couldn't be here today. I know he was very interested in your point of view. He asked me to say that he admires your courage."

Perhaps it was then that the first misgiving slid coldly down Léo's spine. "The proposals are quite extreme, Chancellor. All I was suggesting was that we reconsider—"

"He was also rather . . . surprised." The Chancellor glanced past him at the door. "Come in. Ah, biscuits! Good girl. Yes, put it down there. On the coffee table." The secretary began to unload her tea tray, and the Chancellor gestured to the sofa. "Léo, please . . ."

Léo got up, crossed to the sofa, and sat down again; but the Chancellor hesitated and walked to the window, gazing out with his hands behind his back. "What was I saying?"

"You said the Old M——that the Prime Minister was interested in what I wrote."

"A better phrase would be *taken aback,* I think." He waved a hand at the glinting array of china. "Please don't stand on ceremony, young man. Help yourself to a cup of tea."

Léo poured a cup of tea, added lemon, stirred it, and raised it to his lips. Then he put the cup and saucer down, conscious of the tension in his wrist. How many times, sitting here with the Old Man, had he heard the telltale rattle of porcelain as other men tried to master their shaking hands? But this was different; *he* was different. It was simple hospitality, surely——not a test, not an ordeal.

When he looked up, the Chancellor was smiling at him. "Ah, Léo, my dear boy. Well, not really a boy——forgive me, the privilege of age . . . How old are you, remind me? Twenty-eight, twenty-nine?"

"Thirty-two."

"Really? Well, never mind . . ." He turned to look out of the window, idly tugging at the curtain cord. "The point is, Léo," he said, "that your letter was rather unfortunate."

Léo didn't answer. For a vertiginous, dislocated moment he expected the Chancellor to draw the curtains across, as if someone had died.

"To put it frankly . . . We are disappointed, Léo. You seemed to have such a promising career in front of you. We were confident in your abilities. Here is a young man, we thought, who can help bring the country into a new, prosperous, liberated era, who understands the Party's vision, who will lead the next generation when we are too old to carry the burden anymore . . . I thought you shared that dream, Léo."

The past tense was like a needle, digging deeper and deeper. "I do, Chancellor——I absolutely share the Party's ideals."

"And yet your letter suggests that you do not."

"Only this one particular——this one section of the bill . . ."

"You find the measures to be—what was your phrase?—'irrational and morally repugnant,' in fact."

"Did I? I don't remember saying repug—"

"Please, feel free—if you would like to refresh your memory." The Chancellor waved toward the desk. The letter was there, on the blotter, Léo's signature a dark scrawl at the bottom. There was a pause.

Léo swallowed. His mouth had gone very dry. He shook his head. "I may have been slightly too emphatic, Chancellor. I apologize if I—"

"No, no, dear boy." The Chancellor flicked his hand at the words. For an instant, Léo almost saw them dropping to the carpet like dead flies. "Too late. I regret your impulsivity as much as anyone, but it serves no purpose to dwell on it." Finally he turned and met Léo's eyes. It was the way Léo's father looked at broken objects in his scrapyards, wondering whether they were worth the space they took up. "The question is," he said, "what do we do with you now?"

"I—what? You mean—"

"We cannot possibly have a cabinet minister who is lukewarm about our policies." The Chancellor frowned. "You are an astute politician, Léo, you must understand that."

"Hardly *lukewarm.*"

"Please." He held up his hand. "I am as sorry as you are, believe me. As is the Old Man. But if we cannot trust you . . ."

"Chancellor, please . . . I honestly don't think—"

"Be quiet." The bell of an ambulance clattered past, distantly. Léo's mouth tasted bitter, but he didn't trust himself to lift his cup of tea without spilling it. The Chancellor strode to the desk, picked up a piece of paper, and put it down on the low table in front of Léo. A letter. *To whom it may concern . . .* "Here is a letter of resignation." He put a fountain pen down next to it. "Be sensible, Léo. If you read it, you will find that we have made matters easy for you. In recognition of the work you have done for the Party. The Old Man is fond of you, you know. I think you will agree it is an elegant solution."

He had to blink to make the words come into focus: *honored to have served . . . contribution to the Prime Minister's vision . . . glorious prosperity, unity and purity . . . but others are better fitted . . . in my heart of hearts, I have always yearned . . .* He looked up. "I don't understand."

"I would have thought it was fairly self-explanatory."

"You're saying—you want me to say . . ."—he stopped and looked again at the letter—"'I am proud to have done my best as Minister for Culture, but it is as a humble student of the *grand jeu* that I long to leave my mark.' What is this?"

The Chancellor sat down opposite him. He poured a cup of tea and tapped the spoon on the gilt edge of the cup with a brittle ting. "You were the only second-year ever to win a Gold Medal at Montverre, were you not?"

"You know I was. Is that relevant?" It sounded more belligerent than he meant it to.

"You have played a very highly regarded part in the election of this government, Léo. But you were never cut out to be a politician. Although you repressed your personal wishes for as long as you could, in order to help bring about the greatest political success of this century, you have never been able to forget the dream of going back to Montverre to study our national game. Now that the country's future is assured, you finally have the opportunity . . . It is a touching story, the artist returning to his roots, fulfilling his vocation. Who knows, it's possible you will be of use to us there."

"But I don't—"

The Chancellor put his teacup down. It was a smooth movement, almost casual, and yet it made Léo flinch. "Either you are being deliberately obtuse," he said, "or you are a complete idiot. Which, until yesterday, I would have sworn you were not." He sighed. "I don't know how much more clearly I can put this."

Léo heard himself say, "Perhaps in words of one syllable."

The Chancellor raised his eyebrows. "You have a very simple choice. Either you sign this letter, tell the papers the same story, and retire to Montverre for as long as we deem it necessary, or the Prime Minister will be forced to deal with you more . . . forcefully."

"You mean someone will find me in a ditch with my throat cut?" He meant this as a joke. But the words sat leaden in the silence, solid and monstrous, until he realized it hadn't been a joke at all. He fumbled to get the cap off the fountain pen and signed the letter without reading the rest of it. His signature was hardly recognizable. Underneath the first copy was another. He paused, without looking up. "There are two of these."

"One is for you to keep. For future reference. We'll see about arrangements for Montverre—it'll be a few weeks, I imagine. Your resignation will be formally accepted then. In the meantime, Dettler will carry out your duties." The Chancellor took a sip of tea. "It goes without saying that you won't attempt to interfere with the progress of the bill."

"I see." He hesitated. Then he put the lid back on the pen, focusing on his fingers as if only his eyes could tell him what they were doing. "Chancellor . . . please believe that I had no intention—"

The Chancellor got to his feet. "I don't think I need keep you any longer."

Léo folded the second copy of the letter and put it in his jacket pocket, next to his heart. Then he stood up, too. Somewhere a phone was ringing, a secretary was typing, the business of state was rolling on. It was as if he'd taken his hands off a keyboard and heard the music continue. He straightened his tie. "Well . . . thank you, Chancellor. If we don't see each other again, good luck with government."

"Thank *you,* Léo. I hope our paths will cross again eventually." The Chancellor made his way to the desk and sat down, reaching for his address book. "Good afternoon, Léo. From now on, if I were you, I would be very, very careful."

Léo shut the door behind him. The secretary—Bella—glanced up at him and then quickly down again. He smiled at her, but she kept her head down, scribbling something in a notebook. When he walked past her desk he saw over her shoulder that it was a tangle of meaningless lines, not even shorthand.

He came out onto the landing. Two civil servants climbed the stairs, halfway through a conversation: ". . . measures only reflect the times," the first said, and broke off to nod at him. Automatically he nodded back; then, with a jolt, he saw that the second, lagging a little behind, was Émile Fallon. It was too late to duck away. Instead he said, "Émile, long time no see, how are you? I'm afraid I must dash," all in one tight breath.

"Ah, Minister," Émile said, "yes, indeed, let's catch up soon," twisting mid-step to give Léo a sliding smile as he passed. There was something worse than straightforward malice in his face: irony, maybe, or—oh, god, worst of all—compassion. Clearly news of Léo's resignation had already spread to the Ministry for Information. Léo waited for them to disappear through the door, holding his own smile in place as if it was a physical test.

He was alone. Cadaverous portraits of statesmen watched him impassively from the walls. The dark carpet muffled every sound; he might have gone deaf. He leaned against the wall; then he slid down into a crouch, his blood singing in his ears, nausea wringing sweat from every pore. His chest hurt. The air made a faint rasping sound as it went in and out of his lungs. He shut his eyes.

Slowly the sickness eased. He pushed himself back to his feet and placed one hand on the wall, fighting for balance. If anyone saw him like this, if the Chancellor emerged or Émile came back . . . He stood up straight, wiped his face on his sleeve, and smoothed his hair. Now only his damp collar could give him away, and it was a warm day; he would walk past the girl in the lobby downstairs and she wouldn't look twice. He could pretend that nothing had happened—that in fact he had sent in his resignation, explained himself to the Chancellor, and been set free. He almost believed it himself.

But when he reached the half landing, something made him look back. There on the wallpaper, almost black on the green pattern, was a dark smear: the mark his sweaty hand had left as he tried not to throw up.

He shaves, puts on his jacket and tie, and orders more coffee. The maid offers him breakfast, but he can't bring himself to accept. By the time he's drunk the coffee, the sun has cleared the houses and is shining into the street. Warmth creeps along the floor, reaching out for him. He can't sit here all morning. He walks to the railway station and buys a paperback novel from the bookstall. There's a line of porters waiting for the first train; the third- and second-years must have gone up last week, a few days apart, and today it's the first-years' turn to flood the town for a night. The train arrives as the bookseller gives Léo his change. He pauses, squeezing the coins in his hand, watching the young men pile excitedly onto the platform. There are a few families, too—bluestocking sisters, proud mamas, mulish younger brothers—who've come along to give their clever boys a good send-off and get a few days of mountain air while they're at it. They're not allowed up to the school, of course, and they probably won't even be awake to wave goodbye tomorrow when the new scholars slog up the path at dawn. "Oh, how lovely," a woman calls to her son, staring across the valley toward Montverre-les-Bains. She points at the Roman bathhouse in the distance. "That must be *it*."

Léo shoves his change into his pocket. He bends his head as he joins the stream of people surging through the ticket office, afraid that someone will recognize him, but they're all too intent on themselves. They have to summon taxis, load their trunks, find the grandly named hotels before the sun gets too fierce. No one looks twice at Léo. He ducks into a grimy little café and watches until the square in front of the station is empty again, waiting in the quiet sunshine for the next train. There's a newspaper on the bar, and he catches sight of the headline: *Minister for Culture's Shock Resignation.* But he doesn't reach for it. Dettler showed him a draft a couple of days ago. "If there are any suggestions you would like to make, Minister?" he said, offering Léo a blue pencil with a funeral director's delicacy. "It'll be in Monday's paper; that way you'll be safely—that is, you won't be too troubled by the attention." But Léo waved the pencil away. He didn't care anymore what they said about him, and he still doesn't.

He drags his eyes away from the paper, sits down at a table in the window, and opens the cheap novel he's bought. It's a translation from the English, a detective story: the sort of thing Chryseïs devours in one go, curled on the chaise longue with a box of chocolate creams. He doesn't know what made him buy it, except that he can't think of any other way to pass the time. But after he's read the first page three times, he sets it aside. When the National Heritage Bill goes through, fiction will be taxed to the hilt and foreign fiction will be virtually unaffordable, even for people like him. What was it the Old Man said? *We must find ways to cherish and protect our national game, which—as you know, Léo—is so much more than a game . . .* At the time Léo thought he was right; or at least not wrong enough to warrant disagreement. He never disagreed with the Old Man; that was how he rose so high, so quickly. Not until the Culture and Integrity Bill.

He gets up. The waiter, who has been slouching in the shadows doing a crossword, jumps to his feet and says, "What can I get you, sir?" but Léo is already slipping out the door. The station clock chimes ten. Only ten! Maybe he'll get the car sent early. He walks up the hill toward the Palais Hotel, but when he gets there, the foyer is full of people. A portly woman in a plumed hat is gesturing fiercely at the proprietor. "His father stayed in the Arnauld Suite thirty years ago," she says. "I requested it especially—yes, but *why* hasn't the maid been able to . . . ?" Léo turns aside without bothering to listen to the rest. He walks up the street until he reaches the end, a little run-down church and a few ramshackle houses. A path leads up into the forest, climbing steeply, but there's no signpost. It might be a shortcut to the school, or it might be merely a goatherd's track to the high pastures or Montverre-les-Bains. It's not the road he slogged up on foot as a scholar at the beginning of every term—the road he'll be driven up this afternoon, while the gradient pushes him back in his seat and the chauffeur winces at every pothole. He can pause here, leaning on a tumbledown wall, without being reminded of anything.

He shuts his eyes. The sun is bright through his eyelids. He wonders whether the Palais does a decent lunch, or whether it'll be the same indigestible mixture of cheese and stodge that they gave him for dinner. "The best hotel in Montverre, sir," Dettler's new secretary had said as she held out his tickets and itinerary the day before yesterday, without meeting his eyes. "I do hope it will be suitable." Part of him wants to write a terse note to her, suggesting that if she wants to ingratiate herself with Party officials, he doesn't recommend exposing them to bedbugs and heartburn; but it's not worth it, as now he's not even a Party official.

Anyway, he's spoiled. The first time he stayed in Montverre he didn't even have a hotel room, just a bed in a smelly lean-to that was clearly a scullery for the rest of the year, in a house where the family looked at him without warmth and asked him for extra money for the soap he'd used. Yes, now he remembers—it had been one of his father's clerks who had booked it for him, which meant his father must have given instructions not to spend more than necessary. But he hadn't minded much, even though he had to walk for ten minutes in the predawn chill before he got to the signpost that first time; he can still remember looking up at it, *Scholae Ludi 5½*, and the electric jolt of realizing that at last he was really here. He'd woken up hours earlier than he needed to, determined to be the first at the school gates, and the stars were still out. The sweep of the galaxy above him was richer and clearer than he'd ever seen. He stood and breathed, glad to be alone, his head full of ambition and the *grand jeu*. He'd left his trunk at the Town Hall the day before to be picked up by the porters, so all he had to carry was a knapsack. He knocked on the signpost for luck, took a deep breath, and set off as if he had a whole range of mountains to climb before dawn.

His pace slackened quickly and the burn in his calves started to spread upward. After a while he forgot to look about him and walked in a dream, his head bowed. It nearly made him trip over his own feet when some unconscious impulse made him glance up and he saw someone on the path in front of him, in a dark uniform similar to the one he wore. The first thing he felt was outrage: *he* was going to be the first to Montverre, not this skinny youth standing still in the middle of the track, staring at nothing. The sky was deep blue now, ripe with the promise of sunrise, and the shapes of things were starting to emerge from the shadows, newly solid. It should have been beautiful, but he wanted to be alone, the first . . .

"What are you doing?"

The youth looked around. There was something unexpected about his face, something Léo couldn't put his finger on. "Looking," he said. The softness of his voice seemed to mock Léo's rudeness.

"Looking at what?"

He didn't answer. Instead he raised his arm, his hand open. Something in the grace of it reminded Léo of the opening gesture of the *grand jeu*: here, it said, is my creation, which you have no choice but to admire.

Léo squinted. "I can't see anything." Then he did.

A cobweb. It was huge, a billowing sail of silver, glinting and flickering as the breeze tugged it back and forth, stretching right across the path. Trembling on every intersection were tiny beads of dew, sparkling blue where the light from the sky caught them, dim and star-ridden in the shadows. Léo stared, full of a strange rush of elation and melancholy that was like homesickness for somewhere he'd never been. It was the feeling he got when he watched a perfect *grand jeu*—and this was as symmetrical and intricate as a game, a perfect classical game. He wanted to have discovered it himself; if this other boy hadn't been here . . .

He stepped forward—felt the infinitesimal cling of threads on his face—and through. A broken shred of gauze clung to his sleeve.

"Didn't you see? You tore right through—there was a spider's web."

"Oh," he said, picking the gray strands off his coat. "Right. Is that what you were gaping at?"

"It was beautiful," the other scholar said, as if it was an accusation.

Léo shrugged. "I have to get going," he said, and jerked his chin toward the path that led upward. "I guess I'll see you around."

He felt the scholar stare after him. But what else was he supposed to do? The cobweb was across the whole path; someone would have ripped it down eventually. He refused to let it bother him. He was on his way up to the school, and he was going to be first.

In the excitement of going through the gates and crossing the famous threshold, he had almost forgotten about that encounter. Then later, when he was trying to find his way from the scholars' corridor down to the dining hall, Felix had bounded toward him, hand outstretched, and said, all in one breath, "Are you new, too? I'm Felix Weber, I'm lost, this place is a maze, let's try this way," and they turned down a new passage as a door opened farther along. There, dark-eyed and disheveled, was the young man he'd met on the path. Automatically Léo's eyes went to the name above the door. *Aimé Carfax de Courcy.* "It's you," he said stupidly. "Hello."

"I'm Felix Weber," Felix said. "We're going to find something to eat. Are you a first-year, too?"

He glanced at Léo and then nodded. "Carfax," he said.

"Carfax de Courcy?" Léo said, pointing to the neat white-painted lettering. "De Courcy, as in the Lunatic of London Library?"

"Edmund Dundale de Courcy was my grandfather."

Léo whistled through his teeth. A perverse bolt of envy went through him. What wouldn't he have given to be here by birthright, not just exam results? He grinned, trying to conceal it. "Well, I hope the porters frisked you for matches."

Carfax looked at him, unsmiling. Without a word he pushed past them both and disappeared around the corner.

"What's the matter with him?" Léo said. He'd only been trying to be funny; surely no one should be that sensitive about something that happened decades ago? "It was a joke."

"Obviously inherited the crazy strain," Felix said and caught his eye. They both started to laugh at the same time, Felix with a high yelping giggle that echoed off the walls.

But it was true, Léo thinks now. Wasn't it? The signs were bloody obvious even then.

He opens his eyes. The sudden brightness is dazzling; he blinks and wipes away automatic tears. After a moment the bleached wavering shapes settle into houses and trees.

He catches a movement at the edge of his vision. A man moves backward into a patch of shade; a second later he drops to one knee and fumbles with his shoelaces. But although his head is bent, his eyes keep flicking back to Léo. He stays where he is for an improbably long time before he gets to his feet and lights a cigarette. The smoke drifts along the path, grayish in the sunshine.

A watcher. It shouldn't come as a surprise. But somehow it does, a sick shock of outrage rising in Léo's belly. He wants to shout or throw a stone, as though the man is a vulture he can scare away. He clenches his jaw. Stupid. Childish. Of course they'd send someone to follow him; of course they want to be sure he goes to Montverre.

Possibly it's a kind of courtesy to have let him spot the surveillance. Or a warning. Do as you're told. Otherwise there are steep cliffs and treacherous paths . . . He holds on to the fury because he knows that underneath he's afraid; and when he turns and walks down the path to the village—passing so close he nearly knocks the cigarette to the ground—it's the other man who flinches, and he's glad.

He orders the car for an hour earlier. He has lunch in the hotel restaurant, looking out at the slope of the village, watching the rising trail of steam as the next train puffs into the station and away again. More first-years pour into the streets as he sips bad coffee and brandy. At last the clock chimes, and he pays his bill and makes his way out to the car. The chauffeur has already loaded his suitcases. He gets in and shuts his eyes. The road up the mountain is as steep and bumpy as he remembered. A tune goes around and around in his head, almost but not quite keeping time with the potholes. The *Bridges of Königsberg* again. He opens his eyes and looks out of the window, trying to distract himself, but the game has taken hold of him and won't go away. The bloody tune, the move into the Eulerian path, the mathematical proof, the sweep of Prussian history . . . It's ungainly, awkward, and he's always hated it. It's the most overrated game ever played. As they drive up the final bend and come within sight of the gates, it reaches a crescendo. The chauffeur climbs out of the car and knocks on the porters' door to ask them to open the gates, and Léo gets out, too, suddenly desperate for some fresh air. The music sings in his ears. He turns to look back the way they came, down toward the valley, the forest and the scattered waterfalls, the road disappearing out of sight. It's almost the view he had from his cell when he was a scholar. The air is thinner up here and it's hard to breathe.

The gates open. The chauffeur says, "Excuse me, sir," and gets back into the driving seat.

The tune pauses and then resumes with a new venom. Léo stays where he is. In a moment he'll turn and smile at the gatekeeper, allow one of the servants to take him to his quarters, show himself to be charming and humble and achingly enthusiastic about the *grand jeu*. But this is his last moment of freedom, and he wants to make it last.

Then he realizes why, out of all the games in the world, it's the *Bridges of Königsberg* that's got stuck in his head. It's more than just his subconscious making him a snide present of a game he's always despised. It's because of the theme of the game: the impossible problem, the way it brings you back to the same bridges over and over, the way you never escape.

3

THE MAGISTER LUDI

She is standing at a window in the middle corridor, looking out over the courtyard at the Great Hall, letting the breeze cool her damp forehead and neck. She pushes one finger under the band of her cap, wishing she could take it off, irritated by the hot weight of her hair. Her undershirt is sticking to her. She has been working in the class-room behind her, enjoying the last quiet day before term begins, the calm away from the laughter and noise of the scholars, but the sweltering sun has finally driven her out. She puts her notes down on the windowsill and draws a long breath. The air that plays around her has a faint delightful chill to it. On this side, in the shade, you can smell autumn coming.

The clock chimes two. Then, droning underneath the bell, there's the slow crescendo of an engine. At first she thinks it must be the bus, struggling up the road with the first-years' trunks; but the note is too smooth, with a deep rumble in it like a cello. She turns her head to listen. The wind sings a descant in the slates of the roof. She puts her elbows on the sill and leans out to look.

The gate opens, and the sound sends a bird skirling up from the flagstones in a flash of wings. A couple of third-years—she recognizes Collins from his walk, cocky as always, which means the other must be Muller—stop in the doorway of the refectory to watch. Then, slow as a drop of crude oil, a car rolls into view. It purrs to a halt outside the Magisters' Entrance, and a man in a cap gets out, opens the trunk, and drags a leather-strapped suitcase to the door. He dumps it there, goes back to the car, and brings out two more.

She blows air out between her teeth. Where are the porters? Or the gatekeeper? There should be someone already hurrying up to explain that scholars are not allowed more than one medium-sized trunk, and that on *no account* may a car drive into the school itself—that the violation of the environs of the Schola Ludi is grounds for immediate expulsion—that use of the Magisters' Entrance is only for—

The gatekeeper comes out of the lodge. He can't miss the chauffeur and that ostentatious pile of luggage blocking the Magisters' Entrance, but he doesn't say anything. Instead he pauses and waits for another man, leading him into the courtyard with a sweeping gesture of welcome. ". . . changed too much," she hears him say, the breeze scattering his words. The man behind him emerges into the space and looks around. He's wearing a tan suit and fedora that looks out of place—absurd, in fact. Even from this angle she can make out the width of his lapels and the eau de nile handkerchief in his pocket. "Like going back in time . . . the old place . . ." she hears now as he tilts his head back to take in the height of the Great Hall; then he swivels slowly, his face tilted as if he's absorbing the grandeur of the buildings. For an instant he looks straight up at where she's standing. She catches sight of his face.

For a moment she thinks she's mistaken. She holds on to the sill, so still she's hardly breathing.

His gaze slides over her. The gatekeeper says something and he laughs, pushing his hands into his pockets. They saunter to the Magisters' Entrance. The chauffeur tips his cap to them both and gets back into the car. He turns it in a wide half circle and drives out through the gate. No one closes it behind him. Collins and Muller cross to the middle of the courtyard and stare admiringly after the car as it goes down the road. The noise of its engine fades as Collins says, ". . . *kill* to have one like that."

She draws back from the window. She looks down at herself. Her cuffs are grimy. There's an ink stain on her thumb. Her heart is beating so hard the rest of her feels unreal: she could be floating in space, a ghost with a thundering pulse.

She doesn't know how long she stands there. When she looks out of the window again, the courtyard is empty. Someone has finally shut the gate. The suitcases outside the Magisters' Entrance have disappeared.

She picks up her notes. Distantly she remembers writing them, but the ideas have lost their clarity; it's like seeing them through a cloud of dust. All she can do now is try to find her way through to cleaner air. Her heartbeat has eased and some of the feeling has come back into her fingers and toes, but she still can't quite catch her breath. She pauses, staring out at the courtyard, chewing her lower lip. Then she turns and begins to walk down the corridor rapidly, as if she doesn't want to have time to think.

The Magister Scholarium is at his desk. He looks up when she opens the door, startled, as if it wasn't his voice that told her to come in. "Ah," he says, "Magister Dryden. Do . . ." He points at a chair, but she's already sat down. "How can I help you?"

"I saw——" She sees his eyebrows go up. She takes a deep breath, folds her hands in her lap, and starts again. "Excuse me, Magister . . . A moment ago I was looking out of the window from the top corridor, and I saw a car drive in. And I thought I saw Léonard Martin getting out. He had quite a lot of luggage with him." She is trying so hard to keep her voice low that she sounds like an automaton.

"Ah, yes," the Magister Scholarium says. "Yes, indeed. I've been meaning to have a word with you about that." He glances down at the page in front of him, hesitates, and puts the lid on his fountain pen. "You're quite right, it was Mr. Martin you saw. He's going to be staying with us for a little while. To study the *grand jeu*. I wondered whether you could possibly—"

"Staying with us? Here?"

"Indeed." He smiles at her and raises his hand to cut her off. "Now, I know it's unusual."

"Magister." She clears her throat. "We don't take guests. Of any kind. Let alone—"

"I think you'll find there is a precedent. Arnauld spent nearly two years here as a guest before he was elected Magister Ludi. In the past we have sometimes offered hospitality to those wishing to expand their understanding—foreign scholars, players . . ."

"Léonard Martin is not a *player,*" she says, struggling for control. "He's Minister for Culture."

"Not anymore, as I understand it."

"What?"

He sits back with a sigh, as if his bones ache. "I believe the announcement is in today's papers. Mr. Martin has resigned from government and intends to devote his life to studying the *grand jeu*. The Chancellor himself wrote to me on his behalf to ask if we could possibly support him in that—it having been Mr. Martin's deepest wish to return ever since he studied here."

"That's nonsense." She leans forward. She has to keep her fists clenched or she'll reach out and smash something. "I beg your pardon, Magister, but it is. Léo Martin has shown himself to be a cynical pragmatist of a politician. To allow him here—into the heart of the *grand jeu*—"

"He was a Gold Medalist, I seem to recall."

"I know that. But since then . . ." She stops, trembling on the edge.

"And I am assured that his political career is over. He will be devoting his time here to scholarship. Remind me, was there some personal connection . . . ?"

"It's not that!"

He blinks. "But then—forgive me—what *is* it?"

"It's sacrilege."

He goes very still. They stare at each other, and for a moment she can feel the weight of the *grand jeu* on her side, the tradition of the school, the stone of the very walls ranged behind her. She swallows.

"Very well, then," he says. He gets up and walks to the window, drawing the casement shut with a sharp click. "Tell me, Magister. What do you suggest?" The warmth has left his voice.

There's a silence. "I suggest sending him away."

"Perhaps you would help me draft a letter to the Chancellor to explain."

"This is no place for someone like him."

"Someone, you mean, with power?"

She opens her mouth and closes it again.

"Someone," the Magister Scholarium goes on, "with friends in government? Someone whose connections could replace me with a puppet of the Party? Or you? Who could rescind the school's privileges? Perhaps even shut it down?"

"No one could shut down the school."

"You would gamble with the very future of Montverre—of the *grand jeu,* no less—because you personally dislike a man who may not be one of us?" He raises his voice as she takes a breath to speak. "No, I concede, he is not a magister or a scholar, he will perhaps feel himself to be an outsider—but what do we lose by welcoming him? By all accounts he is a charming, erudite, intelligent man. He will be an honored guest until he gets bored—which may be very soon— whereupon he will leave of his own accord, with happy memories and a renewed affection for the school. You honestly think that is a worse alternative than refusing the Chancellor's . . . request? Which,

I may add, was hardly presented as such." He clenches his fist and brings it down slowly onto the windowsill.

She bites her tongue until her mouth floods with the taste of salt. "They want to use the *grand jeu* for their own ends," she says. "They call it our 'national game.'"

"It *is* our national game."

"Not in the way they mean it."

"Magister . . ." He breaks off and turns to look at her. "Your scruples do you credit. Truly. But we cannot avoid politics. Not even here."

"Surely we have an obligation to—"

"We do what we can. And what we must." He opens his arms, and there's something despairing in the droop of his hands. "Very well, Magister. What shall I do? If I send him away, I run the risk of far, far graver consequences—for myself, for you and the other magisters, for the scholars. I remember how strongly you felt about having a Party member on the entrance panel, and the problems we've had with accepting Christians . . . We are, I would venture to say, privileged; we're partly funded by the state, and yet we have more autonomy than the civil service or the legal profession. We were lucky to be exempt from the Culture and Integrity Act. For as long as the Party's input is merely advisory, I am grateful. It might be much worse. But what is your advice? Should I stand on principle? Please. Tell me."

There's a silence. She looks down. Her hands are so tightly interlaced that the veins in her wrists are standing out. She says, hardly loud enough to be heard, "It will be a distraction for the scholars."

"You will have to make sure they weather it."

She nods once.

"I'm glad you've seen reason." He sits down and fumbles with his pen. "I think it would be useful for you to speak to Mr. Martin as soon as possible. He has been given a room under the clock tower. He should be there now . . . He will be interested in meeting you,

I'm sure. And during his stay, from time to time, you should offer him guidance and help with the *grand jeu,* if he wants it. Tactfully."

"Yes." She ignores the cold lurch of her insides.

"Thank you." He sighs and runs his hands over his forehead. The movement pushes his cap up over one eyebrow, so that it sits at a jaunty, incongruous angle. A tuft of white hair escapes and sticks out sideways. "I know you will be able to put your feelings aside in the service of the school."

She gets to her feet. "Thank you, Magister."

He smiles at her with a vague benevolence that tells her his mind has already gone back to his work. At least she thinks so until she reaches the door; then he says unexpectedly, "Magister?"

"Yes?"

"You may not like him or what he represents. But please remember that there are always voices that speak against an outsider. There were many, for example, who spoke against you."

There are no mirrors at Montverre. That is, not officially: although among the third-years *scab-face* means a new, naive scholar who hasn't got the nerve to break the rules, and the Magister Cartae had perfectly smooth cheeks from the day he arrived, without the nicks and grazes you'd expect as he grew used to shaving by touch. It must be the only rule that affects Magister Dryden less than the men; she can still remember her first day as Magister Ludi, and the way the Magister Domus's expression turned from sympathy to surprise when she said, "I'm a woman, for god's sake, I don't need a mirror." She almost laughed. But now it's different; now she bends over a basin of water, suddenly desperate to scry her own face. The room is too dim for her to make out more than shadowy eyes and mouth. A swirl of soap scum marbles the surface. She leans closer to her reflection, imagining how she might look to someone else; then with a hiss of frustration, she crosses to the window and empties the basin onto the grass below. She turns back into the room, catches her wrist on the casement, and drops the basin with a clang. She stares at it as it rolls to a halt against the wall. In the bare room—bed, chair, closet, washstand—the stranded basin draws the eye: already the tidy austerity of her life is disrupted, ruined. She shuts her eyes and tries to summon the silence of the *grand jeu,* that empty waiting that wipes out everything but the present moment. She fails.

The clock chimes three. It brings to mind the Minister for Culture—*former* Minister for Culture—in his rooms beneath the clock tower. Her skin crawls at the thought that he's so close, within the call of the bell; but he'll be here for a long time, so she'd better get used to it. She gnaws at her lower lip. She doesn't have any choice. Sooner or later she'll have to talk to him. Better to get it over now, before she has too much time to think.

She picks up the basin and puts it back on the washstand. Then she goes down the little wooden staircase into her study and collects the books she'll need for her tutorial with Grappier at half past three, and the dusty reading glasses she uses only for Artemonian notation. When she puts them on, the world looms up in front of her, so close she takes an involuntary step backward. Never mind. If she goes now, she can be brisk, on her way to the top classroom to see Grappier, polite but unable to linger. She pulls her cap down over her forehead until her hairpins dig into her scalp. Blinking at the over-magnified world—willing away the incipient headache—she hurries out into the corridor and turns left, toward the clock tower.

The door is open. He is standing at the window, his hands in his pockets, whistling a tune that dances just out of reach, mocking her with its familiarity. She pauses, unsure whether to go in: Is this his territory or hers? Some remnant of good manners takes over, and she knocks lightly on the doorframe. He glances around briefly, his lips pursed. "Come in."

She is suddenly breathless. It's ridiculous not to have planned what to say; even more ridiculous that the idea that she's going to have to speak comes as a shock. She steps forward, but no words come.

"I'm not sure this room will be suitable," he says over his shoulder. "Does that bloody clock strike all night?"

"I——" She stares at him. This is not what she was expecting; even if her face means nothing to him, surely he should be suave, smiling, the politician she has always imagined him to be. "Yes. Every hour."

"Well then, it won't be——" He turns, stops, checks himself. "I beg your pardon. I thought . . ."

She doesn't understand; then she does. He took her for a servant. He read the subtle shape of her body before he noticed the white gown and drew his own conclusions. There was no need for the glasses, after all; he's not even observant enough to realize she's a magister as well as a woman. "I'm Magister Dryden," she says. "Welcome to Montverre."

"Magister Dryden, of course. Forgive me." But the flicker of embarrassment is gone in a second, replaced by something colder. "Yes, I should have recognized you."

Her heart thumps. "What?"

"I believe I saw your picture in the papers when you were elected. Quite the coup, an unknown woman in charge of the *grand jeu.*"

She lets her breath out slowly at the thought of his having seen that blurry, badly posed photograph, accompanied by headlines like *Brainy Little Lady Beats the Odds* or *What a Treat for the Scholars!* But she won't give him the satisfaction of seeing her wince. "Thank you," she says. "I was fortunate."

"Fortunate!" he says. "You certainly were." He turns his head sharply back to the window, craning sideways as if he's watching something at the base of the clock tower. She should be glad that he's so uninterested, that she is free to look at him without worrying that he'll look back; but a fierce, deep anger rises until she could scream. She forces herself to take an inventory of him, as though he's an object. He is good-looking, of course, but he's starting to go to seed; his beauty is dog-eared, well-thumbed, as if he's used it once too often. The blond of his hair is dull—not exactly gray, but beginning to fade—and there's a flush in his cheeks that will eventually be the fine red veining of a drunkard. Good.

"Well then," she says, "if there's nothing more—"

She shouldn't have said anything. He can't let her go like that, of her own accord: he swings back to her, his whole body this time, and suddenly the famous smile is there as if he's asking for her vote. "Magister Dryden," he says, "forgive me. I'm afraid the hotel was somewhat primitive, and I didn't sleep well . . . It's an honor to meet you."

She says nothing.

"I'm Léo Martin." He holds out his hand. "Minis—*former* Minister for Culture."

She doesn't move. "I know."

"Really?" He drops his hand with an ease that suggests he's used to being snubbed, although she imagines him storing it away for later. "I didn't think you were allowed newspapers here."

"The magisters are. If they choose."

"And you do choose . . . ? I see. Well, I congratulate you. So many people think Montverre is an ivory tower. I'm glad it isn't. Although I hope it will be a retreat for me, at least."

"Retreat from what?" She shouldn't have asked. She bobs her head, avoiding his gaze.

"Oh, you know," he says, in a tone that suggests he doesn't think she does. "Politics." His smile turns into a grin that is meant, she imagines, to be endearing. "Real life."

She is used to keeping her face blank. She nods, and glimpses his disappointment that she hasn't responded to his charm. It gives her a secret twinge of satisfaction. He should know better than to think the *grand jeu* is a refuge from life; if anything, it's the other way around. But she has more important things to do than explain that to him. "I do hope you'll enjoy your studies," she says. "The Magister Scholarium has asked me to tell you that if you need guidance, I will try to find time to help you. If I can."

His eyes flicker, but all he says is "Thank you."

"You know where the library is, of course. If there is anything else you need, please let one of the servants know."

"I will. Thank you."

She starts to leave.

"I wonder . . . have we met before? There's something about your voice."

She turns back to him. The light catches in a smear on one lens of her spectacles, but she resists the urge to clean them on her sleeve. "No, I don't believe we have."

"Well," he says, "anyway, it's a pleasure to meet you, Magister. I'll be interested to see what you can do." There's a fractional pause; then as she takes a breath to answer him, he waves a hand at her. "Don't let me keep you. I'm sure the *grand jeu* is calling."

Such casual dismissal. It would be perverse to insist on staying; she doesn't *want* his attention. But it takes all her willpower to drop her gaze and turn away.

As she does, he whistles that scrap of melody again, and with a jolt she recognizes it. The *Bridges of Königsberg*. She shoots a glance at him over her shoulder, but he's looking out the window again.

"Goodbye," she says. She feels herself relax, but just as she pauses to shut the door after herself, he stops whistling mid-bar.

"By the way," he says with a smile, "your being the first female Magister Ludi . . . I'm curious if you could tell me—would you translate it as *master* or *mistress*?"

She's walking in a dream. She looks down at her feet and suddenly the ground is black and white. She raises her head, blinking. She has

come out of the Magisters' Entrance into the courtyard. In front of
her the pattern of black and white is tinged blue by the afternoon
shadows, turning it to watered milk and charcoal. It's nothing like
the pattern the moonlight left on the floor of the Great Hall a few
days ago: and yet, in its stark clarity, it recalls exactly the sense of
a board waiting for the first move. She can't shake that feeling out
of herself; ever since that night it's been lurking, prickling in her
thumbs like the promise of a storm. She tells herself—has been telling herself—that it's merely anxiety about her Midsummer Game,
the early creep of understandable nerves: it's her first, and she hasn't
started work on it yet. That her imagination becomes overactive at
night, especially when she walks the corridors, watching the moon
slide from window to window, until she ends up in the Great Hall as
if summoned there by some silent bell. That anyone, staring into that
pale geometry of light on stone, would feel watched; that the sensation of a hostile gaze from the darkness was nothing but the silence
and chill of a night in the mountains . . . But it felt like an omen. And
now Léo Martin is here, under the same roof as her, whistling the
theme from the *Bridges of Königsberg*.

She crosses the courtyard and steps through the doorway into the
soft seasonless hush of the library. Here and there second- and third-
years are bent over their books, brows furrowed in concentration.
As she walks past one of them, he moves his hand unconsciously back
and forth as he plots a move, testing the weight of the gesture in the
air. She almost pauses to glance over his shoulder at the page in front
of him, but today she has no appetite for teaching. She makes her
way through the high bookshelves to the staircase and then up the
stairs. In daylight, this is her territory—her hunting ground, where
everything she could possibly need hides in an index or a footnote—
but after the clock strikes midnight, she's glad to leave with the last
scholars, while the bleary-eyed attendant extinguishes the lamps.
No one has been allowed here alone since the London Library was

destroyed: but even if she could, she wouldn't. On bad days it's too easy to imagine losing control, dropping a match, and the dance of flame shadows on the plaster ceiling . . . She passes the attendant's desk now and nods to him. Then she turns aside, fumbles for the key, and unlocks the narrow door of the Biblioteca Ludi, her own private library.

It smells of dust. After she has locked the door behind her, she crosses to the windows, stepping over boxes and piles of books, and pushes the casement open as far as it will go. From here she can look out over the road and the valley: somewhere out of sight is Montverre village, and beyond that, the foothills and the fertile floodplain, and somewhere, miles and miles beyond that, is home. But it's not her home anymore. She swings around, turning away from the view as if she's afraid someone is looking back at her. She takes a deep breath, frowning at the tight-packed bookshelves, the untidy floor, the draped cobweb in the corner of the ceiling that hangs so thickly she could have mistaken it for a detail in the plaster.

Once, perhaps, the Biblioteca Ludi was the secret heart of the school, a priceless collection of texts on the *grand jeu* that were too precious to be looked at by mere scholars. Some of these books are unique, illuminated in gold and lapis, chained to their shelves against the far wall; others are handwritten by the Grand Masters or are the sole surviving copies of ancient codices or contemporary notes from witnesses of classic games. But it has been years—generations— since anyone has catalogued what's here. Since then, the shelves have accumulated piles of dark-bound volumes, labeled tersely with names that even she doesn't recognize; tiny octavo notebooks crammed with Artemonian notation; and portfolios of unlabeled notes in cramped illegible writing. Some magister of the last century decided to keep not only his games but his research material: the floor is cluttered with boxes of sheet music, mathematical and scientific journals, books of philosophy and verse. Scattered among the dubious treasures chosen by her great-great-grandfathers are things that she is almost sure must have been left by mistake: a pipe, a Latin dictionary, a scholar's essay. The last time she was here, she found a dingy copy of a thirty-year-old *Gambit* next to a first edition of Philidor; she imagined Magister Holt leaving it there absent-mindedly while he searched for something else, his lumpy rheumatic fingers brushing gently along the spines. After she was appointed, she spent hours exploring, like a priestess taking possession of her domain, but her enthusiasm palled before she had even made it halfway around the room. Now she has neither the desire nor the arrogance to organize the collection: she treats it as a sort of hiding place, a tomb.

She goes to the corner farthest from the window and bends down to reach behind a bookcase, dragging out a little metal trunk. She sits back on her heels and wipes a clinging cobweb from her forehead with the inside of her wrist. Then she digs in her pocket for a key, unlocks the trunk, and lifts out a package. The old oilskin crackles as she unwraps it. It's a ledger, covered in blue-gray marbled paper like pebbles underwater; the corners and spine are scuffed leather. An inkblot bulges across the front. When it was fresh, the stain gleamed like a coin, a blue-and-copper sheen rising to the surface where the ink was thickest; but time and desiccation have dulled it to a flat black. It still leaves a smear on her finger when she brushes her hand over it, and unconsciously she raises her fingertip to her mouth and sucks it clean. She raises her eyes to the window for a second, letting her gaze linger on the sky over the valley; then she bows her head over the book and opens it.

4

FIRST DAY OF SEROTINE TERM, SECOND YEAR

I meant to get up at dawn this morning, but I overslept, so by the time I was slogging up the hill it was getting warm and I arrived at the gate thoroughly drenched in sweat. It's bloody annoying, having to walk all the way—not because I resent the exercise particularly, but because after all they've got a bus and they could perfectly well ferry us all up at the same time as our trunks. I have a theory it's deliberate: they make us *earn* the first sight of the school, so that we're already breathless and reeling when we step into the courtyard for the first time. And then we stand there and look around at the Great Hall and library and the towers, etc., etc., and feel overwhelmed and insignificant. The scale of it all, the site up here where the air is thin and you have to struggle to catch your breath, the austere grandeur of the buildings . . . It's pure theater. (I couldn't say that aloud, of course. Imagine, *theater*! In the same breath as the *grand jeu*! I remember in the first term, letting slip something about having seen *The Knight's Check* at the Empress, and the way everyone turned to look at me. There was a pause, and then Émile waved his hand languidly and said, "Don't judge him, my dears. I have a vast collection of erotic postcards, and Felix here is a great connoisseur of farts." We all laughed, and I never mentioned going to the theater again.) They like to pretend that the *grand jeu* has nothing to do with "entertainment," but deep down, the school is nothing but a playhouse. It's drama, that's all.

Maybe I'm being disingenuous. There was a moment this morning, on the last stretch of road with the towers looming into sight, when I felt pleased as Punch to be here again. I felt myself swagger as I walked through the gate. It still comes as a surprise that I'm a scholar of Montverre. And second in my class, no less. I didn't expect *that,* this time last year. This time last year I was afraid they'd realize there'd been a mistake.

It doesn't matter, anyway. I'm back. Two more years to go.

LATER

Had to break off because Felix came and knocked for me and we went down to get some lunch. He's worrying about being near the bottom of the class; apparently his parents gave him a hard time over the summer and they've threatened to make him find a job if he doesn't get at least an upper second next year. I told him it was a bit early to be worrying about leaving, but I couldn't muster much sympathy. He clearly thinks getting a job is about the worst thing that can happen to him. *Any* job. Presumably earning a living is the sort of thing only the middle classes do. I'd like to see him slaving away in Dad's scrapyards, the way I did all summer. For goodness' sake, all these people whose dream is sitting in a country house somewhere, studying the *grand jeu* while the country goes to the dogs . . . Not that I'm much better, if what I want is to be Magister Ludi—but at least that's an honest ambition, it isn't just trying to avoid hard work. I bit my tongue and didn't mention the scrapyards; but then, there are a few other things I did over the summer that I'm not going to mention, either. That bit of my life (manual labor, colleagues who read only *The Flag*, occasional sweaty fifteen-minute-stand behind the architectural salvage pile) is staying firmly in another compartment. Every so often I wish I *could* tell him, if only to see his face. But I'm not an idiot.

Lunch was plain wholesome food suitable for the *grand jeu* players of tomorrow, as per, but at least it was copious. Most of the class

was already down there, swapping the usual Long Vacation stories. Émile had been in France for most of it (naturally, my dears!)
and was regaling the others with tales of the conquests he'd made
chaperoning his cousins around Paris—whereupon Matthieu tried
to outdo him by announcing that *he* had met an obliging dairymaid
(or was it a shepherdess? I forget) in the Alps and had actually lain
hands on the most perfect pair of . . . etc., etc. Jacob (who has
never quite mastered the idiom) was boasting that he'd been invited to Oxford to study. He was telling Felix about the Abacus
Collection—his uncle's the curator, he was invited to the *grand jeu*
soirées with the best players in England, blah-blah—until I said,
"Jacob, the Abacus Collection is in Cambridge," and he choked a
bit and went quiet. Sometimes I wonder whether any of us tells the
truth about anything.

After I'd picked up my schedule—we have fewer lessons this
year, to give us time to work on our games—I came back up here.
As I turned the corner I caught sight of Felix outside Carfax's
room, pinning something up on the door. I paused and looked over
his shoulder, and he turned and grinned at me. "Like it?" he said.

It was an advert for fire extinguishers, with a picture of a burning
house and two wide-eyed children loitering on the lawn, hand in
hand. *Why take the risk?* it said.

"Are they meant to be the survivors or the culprits?"

"They've definitely got the de Courcy look, haven't they?" Felix
pushed in the last drawing pin, and stood back to appraise his work.
"Slightly manic . . . guilty expressions . . . ash-smeared hands . . ."
He looked around and grabbed my arm, but it was too late. Carfax
was coming down the corridor toward us. He must have been in the
lavatory, because his hair was wet and he was carrying a damp towel.
He paused in front of us and read the poster. His face went tight. For
a second I thought he was going to go inside without saying anything,
but then Felix giggled.

"Hilarious," Carfax said. "Did you spend the whole vacation planning that?"

"No," Felix said, "I just saw it and thought of you."

"Maybe if you thought less about me and more about the *grand jeu* you wouldn't be in line for a third."

Felix's grin slid off his face. "You really can't take a joke, can you?"

Carfax turned so suddenly I thought he was going to hit one of us. "For pity's sake, will you *leave me alone?*"

"Or what? Will you burn us in our beds?"

"I'm sorely tempted." He looked past Felix at me.

"What have *I* done?" I said. "I simply happened to be walking past—"

"I hope one day you realize what a bastard you are, Martin. That's all." He pushed the door open and then paused, as if something else had occurred to him. "Oh, and by the way—congratulations on coming second. Your family must be very proud."

The door shut behind him. Felix grunted, and peeled the poster off the door. "He is such a sanctimonious prig." He caught my eye. "Shall we catch him off guard somewhere and scrag him?"

I shook my head. For Felix, it really *is* a joke. He likes teasing Carfax because he gets a reaction. He doesn't realize how much I loathe him. How much I would like to see him . . . all right, maybe not hurt, not badly, but humiliated. No one knows that except possibly Carfax himself. In some ways we see each other more clearly than anyone else does, I think.

Felix said, "Reckon you can knock him off his perch this year?"

I took a deep breath and tried to sound casual. "If I get the right partner for the joint game. I'm thinking of asking Paul."

"It should be a walkover. It's not like anyone's going to want to work with Carfax, even if he's the best player. He'll get stuck with one of the no-hopers at the bottom of the list." He paused. "I hope it's not me."

"Find someone else quickly, and it won't be."

"Right. Yes."

It shouldn't have bothered me, that Felix called him *the best*. I mean, he *is* the best, at the moment. But it galls me even to write the words. Damn him. I am going to be top of the class this year. I swear it. Whatever it takes.

And one day, I promise, I am going to see Carfax de Courcy cry.

THIRD DAY OF SEROTINE TERM

First *grand jeu* lesson today, but we didn't do much. Magister Holt told us about our joint games, which are due in at the end of this term. I caught Paul's eye as Magister Holt was speaking, and he gave me a look to ask if I was up for partnering him. I gave him a thumbs-up, so hopefully that's that sorted out.

Afterward, as I was picking my exercise book off the floor (Felix had sent it flying in his eagerness to sprint downstairs for lunch), Magister Holt said, "Mr. Martin, I'd like to speak to you, if I may." Everyone else was already pushing out of the classroom door, and the Magister waited for them to leave before he shut it and gestured to me to sit down. For a moment I thought he was going to stand on the dais and address me from there, but he stood staring at the diagrams of notation on the wall and didn't say anything.

"Yes, Magister?" I said, finally.

"Well done," he said. "On your coming second in the class. No doubt you're pleased."

I said, "Yes, I am. Naturally." There was such a long silence that I had time to wonder why, if congratulations were in order, he hadn't kept Carfax behind to congratulate him; but then, of course, they'd be surprised if a de Courcy *wasn't* at the top of the class.

"How would you say you were getting on, Mr. Martin?"

"I beg your pardon?"

"At Montverre. You are the first of your family to come here, I believe."

I thought about making some crack about having crawled to the top of the rubbish heap, but I didn't. "That's right, Magister." I was hoping I could leave it at that, but he was giving me the Magister Ludi look, which makes you squirm until you've come up with a better answer. "I'm . . . all right, I suppose. Glad to be doing okay."

"Do you feel at home here?"

"Does anyone?"

That got a smile out of him, but only for a second. "Please, Mr. Martin," he said, "don't imagine that I am trying to make you feel uncomfortable. But I . . ." He sighed and went back to looking at the notation charts. I dug my hands into my armpits to stop myself fidgeting. "When we marked the games, at the end of last term, I must say I was very impressed with your progress."

I said, "Thank you," but he hadn't finished.

"You have certainly developed a great vocabulary, a sophisticated grasp of the *grand jeu,* a facility with the idiom," he said, with a glance at me to acknowledge my interruption. "But I don't think I would have awarded you quite those marks if the rest of the masters hadn't insisted."

I said, "Oh."

"Not that your game was in any way deficient. Not at all. But there is . . . how shall I put this? I worry that there is something . . . inauthentic. That what you produce is a very clever imitation of what you think the *grand jeu* should be, rather than a true game. Do you understand what I mean?"

I think I said, "Not entirely, Magister."

"You are intelligent. Very intelligent." He paused, but this time I didn't thank him, and I don't think he expected me to. "You have assimilated the culture of Montverre, the practice of the *grand jeu.* You produce, let us say, a flawless imitation of a Montverre scholar,

complete with flawless, accomplished games. And yet there is something . . ." He plucked at his ear. "I hesitate to say—cold, but . . .
insincere, perhaps. There is something missing."

I cleared my throat. "What is that?"

He gave a rueful laugh, as if this was some intellectual problem
we were trying to solve together. "I'm not exactly sure. But I think
I would know it if I saw it. And without that, I think you will never
be more than a competent player. Extremely competent—but *only*
competent."

There was a pause. I was trying not to let anything show on my
face. I said, "Are you saying, Magister, that I play the game as if it's
a game?"

I thought he'd tell me not to be impertinent. But he said, "No, Mr.
Martin, I'm saying you play the game to win."

I stood up and swept my books into my arms. I nearly knocked
them all on to the floor and had to scramble to catch them. "Well,
thank you, Magister," I said. "Next time I will do my best to lose."

He held up his hand. "Don't get angry, Mr. Martin. I'm telling you
this because I think you have promise."

It took an effort not to reply. I stared at the diagrams of notation and tried to estimate how often I'd used each symbol in my last
game.

"Tell me, Mr. Martin . . . It has occurred to me to wonder whether
your admirable work ethic is driven by a rivalry between you and
Mr. de Courcy."

He waited, but it wasn't a question, so I didn't answer.

"From what I have observed, that rivalry strikes me as somewhat . . . unfriendly. Am I right?"

"I don't particularly like him."

"I believe I know the reason for that."

"I don't know what you mean, Magister." Lucky I was still holding
all my books, or I'd have been tempted to pick up the volume of

Hondius on his desk and hit him over the head with it. I thought he was going to say something else, so I added, "I don't think anyone likes him much, to be honest."

"A shame. I believe you could learn a lot from each other."

I didn't reply.

"I'm sorry. I see that I have upset you."

"I'm not upset."

"No doubt you need your lunch." He took a step back and gestured to the door. "Anyway, Mr. Martin, welcome back to Montverre."

I wrote all that down this afternoon and then went off to meditation, but I'm still furious. What gives him the right to judge me? My life isn't a game that he gets to mark out of a hundred and pontificate on. If he wants to dispense his infinite wisdom, he can stick to his bloody *grands jeux*.

Right. I'm going back to the library. If the Magister wants authentic, that's what he's going to get. It can't be that hard. I have a cunning plan: I'm going to find the most authentic game ever written and work out how to copy it.

I cannot fucking believe it.

5

THE MAGISTER LUDI

The first-years fall silent as she walks into the classroom for their first *grand jeu* lesson. She's late, deliberately; they're all seated, tense and waiting, unsure of themselves and one another. It's an art, finding the right moment, before their unease tips over into nervous chatter or bravado, but it's the same instinct that guides her through a *grand jeu,* and she knows as she crosses to the dais that her timing is exactly right. She pauses before she looks up. Then she lets her eyes sweep across their faces, noticing who meets her gaze and who looks away, which ones shift in their seats or cross their arms. Who will resent being taught by a woman.

There's a small movement by the window. It's a tousle-haired young man with a thin, good-humored face, fiddling with his collar.

She recognizes him. Simon . . . Charpentier, is it? She was at his viva voce. He was charming then, incoherent with enthusiasm, stumbling over his words. He described the *Four Seasons* as if no one else had ever heard of it. The thought of it makes her want to smile, now. "It's the way it isn't . . . It shows how music and math and . . . It's all different but it isn't, it's still the game, the game is . . ." he'd said, and stuttered to a halt. She had leaned forward in the pause and said, "I think, Mr. Charpentier, you're talking about beauty." Yes. He was so young; but everyone is, to start with.

Abruptly he realizes what he's doing and drops his hand, ducking his head. He was trying to cover a stain, was he? No, a rip——no. Her heart gives a little flip. There's a cross sewn to the fabric of his gown. A Christian. She knew that, although she'd forgotten. There'd been a Party official at the viva, too. "I'm afraid," he'd said, with a sort of sigh, "that no matter how enthusiastic you believe yourself to be, there may be a time when you realize that as a Christian you are not quite fitted——and you have your own culture of course, far be it from me to disparage your faith; it is a very ancient one, if somewhat melodramatic——that in fact you cannot participate fully in the life of the *grand jeu* and thus in the life of Montverre." She'd bitten her tongue, raging. Later she'd taken particular pleasure in signing Charpentier's acceptance letter.

He looks up and registers her eyes lingering on his gown. He shrinks down in his chair, hunching his shoulders so that the cross disappears into a crease of material. There's something in the gesture that looks habitual. The pang in her chest turns into a deeper misgiving. The crosses have been law for only a few weeks——this is the first time she's seen one——and yet he has already developed this reflex, to make himself appear smaller. She wants to snap at him to sit up straight. Show weakness here and you're doomed.

She draws in a long breath. She has given this lesson over and over again, but now for some reason she hesitates. Part of her wants to speak to Charpentier directly, but what would she say? Launch into a brief history of the *grand jeu* that explains its origins in the Christian Mass? A diversion into the *Cordoba* and *Jerusalem* games, a short essay on the compatibility of scriptural religions with the new forms of worship? That would get her into trouble, but nonetheless it's hard to resist. *We search for the divine everywhere,* she could say, *and we may find it in the* grand jeu *or in the liturgy or both. There were* grands jeux *played in the Hagia Sophia and in the Al-Aqsa Mosque and at the Western Wall. It is modern arrogance to imagine that the divinity we hope to touch through the* grand jeu *is better than, or even different to, the deities of other religions. A younger way to worship is not necessarily a better way, nor is it the only way . . .* A brief attack on anyone who can use the *grand jeu* and its theology as a basis for discrimination, when the whole point of it is humility, attention, silence? Or on the people (she's not an idiot, she wouldn't name the Magister Cartae specifically) who seem to resist regarding it as worship at all, who wince at the word *God* as though it's embarrassing? Or merely a few acerbic words on the government and the long years of economic unrest and its choice of scapegoats?

But there is no protecting Charpentier from the other scholars, who are even now distancing themselves, refusing to meet his eyes; she would only make things worse. And part of her resents him for reminding her that she's an outsider, too; she knows full well how cruel Montverre can be.

The silence has gone on too long. She raps on the surface of the dais, dragging her mind back to her beginning-of-term speech. The old rhetorical question: "What is the *grand jeu,* gentlemen?" Then a pause, of course, as if she expects one of them to reply. "I find it hard to believe that no one can tell me," she says. "You've done well in the examinations. You've passed your vivas. Anyone?" And she pauses again, just enough to make them shift in their seats.

"Good," she says. "I'm glad that none of you is under the illusion that you can define or even explain the *grand jeu.* That is a good place to start. In the meantime, let us consider the things that it is not. It is not music." She counts off the points on her fingers. "It is not math or science or poetry. It is not art. It is not fiction. It is not performance. It is not even, strictly speaking, a game." By now she is fluent again, the words so familiar she hardly has to concentrate. "In your time at Montverre you will study all these things and more, but they are merely aspects, elements, of what constitutes the *grand jeu.* You may make something of all of these things that is not a *grand jeu,* and equally, a *grand jeu* may have none of them at all. There is only one possible way to answer the question *What is the* grand jeu? And that, gentlemen, is by playing it. That is what you will study with me in this classroom." She leans against the desk. "This term you will sketch a game every two weeks, and play and critique one another's games. At the end of Vernal Term you will write one full-length game each as well as taking your preliminary examinations. Please remember that everything you learn in every other class is for the *grand jeu*; this class must and shall be your highest priority. And—"

There's a movement on the other side of the frosted windows that let in light from the corridor. A figure is outside, at arm's length from the door: the brownish silhouette of a man in a suit, no gown. Léo Martin. He is waiting there, listening.

She takes a step toward the door, ready to fling it open and confront him, but before she reaches it, he's gone, sliding away. Footsteps click along the passage.

What was she saying? She can't remember. She has lost her train of thought entirely. She turns carefully toward the blackboard, conscious of the scholars' eyes on her. Five more seconds of silence and they will realize. Her armpits are damp, her mouth dry. She is afraid; and suddenly the realization makes her angry.

"Gentlemen," she says, without thinking, "if you are here to be a great player of the *grand jeu* . . . you should leave now."

A couple of scholars swap a glance; one frowns, another crosses his arms.

"If you are here," she says, "to win the Gold Medal. If you are here because you want your face on the cover of *The Gambit*. If you are here"—she pauses, and her hand goes to the headband of her cap—"because you want to be standing here in my place as Magister Ludi, you would do better to walk out of that door, and find another route to success." She shakes her head. She has never said this before, but the words are there waiting, like a game she can play without notes.

"Or you may even have lower ambitions. You may be here because you want to go into the Civil Service, or because your father was here before you, or because you want to boast about being an alumnus of Montverre or keep up with intellectual conversations with business acquaintances over a glass of port. You may think that the *grand jeu* is our 'national game' and that therefore it is simply one more accomplishment to master, a creditable hobby for when you reenter the real world. You may think that, because you have won a place here, you are being rewarded. That learning the *grand jeu* is some kind of prize."

She takes a breath. "But you would be wrong. The *grand jeu* has nothing to do with glory. It is a vocation, gentlemen. It is harder and lonelier than you can imagine, and the higher you go, the colder it will be." Almost to herself, she goes on, "The *grand jeu* is not a game. It is the opposite of a game. It is our way of paying attention to something outside ourselves. And what is outside ourselves—whatever truly exists—is the divine. We remake the world so that we can submit to it, and what we encounter, in the act of playing the *grand jeu*, is the truth."

Someone fidgets in the back row, scraping a shoe against the floor.

She smiles. "You don't understand now," she says, "and you will understand less and less . . . It is very easy to start on the path. But be wary, because at the end of it is God."

6

LÉO

The clock strikes two. Léo hisses through his teeth into his pillow, squeezing his eyes shut as if he can will himself into unconsciousness. Then he rolls over, swings his legs out of bed, and stands up, abandoning any attempt to sleep. Eventually, maybe, he will get used to this room below the clock tower, but for now he jerks awake every hour when the bell chimes and passes the days in a haze of sleeplessness. A few days ago he had asked the Magister Domus to move him, but the man only shook his head and said, "I'm sorry, Mr. Martin."

"You don't understand," Léo said. "I can't stay in that room. I can't sleep."

The Magister Domus smiled. He wasn't the same Magister Domus who had been there ten years ago, when Léo was a scholar. This one was plump and younger, with a placid look on his face that made Léo want to take him by the collar and shake him. "*You* don't understand, I'm afraid," he said. "We don't have any other rooms suitable for a guest."

"I'll sleep in a cell, I don't care."

"I'm sorry. Those are the only rooms we can offer you."

Léo stared at him. In his office, he would have sacked someone for a flat refusal, especially if it came with a smile; here, he felt his own helplessness, as if suddenly his fingers had decided not to button up his fly. "If it's a question of money . . . ?"

"Not at all. It's an honor to offer you our hospitality," the Magister said. "I'm very sorry not to be able to help." He nodded with deliberate courtesy. "Now, if you'll excuse me . . . I must hurry, the clock has to be wound every morning. It's never run down in two hundred years."

Léo watched him go, feeling queasy and murderous. He was too used to having enemies to mistake hostility when he saw it; but to encounter it here, at Montverre, when they should have been grateful to have him . . . He straightened his tie, as if someone was watching, and walked down the corridor back to his rooms with his hands in his pockets, whistling the tune of a risqué ballad.

Now in the dark he crosses to the washstand and splashes his face until the grit washes out of the corners of his eyes. He pulls on a shirt and trousers. He fumbles for a match and strikes it, squinting at the flare of the flame, and then lights the lamp. If he reads, eventually he'll fall asleep. But he has long since finished the detective novel he bought at the station. He picks up the lamp and takes it out into the corridor before he remembers that the library will be shut for the night. He can't bring himself to go back to his room, so he goes down the staircase into the little cloister that joins the clock tower to the magisters' building. Summer is over: out here the night air is chilly and has the clean, sharp scent of autumn coming, with winter on its tail. He pushes the heavy door open and turns right, past the Magisters' Entrance, past the music rooms and offices, up the spiral staircase, and into the wider passage of the scholars' wing. The Square Tower houses the scholars' cells; he turns in the other direction, toward the classrooms. He has been up here only once since he arrived, one morning when he was pacing the corridor and paused outside the *grand jeu* classroom to listen.

Now he walks to the classroom door, puts his hand on the doorknob, and hesitates. He's half afraid that he'll open the door on a

silent class, turning to look at him with vacant eyes. The image sends
a chill down his back. His lack of sleep and the lamplight are sowing
shadows in the corners of the corridor. If he walks away, it'll be cowardice or hysteria. He throws the door open with a kind of daring
flourish. Of course the room is empty, quiet, the moonlight spilling
through the windows so strongly he can see every outline, every
desk and chair. There's no need for the lamp; he puts it down on the
windowsill in the corridor, and goes into the classroom without it.

It's changed since he was last here. When Holt was Magister Ludi,
the walls were covered in diagrams and charts and *grand jeu* scores,
but as Léo looks around now, there's nothing on them but austere
planes of moonlight. The notation graph has gone. Even the blackboard is wiped clean. He runs his hand along the shelf below it to feel
the thick softness of chalk dust on his fingertips.

Then, without knowing why, he goes down the aisle to the desk
beside the window and sits down. It's the same desk, his desk: the
same nick beside the inkwell, the same scars and dents, the same *L*
carved into the top. He touches it, like a blind man trying to read,
and his heart gives a thud. He remembers scratching an old pen nib
into the wood, one lesson early in Vernal Term of his first year, anticipating two hours of boredom while they critiqued other people's
sketches for *grands jeux*. He had his head down, listening with half
an ear to Carfax summarizing his *ouverture*. Carfax's games were always clever—and flashy as well—but Léo was determined not to
show any interest; when he'd presented his own sketch a few days
before, Carfax had watched with insolent attention, suggesting improvement after improvement with overstated courtesy until Magister Holt sighed and said, "Perhaps . . . someone else?" Léo knew
he wouldn't be able to retaliate in kind—Carfax was the top of the
class, week after week—but at least he could pretend complete in-
difference. And later, when they were at dinner, there would be a
joke or a snide comment to be made, another opportunity to balance

the score. He drove the point of the nib across the grain of the wood, deepening the bottom line of the *L*. On the dais, Carfax cleared his throat and said, "So I've decided to focus on the first development of the musical theme and the transition into the lyric element."

Léo kept his pen moving, scraping splinters out of the groove he'd made. In a moment it would be clear enough to last for years, and he could move on to the *E*.

"So with that overview, we have the introduction of the first theme: the potato."

Léo looked up. Felix caught his eye and gave a tiny, bemused shrug; other scholars were stifling smiles. Carfax had noticed their reaction—you could see that from the way his eyes swept across the room—but his composure didn't flicker. He used his notes to gesture, with the insouciant authority that set Léo's teeth on edge. "We begin with an exploration of musical notation as both itself and an almost literal pictogram: that is, the whole note acts as a kind of pun, providing both the melody and a portrait of the potato. Thus—" He demonstrated the musical theme: a single dull thump of a note, repeated. It was like something heavy falling into a bucket. For a few bars, everyone sat silent, watching him; and then the first snort came from Dupont in the back row. It set off a ripple of smothered amusement. Carfax tilted his head, with a tiny acknowledgment.

It was then that Léo realized Carfax was doing it deliberately. He leaned forward, his pen loose between his fingers.

"I've used that melody"—he paused for the tiny incredulous giggle from Émile, as if he knew it was coming—"as a cantus firmus. For the elaboration, I have composed a baroque variation." He consulted his notes and turned to the blackboard to sketch the movement. "While maintaining a continuo for the theme, I've indulged in some compositional extravagance—" He broke off, adding diacritics to the structure. Then he stood back to assess what he'd written, as if for a moment he'd forgotten that the rest of the class was there. Léo frowned. Carfax's game was absurd, grotesque, completely unlike his usual style, and yet he was surveying it as if it was the best thing he'd ever done.

"Now, following the classic structure, I introduce the mathematical proposition—a combination of lyric poetry and an allusion to the philosophical tension between integers and the looming infinite."

Léo couldn't concentrate on what Carfax was saying. He stared at the elaboration of the musical theme on the blackboard. It was familiar, somehow. Not that he had ever seen it before—he would have remembered that—but the style, the shape . . . His own game had been called the *New World*—had there been something about potatoes? Maybe he'd read something similar when he was doing his research. It seemed unlikely, but he couldn't deny the twist of recognition in his gut.

"One potato," Carfax said, "two potato, three potato, four—five potato, six potato, seven potato, more."

This time everyone laughed. From his seat in the corner, Magister Holt said, "Gentlemen . . ."

Léo narrowed his eyes. He ignored the joke. There was something . . . It was a standard structure, the sort of development he used himself—so what was it? He leaned forward, wrestling with a complex knot of notation, and caught sight of Émile glancing at him. There was something in his expression that Léo couldn't read. He mouthed, "What?"

Émile shook his head and turned back to face the front of the room. After a moment he sent another curious look over his shoulder. Felix and Jacob were nudging each other, and almost everyone was smirking. Carfax said, ". . . as demonstrated here, in the transition," and another wave of mirth broke over the room. Léo rolled his eyes and slumped in his chair, folding his arms. He wasn't going to laugh; he wasn't impressed. He kept his eyes half closed, staring at Carfax with deliberate blankness. Carfax held his gaze and smiled. Léo raised an eyebrow and let his eyes drift past Carfax, back to the blackboard, trying to show his contempt in his expression.

He felt his face go slack as he realized.

It was his own game.

No, not his game. But close enough. With his habits, his structure, his style—all of them skewed, caricatured, but recognizable, the whole thing a vicious parody of his *New World*. A high piercing note rang in his ears. He shut his eyes. When he opened them again, the game was still there, still monstrous, still sickeningly familiar. Was he imagining it? No. It had the same architecture as the *New World*—as all his games, for god's sake—and every detail was as precise as a needle prick. He jerked in his seat, mastering the impulse to twist around to check if anyone was watching him; if they were, he couldn't let them see his face. He clenched his jaw. The singing in his ears intensified, drowning out Carfax's voice.

He sat very still. There was nothing he could do but try not to attract attention. Perhaps no one else had realized—please, let no one else have realized . . . Had Émile's look been pity? Waves of heat went over him. Sweat crawled down his scalp and soaked into his collar. There was a piercing pain in the base of his thumb; he looked down and saw that he'd driven the grimy pen nib into the flesh, so deep he'd drawn blood. He spread his hands flat on the desk and looked down at them, and after a while a bubble of red oozed out from under his palm. Carfax's voice came and went in his ears while the class murmured and chuckled. He told himself that they didn't know, they weren't laughing at him; but they *were*, whether they knew it or not.

The class fell silent. He looked up, in spite of himself. Carfax had finished. He held Léo's gaze, a long level look of victory. No one moved or spoke; they might have been the only two people in the room. Then, although Carfax hadn't performed a whole game, he gave the low, graceful bow of *fermeture*.

The class applauded. It was only for a second or two—stifled quickly, amid laughter, when Magister Holt raised his hand to cut them off—but there was appreciation in the sound, even a whistle from Dupont. Léo heard it in his bones like thunder: applause, when even the best games at Montverre ended in silence. Carfax put his hand on his heart, like an actor. "Thank you, gentlemen," he said.

Magister Holt stood up. "Thank you, Mr. de Courcy," he said. "I think I will discuss this game with you privately after class. Please sit down." He walked to the dais and consulted his list. He ignored the mutter of confusion. "Mr. Legrand, I believe."

Carfax bent his head, collected his notes, and went to his desk. There was a flush on his face and a hint of a private, triumphant smile. His hands had been steady all the way through his presentation, but Léo saw them tremble as he drew up his chair and sat down. Someone leaned across and said, "That was brilliant," but Carfax seemed not to hear.

Léo sat through the rest of the lesson without moving. The furious heat of humiliation burnt through his body, leaving a dull inertia; he said nothing about Matthieu's game, even though he could see quite clearly what was wrong with it. It didn't matter when the thought of his own games made him feel sick. If only Carfax hadn't got it *right* . . . After a long time he looked up to see Felix standing over him, and the classroom half empty. "Come on, Martin, I'm starving. Poor old Matthieu, what an act to follow. Who would've thought Carfax had a sense of humor? Amazing. Magister Holt didn't look too pleased, though, did he?" Felix peered into his face. "Are you all right? You look like you're going to throw up."

"Fine," Léo said. "I'm fine." At least Felix hadn't spotted it; but then, Felix was never the sharpest observer in the room.

"I don't know why he didn't let us discuss it. I've never seen a comic game. It was fantastic. We could've had some real arguments about that—you know, the place of laughter in worship, the . . . who was it who said laughter is what distinguishes men from beasts? Was it Socrates?"

"Aristotle." Léo got to his feet. "He said we laugh at people we feel superior to." He pushed past Felix and out of the classroom. He wove through the current of people in the corridor until he reached the bottleneck at the top of the stairs; then he had to slow down, resisting the urge to shove. The group in front of him was laughing. Behind him, Felix was saying something, but he didn't look back.

"Hey, Martin, where are you going?"

He turned aside, ducked into the lavatories, and stumbled into a cubicle. He had time to slam the door and slide the bolt across. Then he vomited.

He raises his head, blinking away the memory. It was a long time ago. It's absurd that he still remembers the taste of bile and the splash of freezing water on his face. And the way he strode into the refectory a few minutes before the end of lunch, glanced at the damp fire smoldering in the hearth, and said, "Hey, de Courcy, can't you find a couple of books to throw on that?" He grimaces, and somehow the grimace turns into a long shuddering exhalation, not quite a laugh. It's loud in the moonlit classroom, and it brings him back to himself. He rubs his thumb over the L on the desk. He doesn't know if he wants to erase it or finish his name. It doesn't matter now; he can't do either.

For days afterward he dreamed of killing Carfax. He found the idea returning to him again and again: some silent poison, or—no—a pillow held over Carfax's face. There would be pleading, then a spasm of terror, a final gasp—or maybe flailing hands, if the pillow made gasping impossible—and then Léo would walk out, shut Carfax's door gently behind him, and stand in the corridor brushing nonexistent dust off his sleeves, smiling to himself. It was easy to imagine: so childish, so like the villain of a melodrama, so satisfying. No retribution, no guilt—only that orgasmic moment of power, and then he could walk away. It comes back to him now so vividly it sends a shiver down his spine, as if it really happened. Abruptly he stands, stumbles to the dais, and turns back to face the rows of empty desks. Carfax's desk was at the other side of the room, next to the aisle. He looks at it now—or rather, at the emptiness where Carfax would be. How many times did he stand here, meeting Carfax's eyes? And hating him, wishing him dead?

He jabs his thumbnail into the base of his thumb, where there's still a tiny scar. It was stupid of him to come up here, especially when he hasn't slept. He has to pull himself together. If he goes on like this, he'll have a nervous breakdown. Carfax is long gone; there's nothing to be gained in thinking about him.

He goes out into the corridor. He's clumsy when he picks up the lamp and nearly drops it. He fumbles, steadies it, and puts it back carefully on the windowsill; then immediately has to bend over, trembling, trying to get the breath back into his lungs. What's happening to him? If he wanted to burn himself alive . . .

"Who's there?"

He jolts upright. There's a slim figure at the end of the corridor. "It's me, Léo Martin."

"Martin? What on earth are you doing up here?"

His vision steadies. White gown, bare head, a rope of dark hair falling over one shoulder. Magister Dryden, of course, with her plain square face, the narrow shoulders and hips . . . Of all the people in the school, the one he least wants to see him like this. She's not wearing those thick bottle-glass spectacles, and it makes her look quite different; in the jumping, treacherous lamplight he almost thought—

He shrugs. "I couldn't sleep."

She doesn't reply. A wave of intense fatigue goes through him. He could be at home now, in bed with Chryseïs; he could pull her into his arms, bury his face in the space at the base of her neck while she muttered and went back to sleep. Instead he's in a chilly stone corridor, staring at this plain lanky woman who thinks she owns the place. "I'm sorry," he says, too weary to defend himself. "I'll go back to my rooms." He picks up the lamp with both hands.

"Were you meeting someone?"

"What?" It takes him a second to understand, and then he can't believe what she's suggesting. "No, of course not. There's nothing up here but the classrooms."

She crosses her arms over her chest. "So? What are you doing here, then?"

"I—I was . . . It's been a long time, I wanted to see if . . ." He shakes his head. "Look, what's the problem? I haven't touched anything."

"You can't wander about like this."

"Why not?"

She opens her mouth, but she doesn't answer immediately. She runs her plait through her hand, letting it whisper against her skin. At last she says, "Has it changed?"

"What?"

"The school. Since you were here."

"I—" He stares at her and she glances away. He'd never met her before he came back here, and yet . . . No, he's never known anyone called Dryden. He's so tired that his brain is playing tricks on him. He tightens his grip on the base of the lamp. "In some ways. Hardly any of the magisters are the same."

"There was an influenza epidemic here, a few years before I was elected."

"Yes. I heard about that. A very bad business," he adds, with a politician's automatic gravity. Not that he cared much, at the time: Montverre seemed so far away that the list of deaths was no more than a number.

She twists the rope of her hair, pulling it forward so that it lies across her cheek. In this light, her face could be anyone's: especially now, with her eyes turned away, her gaze searching the window as if she can see beyond their reflections in the glass. "What was it like?" she says. "When you were here before?"

"It was . . ." He stops. His head is spinning and his throat is tight. He's done enough remembering tonight. He shrugs. "Much the same as when you were here, I imagine."

There's a fractional pause; then she says, "What?"

"No, I'm sorry." He turns aside, stuttering.

"Sorry? What for?" There's a strange warning note in her voice.

"I forgot I was talking to—that you didn't come here—that you're a—" What's *wrong* with him? He's blathering.

"You're sorry I'm a woman?" She laughs shortly.

He opens his mouth, on the verge of saying, *Yes, exactly.* It's true; she shouldn't be here at all, let alone Magister Ludi. He can still remember the day she was elected, and the aide who brought him *The Beacon*, grimacing as he set it down on Léo's desk. "What a balls-up," he'd said. "Goes to show Montverre can't be trusted to run its own affairs." When Léo put down his pen and dragged the paper closer to read the headline, the aide added, "At least we didn't get a crosser or a commie. The Minister did something right. But honestly, we should've stepped in before they got to that short list. Blind submissions, give me strength! Everyone knows what that's *supposed* to mean. Next time . . ." Léo stared at that blurry photo, furious. How could they have let it happen? Someone who hadn't even studied at Montverre, chosen faute de mieux, because the others were even more unelectable. He could have thrown something.

But he doesn't say so—partly because he's too tired, and partly because his own promotion came soon afterward, when the Minister for Culture stepped down. He takes a breath. "It's unusual, in the world of the *grand jeu*. How did you even learn to play?"

"My family. I lived with my cousins for a while, in England. They were good players."

"They must have been." He smiles. "Do you ever wonder what your games would be like if you'd been a man?"

"No."

He waits, but she doesn't say anything else. "No," he says eventually. "Well. It's a waste of time to speculate, I suppose." Something makes him glance at the door to the classroom and the rank of frosted windows. He can just make out the milky pallor of moonlight on the other side. "I dare say it wouldn't have suited you here, anyway. It's very competitive. A lot of ambition, rivalry, and so on. Not a suitable place for a woman. That is, I'm sure you do a very good job as Magister Ludi."

"Good night, Mr. Martin," she says, turning away. "Please return to your rooms without waking anyone, won't you?"

He watches her go. She doesn't have a lamp, but she knows her way. She brushes the wall with her fingertips as she turns the corner toward the staircase. He catches himself thinking that she's doing it deliberately, to show that Montverre is hers, and clenches his jaw. He shouldn't let her get under his skin—she's only a woman, why should he care if she loathes him?—but she's not like any other woman he knows. It's as if she's forgotten who she's supposed to be, and he can't help being drawn into her world, where he's not only alien but inferior. Perhaps she would have fitted in as a scholar, after all.

He leaves it a long time before he follows her down the stairs and into the magisters' wing. There's no sign of her. He's glad. He goes back to his rooms without pausing. The clock strikes three as he walks along the corridor. When he finally reaches his bedroom he's too cold to undress. He crawls under the blankets as he is, in shirt and trousers, and within seconds he's asleep.

7

FIFTH DAY OF SEROTINE TERM

I was too fed up to write yesterday, but I suppose I should explain—
if only for when this is consulted for my biography (working title:
Léonard Martin: The Life and Times of the Youngest Magister Ludi).

So. Yesterday. After meditation I went to the library—I've been
looking at the *Oxford*; Paul said the other day that it "reeks of histrionic Christ worship," but it seems okay to me—and stayed there
until dinnertime. I was crossing the courtyard to the refectory when
I saw Émile and Dupont coming out of the classroom wing. Émile
called my name and beckoned me over. "Have you seen?" he said.
"Did it come as a shock?"

I said, "Seen what?"

They exchanged a look. A smirk, I should say. Dupont jerked his
thumb over his shoulder. "It's on the noticeboard," he said.

"What?" It was too early for the first week's marks to be out.
"Have I—has someone been kicked out?" I had a tiny moment of
panic in case the school had found out about some of the stuff I did
over the summer. I've never heard of anyone being sacked for lack
of chastity off the premises, but technically bringing the school into
disrepute is a sackable offense.

"Don't worry, dear boy," Émile said, "it's nothing like that." He
swapped another glance with Dupont and tittered.

I didn't pause long enough to give him a dirty look. I walked
with speed but dignity into the scholars' wing and broke into a
run as soon as I was out of sight. There was a crowd in front of
the noticeboard, and when I arrived Felix turned around. He was

grinning, but when he saw me, his face changed and he looked at me like a vet who was about to shoot my dog. "What's up?" I said. "Has something happened?" My only thought by then was that the government had fallen or some crisis like that, but there was something too personal in the way Felix was attempting a sympathetic expression.

"Have a look," he said, and pushed someone aside so I could get close enough to see.

Second-Year Pairings for Joint Games. The first time I read it, it didn't make sense; then it did. I felt my heart start to thud as I read down the list until I got to my name. But I'd known what it would say from the moment I saw the title, written out in Magister Holt's neat block capitals and underlined in red.

Léonard Martin & Aimé Carfax de Courcy.

Someone said, "But they've never assigned partners before! I was supposed to be with Mirabeau."

I couldn't speak. I stared at the list. Most people had been averaged out—Felix was with Paul, Émile was with Jacob—which meant it was even worse that Carfax and I had been put together.

Felix said, "At least you two will be top of the class. You'll walk it."

I didn't deign to answer that. I would rather be with anyone—anyone, Felix and Jacob included—than Carfax. And I may sound self-absorbed, but this whole thing is clearly about me (well, us). Magister Holt has some kind of bee in his bonnet about our "unfriendly rivalry" and thinks this is a good way to make us work together. Damn him. I can't even go to the Magister Scholarium, because I know what he'd say: you're here to learn, trust the Magister Ludi, set aside personal differences, the game is after all an act of worship, blah-blah-blah.

At dinner it was all anyone could talk about. Everyone was sympathizing with me, which should have made me feel a bit better—at least no one else likes Carfax, either—but it didn't. And Carfax was nowhere to be seen.

It's hard enough to write a joint game at all, but with someone you can't bloody stand—

LATER

Well, that was perfect timing.

As I was writing that last sentence, there was a knock at the door. When I opened it, Carfax was standing there. He sort of blanched when he saw me, as if he thought I was going to hit him. Apparently he thinks I'm a psychopath as well as an idiot.

He said, "Have you seen the notice about joint games?"

I said, "Yes."

"Right."

I started to close the door. He said, "Is there any chance we can talk about this like grown-ups?"

"What do you want to talk about?"

"Well, what sort of game we want to play. How we want to work together." He pushed the door farther open so that I had to step backward. "Look, let's make this as easy as possible, all right? Let's write the game and move on."

I didn't want to agree with him, but in fact he was right. "Fine."

"We don't have to be friends."

"Just as well," I said. "You don't have friends, do you, Carfax? You only have inferiors and enemies."

"At least we're not enemies, then." He gave me that look, as if he's inside my head and faintly amused by what he can see.

"Very fucking funny," I said, and shut the door on him. This time he didn't stop me, but a second later he knocked again. I didn't open up. "Go away."

"We've got a free class tomorrow after Historiae. Come to my room and we can talk through some ideas."

"Your ideas?"

"Any ideas." I heard him add something obscene under his breath. "Do you have a better plan?"

"Yes," I said, still without opening the door. "Let's do this by correspondence. Write it all down and put it in my pigeonhole. I'll do the same for you. That way we never even have to speak to each other."

He said, "Perfect." I couldn't tell whether he was being sarcastic or not, but he didn't say anything else, and when I opened the door he'd gone.

So I guess that's the way we'll do it, then. Obviously it involves a certain amount of effort. I was going to write *unnecessary effort*, but frankly anything that means I don't have to look at his face is worth every moment.

You know, what I hate most about him is the person he makes me into.

SEVENTH DAY OF SEROTINE TERM
Just got back from leaving my notes for the joint game in Carfax's pigeonhole. I've been thinking about surrealism and dreams—something weird and disjointed, a kind of beautiful monstrosity—Shakespeare, Purcell, "a change came o'er the spirit of my dream," a recurring motif that develops into something else . . . I don't know, all very vague ideas at the moment. Different from my usual stuff, where I plot it all precisely and make sure everything is clever and harmonious . . . I have to admit I'm thinking about how to do "authentic," because I really want to do well this term. It galls me to try to placate

Magister Holt, especially now, but I imagine it's the politic thing to do. (Curse him.) Anyway, I reckon it could work. Assuming Carfax doesn't deliberately sabotage it or insist we do something deadly dull. No doubt he'll come up with some complex, esoteric idea about math and music to make me sweat. All served up with the usual de Courcy arrogance, and technically perfect, of course. (Curse him, too.)

On my way back I came past Jacob's room. He was loitering outside, looking helplessly from side to side as if he was trying to cross a busy road. As soon as he saw me he called, "Martin! Come in here," and steered me into his bedroom. (I thought about making some crack about most people buying me a drink first, but didn't.) "Listen!" he said, and hissed at me when I started to ask what we were listening for, so we stood there in silence for a couple of minutes. "Can you hear it?"

"Hear what, Jacob?"

"The crying!"

I listened again. "Er, no," I said.

"Oh, bugger," he said, "it's stopped. It did this last time."

"Right," I said. His cap was standing up like a mushroom, and he'd got ink stains on his face. "Are you having a funny turn? Do you want me to call the Magister Domus?"

"Oh, forget it," he said, and collapsed onto the bed. "You all think it's a bloody joke. I tell you, every time the east wind blows, there's a child's voice in here, sobbing its heart out."

"Jacob—" I was going to laugh at him, but he looked genuinely pathetic. "It's most likely someone practicing the violin. Coming through the pipes or something."

"Never mind," he said, waving me away. "You think I'm crazy. They refused to move me, you know. I should've said there was a smell of drains."

"You think so? Rather than ghostly wailing? Ah, the magic of hindsight."

"Go away," he said, which was ungrateful considering he'd frog-marched me in there to begin with. When I left, he was turning his head from side to side compulsively, like a caged bird.

Actually, as I went out, I wondered if I *did* hear something.

NINTH DAY OF SEROTINE TERM

I woke up early this morning and found myself checking my pigeon-hole before breakfast. He'd replied. It was a single sheet of paper covered with tiny symbols and a lot of lines. For a second I thought it was Artemonian notation, but I didn't recognize any of the ideograms, and none of the transition marks were the same. It looked a bit like a spider's web, if a spider had made prolific, drunken notes at every junction. It was unreadable. After breakfast I went straight up to his room and banged on the door. There was a scuffling sound before he told me to come in, and I had the impression he'd only just got dressed. His hair was all over his face and his gown was inside out.

"Thanks for your contribution," I said. "That is, I assume it was from you."

He sat down at his desk, facing me. "So, what did you think?"

"I think it's illegible." He didn't answer. I pulled the page out of my pocket and flattened it on the desk in front of him. "What notation is this meant to be, exactly?"

He reached out and rotated the page through ninety degrees. "It's a variation of Artemonian."

"A *variation*? What kind of variation?"

"I find it useful for sketches. The Imaginists developed it from Artemonian and Occidental ideograms, with some influences from Mandarin and Persian. My grandfather used it for the *Fireseed*—" He stumbled on the word but went on before I could say anything. "I suppose I've put a personal emphasis on some aspects, but—"

I said, "You write your sketches in the *family dialect of Artemonian*?"

There was a pause. I mastered the urge to grab him by the collar. "Well," I said, "if you think I'm going to waste my time on your particular brand of de Courcy mumbo jumbo, you've got another think coming. Put it into classical."

"What?" For the first time he looked as if I'd said something unexpected. "Do you have any idea how many pages that would take up in classical notation?"

I didn't, obviously, as I had no idea what it said. "I don't care."

"It's not that difficult to learn——"

"I never said it was too difficult."

"Listen," he said, getting to his feet. "I'm sorry, but this is how I work. I can't write everything out longhand, it would take forever. It's a sketch. I could explain it to you——"

"Just translate it, Carfax."

He ran his hands through his hair. "This is ludicrous. I'm not spending hours expanding on my notes because you refuse to behave like an adult. We could *talk,* Martin. That way, if you didn't understand something——"

"I'd understand it all if it wasn't in hieroglyphics!" We glared at each other. I was shaking. There's something about him that gets under my skin—always has, from the moment I saw him on the path to Montverre that first morning. "Don't patronize me."

"I wasn't! *Patronize* you? My God." He turned his face away from me. He looked down at a pile of books and straightened their spines. "I don't like you, Martin," he said. "You're arrogant and unkind and self-absorbed. But I've never thought you were stupid."

Later, coming down the stairs (literally *l'esprit de l'escalier*), I wondered why, if I'm *not* stupid, everyone feels such a need to reassure me on that point. But I think all I said was "Thanks."

He finished adjusting the tower of books. For a second I thought he'd forgotten I was there. At last he looked up at me. He said, "We could scratch it, of course."

"What?"

"The game. At the end of next term. If you really can't bear to work with me."

"Scratch it? What do you suggest, that we hand in a blank sheet of paper?"

He tilted his head, as if I'd made a good point. "That's an interesting idea," he said. "They're always telling us how important silence is. A blank sheet is about the most silent game you could play."

"Are you serious?"

"What I'm saying is, no one can make us work together. We can hand in a bad game. Or nothing at all."

"They'll fail us."

"One bad mark. What are you so afraid of?"

He was looking at me like I was five. I wanted to reach out and topple his beautifully stacked books on to the floor. "Are you mad?" I said. "Or is it because you're a de Courcy? You think they wouldn't dare expel you."

"They wouldn't expel either of us."

"How do you know?" My voice cracked and I swallowed. Imagine Dad, if I got sent home in disgrace. He'd be mortified. And I'd be stuck forever in the scrapyard business. "Look, this may be a trifling aristocratic hobby for you, but I want to stay at Montverre. If you refuse to work with me—"

"On the contrary, I'm simply pointing out that if you're not prepared to take the risk, then we have to work together."

"On your terms."

"On civilized terms." He slid a glance at me. "I realize that might take some getting used to."

I walked to the fireplace and then to the window. I had a ridiculous sense that somewhere, if I looked in the right place, I'd find a good answer. A winning move. In the shape of the marks in the dust or the light or the mountain. But I couldn't see it, and in the end I knew the fight was over. "Fine," I said. "When do you want to start?"

"We've already started."

"Tomorrow, then. You can explain your . . ." I waved at his notes, but he raised his eyebrows as if he didn't understand what I was talking about. "Your whatever it is."

"I won't have to. It was only a sketch." He leaned back against the desk, crossing his legs at the ankle. "Don't think I'm any more eager than you are, Martin."

For once I believed him. I strode past him, so close he had to flinch. I paused at the door and looked around. He was already flicking through one of the books, too quickly to be reading it.

"Be careful, Carfax," I said. "Making up your own language . . . Madness runs in the family, after all."

8

THE MAGISTER LUDI

She wakes up in sheets stained with blood. Somehow she has managed to spread it in her sleep and there is a rusty smear on her pillow, a deep blot on the cuff of her nightgown. She sits up, her mind still hampered by the weight of her dreams. For a moment, confusion and memory overlap and panic floods through her: a floor puddled with red, a handprint on white porcelain, her fault. She squeezes her eyes shut and opens them again, hugging herself until her shoulders crack. Slowly her heartbeat slows. The ache in her bones softens, her breath comes more easily. She is here, at Montverre, and it's nothing. Only her own blood. Only the magic trick of being female: look at me, I can bleed without being wounded, I can empty myself again and again and still live. She gets to her feet and her nightgown clings to the back of her thighs. There is a meaty, metallic smell in the room. She bends over the basin, her fingers already turning the water pink.

The clock chimes. She has overslept. She has missed meditation and breakfast; at this moment she should be hurrying along the corridors to the Capitulum, fully dressed, instead of cursing as she strips off a bloody nightgown. She rinses herself as quickly as she can—hastily, so that water goes everywhere, spattering her feet and the floor—and fumbles for the rubber cup that Aunt Frances posted from England. *My dear Claire, I've taken the liberty of sending this little gift, which might make you a little more comfortable when you are feeling delicate . . .* From her note, she might have been talking about a negligée or silk stockings or lavender water—glamorous, frivolous, feminine; not an inverted bell of vulcanized rubber. Trust Aunt Frances to send something utterly practical and still be too squeamish to refer to it directly.

She inserts it, rinses her hands, gets dressed. She bundles her ragged plait into her cap; she doesn't have time to brush it or pin it properly. Nor does she have time to empty her bladder or brush her teeth. She splashes her face with one swift movement and hurries out into the passage. It is only as she crosses the courtyard and climbs the stairs to the Capitulum that she has time for resentment. Her body is normally trustworthy, warning her in advance with a familiar ache, holding on to the first moderate gush of blood until she visits the lavatory. Today it is treasonous.

The meeting—the first Council of Serotine Term—has already started. She straightens her shoulders and walks through their sudden silence to her seat beside the Magister Scholarium. He waits until she has sat down before he gestures to the Magister Cartae to continue.

The Magister Cartae gives a fussy, multisyllabic cough. "My dear Magister Ludi," he says, "good morning. Did you perhaps lose track of time in inspiration? What a pity that your genius must be bound by the humdrum routines of bureaucracy."

"Excuse me, gentlemen," she says. "I was unavoidably detained." She wonders how often they have to apologize for their bodies.

The Magister Cartae waves his hand. "As I was saying . . ." He peers down at his notes as though he has entirely lost his train of thought. "Yesterday I received a letter from the Minister for Culture," he goes on. "He sent us greetings and thanked us for our hospitality toward Mr. Martin, but his primary point . . . Well." He brings a sheet of notepaper closer to his face and reads:

"We are keen to examine ways in which Montverre might increase its contribution, not merely as a beacon of academic achievement but also as a crucial influence on developing minds. It gives me great pleasure to know that the traditions imbibed at Montverre are carried through into our Civil Service, and indeed the very highest levels of government, and I continue to wonder how we might ensure that every scholar who graduates is of the greatest possible service to our country."

There is a silence. The Magister Corporeum scratches his ear. "Well," he says, and grimaces. "I'm not sure I know what that means."

The Magister Cartae sighs. He smooths his top lip; she suspects that before he came to Montverre he had a mustache, and he still pets the ghost of it. "I think perhaps the Minister for Culture is suggesting that we bear in mind our duty to keep the game and its players . . . pure."

"And what does *that* mean?" She should have taken a breath before she said it.

"I'm afraid you've missed the context of this discussion," the Magister Cartae says, with a tilt of his head. "While you were— unavoidably detained—we were discussing this week's edition of *The New Herald*. Very concerning, the report on Christian infiltration—"

"*The New Herald* is pure propaganda! It's not worthy of serious consideration." The Magister Scholarium stirs, but she can't stop herself. "Next you'll be saying the Game of the Bloody Cross isn't a forgery. Or that Christians are cannibals."

"I don't think we can dismiss the government's very real concerns about the compatibility of the older faiths with modern enlightened—"

"Oh, for pity's sake!" Now they're all looking at her. "Christianity and Judaism—and Islam, come to that—have never been in conflict with the *grand jeu*. Not in themselves." She stutters and goes on before anyone can bring up the Renaissance popes. "There's no reason to exclude them—just because the Party has got a bee in its bonnet—"

"I find it very hard to believe that you are so relaxed about the survival of Montverre."

It takes her a moment to understand that it's not a non sequitur; and by then it's too late to answer.

"Magister . . ." the Magister Religionis says, leaning toward her, one crumple-skinned hand stroking the air as if it's an animal, "I understand your concerns. We all do. They do you credit." He doesn't look at the Magister Cartae, who snorts. "We don't want to *persecute* Christians. But these days Montverre has a political role. There is more and more pressure on us to pull our weight. Not to be complacent in our privilege or to encourage parasites. To waste spaces on scholars who can never repay their debt to society—"

"Who are barred from the Civil Service, you mean."

He smiles gently, as if she hasn't spoken. "And as *you* know, my dear Magister, it is perfectly possible to become a great player of the *grand jeu* without attending Montverre. Those who are truly talented, truly called, will still find a way to study it."

She bites her lip. Her insides are being wrung out like a wet cloth. The back of her neck is sticky. "It isn't that easy," she says.

"You are yourself a shining example," the Magister Religionis says. "Evidence that the *grand jeu* is open to everyone, regardless of their sex or race or religion. If a young woman of no education can become Magister Ludi—"

"All right," she says. "I understand." There are things she could say: that she was hardly of *no education*; that the *grand jeu* was in her blood; that everyone knows that when they found out she was a woman, they tried to repeal her election. But her throat is tight, and the battle is already over.

The Magister Scholarium sighs. "We must be practical," he says. "It might be expedient to concede certain . . . measures to the government. Temporarily." He stares into the middle distance, and for a second she imagines what he's seeing: hundreds of young men slaving over their essays, their exam revision, their submission games, all hoping for a place at Montverre next year. How many of them are Christian? How many of them are like—what is his name? Her Christian first-year, who seems promising: not brilliant, yet, but promising. Stephen? No, Simon.

"No Christians," the Magister Corporeum says. "Is that what we're talking about?" He glances around, like a scholar who has ventured a risky answer and wishes he hadn't. No one responds.

She should fight. But she can feel the decision in the room, as blank and solid as a brick wall. Nothing she can throw at it will make a mark. She says, "And what of our current scholars?"

The Magister Scholarium catches her eye. There's a flash of relief in his look, gratitude for her capitulation, and she swallows a faint taste of bile. "It goes without saying," he says, "that we will never ask an existing scholar to leave the school purely on the basis of their background."

"Well then," the Magister Cartae says, "that's settled. I will draft a memo."

She sits back. She still feels sick. Cramp settles deeper in her abdomen and drags downward. The blood roars in her ears. Someone says something about the next item on the agenda. She lets their voices blur, like the smeared notation on the paper in front of her. None of it is important. It is all she can do to stay where she is, as the nausea comes and goes.

After what seems an age the clock strikes and there is a mutter of cracking joints and creaking wood as the men lean back in their chairs. The Magister Scholarium says, "Well, thank you, gentlemen."

The Magister Cartae is the first to stand. He nods to the Magister

Scholarium, pats his papers into a pile, and drifts toward the door.
The others get up and follow him, breaking into knots and couples,
murmuring to one other. Slowly she levers herself to her feet. She
is light-headed. She can smell the others' claggy lungs, their wind-
pipes, their tongues.

"Excuse me," she says, and pushes past to the door. Voices come
down the stairs behind her. She swerves right, past a row of identical
doors, heading for the little walled cloister below the clock tower.
It's out of bounds for the scholars, which makes it a good place to be
alone; and at this time of year it catches a few brief hours of sunlight
and some precious warmth. She pushes open the door; after the dark
passage, the white arches and green knots of hedge are like a painting, too bright to be real. A gust of cool air wraps her gown around
her legs. A wisp of hair tickles her cheek. The sky above the clock
tower is a limpid autumnal blue.

But she's not alone. Léo Martin is sitting on the bench, a cigarette
between his fingers. He's rattling a matchbox in his other hand. It
makes a scratchy, ragged tattoo in the sheltered quietness. Next to
him, the pages of a discarded newspaper flutter gently in the breeze.
She catches sight of the headline: *Bible Bonfire Engulfs Church*. The
picture is stark, a blaze of white and gray against black, a cross in
flames. Below it, a smaller headline announces: *Overwhelming Enthusiasm for Social Purity*.

He turns his head and sees her. He smiles politely, welcoming her,
as if she's the one who's intruding. For a few seconds she is frozen,
not quite believing that he is here, with his tobacco smoke and his
despicable newspaper.

"Put that out!"

He blinks. "What?"

She points at the cigarette. The muscles in her arm are as tight as
wires. "You're not allowed to smoke here. Put it out."

"I——" He hesitates. "Why?"

"It's against the rules."

"Yes," he says, "but why? I'm outside. What harm is one cigarette going to do? There aren't any scholars here to see me." He blows smoke into the blue sky, as if he's inviting her to watch it evanesce. "Unless you're afraid I'll corrupt *you*," he adds, laughing. Of course, laughing.

"There are priceless books here," she says. Her voice grates in her ears. "There is a library which—if someone was careless with a naked flame, a spark—"

"On the other side of the school," he says. "Not in this cloister."

She draws in her breath. There are flickering lights at the edge of her mind's eye, the image of thousands of matches scattered across a stone floor. "Don't you have a healthy fear of being burned to death in your bed? You of all people—" She wants to shame him, to throw his endless merciless jokes back in his face; but that would mean admitting to having read his diary.

His eyes narrow. "What are you talking about?"

"It doesn't matter, Mr. Martin. Put out your cigarette. Now."

He holds her gaze. Something hardens in his face. He says, "Perhaps if you said *please*."

She grabs his arm, and before he has time to react, she has reached across his body and plucked the cigarette from between his fingers. She dashes it to the ground and grinds it out with the toe of her shoe, and then they are staring at each other. She is so angry she finds it difficult to breathe. Even though she has let go of him, she can feel the warmth of his body, the sturdy flesh and bone of his arm; the feeling is so strong that she wipes her hand on her gown. She is shaking.

He says, "What on earth . . . ?"

He is looking at her as though she is hysterical. Is she? She wants to cover her face, but it's too late. Instead she bows her head and fusses with her cuffs until her fingers are steady and the heat has left her cheeks. She says at last, "While you're here, Mr. Martin, you must obey the rules. This isn't a holiday camp."

"You're telling me." A new angle of light falls on his face as he turns his head, and for the first time she notices the dark circles under his eyes, the gaunt cheekbones. The fine-veined flush of good living he had on arrival has faded, but there's a pallid tinge around his mouth that doesn't look any healthier. He hasn't shaved, and it gives his jaw a gritty, silvery look.

"Mr. Martin," she says, "you've chosen to be here. If it doesn't suit you, why don't you leave?"

He fiddles with the matchbox, pushing it open and shut.

"You're not actually studying the *grand jeu,* are you?" When he doesn't answer, she shakes her head. "This is a sacred place. If you want to sit and read the paper, go somewhere else."

He glances up at her. "Where do you suggest?"

"Go back to government," she says. "Go back to the Party. Draft more Purity Laws. Exile more Christians." She gestures at the paper. "That's what you do, isn't it? Burning Bibles, burning churches . . . Go back to *that.*"

He takes out a match and strikes it. The flame hisses and dies. "I can't."

"Really? Why not?" There's a silence. He throws the spent match aside, into the flower bed. She wants to pick it up and press the hot end into his skin. "You think I don't know why you're here?" she says, fighting to keep her voice under control. "The Party wants to take over Montverre or to close it down. You're a spy. You're here to give orders to the Magister Scholarium. Well, I can't stop you. But don't imagine you're welcome. You're not part of this place, and you never will be."

He pauses, his head bent, another virgin match ready in his fingers.

"Today we agreed that next year no Christians will be admitted. I expect that makes you happy, doesn't it?"

"No," he says. Suddenly his voice has an edge to it, as if for once he's telling the truth.

"Oh? Well, at least you must think it's a step in the right direction."

"For goodness' sake!" He's on his feet, turning on her, the matches and their box scattered in the soil underneath the bench. "I'm not part of the Party anymore. I'm stuck in this blasted place because they don't want me back." He grimaces, as if he's said too much, but after an instant he goes on. "You really want to know why I'm here? I tried to water down the Culture and Integrity Bill. I thought it was going too far. That's why they sacked me. I'm here in disgrace."

"Going *too far*?" she echoes, trying to cling to her advantage, but it comes out sounding thin and petty.

He shoots a look at her. "I don't see *you* packing your bags in protest."

"That's unfair. I did my best—"

"As did I." He scuffs his heel at the matches on the ground, driving them deeper into the soil. "Unfortunately, our best isn't much good, is it?"

There's a silence. She tips up her face to the sky. Her head is spinning. Perhaps he's lying, but she doesn't know why he'd bother; it's not as if he cares what she thinks of him. Why would he?

He sits down. After a moment he picks a match and the empty box out of the earth and lights another cigarette.

"You might as well work on the *grand jeu*," she says. "While you're here."

He raises one shoulder, without looking at her.

"You were a promising player, once." Now he does flash a glance at her. She stoops and brushes her hand along the top of the hedge, releasing the scent of box. "I've . . . I heard that your Gold Medal game wasn't bad."

"Thank you." She can't tell whether he's being sarcastic.

"If you put your mind to it, you might write something . . . good."
It sticks in her teeth, the word, but it's true.

"How kind."

"This is Montverre. It's a waste to be here and—"

"Yes, it's a waste! You think I don't know that? It's a prison."

She folds her arms. "Then do your time."

He blinks. After an instant, a reluctant half-smile tugs at the corner of his mouth.

"By all means," she says, "leave as soon as you are able. In the meantime—write a game. Study. You may tell the librarians that I said you could look at the archives."

A silence. "Are you trying to keep me out of mischief?"

"Ideally." And for a second, swift and elusive as a breath of wind, there's warmth between them. Not as much as a smile, but a kind of . . . complicity. She turns away, disgusted with herself. The smell of tobacco is half nauseating, half seductive. When was the last time she smoked? A memory catches her off guard: wide night sky, endless stars, a voice laughing in her ear. She shakes it away. That life has gone. She's here now, in the autumn sunshine, with a man she doesn't know. "I must go," she says, and immediately despises herself. She doesn't have to make excuses to him.

He doesn't answer.

She pauses in the archway. "Oh," she says, "and please don't use this courtyard again. It's reserved for magisters."

She can't settle down to anything. She teaches her third-years like a five-finger exercise—automatic, joyless, distracted—and lets them go before the clock strikes. Afterward she hurries down to the Great Hall. Part of her flinches from the prospect of silence, but she is still enough herself to know that it will be good for her. To let go of routine—to let go of the *grand jeu,* of God—would be dangerous;

now more than ever she needs the reassurance of it, the bedrock. She collapses onto a bench and bows her head. She tries to breathe slowly, but now that she's sitting down, her heartbeat seems to grow louder instead of softer.

She can't keep still, so she tries to focus on listening. Beyond the dominant thump of blood in her ears, there are other sounds. The wind is a whole orchestra. Deep notes surge in the trees outside, a loose windowpane rattles, the stone chimney sings. But she can't concentrate. She rubs her hand on her gown, as if her palm is sticky: but the memory of grabbing Léo Martin won't be wiped away. It makes her grit her teeth with shame for having lost her temper— what would the other magisters think if they'd seen her?—but there's a deeper unease, a creeping sensation under her skin.

When was the last time she touched someone, was touched? She can't remember. Magisters bow, they don't shake hands, and she trims her own hair when it gets too long. Can it have been when Aunt Frances said goodbye to her, when she left England? Surely not; that was years ago. But she has been at Montverre continually since then, in spite of being allowed to travel in the vacations; she has kept herself impris—no, protected, safe—here. And she doesn't *want* to be touched. When she was elected Magister Ludi, it was a relief to know that she would be celibate now forever; she'd almost laughed at Aunt Frances's concern, her gentle questions about children and marriage and . . . well, *you know what*, darling . . . Maybe the other magisters had secret mistresses, maybe not; it didn't matter that they'd treat her differently, that she'd be out at the first hint of scandal, because scandal was the last thing she wanted. The thought of someone else's flesh made her skin crawl.

But now . . . She tries to evoke the feeling of an embrace, the brush of a mouth on her cheek, but it is like something she once read about. It's certainly nothing like remembering Martin's jacket under her fingers, the solidity of his arm, muscle and bone . . . He smelled of tobacco and newsprint. It surprised her; now that she is alone, she can admit that to herself. Which is foolish, of course, since he was smoking and reading a newspaper. What had she been expecting? The scent of tweed and cheap soap? The mustiness of the scholars, of too-seldom-laundered linen? Or something more . . . glamorous?

She opens her eyes. She hadn't realized that she'd closed them. How can she sit here in this sacred space, thinking about Martin? Or rather, how dare he worm his way into her head, when she has earned the right to be here alone, her own master, Magister Ludi? And why did she tell him he could look at the archives? She wants him gone as soon as possible. He should be playing his own, more puerile games: politics, oppression.

All of a sudden, without meaning to, she gets to her feet and steps into the silver-edged space where the *grand jeu* is played. She sketches a gesture of *ouverture,* a deep unflourished bow that she knows would make the Magister Motuum nod in appreciation. But for once it feels theatrical, the triumph of technique over inspiration.

She bows her head. There are always days when the *grand jeu* is out of reach. There's no reason to feel that today is especially significant. She's distracted, that's all.

Something on the floor catches her eye. A dark stain between the stones. Rust, soil, paint.

Blood.

She crouches down. For a stupid, dislocated second she thinks that somehow it is her fault: as though she could have bled here without noticing. But it's dry and the stones have been scrubbed, the stain lingers only in the crevices. In a different light, you wouldn't see it. There's no way of telling how long it's been there. If not her, then who?

She stares at the neat dark runnel between the stones, her mind racing. Perhaps she's mistaken. How can there be blood here? Have the scholars been fighting? Scholars do fight, sneaking down to the gymnasium at night. In general it's simpler to let them get on with it, so the magisters pretend they don't know. But it would be different, if they came here; if they were caught, they'd be expelled for sacrilege. To defile the very ground of the *grand jeu*—yes, that would be unforgivable.

But someone has done it.

In a rush, out of nowhere—unless it has been shadowing her all day, trailing red footprints behind her, breathing hotly down her neck ever since the moment when she woke in a bloodstained bed—a memory punches into her and she is staring at a crimson smear on white porcelain, so vivid she can't see anything else. For an instant—a few seconds, an eternity—she is caught in the clarity of shock, where everything is simple. She is at home, and a minute ago she had dropped her suitcase in the hall and come upstairs, wincing at the new rot in the staircase and the crumbling plaster, calling her brother's name; but all that is already forgotten. The bathroom door is ajar. She pushed it open. And there must have been a moment when she saw what was there, but for some reason that, too, has disappeared, as if her whole life starts now—now, as she steps over the scarlet puddle on the clay tiles, which creeps outward, silently encroaching on the painted birds and fleurs-de-lis. Now, as she takes in the handprint on the washstand and the looser smear on the bathtub, her mind following the logic: here he grabbed for balance, here he slipped to his knees, losing consciousness, and here . . . And inexorably her gaze goes to the thing on the floor, the thing she has in fact been trying not to look at, the thing that is, or was—and her mind teeters on the tense of the verb like the edge of a cliff, as if she can still stumble back to safety—is or was, was is *was*—

Her brother. Her brother who was her own self, only not; so close he was like a twin, like a mirror, only so different he was always out of reach—

Who has poured all the color in his body out onto the floor.

Who has come to the end of color, and air and light. Has gone—
has *chosen*—

Who is dead. He's dead.

And it is her fault. If she had been here. If she had come straight
home when he telegrammed. If she had, had not, had—

She wrenches herself back into the present. Or tries to. The Great
Hall of Montverre blurs and wavers as if she is seeing it through water. She staggers to her feet. She can't shake it off.

There is someone watching her. She spins around, damp-faced,
off-balance. But the doorway is empty.

Then the clock strikes, making her jump; and gradually—barely
audible at first, until it broadens and swells into cacophony—a cho-
rus of young male voices trickles along the passage, joking and arguing as if they've never heard of the divine or the *grand jeu* or death.

9

LÉO

He'd forgotten what rain was like in the mountains, until this morning. It has set in like gravity: impersonal, unchanging, the inexhaustible sky falling on and on. After an hour, it's hard to imagine a world without it; after two hours, he stops trying. After breakfast he takes the long way round to the gatehouse to pick up his paper, but the final dash across the corner of the courtyard leaves him soaking and wet-footed. He might as well not have bothered. He pauses in the doorway to shake himself off like a dog. The porter nods at him and holds out his post. "Filthy, isn't it, sir?"

He takes the proffered bundle and looks through it. A headline catches his eye: *New Security Measures Welcomed*. Later he'll read the paper all the way through, but out of duty, not curiosity. These days, every edition seems the same, full of the same story, the same people. Dettler, the new Minister for Culture, announcing a festival of the arts, defending the tax on books; the Old Man exhorting the army to keep the peace in lackluster rhetoric that no one believes. Violence. The absence of his own name . . . There's a letter from Mim; he tries not to notice that her handwriting is shakier by the week. An envelope addressed in an unfamiliar hand, but franked, not stamped, and with the crest of the Ministry for Information on it—a Party circular, which must be someone's idea of a joke. And . . . He hesitates, an unexpected warmth running through him.

There's a letter from Chryseïs. She has never written to him before, but he recognizes her *e*'s and *r*'s from her signature. It's thick, too— two pages. They parted on bad terms; perhaps this is an apology or at least some news, government gossip or something about the latest fashions . . . Right now he's hungry for all of it. He turns his back on the porter and rips the envelope open.

It's the tailor's bill, forwarded from his previous address. She hasn't included a note. He crams the whole bundle of post into his pocket and stares out into the courtyard. Rain, gray light, gray stone, a sky so swollen it gives him a headache.

That's it. He has lost. It's not exactly that he's made a decision: more a realization that at some point, without noticing, he's swallowed his pride, like a rotten tooth. There's nothing but a sore gap where it used to be, and the weary knowledge that today, finally, he'll go to the library and begin work on a *grand jeu*. He's lasted less than three weeks; boredom has broken him faster than he thought possible. Well—boredom and regret, and the clock that strikes every blasted hour above his bedroom. And Mim's plaintive letters, and Chryseïs, and the way the world goes on turning without him. He hates the *grand jeu,* it's a waste of time; but right now he wants to waste time. He wants time to pour through his hands like water.

He dumps the newspaper in the bin and steps out into the courtyard before he can change his mind. Rain slides down into his collar. He sprints the last few meters, ducks into the doorway of the library, and pushes the door open. Drops of rain patter on the floor and the scholar at the nearest desk looks up from his work, frowning.

Léo puts his hands in his pockets. Good God, the smell . . . Dust, books, damp wool, and male bodies, and under it all a perverse woody sweetness. He draws to a halt, his stomach tightening, tempted to leave again. But the door has already swung closed with a clunk. Instead he makes his way to the stairs that lead up to the

Biblioteca Ludi and the archives. The attendant is making a note; he finishes it before he glances up. "Yes?"

"Léo Martin. I have permission to work in the archives. From Magister Dryden."

The attendant says nothing until he has found the right ledger and flipped to the right page to check his name; then he nods and stands to unlock the door. So Magister Dryden kept her word; Léo isn't exactly surprised, but he isn't grateful, either. She's the sort of woman he would never have looked at in his last life—not beautiful or charming, not even amiable—and he resents being indebted. She thinks she owns Montverre, but she was never a scholar here; *he's* the Gold Medalist, and one who could have been in her place now if—well, if he'd wanted to be. He used to be Minister for Culture, damn it. Why should he—

"Sir?"

"Yes?" He hopes he wasn't thinking aloud, in a petulant childish whisper. He summons a reassuring smile to show that he's not a madman.

The attendant beckons Léo up a little corkscrew of a staircase and through another door. Léo never knew that the archive was so big; the room stretches the whole length of the main library beneath, cabinet after cabinet, shelves and shelves of books and files. The assistant says, "Do ask me if you need anything," without meaning it, and scurries away. The door shuts with a quiet thud.

There are desks set between the cabinets, a long way apart from one another. A few are piled with papers and books, but most are empty. Léo chooses one in mahogany with green leather and gold tooling, next to a low, round window. Rain patters on the glass, and a damp draft slides like a blade around the edge of the central casement. He leans forward and wipes the pane with his sleeve, but all he can see is lowering sky and—if he bends at an undignified angle—a glimpse of treetops.

It's as good a spot as any. He sits down. The desk has paper in one drawer, pen and ink in another. He wipes the leather with his damp sleeve until it gleams, sets the blank paper out, and lays the pen neatly beside it. He rests his chin on his fist and looks down at the page. It's very empty.

The theme of the *Bridges of Königsberg* stutters into life. It's so loud he looks around, ready to complain, before he understands that it's inside his head. It has a reedy, whining timbre to it that makes his jaw hurt.

He gets to his feet again. He rattles the change in his pocket. Enough for a train ticket to somewhere else. Anywhere else.

But if the Party heard he'd escaped . . . Maybe they're still watching him somehow. Any one of the servants could be a spy—or an archivist, a scholar, a magister . . . The back of his neck prickles. There have been too many accidents: a car crash, the Minister for Business and his mistress; another minister dragged from an icy river after rumors that he was going to defect; a journalist found in a ditch with a smashed skull. He remembers the man who was watching him on the path to Montverre, the day he arrived; he shuts his eyes and tries to recall whether there was the telltale bulge of a weapon in his jacket. No. Yes. Perhaps it's his imagination. But his mouth is dry. The *Bridges of Königsberg* mocks him in 7/4 time. He can't leave.

And since he's here, he might as well do something. Read a game. Make notes. It doesn't matter what. Blindly he strides to the card index, opens a drawer at random and stares at the rank of dog-eared cards, packed tight. He pulls one out and forces himself to focus. It's handwritten, in a thin looping script that has faded almost to invisibility. *CORNIER, Gaultier. M. Corporeum MV. (1816), sch. MV (mat. 1801)* . . . He replaces it without reading any more. There must be centuries of names, here, most of them unknown; and every one has a file somewhere. He'd never realized the archive held so much material. He glances up, imagining the ceiling joists bowing under

the weight. How much of it will ever be read? Then before he admits
to himself what he's looking for, he slides out a different drawer.
MAB–MAS.

> MARTIN, Léonard. Sch. MV. (mat. 1926) Gold Medalist. Notable
> games: *Reflections* (GM, 1.1927. 2.17.1). Other games: 2.1926.17.1.1.
> (*Danse Macabre*, c. A. C. de Courcy), 2.1926.17.1.2 (*Prelude*, F.G. 2.I).
> Papers: 2.1926.17.2, 2.1926.17.3.

It's like looking at his own tombstone.

He turns the card over, checking for a thumbprint or a bent corner
where someone has jammed it carelessly back into its place. But it's
pristine, neat and white, every edge sharp. No one but the archivist
has ever touched it. Ten years, and not one glance . . . Deliberately
he twists the edge until a deep crease spreads like a root across the
typed numbers. Then he slips it back between *MARTIN, Lazare* and
MARVELL, Philip and shuts the drawer with a bang.

He stands still for a long breath; surely he hasn't come here to
moon over his own games, like an old woman brooding on aged
billets-doux . . . But it's one way to distract himself. Section 2 is at
the far end of the room, where the glass-fronted cabinets of Midsummer Games and Layman's Prizes and Gold Medals give way to
shelf after shelf of bare foolscap files, crammed so tightly he can't
read the labels. He turns left into a little windowless alcove, counting back the years. He pulls a folder out to see the whole number,
but it's *2.1926.11.1.3* (*FALLON, Émile, Mask of Tragedy*), and the next
one he chooses is *2.1926.16.3.3* (*LANTZ, Friedrich, Final Exams*). For
a fleeting moment he's tempted to see what idiocies earned Freddie
his third—was it a third, or a lower second?—in his finals, but even
as he's wondering, he replaces it and moves on. And with a jolt, as if
he never truly believed it would be there, he stares at his own name.
MARTIN, Léonard, c. DE COURCY, Aimé Carfax, Danse Macabre.

The *Danse Macabre*. His throat tightens. He has never reread it. He burned his old games—and his notes, textbooks, everything—after his final exams; this must be the only copy in the world. Or no, one of two; it'll be filed under Carfax's name as well. There are moves he can still remember: the chime of a bell, the swell of a melody, the algorithm dying while the breathless tune went on . . . But time has broken the threads that held it together. In his head, it's in fragments: the clicking of dancing bones, flowers and rigor mortis and worms. A feast in a catacomb. A poet being painted in his shroud.

The thought of it fills him with contempt, and something else, an elusive unease that flickers away if he tries to identify it. It was clever, he can remember that—overflowing with ideas, baroque with excess, like a body teeming with rot. English revenge tragedy, *Ars Moriendi*, lullabies, superstitions. And Carfax's melody, that brilliant jaunty allegro that made you consider the human body, the echoes and hollows of it. And the math that Léo discussed and criticized without ever admitting that he didn't *entirely* understand it. Words, images, abstractions. A dark tapestry. Yes, it was clever. But what did any of it have to do with death? Not a scythe and a skull, but—*death*?

He raises his head and sees, not the library shelves, but Carfax at his desk, chewing his pen, oblivious to the black stain on his lower lip. Carfax lost in a problem, staring at nothing, muttering, "I like your variation, but it's not quite right . . ." Or writing furiously, so absorbed he didn't hear the clock strike; or adding diacritics to Léo's notes with a flourish, as if every one was a plucked string. Carfax, whom he could happily have strangled, or thought he could.

Carfax, who killed himself six months later.

Léo sinks down until he's crouching, his head bowed. He closes his eyes. He's here, now. He's not stumbling to a halt in the scholars' corridor, to stare through the half-open door of Carfax's cell at the empty desk and stripped bed; he's not in the Great Hall, frozen in his seat while the Magister Scholarium clears his throat and says, "I'm afraid, gentlemen, I have some very bad news." He's not even in his first government office, opening a police report with clumsy fingers while his private secretary murmurs mutinously about interdepartmental relations. *The deceased, a young man of twenty-two . . . No foul play is suspected . . .* It was a long time ago. It's over.

If Léo hadn't . . . but he won't let himself finish that sentence. It wasn't his fault. It couldn't have been. No one ever said it was his fault. Even if they'd known . . . if someone, anyone knew—

He slaps his own face, hard. It shocks him; it's the gesture of a madman, or one of the Party's political prisoners who've been in solitary for too long. He's a grown man; what is he doing, losing control like this, groveling on the floor like a child? He drags himself to his feet, fumbles with his tie and his cuffs, as if he's being watched. He wipes his face on his sleeve.

Carfax killed himself. He chose to. His mind gave way. That's what it said in the police report: *while the balance of his mind was disturbed.* It was nothing to do with anyone else—with any of it, with Léo or Montverre or even the *grand jeu.* Carfax was a de Courcy, what did they expect? His father drank himself to an early grave, his grandfather was the Lunatic of London Library . . . It was almost bound to happen, sooner or later. They were lucky he didn't murder the rest of the class in their beds. But even to himself, he sounds like a politician under attack, with the shrill slippery tone of a minister caught embezzling public funds; and abruptly he's filled with an enormous weariness. It doesn't matter. Carfax is dead, long dead. There are no amends to be made.

The clock strikes, muffled by distance. Faintly there's the sound of voices crossing the courtyard, yelling and laughing as the scholars sprint through the rain to the doorway of the Square Tower.

He slides the *Danse Macabre* off the shelf and flips the folder open. He is holding himself steady for the sight of Carfax's handwriting alongside his own. He can remember pushing his half-complete fair copy across the desk, gesturing to the nodes of math and music. "Fill in the Artemonian, will you? Since you're so good at it." And Carfax giving that wry sideways nod, taking the paper without a word, as if it went without saying that Léo needed his help. But the folder is slimmer than he expects, and the sheet on top isn't the cover sheet of the *Danse Macabre* itself but the Magisters' Remarks. *While somewhat overelaborate,* Danse Macabre *shows an unusual mastery of . . . exuberance, which is paradoxical but fitting . . . in the future we suggest cultivating restraint . . .* He slides out the papers and flips through. Behind the Remarks are his rough notes—yes, he remembers now, he sketched out new ones the night before the game had to be handed in, scribbling frantically, because his real roughs were covered in obscenities and stupid jokes, he can still feel his arm aching . . . And then he reaches the end of the pile and the folder is empty. There's nothing else. The game itself is missing.

He flicks through again, to check. It's gone. So much for the archives. He pulls out the next couple of folders (*MARTIN, Léonard, Prelude,* and *MARTIN, Léonard, Final Exams*) to see if it's been put in one of those by mistake; but it isn't there, either. He hesitates. When he burned his notes he never wanted to see or play or remember the *grand jeu* again—any *grand jeu,* but especially his own. He can still remember the fierce pleasure of dumping the canvas suitcase of books into the brazier at his father's scrapyard and watching the fire devour it. It was late at night, the summer after he graduated, and the sparks floated up like flags and fireworks into the hot dark. Behind him, reclaimed statues bent their heads together as if they'd moved while he wasn't looking; opposite, windows were stacked like blind eyes, reflecting the flames. He could taste soot and sweat, and yes, salt—perhaps he was crying, because he'd brought a bottle of brandy with him in the taxi and he was a mess, swearing and yelling into the fractured echoes. His voice bounced back from piles of bricks and broken fountains. That was the real world, where even houses died and were ripped apart; the *grand jeu* was a gigantic empty charade. He'd made it through his finals, putting in a lusterless, competent performance that disappointed everyone except himself, and then he was free. Three weeks later the head of the office where he was working came to him and asked if he'd ever met the Old Man; a month later he'd joined the Party. And then . . . But the point is, the point *is* that he burned his notes. He didn't hesitate when he threw them into the fire—not for his own games, and not even when he found the *Tempest* at the bottom of the pile, Carfax's handwriting as familiar as the smell of his own sweat. He didn't care if they were the last copies; he would have been glad to think they were. So to be bothered now—to flick back and forth through the file, as if he could conjure the *Danse Macabre* back into existence—is absurd. Why does he suddenly yearn to see it? What's he going to do, check the diacritics?

A second later he remembers, with the same sort of jerk as when he makes an idiotic mistake in a report or trips drunkenly on a curb, that it's a joint game: so it will be filed under Carfax's name, too, with Carfax's rough notes and the Magisters' Remarks. There's no need to be histrionic. Some fool has probably put both copies into the same folder. He slides his finger back along the shelf. *2.1926.4, 2.1926.5* . . . Yes. *DE COURCY, Aimé Carfax, c. MARTIN Léonard,* Danse Macabre. His stomach twists a little. He tastes ersatz coffee on the back of his tongue.

This file is empty, too. Or rather it has two sheets of Magisters' Remarks and nothing else. Not even Carfax's roughs. They were beautiful in their way, strong-boned and intricate, as if all his ideas came out fully formed; he could swear he remembers Carfax handing them in with his fair copy, his ironic murmur as they left Magister Holt's office together: "*Alea iacta est.*" Now he stares at the Magisters'

Remarks, but although phrases rise to the surface, he hardly sees them. *A new freedom . . . departure from classical simplicity . . . energy, a sort of serious hilarity . . .* But where on earth is the game itself? Automatically he reaches for the next folder along. It's *JANSEN, Pierre*, Circles and Triangles. He flips through the files on either side: nothing.

He returns to the card index. There is nearly an entire drawer for *DE COURCY*; a couple of entries run on to five or six cards. But Carfax isn't there.

He shuts the drawer with a thud and stands staring into space, frowning.

He didn't come to the archives to look at his own games; still less, to pore over Carfax's. But this . . . He should check again or ask an archivist, but he already knows it wouldn't do any good. Carfax is gone. Wiped out of the archive as if . . . He thinks suddenly of the Party photographs, the early ones, with rows of young men grinning, clustered around the Old Man outside beer houses. Or the picture that was taken after the first election, on the steps of the Capitol. The version that hangs in the Old Man's office has fewer faces in it than it used to. But Carfax's games? It doesn't make sense. And it isn't the same. It's only the games, not Carfax himself; his name is still there, the empty files . . . And what is there in those games that anyone would want to erase? Only the magisters have access to the archive, and which of them would care?

He gnaws on a fingernail, tasting soap. Rain runs in columns down the window, splitting and rejoining like some arcane graph. He can't bear to admit defeat, but what can he do? It's as though he's staring at a blank wall, waiting for a door to appear. It doesn't. And finding Carfax's games wouldn't bring him back from the dead. It would make it worse, even. He shuts his eyes, imagining how it would feel to see that handwriting again. Pain, like breathing into a cracked rib cage. A scratched eyeball. Stupid to long for it.

When he shifts his weight, something crackles in his pocket. He pulls out his letters, uncrumples Chryseïs's bill, and folds it neatly into four before throwing it into the nearest wastepaper basket. He opens Mim's letter and skims it. The usual. He forgets it as soon as he drops it on top of the bill. He opens the Party circular, watching the patterns of water on the windowpane, and glances at it as he leans over to put it in the rubbish, too.

It isn't a circular. It's handwritten, and the writing is . . . Perhaps it is familiar, after all; it sets off an elusive tingle of recognition. Perhaps it's only because he was thinking about Carfax, and ten years ago— but no. He knows it. *Dear Léo* . . . He flips it over to the signature. *Yours affectionately, Émile Fallon.* He hasn't seen Émile's handwriting since . . . for years. It leaves a strange taste in his mouth. Why is Émile writing to him?

In a way I envy you. The Ministry has never been so dull. I'm contemplating a change, maybe to the Ministry of Culture—but don't worry, I have no intention of stepping into your old job. You're too much to live up to, as Dettler is finding out fast. Think he must have been blinded by the office and the pretty secretary (she really is, isn't she?) and didn't realize there was any responsibility attached. Only a matter of time before he goes, I imagine.

Funny how your name still comes up in conversation. I do my best to mention you when I can, of course; otherwise people forget so quickly. Out of sight, out of mind. How are you getting on at Montverre? I'd be fascinated to hear what you make of the place now. I've been told the atmosphere has changed a lot. Do be careful, won't you? Since the Arts budget was cut, I expect the place will be starting to crumble. You don't want to slip on the stairs.

Oh, and if you need anything, let me know. Books, music, magazines, and so on. Anything I can do to help. You can pay me back when you're out of exile . . .

Léo clenches his jaw, folds the letter, and puts his hand over it. He can almost feel the words crawling under his palm like ants. It seems chatty, but it isn't, of course.

The doctored photograph in the Old Man's office flashes again into his head, but this time the absences are sharper, more glaring. Will his own face disappear from the front row? Has it already? First his face from a picture, then his name from the records, his body . . . He looks down and sees that he's gripping the edge of the desk, fingers splayed. He's getting morbid; it's the solitude, the boredom, this bloody place . . . The *Bridges of Königsberg* rings in his ears like tinnitus.

He picks up his pen and unscrews the cap. He's trying not to think, trying not to despise himself for his own cowardice. He finds a piece of paper.

My dear Émile, he writes. *Thank you so much for your letter.*

10

FOURTH WEEK OF SEROTINE TERM
(Lost Count of the Days)

I know, I haven't written for ages. I skipped Factorum this afternoon to catch up on sleep, which is why I have the energy to write this. I shouldn't, really, I have a paper to finish for tomorrow ("To what extent did the Pythagorean School of the sixth century BCE prefigure the modern study of the *grand jeu?*"), but the thought of it makes me want to bash my head against the wall. It'll only get harder and harder the later I leave it, so obviously I'm procrastinating.

The joint game, though, is coming along. At least I think it is. Don't get me wrong, I still think Carfax is an arrogant toad. We spent a whole evening last week bickering about our theme: he wanted something mathematical that we could use to explore other ideas (i.e., classical structure, utterly static and boring—imagine the offspring of an encyclopedia and an abacus), and I wanted something bigger, more ambitious, which made him screw up his face like I'd proposed jumping off the roof of the Square Tower. I pushed my ideas about dreams and storms, but he refused point-blank. He kept saying, "We have to start with something true, something *real*," and I kept saying, "Don't be so bloody difficult, Carfax, it's all real, *reality* is real." We got stuck like that for ages, as if the wind had changed mid-conversation, until suddenly for no reason he raised his hand to shut me up. I nearly lost my temper then. He scribbled something on a bit of paper and pushed it toward me. I swear if it had been in Artemonian I would've punched him and risked being expelled for it, but it was math.

"De Moivre," he said. "Heard of him?"

"Didn't he write something to do with complex numbers?"

"De Moivre's law is a hypothetical model that can be used to predict how long people are going to live. For calculating annuities and so on. De Moivre was commonly held to have predicted the date of his own death."

"Math as magic," I said. "Nice."

He smiled. It must be the first time he'd ever smiled at me as if he agreed, not as if he was smirking at my stupidity. It was surprising how it nearly made me forget to despise him. "Exactly," he said. "Since you want to work on something risibly difficult . . . how about death?"

"Death?" I repeated, like an idiot.

"There's a lot of material. I mean, it's huge. Enormous. I think we'd be mad——" He caught himself and looked away, tensing, as he waited for me to make the inevitable comment about his family. There was a second's pause, and then he went on in a kind of rush. "We'd be mad to do it. But . . . there's a musical precedent. The *Danse Macabre*——Saint-Saëns, Liszt."

"Shakespeare, Dante," I said. "'I had not thought death had undone so many.'"

He grinned. "The structure of the Requiem Mass, the tension between an individual and infinity—asymptotes . . ."

"Yes! The rituals of mortality, decomposition, and belief in the eternal."

"The impossibility of comprehending the magnitude of our own demise—our own insignificance." He was teasing me, but he was excited, too, I think.

"The undiscovered country—the deepest mystery of existence itself!" It tipped me over the edge, and I started to giggle like a little kid. And suddenly he joined in, in a sort of high-pitched splutter, his shoulders shaking. I'd never heard him laugh like that. I didn't know he *could* laugh. I thought anything more than a contemptuous snort would make him rupture something. "All right," I said when I could speak again. "You're on."

"If we fail—"

"We fail?" I said, in my best Lady Macbeth voice. As soon as I said it, I was sure he'd raise an eyebrow and say something snobbish about the theater, but to my surprise it made him catch at another gulp of laughter. Then that set us both off again. It was—I've only thought of this now, but it's true—it was as if he'd never laughed before and didn't know how to deal with it. Or like someone who's been holding back tears until finally something snaps . . . But the strangest part of it was the way he got hold of himself—in a split second, from hysterical to sober, swallowing it all down. One moment he was giggling, like me, and I swear he meant it; but the next he was on his feet, his face set, almost angry. I drew back—maybe I'd touched his sleeve or something, I can't remember, but nothing important, nothing that might have made him react like that, surely—and said, "What? What's the matter?"

"That's settled, then," he said, without meeting my eyes. "The theme for our game is—death."

"We who are about to die, etc.," I said. "Yes."

He still wouldn't look at me. I suppose he was furious at himself for getting chummy with someone so thoroughly beneath him. He'd let me glimpse something real about him, and he couldn't stand it . . . I felt all the dislike flood back. As if I'd thought one bout of *fou rire* could make him into a decent human being.

"You'd better go," he said. "I've got work to do."

I said, "I thought this *was* work. I'm certainly not here to enjoy myself."

He shot me a glance. I glared back at him, daring him to say something snide about my Lady Macbeth impression. He didn't. Not aloud, anyway.

I scraped up my notes. "You're right. We both have better things
to do." One of his pages was on top and I dropped it on the floor.
"Work up the de Moivre theme for tomorrow. I'll have a look at
some of the text."

He blinked. You have to give him credit for realizing that he
couldn't take exception to my tone, given how he'd spoken to me.
"All right," he said.

"Good."

There was a sort of tense pause while we tried to work out who
was backing down. (For the record, he was.) Then I left and slammed
the door on him.

It's dinnertime. I'd better go.

BEGINNING OF FIFTH WEEK, SEROTINE TERM

Where was I? Oh yes. We were making progress. Still are, actually.

Yesterday evening we worked straight through from meditation
to past midnight. Halfway through dinner I caught sight of Felix
and wondered why he was looking at me oddly; later I realized
that it was because Carfax and I were sitting together, thrashing
out one of the bits of counterpoint. It's true that I'd never choose
to sit with him normally, but it didn't make sense to break off our
conversation. We're at that stage where everything is fermenting
so fast you have to keep siphoning off the top or it'll all overflow
and be lost. I didn't realize what a joint game would be like; even
though it's Carfax, it's exciting—more exciting, I think, than writing a *grand jeu* on my own. Less lonely. And there are those moments
when something uncanny happens, something else steps into the
space between us, and we're both left marveling at a move neither
of us would ever play. I love the way the game is held together by

the music—Carfax's music, I have to admit he's a much better musician than I am—and the way that gives us more freedom, not less. I can let him look after the structure and add my own harmonies and ideas . . . It's funny, his style is classical and clean, so I don't understand why he makes me feel more exuberant, more daring. Maybe I'm trying to outdo him. I love it when I add a move to something he thinks is already finished and pass it back to him, thinking, *Take* that! Especially when he pretends to bang his head on the desk or gives me a filthy look.

It's bloody hard, though. He was right, we're mad to be trying it. I keep waking up in the middle of the night, imagining the Magisters' Remarks: *This subject is an audacious and indeed distressing choice for second-year scholars, since what might otherwise have appeared confidence is necessarily exposed as the grossest (and most unfounded) arrogance.* Or maybe, even if we stick with the themes, we should take out the Christian stuff? It works, and Magister Holt wouldn't mark us down for that, but it might be frowned on by some of the others. Argh. It's driving me off my onion. My only consolation is that if they pan it, at least Carfax will get the same mark.

Felix keeps asking what we're working on. He was quite persistent this morning, and I don't know why it gave me such satisfaction to tell him it was none of his business. It might have been something to do with the way he sank down next to me at breakfast, as if he was my best friend. (Best friend! Ugh, it's like schoolgirls.) I stood up to leave quite soon after that, as I had to go to the library to look up a bit of Webster, and he gave me a very funny look. "You and Carfax," he said. "Are you . . . ?"

"What?"

"You still hate him, right?"

His voice carried. I saw Émile turn his head, and Pierre.

"Of course I do," I said. I suppose I misjudged my voice, because suddenly the noise in the hall dipped. Carfax was at the end of the far table, with a book; he glanced up and met my eyes for a fraction of a second.

LATER

I am pathetic. I couldn't sleep. I kept lying awake, thinking about what I'd said. It kept going around in my head. In the end I got up, slung my robe on over my pajamas, and went and knocked for him.

When he came to the door, he didn't say anything. He stood there with raised eyebrows and waited.

I said, "Listen, Carfax . . . this evening . . ."

"What are you talking about?"

"When I said to Felix that I still—um, that I hated you . . ."

"Yes?"

I didn't say anything—I hoped he'd just get the message—but he was determined not to help me. Finally I managed, "It was stupid. I shouldn't have said it."

"Why not?"

"Well, because . . ." I trailed off.

"What makes you think I care that you hate me?"

I was too tired to think properly. "I don't hate you," I said. "I mean, occasionally I do, obviously. But mostly I don't."

"How kind."

"Forget it." I turned away. I don't know what I'd been trying to achieve. Of course he wasn't going to admit that he cared a toss. I started to walk away.

Then abruptly he said, "Don't worry, Martin. It's all right." I glanced back at him. He had that glint in his eye that isn't quite warmth. We may not like each other, but it almost feels as though we understand each other better than anyone else in the world. He took his hand off the doorframe and made a mocking gesture of *resemblance* that ended with his hand on his heart. "I only hate you occasionally, too."

He didn't exactly say he'd forgiven me. But it was enough.

FORTY-SECOND DAY OF SEROTINE TERM
(I went back and counted)
Sunday today, thank goodness. And the Magister Cartae forgot to give us any prep (presumably because senile dementia is setting in, but I'm not complaining), so I have hours and hours of free time. Well, hour and hour. Hurrah.

I ought to write to Mim. I've got five unanswered letters sitting on my desk. The last one I haven't even read yet. If I don't reply soon, when I go home at the end of term she'll say something very gentle like "I was so afraid you were ill, darling," and wave me off with a brave, bewildered smile if I try to explain. (Honestly, if something was wrong with me, they'd tell her. It's a school, not a prison camp.) Then again, unless I dash off five long letters and backdate them, she'll do that anyway.

Someone's knocking. I hope it's Carfax, I'm waiting for him to get back to me about the middle movement of *Danse Macabre*. It's infuriating—he must know I'm anxious to get that motif sorted. We've got another four weeks, but that's not as long as it sounds. Every second he wastes feels like an eternity.

LATER
He liked it! Maybe he's not such a toad after all.

What am I saying? Obviously he's a toad. Five seconds after saying, "I think this has definite possibilities," he was explaining all the corrections he'd written on it (in Artemonian, naturally). He was sitting at his desk, his head bent over the bit of paper, scratching tinier and tinier hieroglyphics in the margins, talking so quickly I lost track of what he was saying. I stared at his hand on the paper, and the veins running across the knuckles. Then he looked up. "Hey, Martin," he said. "Are you listening?"

"Sure," I said.

He narrowed his eyes at me. "What did I say?"

I was going to bluff, but I couldn't think of anything. It wasn't just that I was annoyed. There was something about the light—late afternoon light turning gold—and the shape of his profile. It was like a painting. The bones of his neck, the line of shadow under his collar. I had a crazy impulse to put my palm on the lowest vertebra to feel the heat of his skin. At least it might have made him shut up, even for a few seconds. "I'm . . . surprised you like it," I said.

His mouth twitched. "Well," he said, "so am I, to be honest."

I had to walk over to the window and look out, turning my back on him. I didn't trust myself. Ugh, he is so exasperating.

It's ridiculous that I feel euphoric because some supercilious inbred bastard thinks my move has *possibilities*. Get hold of yourself, Martin.

EVEN LATER

I went down to the Lesser Hall with Émile and Jacob to play a few bouts, but my mind wasn't on it and I lost. Fencing is a stupid sport, anyway; wish we could have punching bags instead. After a while I sat down on the bench and watched the others. Even then I couldn't concentrate. I watched the sky darken through the windows, feeling light-headed, sort of dizzy and breathless. I've never had a problem with the altitude, but suddenly I could feel how high up we are, how thin the air. My heart seemed louder than usual, too. It wasn't exactly bad, just odd. I haven't been sleeping well recently, so it's probably that. Or I'm coming down with something.

FORTY-FOURTH DAY OF SEROTINE TERM

This afternoon we only had math and meditation, so Carfax and I decided to spend the rest of the day in the library. The middle movement is pretty much complete, or at least as complete as it can be before we go back for another look, and we're trying to work out how to fit the algorithm and the tune together. We sat there in silence for half an hour, both of us making notes, but I wasn't getting anywhere and I don't think Carfax was, either. I found myself staring into the middle distance, and then realized I was staring at him. He looked pretty exhausted, actually—pale, red-eyed, chapped lips—and I put my pen down and said, "Are you all right?"

"What?"

"Never mind." I don't want him to get ill; if he went under now, I don't know what would happen to our game. The thought of having to finish it on my own brings me out in a cold sweat.

"I'm fine," he said after a moment.

"You look terrible."

He gave a twitchy shrug. "I had some news. My . . . a family matter."

I opened my mouth to ask whether someone had escaped from the lunatic asylum. Then I shut it again; but I saw him notice. He gathered his stuff together and stood. I said, "Where're you going?"

"What's it to you?"

I rolled my eyes. "What's up? You can't take offense at something I didn't *say*—"

"I know what you're thinking. You don't have to pretend."

"Really? So what am I thinking?"

He hesitated. Then he shut his mouth again and walked away. I started to go after him, but then I remembered my notes—if I lost my notebook, I'd be scuppered—and went back for them; so by the time I got outside he was already disappearing into the Square Tower. I called his name, but either he didn't hear or he was ignoring me. I sprinted across the courtyard, slipped on the tiles, and cannoned into Felix, who was emerging from the doorway. He said something to me, laughing, but I pushed him aside and climbed up the stairs two at a time.

Carfax was standing on the threshold of his cell, looking in. Then belatedly I made sense of what Felix had said: something about my having missed the fun.

Carfax looked around. Then he spread his arms and stood aside, inviting me to look.

I have no idea where Felix had found so many matches. He must have got someone to send him parcels full of them. They were scattered everywhere, like a mad game of spillikins: on the bed, the desk, the windowsill; in the washbasin; all over the floor. I caught a faint whiff of sulfur. I think I made a noise that wasn't quite a laugh.

"Well done," Carfax said in a tight voice.

"I didn't—"

"Very impressive. Very . . . amusing."

"It wasn't me! I was with you in the library."

"Oh, I know," he said. "I'm your alibi as well as your victim." He smiled at me, without warmth. "Why did you follow me? To see me open the door?"

"It *wasn't*," I said, and then, before I could stop myself, "It must have been Felix. I saw him a moment ago, coming down. Didn't you see him, too?"

"Yes. But . . ." He tilted his head to one side, his eyes hard. "So the familiar demon has got free of the sorcerer, has it?"

"That's—" I broke off. Bloody Felix. "It's not my business what he does."

Carfax pushed at the matches on the floor with his toe, clearing a tiny patch of floorboard. Then he leaned against the side of the door, his shoulders sagging. In a different voice, he said, "You know, Martin . . . I looked forward to coming to Montverre. I dreamed about it for years. All those people studying the *grand jeu*, praying, making music and math . . . I thought it would be like a kind of retreat. Hard, because the *grand jeu* is hard, but not—not like this."

I didn't say anything. I didn't know what to say. The bloody matches weren't my fault.

"The *grand jeu* is worship, isn't it? One way for humans to approach the divine. Trying to embody truth and beauty. A testament to the grace of God in the minds of men."

"Is that a quote from Philidor?"

It was as if he hadn't heard. "Shouldn't the *grand jeu* make us better people?"

I said, "That's an essay question—"

"No!" he said. "No, it isn't. It's a real question, and the answer is yes." He shook his head, with a kind of grimace. "So why are you all such bastards?"

"Carfax . . . It's only a joke, there's no need to be so—"

He swung around to stare into my face, his eyes narrowed. "Do you know why your games are shit, Martin?"

"What?" It took me a second to take in what he'd said. "They're not *shit*. I came second in the year."

"Yes, yes, I know. Second in the year. That's not because your games are any good, it's because there's nothing wrong with them. Nothing to mark down. They're completely empty. There's nothing in them at all, no emotion, no truth."

"You've been talking to Magister Holt," I said. "I don't know why I'm surprised, everyone knows you're his pet."

"He agrees, does he? Well, he's right. You're a bad player. And you know why? Because you're nothing but a bully. The only authentic feeling you ever show is contempt. When I wrote that parody of your games last year . . ." He stumbled a little, as if he hadn't meant to admit it, but I didn't have time to react. "When they all laughed. It was because they recognized you. *You.* It wasn't your juxtapositions or your minor fifths or your pretentious three-level note play that they were laughing at. It's what those things cover up. You rely on gimmicks because never, not once, have you put anything of yourself into a game. We can all see it. You're a thug and a coward and you'll always fail at the *grand jeu* because you fail as a human being."

I forced myself to hold his gaze until he blinked and looked away.

"They don't hate me," I said, and I was pleased at how steady my voice was. "The rest of the class. They laughed at me once. So what? None of them think I'm a failure. They think I'm clever and amusing. They hate *you.*"

"Yes, I know," he said. There was a pause, and he added with a dry edge, "And not just occasionally." Then suddenly I wasn't exactly angry anymore.

He turned and went into his cell, kicking a path through the matches. He shook them off his blankets on to the floor, sat down at the foot of his bed and bowed his head.

I cleared my throat. "Do you think the *Danse Macabre* is shit?"

Another long pause. I could feel my heart beating in my jawbone and between my teeth. "No," he said at last. "No, that's different."

"Because of you? You're my savior, are you?"

"I don't know. I don't know why."

"And of course," I said, "*your* games are a model of self-revelation."

His shoulders jerked with a single, ironic cough of laughter, as if I'd made a bad joke. After a moment he reached out and brushed the matches off the nightstand. They pattered on to the floor. There was one left on his pillow and he rolled it between his finger and thumb. Then, very deliberately, he leaned over and struck it against the wall.

I grabbed it from him. I don't remember moving, but I was there in front of him. It felt like blowing the flame out took all the breath I had. "For pity's sake, Carfax!"

"What?"

"What do you mean, *what*? You drop a naked flame in here, it'll go up like——"

"Like the London Library?"

I checked that the match was properly out and dropped it into the ewer on the nightstand. When I turned back to Carfax, he had a curious little smile on his face. Something about it made my spine tingle. I took hold of him and dragged him to his feet. "Come on," I said, and manhandled him to the door.

"What're you—let go of me——"

I got him into the corridor. "Stop arsing around."

He pulled away and stared into my face, frowning. Then he rolled his eyes. "I'm touched," he said. "Honestly, Martin. You really think self-immolation is my style? I'm not going to burn myself to death. I wouldn't give you all the satisfaction."

"Then what was that?"

He sat down on the windowsill, folding his arms, and stared at me mulishly.

"I'll get a servant to clear it up," I said. "Go back to the library."

He tipped his head back, examined the ceiling. I waited, but he didn't give any sign of having heard what I'd said.

"Look . . ." I could have slapped him, one cheek and then the other. I could actually see the marks my hand would leave, two vivid red prints across his face. "Don't flatter yourself, Carfax. I couldn't care less if you burn to death." He looked at me then. "Stay alive until we've finished the joint game. That's all I ask."

Silence. I felt sick and off-balance, like my heart had dropped into my stomach. I walked away. I didn't think he was going to answer, so it took me by surprise when he said quietly, "Thank you."

"You wanted honesty, didn't you?" But I didn't turn around. I didn't care if he heard.

I'm not a thug. I'm not a bully. Am I? Who does he think he is, to say that?

It wasn't even me. It wasn't even *me*.

LATER

I went to find Felix. He wasn't in his room. When I finally tracked him down, he was in one of the music rooms, bashing out scales. He didn't notice that I was there until I closed the piano lid and he barely got his fingers out of the way. "Hey! What the—"

"Leave Carfax alone," I said.

"What? It took me *ages* to get all those matches, even with my cousin sending me two packs a week."

"It wasn't funny."

He rocked back on the piano stool, screwing up his face. "Yes, it was. What's up with you? I thought you'd—"

"Leave him alone, all right? I've had enough. It's boring."

He stared at me. Then he reached for some sheet music and flicked through. Without looking up, he said, "You're going soft. Or are you scared he'll go running to Magister Holt?"

"No! I don't want him to crack up before the end of term, that's all. Come on, Felix. We're doing a joint game together, I need him compos mentis."

"You said you still hated him. You said—"

"That's not the point!" I pulled the music away from him and slapped it down on the piano. (*Am* I a thug and a bully?) "Once our game's handed in, you can make his life a misery. Until then, hands off. All right?"

He muttered, "All right." There was nothing else to say, so I left him to it.

Once when I was small and Dad took me to the scrapyard, I found a watch on the floor of the office. It turned out it had been dropped by one of his clients. Dad asked me if I'd picked it up. It was beautiful, with a rotating dial for the phases of the moon, and I wanted to keep it more than anything in the world. So I shook my head. Dad got down on his knees and said, "Léo, if you tell me the truth you won't be punished. Did you take the gentleman's watch?"

I started to cry, I think. I nodded and took the watch out of my pocket, held it out to him.

He hissed through his teeth like he was disgusted with me. Then he smacked me across the face, hard.

Why on earth am I thinking about that now?

11

THE RAT

It has begun to snow. For a long time—for days—the clouds empty themselves like old sacks; and then the last rags blow away and the sky clears. The moon slides from one window to the next and the next, without curiosity. The snow reflects so much light you could almost read by it: if you could read at all, that is, and if you were awake to read. Almost everyone beneath this roof is asleep. If the Rat was to pause, she would hear the long murmur of their breaths, the tiny thrum of their collective unconsciousness. Someone else might imagine the school as a boat, drifting on that sea sound; but the Rat has never heard the sea, or of it. And she doesn't pause, creeping on numbed feet along corridor after corridor. As long as she is invisible, she is safe.

It is cold: a deeper cold than ever, now. There are fires in the scholars' hearths. Soon the days will be as brief as a blink and she will hardly move from her knot of blankets beside the blank bulk of a chimney, close under the roof, huddling against the stone for the faintest warmth. She will starve a little and freeze a little and slowly slip into an aching half sleep that will linger till the first thaws. She can feel it coming. But she isn't afraid. Hunger is hunger, and cold is cold, but she is a rat. Rats survive the winter.

She scampers down the narrow staircase. Down here—where the gray ones work—it is dim, lit on only one side by windows set high up on the wall. These rooms are half underground, and the passage smells of damp stone; but when she pushes open a heavy door and slides through, the harsh scent of soap fills her mouth and nose. Deep in the bottom of her mind—beneath layers of shadow, almost lost to sight—a child gags, cries, promises never to say the bad word again. But that child was not yet the Rat; and what do rats care for memories, except of food or traps? She pauses, watching, listening. Opposite her is the dim bulk of the great copper; beyond, beside the banked fire, a flock of shirts droops from a washing line. A single drop of water clicks faintly on the floor.

Quick. She darts across the room and yanks a shirt loose. The other shirts sag and bounce as she pulls them closer together, to hide the gap. She unhooks the loose pegs from the line, crouches and slips them neatly under one of the presses, where no one will ever find them. The shirt flicks a damp arm into her face. Then she is still, straining her ears. Nothing.

She slides through the door at the far end of the room, squashing the shirt up inside the one she is already wearing. It forms a moist knot against her chest and makes her shiver. Most of all she would like another blanket, but the blankets are only washed every few weeks. She is careful to make them think the shirt she has taken is lost, not stolen. She is the wind, the scholars' carelessness, the distracted maid, the accident that leaves the laundry count one short. She must never be a person.

The kitchens are still warm. Her mouth runs with saliva, but she hardly takes anything: the stale heel of a loaf, a cupped handful from the pot of cooling stew, an apple, a bit of cheese. She bolts it all on her feet beside the oven, watching the doorway. Sometimes the gray ones steal food, too—sometimes, even, the others. She has had to hide, holding her breath, while a dark one helped himself from the pantry, loudly furtive in the way that only humans are. Another night there was a white one, old and portly, who smelled heady and rank and knocked a plate to the floor. She was under the table, hud-dled as small and shadowy as she could; her heart nearly choked her as she waited for him to crouch and pick up the pieces. But he only swore and staggered out of the room. She wondered then what it would be like, to break something and not be afraid.

The clock strikes. She doesn't count the strokes, but it reminds her to glance up at the windows. The sky has lost its moonlit sheen. There is no sign yet of morning, but it's time to go.

It is too cold to cross the courtyard in bare feet, so she takes a longer route, up above the Great Hall, the space between the angle of the roof and the curved vault of the ceiling below, and out by a trapdoor. The sudden light of stars breaks on her face like spray. She doesn't look down as she crosses a flat ridge, accepting the freezing squeak of snow between her toes, refusing to let the pain throw her off-balance. She jumps to a ledge and clings to the wall, face-to-face with a leering gargoyle. And here there is a narrow window that only a rat could ease through, then a long drop onto a tiled floor, and finally she is back in the others' world, full of easy paths of corridors and stairs. In spite of the chill she is sweating. But the shirt she stole is safe, tucked into her waistband.

She stops in the middle of the corridor. Out in the open, where anyone could see her.

Someone is crying.

She is always listening; she is the Rat. But what she is hearing catches her by the throat; she can't choose to listen, or not to. She cannot hear anything beyond it. A sobbing voice. She is deaf to every-thing else. It is a man, not a woman—outside her head, not inside—but the Rat is not strong enough to drag herself away from the sound or even to move out of sight; for once, the child the Rat used to be is in control, and she listens and listens, aching. Not for this one, but for another, a long time ago. A half memory, not even a ghost.

Once there was a room with a crack in the wall. There was a

locked door. There was a bucket and a quilt with birds on it. There was a woman who came and went, who brought food and water and songs that ended too soon. And there was the other time, more time, when the ceiling would creep imperceptibly lower unless you watched it, where the only way not to be crushed was to stare without blinking. Or when the floor grew so thin it wasn't safe to tread on it, when you had to stay still (stay here, stay quiet, whatever you do, darling, you must) and every drip from the roof made you tremble. Sometimes smoke would trickle out of the crack in the wall, and if you put your hands to the plaster it would be warm. On stormy days, distant murmurs rose and died, carried on gusts of wind.

The Rat has never been back to that room. She feels it like a numbness deep inside, the one place she will never go. Someone cried in that room—someone lived, waiting, someone waited and slept and tried not to think that anything was wrong, someone stared at the extra food and water that had been left, too much, more than a day's worth, her panic rising until finally she tried the door and found it, to her confusion, unlocked—but it wasn't her. She became the Rat the moment she stepped over the threshold.

She stands still. The crying belongs to what she left behind, not to who she is; every instinct is telling her to run away. It's dangerous to stay here in full view. But she can't. The voice is deep and hoarse, foreign, but the despair is familiar, the choke of suppressed sobs, the fear of being heard. The shame. It's like a loop of wire, tightening as she pulls against it.

The sobs die away, quieter, into gasps. Gradually the sound loosens its grip on the Rat. She takes a breath. But the heaviness is still in her feet, pinning her to the floor: she isn't ready to move yet.

There's a faint rustle, a wet sniff, and the scrape of shoes on stone. A door opening at the far end of the corridor.

Now. Now a rat would run. But it's too late.

For a long time they stare at each other, the Rat and the man at

the far end of the corridor. She should go right now, disappear into
a crevice before he's sure he's seen her. But his stance mirrors hers:
abruptly she doesn't know which of them is prey. He wipes his face
on his sleeve. He is one of the black-robed ones, the young ones; he
has a cross on his collar, standing out stark against the fabric. He sees
her notice it and squeezes it in his fist.

"I'm sorry," he says. "I was . . . I—I wanted somewhere where
no one could hear . . . the cells are so close together, I was afraid
they'd—but I wasn't doing anything wrong . . . please don't . . ."

What does he want of her? She waits, her nerves singing with the
danger. When was the last time she deliberately let someone see her?
It makes her feel raw, prickling all over.

"Are you a servant? I mean—not that it matters, I don't . . . It's
stupid, I'm fine really, it's only . . . the others are—they don't . . .
And the magisters, too. I didn't realize it would be so hard . . ." He
tugs at his collar as if there are teeth on the inside. "You must think
I'm pathetic. Well, the others do. I wish . . ." He stops, starts again,
with a jerk like he's being sick. "And I'm scared for my family. They
keep saying things about Christians being attacked. But we're not
allowed newspapers, and I don't know if they're lying or if . . . Do
you know?"

Silence. She stares at him.

"Um," he says. "Sorry. I'm Simon. Are you, I mean . . . ?"

He is asking her name. As if she has one.

She can't move. She can't remember the last time someone spoke
to her. Asked her a question and expected an answer.

He steps forward.

Whatever there is between them, his movement snaps it. She
swings around, hears him call after her, runs. Perhaps there are footsteps, but they falter and anyway she leaves them behind. She keeps
going, surefooted in the dark, until her breath comes ragged and a
patch of sweat spreads across her back. The shirt she stole is coming

loose from its bundle against her stomach. She clambers onto a pipe to reach a window, drags herself upward, lets herself down again into a storeroom, follows the familiar path through the buckets and brooms to the half-hidden door at the far end. No one is following her now. The door leads to another set of steps; at the top of it is her tiny nook, her nest, where the slates rattle next to her ears at night and the drafts whirl. She drags her stolen shirt out from under her clothes and clutches it to her face, breathing hard. Whose was it, before she plucked it off the washing line? She imagines a young man—the young man she saw—and wonders if she can smell his body under the lingering scent of soap. Abruptly she throws it into a corner. She has never thought this way before. What does she care? What she takes is hers. She drops into the knot of blankets and curls up. She is shaking as well as sweating.

He *saw* her. He thought she was human.

Simon, she thinks. His name was Simon. Since when did she care about names? She is the Rat. She is not one of them. She survives; she does not remember, she does not *feel*. This is wrong. This is dangerous. A rat would smell poison. Simon.

She waits until she has stopped shuddering. Then she lies down and closes her eyes. She is the Rat: she always sleeps dreamlessly, lightly, her mind blank. But tonight she does not. Tonight she stays awake, wrapped in her private dark, listening to the silence in the walls.

12

THE MAGISTER LUDI

The snow below the window of the Biblioteca Ludi is less like a blank page than a primed canvas that has been carried carelessly, buckled and spotted with marks. Any artist would grimace at it and refuse to pay the bill. It's unusable. Unless, the Magister supposes, staring out through the leaded panes until her eyes begin to blur, unless he was one of these modern iconoclasts—the kind of enfant terrible she is old enough now to despise—who might simply exhibit it as it is. She saw a show like that in England once, a childish mess of solid colors, and it made her sick that someone should be allowed to get away with it. That a privileged, pretentious young man should be admired for mere audacity. At her side, Aunt Frances was bewildered, wandering from blue to green and finally coming to a halt in front of a panel of yellow. "Oh my," she murmured, "yes, it is . . . um . . ." The Magister (although she wasn't yet Magister Ludi, she was only Claire, halfway between lives, adrift in a foreign country) said nothing. All the energy she had was concentrated on not looking sideways to where the largest picture hung like a square of new-cut meat, with a thick bloody sheen. Red. If she never saw red again, she would be happy.

Now she blinks away the pink shadows her brain has superimposed on the snow and tries to see what's there. A wide slope crisscrossed by bird prints and flecked with blown fragments of bark. Today is Sunday, and no one has come up the road; it's a seam, a mere ripple under the white. Granite boulders hunch under their caps and burrow into the drifts. The sky is heavy, layered with gray strata. Another snowfall is coming.

There's nothing unusual about snow. She draws back from the window, rubbing her eyes. Every year it falls and stays and melts. It's hardly an omen, even less a surprise. She's being fanciful. Allowing the weather to play on her nerves—is this how the madness begins? One day she feels this vague dread, as if pressure is building on the mountain behind Montverre, waiting for a yell, a dropped plate, a single gunshot . . . and the next she will be creeping to the library, secreting barrels of oil ready to start a conflagration. She laughs. She is so afraid of madness she will drive herself mad thinking about it. She's being self-indulgent. Hysterical. Deliberately she uses the word she hates the most. A womanly state, of no importance. Like the nightmares or the times she can't sleep, the surges of grief that catch her off guard, the new agony of a wound she thought had healed. Neurosis. A feminine lack of detachment. She turns her attention back to her desk and the real blank page. Maybe, after all, this is why she can't look at the snow without a prickling sense of malaise.

At the top she's written *Midsummer Game*. There isn't anything below, not even notes.

She's always been able to compose. That is, in the worst days, ten years ago, the *grand jeu* was an irrelevance, like prayer or food, and no doubt if she had tried to play she would have failed; but it never occurred to her. And for a long time afterward she was too dazed to think at all. Aunt Frances and Cousin Helen taught her feminine pursuits—embroidery, gardening, découpage—and she flung herself into them, soothed by the trivial prettiness of flowers and stitches. It was a relief to let her musician's fingers lose their agility and her brain atrophy until she struggled to remember what day of the week it was. She worked at becoming someone new. Helen helped her to buy new clothes, steering her tactfully toward muted colors instead of black; and she grew to like them, the looser cuts and softer fabrics, the dove gray and mauve and violet of a life in twilight. Everyone was very gentle with her, and she was grateful for that, too. It was as though she were the one who'd died.

But the *grand jeu* was in her blood—no, deeper than that, in her cells, in her nerve endings—and it wooed her back, seducing her slowly with a whistled melody, a chance remark, a copy of *The Gambit* inadequately hidden in Helen's stationery drawer. It took a year or two, but finally something inside her awoke and unfurled. At first it was sly, elusive as the smell of a thaw. Then, like spring, it took her over in a wild rush and left her gasping. She composed the *Primavera* in six weeks, and *Twelve Variations on the Moon* in two months. After that she caught her breath and forced herself to slow down, to study and broaden her knowledge; but that dim half-life had been left behind, and she knew she would never go back to it. There were moments, composing or playing or arguing (because although the Drydens weren't *grand jeu* masters, they were educated, at least, and so were their friends) when she felt an echo of the pure joy she'd felt before her brother died. It would never be the same, not ever, but it was all she had. It was always there. She could step into the clear air of the *grand jeu* as easily as opening a door. Even when she became Magister Ludi, she was never afraid that she'd fail; she'd as soon have doubted her ability to swallow.

Not until now. Not until this blank page.

Midsummer Game . . . She doesn't have a title or a theme. Before, inspiration has come like a wave, knocking her to her knees; or like a trail of sweetmeats scattered along a forest path; or like the beam of a torch, showing only the next step and the next. She's used to the differences between *grands jeux,* the way they have to be trapped or cajoled or even resisted. It makes her think of an old exam question: *Make a case for ONE of the following as a metaphor for the grand jeu: a garden; an automobile; a banquet; a railway accident . . .* But she has never had *nothing*. She has never wondered, with a clench of panic in her gut, whether she will ever compose another game again.

If she can't write her Midsummer Game . . . She can't imagine what would happen if she defaulted. Even if she was ill, another magister would be asked to perform it in her place, from her score. She has no choice. She must produce a game—and not just any game, a game good enough to be worthy of the first female Magister Ludi— or else she will lose everything. In front of the other magisters, the invited dignitaries, foreign professors, journalists . . .

This time is precious. Every second wasted is a second lost. Come on, think. But her mind stays empty. She feels an unexpected surge of sympathy for yesterday's class of scholars, gaping at their first page of Artemonian.

It's no good. She tells herself that it will come. She flicks her notebook shut. The desk is piled so thickly with books and papers that barely any wood is visible. The top volumes have grown a sparse fur of dust. She picks up a few tomes and looks around for somewhere to put them, but the shelves closest to her are already chaotic and overloaded. After a moment she replaces the books in the clean square of dust-shadow. A few old envelopes have been propped half hidden against the wall. She can't tell exactly how long they've been there, but it's too late to bother opening them. She recognizes the franking mark on one; it's from the Ministry of Culture, who've been pestering her about a *grand jeu* festival in the capital, in the summer vacation. *For the common man,* they said in their first letter, as if that was something she would approve of. She drops it straight into the bin, followed by the others. Recently the Council has been arguing about whether scholars should be allowed to receive mail during the term; she sometimes wishes that the magisters weren't. The outside world is a distraction, at best. At worst, it can destroy you. For a split second she remembers the sensation of a curl of flimsy paper between her fingers, a telegram: *COME HOME PLEASE STOP AM AFRAID TO*

BE ALONE. Then she jams the lid on the thought and pushes it to the back of her mind. She resists a sudden urge to get up and check that Léo Martin's diary is safely locked away. Of course it is. She refuses to give in to her paranoia.

She raises her head with a jerk. Did she hear a noise outside? She thought so, but when she winds through the mess of books and boxes to open the door, the corridor is empty. She sags against the side of the doorframe. She has found herself listening too much, recently—raising her head at the slightest noise, wondering if the murmur in her ears is a voice or the rush of her own blood. As if someone is calling her from a long way away. She finds herself straining her ears, trying to make out words in the sound of the wind or the syncopated Morse code of rain on the windows. Some-times she's heard footsteps approaching her room, but then they stop, and if she wrenches open the door to see who it is, it's no one. Not even a draft or a drift of fine snow melting on the floor.

She doesn't believe in ghosts—in spite of the rumors that have circulated here for years, about a phantom child sobbing in the walls. Nothing is haunting her except herself. It's because she can't work: her mind is undisciplined, spinning and sparking like a Cath-erine wheel. The energy she ought to be spending on the *grand jeu* is lighting on other things. Sounds, memories, the constant hot itch of knowing that Léo Martin is under the same roof. She refuses to admit the possibility that it's the other way around, that Martin is the cause and not the symptom.

He walks down the steps from the archive as if she's summoned him into being. Startled, she rocks back into the shelter of the arch-way. The movement catches his eye and he turns his head as he passes. For a heartbeat or less they hold each other's gaze; and then he's gone, running lightly down the lower staircase to the library with a patter of leather soles. She feels heat bloom in her face and scalp and armpits. Thank goodness he can't see inside her head.

After his footsteps have died away, the corridor is very quiet. The librarians have the day off on Sundays. There are probably a few scholars in the library below, poring over their books or gazing vacantly into space: some of them are keen; some are the usual misfits, bullied and miserable, who would rather seek sanctuary with a book than risk encountering their classmates in the Lesser Hall. But they're quiet. From the thick, winter-muffled silence she could believe that she is alone in the building. She looks around, listening; then she walks a few paces to the door of the archive and pushes it open. There isn't anyone here, either. Pale light lies over everything, filtered by the snow that clings to the windowpanes. She shuts the door behind her and leans against it, breathing a faint scent of books and something spicy that might be cologne or scented soap. She walks down the aisle between the bookcases, glancing from side to side. One of the desks has been in use for months, since before the beginning of term, but the Magister Historiae—supposedly working on his magnum opus—hasn't moved the books from their neat pile. The servants clean in here, so there's no dust; but one day she slipped a long chignon-kinked hair between the pastedown and flyleaf of the top volume, and she can still see the tiny glint where it catches the light. She has always despised those who couldn't make progress. Now it gives her a pang of shame.

On the other side, a little farther down under a round window, is Léo Martin's desk.

She approaches slowly, as if she is only going to look out at the weather. Anyone watching her from the doorway would think she was woolgathering, wondering if more snow was on its way. Her glance down at the papers on the desk looks like an afterthought, as if her curiosity is trifling, desultory. His handwriting gives her a little shock, like a sharp-edged stone under a bare foot. It hasn't changed. She could hold his diary side by side with this and not know the difference. She resists the urge to crumple the top page, and then the one underneath, working through until she reaches the leather panel of the desk. Instead she slides the first page aside with the tips of her fingers.

It's difficult to see what he's working on; it's fragmented, full of false beginnings and crossings-out. Here and there he has written the same passage in parallel, Artemonian and classical; the versions have subtle differences, but they both trail off without concluding. In the margins of the third page he has written *bugger this*. She doesn't smile. There's something about the few legible movements that makes her pause and bend closer, as if proximity to the paper will help her understand what she's reading. She turns the pages, uncovering more notes: old roughs, this time, but with something strange and sketchy about them, as if they're faked. Then, with a shock, she recognizes them.

The *Danse Macabre*. He's trying to re-create the *Danse Macabre*.

And he's got it wrong. She curls her hand into a fist, resisting the furious impulse to grab a pen and correct his workings. How could he? It's like a garbled poem, a scratched gramophone record. Can't he *see* that it doesn't work? In fairness, she knows he can—why else would he give up in a scrawl of obscenities?—but that's not the point, what he's written is an insult to the *grand jeu*. When she suggested he work in the archive, she imagined some anodyne course of study—not this, not . . . Why on earth is he doing it? How dare he? And this game, *this* one . . .

There's a movement in the corner of her eye, and she glances up. The library door. Martin, coming through it. She draws in her breath without knowing what she's planning to say.

But before she can speak, he pushes past her, barging her out of the way. She lurches into his chair and her hip explodes with pain. "Hey!" she says, a breath as much as a word. "What the—"

"Get out!" he says.

"I was only looking—"

"That's none of your business." He spreads his arm over the papers, with a gesture that would be childish if it weren't for his expression. She rights herself. Her breath jumps in her throat, refusing to touch the bottom of her lungs.

"I'm the Magister Ludi, I have every—"

"Not to look at—" He seems to catch himself. "I beg your pardon," he says more calmly, "but this is very personal. I'd be grateful if you didn't pry."

She turns her head, focusing on the bookshelves and the windows, the ordered familiarity of the archive. She forces herself to breathe out slowly, until the last shudder of air leaves her. She imagines her anger as a candle flame. By the end of the exhalation it's guttered and gone. Or at least it's an infinitesimal globe of blue, clinging to life but easy to ignore. "You weren't here," she says, finally bringing her gaze back to his face, "and your notes were lying around. I wasn't prying."

He bites his lip, but not as if he's sorry—more as if he still wants to shout at her. A line of his handwriting flashes into her mind's eye: *Am I a thug and a bully?* Yes. Yes, he is. "Well," he says, "you've seen them now. So . . ." He gestures at the door, as if this long room were his own private office. His voice is too loud. "I'd like to get back to work."

The ache in her hip intensifies, overflowing suddenly into her thigh as if the pain was in her pocket and the seams have burst. She reaches out for the back of the chair, because her knees have started to shake. Her body is catching up; it's always slower to react than her mind. He'll think she's emotional. She says with as much disdain as she can, "Of course, Mr. Martin. I'll leave you to your . . . work." She tries to turn away without limping. "The *Danse Macabre*, though," she adds, making it sound like an afterthought. "You really want to spend your time here re-creating a game from your second year? Can't you think of anything better to do?"

"For goodness' sake," he says, "will you *stop* . . ." Then he blinks. "Wait. You recognized it." A pause. "How . . . ?"

She doesn't answer. That was foolish; she shouldn't have indulged the impulse to make him feel small. She can feel the stinging creep of blood along her cheekbones and collarbone.

"You looked at my file. Didn't you? You looked me up. Wait, was it you that took the *Danse Macabre* out of the library? Both copies? Why *both*?" He gives a single incredulous gulp of laughter. "Honestly, I'm flattered, but—" And he is. There's a new note in his voice, ease, a relieved warmth. He thinks he knows what's going on; he's looking at her as if, for the first time, she's a woman.

She can't bear it. "That's absurd," she says. "Don't be so vain."

"But you recognized it, didn't you? How?"

She digs one fingernail into the edge of her thumb. Careful. Whatever happens, she mustn't let slip anything else, that she has his diary in her private collection—or that she knows him better than he realizes, all his dirty secrets.

She cuts off the thought, stupidly afraid that he'll read it in her face. "If files are missing, that's nothing to do with me. I don't know what you're talking about. It rang a bell, that's all." She wants to turn away, but her body betrays her, leaves her stranded in front of him.

"How could you possibly have known what it was called?" Good God, he's almost *teasing* her now. "It's all right," he adds. "I can understand why you'd want to do your research on me before I arrived."

"I had—I have no interest in you whatsoever," she says. It's a lie, of course, and it sounds like a lie; she feels a wave of sweat prickle over her scalp. "I happened to recognize the title—the *Danse Macabre* must have been mentioned in Magister Holt's notes. Or perhaps . . ." Her voice is sliding upward. He's watching her with ironic eyes. "Oh, please," she says, "I have every right to look at old games, I *teach* the scholars—and if I did happen to glance at your file, it wasn't on your account. I certainly wouldn't dream of removing anything."

"Oh, of course not," he says. "A mere accidental glance, I'm sure. And a complete coincidence that the copies have disappeared."

"It was a joint game! It's not all about you, Martin."

"Really?" He smirks.

She has never known anyone who could make her this angry. Reading his diary has always made her seethe—but this is worse, the way he's looking at her, the absolute arrogance . . . "Yes, *really*. As it happens, I was much more interested in Aimé's contribution."

He blinks once. It's only a split second of surprise before he covers it up. But she can see he's irked. "Oh, come on," he says. "I was a Gold Medalist, you know. Not a second-year dropout. Carfax was clever, but I find it hard to believe that you happened to—"

Bile burns her throat. Martin should never have won the Gold Medal. "Don't talk about him like that."

"What? Clever? I'm only pointing out that he's not exactly a credible subject for study."

"Whereas you would be?" It takes all the breath she has to say it, and all the composure.

"It would be understandable if you were curious about me, that's all. And you *did* take those games, I wasn't born yesterday." He smiles. "Look, I'm not saying . . ."

She draws in her breath, furious at him and at herself, because he thinks she is at a disadvantage and she has only herself to blame. "Don't be ridiculous," she says. "I wouldn't waste my time on you."

Perhaps she did say it too sharply, but it's no more than he deserves. He has no right to flinch. "How kind," he says. "But don't spare my vanity, will you?"

Spare his vanity? Who does he think she is, a Party wife? No, only a woman. "I'm sorry your *vanity* can't face the truth."

"Look, there's no need to be unpleasant. I've made something of myself. It's not a laughable idea that you—that someone might be interested—"

"Something? Yes. You're an exiled ex-minister. The sooner you go home, the better." She nods, her neck tight, toward his chaotic notes. "Aimé was a genius. *You're* still struggling with diacritics."

He catches his breath. "I may not be a *grand jeu* player anymore, but at least I didn't cut my own thro—"

Something ignites behind her breastbone like a spark. "How *dare* you? You of all people have no right to laugh at him—you're so *arrogant*, you—he died, my brother *died*. And you stand there telling me he was nothing. Well, fuck you, Léo—fuck you—" She stops.

There's a silence, like the gap between two ticks of a clock.

Then she turns away, unable to look at his face.

No time passes, and yet when she looks back at him, he has aged. The creases around his mouth are deeper, the shadows and pallor of his face starker. He is still staring at her, but she knows that he sees someone else, another face superimposed on her own. He says, "Your brother?"

She swallows. He hadn't realized. Of course he hadn't realized.

But there is no point denying it now. It isn't a secret, exactly. She'll admit it to anyone who asks. She had enough of secrets long ago. She opens her mouth, but her throat feels sore, her tongue swollen. "Aimé Carfax de Courcy was my brother," she says.

He bows his head, as though someone has placed a weight around his neck. "I see."

The words almost make her laugh: he *didn't* see, did he? It was staring him in the face, and he never even looked at her. She glances away. "I remember him mentioning that game. The *Danse Macabre*.

He was pleased with the way it ended up." It's true; let Martin think that's all she knows. No need to mention Léo's diary and the endless jokes about the de Courcys and his sheer childish nastiness . . . When she read it, the first time, it stung like acid: *he'll pay for that.* Well, Aimé did pay, didn't he? But she can't say it aloud. She bites her lip and tries to outstare Martin.

"Yes. Well." He nods again, his chin sagging lower as though the weight has grown heavier. "I didn't realize . . . Your name, you're not a . . . ?"

He can't even say *de Courcy.* "I changed it after—after he died. I went to live with my cousins in England. I wanted to make a clean break."

He makes a small sound that isn't quite amusement. "And did you?"

She doesn't answer. For a second, in spite of everything, something flashes between them, some fleeting warmth. Understanding. He hasn't made a clean break any more than she has. But swift on its heels comes the thought: he didn't deserve one.

"You look . . . I should have known. Even if I didn't see it at first. When I saw you that night, without your glasses, in the dark, I nearly realized . . . But I didn't trust—after he died I saw him everywh—" He stops. His jaw tightens, as though he blames her for his having said too much. "That is, I can see the resemblance," he says more smoothly. "When I arrived here . . . Forgive me, I should have guessed."

"Not at all. He died ten years ago. More. We've all changed."

"We certainly have." Silence. Is he inviting her to sympathize? "I'm sorry," he says. "After he died . . . I never . . ."

She stares past him at a knot in the paneling beside the window, the age-smoothed wood at the level of her eyes.

"I was his friend."

"*Were* you?" she says, and her voice twangs like a cello string. "Were you, really?"

And he blushes. She can't remember the last time she saw a grown man blush. The flush runs right up to his hairline and seeps down below his collar. He stares at her, speechless. She's glad she's silenced him. But the chord of triumph that rings in her head has a lower, softer harmonic. It isn't pity, but it's an echo of it.

"Did he ever talk to you about me?" he asks. "Your brother?"

She takes a moment, not to consider whether to tell the truth, but to be pleased that she can. She says, "Not once."

He reaches down, picks up his pen from the desk, and examines it as if he's never seen one before. He flicks the clip with his thumbnail until she expects it to break. "I see."

"You could have come to his funeral, if you cared so much."

He looks up. The flush deepens into blotches of crimson against red, like a rash. "Yes," he says. "I could have."

"Why didn't you?" She has imagined more than once what it would have been like if he'd been there. How at least then she wouldn't have been the only person under the age of thirty. How he might have looked at her and *seen* her, made her feel more real or less guilty or—she doesn't know. It might have meant catastrophe or redemption, or both. It would have been different, anyway: and nothing could have made it worse.

"I couldn't."

"Oh yes," she says, "you were invited to the Midsummer Game. As a Gold Medalist. You couldn't miss that."

"I didn't go to that." He picks at his cuff as though there's a thread loose, although there isn't. "I went home. I couldn't face it. Look, it doesn't matter, does it? He was dead."

She nods. She recognizes the pain in his voice. She wants to berate him—to see if she can make him crack, admit what he did—but that treacherous note of pity is still ringing in her ears. Whatever he's done, then and since . . . "You're right," she says. "Why should it matter? He's dead."

He meets her eyes. Her pity is reflected on his face, and for a strange dislocated moment it's as if they recognize each other.

She wrenches herself into the present. She looks away and he draws himself up, both of them shaking off whatever has just happened. "I'll dig out some old exam papers for you, if you want," she says, determinedly brisk. "Stop you moldering over old games. It'll be more rewarding than trying to match the glory of your past attempts."

"No need to be sarcastic," he says with a faint gleam of amusement.

She gives him a narrow smile, but she doesn't reply. She goes out into the corridor. But she doesn't close the door behind her; and some unfamiliar demon makes her hum the main theme of the *Danse Macabre*, pushing against the sharp knot in her throat, barely loud enough for him to hear.

13

THREE WEEKS TO GO TILL WE HAND IT IN

Two o'clock in the morning. Woke up, then didn't want to go back to sleep. A dream about a net that was also the *grand jeu*. Thread getting tied around my fingers. Not a net, a web. Ugh.

It's snowing outside. Lamplight from my window catching on the sweep of it. Another window farther along, too. Could be Carfax's. Not sure. Wide darkness, darks of sky and trees, white in dark of snow and slope. And against it all, two patches of gold midair, flickering as the flakes thicken. Uncanny. Nothing here is the same as in my dream and yet it is; whatever story my brain was telling me, it's this. Not making any sense, am I? I'm afraid of what's waiting at the heart, lurking spider, something that wants to suck my insides out. But worse than that, afraid of getting stuck. Afraid of the sticky filaments, afraid of a cocoon. Safety and death.

What am I talking about? Shut up. Waste of paper. Rambling.

So tired. Tired but not sleepy. Wasn't like this last year, this is new. My appetite's gone to pot, too. Most of the time I'm not hungry, and then late at night I'm famished. Tonight—last night—I came back to my room after working with Carfax until nearly midnight, and devoured all the chocolate Mim sent yesterday. Maybe that's why I had a nightmare.

Danse Macabre. Everything's the *Danse Macabre.* I look at snow and see bone. Trees and skeletons. Beds and tombs. Saw Carfax asleep the other day, when I knocked and he didn't answer. On his side, face half in his pillow, unguarded. Thought of Juliet. Asleep only she's dead only she's not. Worms as chambermaids. How sweet that is, like a kid's story, like the footmen rats in *Cinderella*. Sweet and disgusting. Chambermaids that burrow into you. Consumed by your underlings. Supper not where you eat but where you're eaten. Stood there staring at him thinking all that, and then went back to the door and knocked again until he woke up. Strange feeling of not wanting to leave him at a disadvantage. Unfair to look when he can't look back. (Death, I suppose, being the biggest disadvantage of all. But he wasn't. Luckily.)

His tune. Found myself picking it out on the piano the other day when I was trying to practice a prelude. Death waltzing with the lovely young girl. It's *suggestive*. Does he mean it to be? Later I wanted to ask, but I couldn't. Your little melody, Carfax—it gives me a metaphorical hard-on, and I wondered whether you meant it to? No? Oh well, it's probably only me. Perverse, as usual.

Glad no one can see inside my head. Especially glad Carfax can't. At least I hope he can't. Argh, what if he can?

He's so inscrutable. No, not inscrutable. Most of the time I know how he's feeling, or at least I can guess. But underneath it all, there's that constant unknowability. Keeping everyone at a distance. Superiority. Looking down at us, refusing to be on the same level. Always holding something back. It's why it feels like such a triumph when I make him laugh or swear at me. Breaking through. Showing him he's human after all. His lamp's still burning. Wonder what he's doing now? With any luck he'll turn up in the library tomorrow with something clever. Oddly pleasant to know he's there, awake.

Watching the lamplight glimmer gold on the falling snow. My shadow, flickering in midair.

His light's gone out.

Maybe it wasn't even his. Could've been Jacob or Felix or Dupont. Don't know why I care. It's Montverre, getting under my skin.

This blasted place. There are times when you feel more alone here than if you were the last person left on Earth.

TWO WEEKS, TWO DAYS
Letter from Mim. Wish she'd stop. Wish I could send a telegram home: *TOO BUSY TO REPLY STOP SEE YOU AT NEW YEAR . . .* She's worried about Dad and his heart. A good thing I don't have time to answer or I'd be saying, "Dad's heart? What heart?"

Business is thriving, though. Apparently the stock market crash, all the people losing their jobs, all the suicides, depression, austerity (etc., etc.) are a Good Thing for the scrap business. Who'd've thought?

I'm glad I'm out of all that.

TWO WEEKS
Nearly got thrown out of Historiae. I got into an argument with Jacob, which turned into an argument with the Magister. They were basically saying that civilization was buggered up, that technology and weaponry and industrialization mean we're all doomed. Normally I wouldn't care—or at least I wouldn't rise to it—but for some reason I got angrier and angrier. How *dare* they sit there smugly discussing the imminent destruction of society? Looking gently rueful about the economy and the people starving in the streets. And the *grand jeu,* too—accepting that the Golden Age is over and that there's nothing we can do. Such apathy. Everything around us can go down the drain, but we'll stay here in our ivory tower, riding the last melancholic wave of truth and beauty before the end of the world. Looking down on real people. Who do they think they are?

I think I might have said that. That's why the Magister told me to be quiet or leave the room. It made everyone stare at him and then at me. No one's ever been chucked out of a lesson before—not in our class, anyway. I was choking on my words already, so I shut my mouth and sat down. But the *arrogance* of it! And no one else seemed to notice or care. I didn't dare look at Carfax; somehow, if he hadn't understood, that would have been worse than anything.

LATER

Wrote that at lunchtime, when I was still raging. Now it's nearly dinnertime. Feeling calmer, but a bit . . . strange. We had Factorum this afternoon. I was still fizzing when I went in, but I got out my sketchbook and pencil and sat down to draw my still life, as per usual. Two bottles and a glass. I could draw them in my sleep. The Magister used to hover over my shoulder and say things like "How about drawing something *else* today?" and "Or perhaps a change of medium . . . ?" but he finally gave up a couple of weeks ago. It's not quite as good as a nap, but at least it's undemanding. (Everyone uses Factorum as a way to stop thinking. I'm not the only one.)

So I was sitting there, trying to draw, but I couldn't. I don't know why—maybe because I was still seething from the Historiae lesson, or because the others were sneaking looks at me as if I might explode at any moment. I flipped through my sketchbook: dozens of bottles and glasses. All more or less similar. All more or less competent. Not even bad. And I thought: *I've never even* looked *at the stupid bottles.* I draw them how I think they should look. I draw my mental image of them. Pictures of pictures.

I got to my feet, left my sketchbook where it was, and wandered away, winding through the tables and benches. It's the only thing I like about Factorum, the long classroom with all the cupboards and tools and models, crazy paper-and-wire frames hanging from the ceiling . . . Everything's a bit dusty, shadowy, a kind of cave where you can find a corner to be unobserved. There are bits everywhere, rooms off to the side with printing stones and pottery wheels and carpentry tools, but I've never seen anyone use them. At the beginning of last year the Magister tried to encourage us to experiment, but somehow we all knew that the done thing was to sit in a circle around a still life and pretend to take it seriously. Even the people who disappear off to do their own work—Carfax and Paul and Freddie—don't ever actually *make* anything, as far as I can see. There's so much equipment, so many moldering projects (paintings, papier-mâché sculptures, collages, faces in plaster of Paris) that it can't always have been like this. There must have been scholars who entered into the spirit of it. But not us.

I found myself at the far end of the building, in a bitterly cold storeroom. The snow had drifted up against the window, so it was hard to see anything clearly, but there were piles of planks and boards against one wall, and a dried-up palette resting on a back-less chair. I started opening cupboards at random. I found some old tubes of oil paint. They were stiff but still soft. I got one of the bits of wood and squeezed a blob of red paint onto it. First I was only seeing if the color had stayed fresh, but then I began to spread it out with anything I could find—an old bit of rag, the end of a stiffened brush, my hands . . . And then I added other tints, different shades of orange and crimson and burgundy, seeing if I could make the red redder. I covered the whole panel with it. I must have looked like a kid, kneeling on the floor, smearing the color right to the edges. Later I found flecks of dried scarlet in my hair.

I lost track of time. It was only when I heard the bell that I came back to reality. I was covered in paint and dust. The panel was a mess of hot colors. *Study of an Executioner's Block.* Here and there the grain of the wood still showed through, but in other places the color was as thick and shiny as blood. I'd left handprints in it, the shapes where it had oozed between my fingers. It was paint and wood, flesh and oil and pigment. It was real. It was the exact opposite of a *grand jeu.*

I'm making it sound like something mystical. It wasn't. It was childish, like scrawling on a wall. Wanting to leave my mark. Change something. But the thought of it makes me happy. It's stupid. Right now, as I sit here, the memory makes my heart lift. I made it. Me. Something honest.

When I got up, I thought I heard someone in the room beyond, hurrying away. It was probably nothing. But I couldn't shake off the conviction that someone had been watching me.

ONE WEEK, FIVE DAYS TO GO

I am so tired. At prep school they used to play a game where you had to let someone stroke the inside of your forearm a thousand times. I know, it sounds indecent. But after a while it was unbearable. Felt like your skin was coming off. Too much of anything drives you crazy. I've spent so long in the library with Carfax—or in his room or mine, or in empty classrooms, wherever, doesn't matter—that it's taken off a layer of skin. Everything he does gets to me. Last night we were talking through the last movement of the *Danse Macabre*, arguing about whether the transition out of the melody works. I think it's limp, that sort of fading to nothing is cowardly and predictable. He thinks it's the only option, that going out with a bang is vulgar. Frankly I'd rather a bit of melodrama than be bored. But anyway, so we were debating it (with some heat) when I stood to show him what I meant. As if I was performing it. And the bastard started to *smirk*.

I asked him what he was laughing at, and he leaned back in his chair and said, "What's your instrument? It's the piano, isn't it?"

"Yes."

"You must play it like a typewriter."

I glared at him. Thank goodness our music practicals are one to one with the Magister, or he'd be parodying my touch as well as my *grand jeu* style. But he didn't apologize; he didn't even blink. He said, "Do that bit again."

"What?"

He drew a little spiral in the air. "That last bit you did. Show me."

"Why?"

"Please."

I clenched my jaw. I was tempted to walk out, but I realized I was being childish. And he had a sort of considering look on his face, like he was paying attention to the point I was trying to make. I said, "All right. Look—if it stays the way it is, it's like a sort of dying marionette—"

"It's a *Danse Macabre*. Dying marionettes are entirely appropriate."

"No, I mean . . ." I repeated the gesture. "See? It makes *me* look like a—"

"That's because of the way you're doing it. It's got to be smooth. Easy. Not like you're trying to swat a mosquito."

"Look—"

"Let me." He stood up. "You've got to imagine resistance. Like everyone's attention is on you, and it's thick, like cream. Relish it. Even if it's only me, watching you."

"Don't tell me how to—"

"It's all wrong. Your arms. The rest of you, too, actually. You're more than your brain, Martin." He looked me up and down and chuckled. "Listen, do that gesture again—only this time . . ." He reached out and put his palm against my wrist. "Feel the weight of it."

I didn't move. His hand was hot, bony, like—oh, I don't know what it was like, it was just his hand. A hand, that's all. But I'd never been so conscious that my skin was the only thing separating me from the universe. I wasn't thinking about the *grand jeu*.

I said, "Let go of me."

"Come on," he said. "Don't go dead, I want to show you—"

"Get off!" I jerked away. He staggered—maybe I was a bit

violent—and suddenly his face was slack and shocked. "Who do you think you are, Carfax? You're not fucking Magister Ludi yet."

"I only . . ." He stopped. We stared at each other.

"When I want tips on my technique, I'll ask. Till then, keep your sweaty hands off me." I don't know why I was so angry. His wide eyes, his sleeves rucked up, the sound of his breath. His telling me what to do. My wanting to let him.

He started to say something else and bit his lip. "Perhaps you're right," he said after a pause. "There must be a more inventive way to end it."

I went back to the desk. Our notes had stopped making sense. I wanted to reflect his tone back to him, but I couldn't. For once I didn't want to think about the *grand jeu* or any other kind of game.

"It doesn't matter," I said. "The bloody thing's nearly finished. It doesn't have to be perfect."

"Léo," he said, and stopped.

"I've got to go," I said, and went.

ONE WEEK, FOUR DAYS

He apologized, late last night. "I forgot myself," he said. "It won't happen again." I didn't know how to reply. By the time I'd got over my surprise, he'd gone.

SEVEN DAYS

A week to go till we hand it in, and it'll be over. I can't wait.

TWO DAYS TO GO

I think it's a dead loss. The *Danse Macabre*. All this work and it's rubbish. I can't even *see* it anymore.

HANDING-IN DAY
That's it. It's done.

LATER
I hardly slept at all last night. We finished our fair copies at past midnight, and swapped to proofread and correct. By the end, my copy
must have had as much of Carfax's handwriting on it as mine. Then we
went to bed, but my head wouldn't stop spinning. Finally I dropped
off, but jolted awake at five, convinced I'd left out the main theme.
After that I had to get up. I took the opportunity to have a long solitary
wash and shave, and came down to breakfast feeling almost human.

Everyone looked exhausted. It was like the day after a battle:
we were all dark-eyed and gaunt and stubbly (except for me, obviously, and Carfax, who clearly thinks a bit of stubble is some kind of
abomination). The table was covered in files. We were all contort-
ing ourselves, trying to keep butter and crumbs away from them
while keeping them within arm's reach. (Because, after all, if we left
them in our rooms, they might spontaneously combust. Or someone
might steal them, which I suppose is more likely.) When the bell
rang, we all stampeded for the office. I ended up at the back, too
tired to fight, and Carfax and I went in together. We didn't say much
to each other. Not surprising, given that we've been talking nonstop
for weeks. When we emerged, finally empty-handed, he grinned at
me. I started to grin back until I realized he was probably looking
happy because he knows he never has to speak to me again.

We had wine with dinner. (Second-years only.) It's been so long since
I had a proper drink that it went straight to my head. I was sitting
between Felix and Émile. They were in high spirits, and it should've
been natural to mess about and make jokes. But it wasn't. It felt like

an act. It was like I'd been on a long sea journey: part of me was still reeling, struggling to remember how to walk on dry land. I couldn't concentrate. My mind kept going to the *Danse Macabre*, tinkering with it in my head, thinking of things to say to Carfax. Then I'd remember that it was done and handed in. After a while they noticed and started teasing me. That feeling of being in a foreign country, again.

Carfax turned up late, after we'd had the soup. I think he was hoping he'd be able to sit down unobserved, but the only free seat was halfway down our table, a couple of spaces from Felix. He hesitated, as if he was hoping for a better offer. Of course some wag made a snide comment about choosing from a set of one, and then there was an ironic cheer when he clambered over the bench to sit down. It wasn't exactly unfriendly—we would have done it to anyone—but Carfax takes it all so bloody personally. If he could take it like a good sport it'd die down, but he doesn't, he goes all white and hard-faced. It's like he never went to school as a child. Maybe he didn't.

After that first glance I didn't look at him. I was talking to Paul about his joint game—sounds good, better than ours, so I was badgering him, hoping he'd reveal some enormous flaw that would set my mind at rest—and didn't let my gaze wander in Carfax's direction for a second. Now I wish I hadn't, because I don't know if he was trying to catch my eye. Although, let's face it, why would he? We don't have anything to talk about, now the game's done.

Then someone poured half a carafe of wine over him.

I don't know how it happened. I don't know whether it was an accident. It probably was. We were all fooling around, weren't we? There was a smash of pottery on the floor and a burst of noise, and when I looked around, Carfax was on his feet with a big wet stain down the front of his gown. It didn't show up all that much against the black, but his collar was red, and his hair and face were dripping. He wiped his eyes on his sleeve. People at other tables craned over to see what was going on. Someone said, "Oh. Ah. Oops."

There was a silence. Not complete silence, but enough to hear what wasn't being said. Carfax shook himself and spattered drops on the floor.

"Accident, old chap," the same voice said. It was Freddie, I think. He sounded drunk. Or stupid. "Never mind."

Carfax went on standing there. I didn't understand why, and then I did. He was expecting an apology. I wanted to stand up and shout at him not to be an idiot, that the longer he stood there, the worse it was going to look. I took a sip from my glass and had to force myself to swallow.

"Was that the last . . . ?" Freddie reached across a couple of people for another carafe, but when he tilted it over his glass, nothing came out. "Oh dear, what a shame," he said to himself, and then to Carfax: "Come over here and drip in my glass, will you?"

Carfax said, "You stupid shit."

People looked around. Thank goodness it was the table closest to the door; the magisters at the High Table hadn't noticed.

"There's no need to be like that," Freddie said. "I mean, you got more than your fair share. You can suck your gown."

There was a split-second pause; then someone gave a huge snort of laughter. And then we were all joining in—Freddie braying, other people choking and clutching their ribs, even Émile giggling help-lessly. It was the image, I suppose: Carfax bundling his gown into his mouth, his eyes bulging, drips running down his chin . . . Or the words, and Freddie's innocuous tone, and the way what he really meant by *your gown* was clearly "my cock."

It was sheer bad luck, I think, that Carfax happened to look at me.

"Fine," he said. He fumbled with his gown, pulled it over his head, and dropped it on the table on top of Freddie's plate of food. The fabric of his shirt was purple and clinging to his shoulders. "You suck it, Freddie," he said. "And the rest of you can kiss my arse." This time his voice did carry to the High Table. I saw Magister Holt look up with a frown, and the Magister Motuum blinked heavily. For a moment I thought they'd tell him to leave, and my heart gave a lurch. But he was already stalking out of the hall.

There were three seconds of relative silence. Then someone said, with perfect, Montverre-trained timing, "Oooooh, who stole *his* mammy's tit?"

He must have heard, even outside in the corridor. And he must have heard the burst of laughter. It didn't last that long, and after it died down we were a little more subdued, as if after all some of it had been bravado; but that roar of exclusion, of amusement at his expense . . . It made it abundantly clear that he's never going to fit in. If he would join in the laugh *once*. Or pretend he didn't care . . .

I got up a few minutes later. Émile raised an eyebrow at me. "Dicky tummy," I said. "Working this hard has completely ruined my digestion." Felix started to argue, so I added, "Trust me, you *really* don't want me to stay."

I went up to my room, but I didn't go in. I walked along to Carfax's cell and raised my hand to knock. But I couldn't. There was a strip of light under the door. Maybe he'd heard me approach, because I saw a shadow cross it and then stay still, as if he was on the other side, listening. I still didn't knock, though. I stood there for a long time. I tried to imagine what I'd say to him, but all the words were flat and empty. And even if I dredged up some kind of excuse or consolation, I knew how he'd react: disdain, contempt, faint bewilderment. He probably hadn't even noticed that I'd smirked along with the others. And then I remembered how he'd made the others laugh at me, last year, and how he never apologized for that.

Now the game's handed in, we're back to where we were. We were civilized adults, doing a job that had to be done. We're not friends.

I thought I'd be triumphant, tonight. Full of relief. Euphoric. But I feel terrible.

14

LÉO

A few days before the end of term Léo finds himself in the magisters' corridor. He hasn't planned it; he doesn't know where it's sprung from, this sudden heart-quickening impulse. The last couple of weeks have slipped through his hands like a string of leaden beads, each day too heavy to hold but gone in an instant, followed by the next. It's easy to be numb, absorbed in intellectual pursuits, essays, the games and theses and reading lists that the Magister—true to her word—has been leaving in his pigeonhole. This is how he felt in his third year here, as a scholar. The Gold Medal meant nothing, as though it had gone to someone else: now he was numb, conscientious, stoic. Nothing happened, nothing hurt. Or not much. He made his way carefully through the treacherous landscapes of his mind, treading lightly, avoiding the quicksand. The *grand jeu* was a path, that was all, and he kept his gaze on his feet. Now he's doing the same thing. He navigates between the archive and the library and the refectory and his cell without pausing. He answers Émile's letters mechanically, refusing to reread them. Every envelope, safely sent off, buys a week of safety, another week of not having to glance behind when a servant comes too close or keep a brown glass bottle of emetic beside his bed or check his pillow for needles. It's worth it. And in a peculiar way it gives him something to think about: how to explain the intricate animosity between the

Magister Cartae and the Magister Motuum, or the Magister Scholarium's tacit avoidance of politics, or the bubbling overconfidence
of the scholars who've got family in the Party? At meals he glances
from face to face, letting his attention flit from one conversation
to another. It's like trying to see the currents in clear water. He's
good at it. It keeps his mind off the other things: the ache of missing the Ministry, the physical strength it takes not to turn his head
and gaze at the Magister Ludi . . .

Mostly, his attempts not to think about her have been successful.
That Sunday afternoon in the library, after she left, he was too dazed
to do anything but sit and stare into space; he didn't realize he was
gritting his teeth until he staggered to his feet at the sound of the
clock chiming and felt the tension like a metal band around his temples. He couldn't eat; he couldn't sleep that night, either, but he lay
in bed watching the stars come and go in the black sky, like blown
drifts of sand. And the next day, passing Magister Dryden in the
corridor, he was in control enough not to stare, although he wanted
to. How had he not realized? He should have seen the resemblance.
Maybe he did see it; but he thought it was because he was back at
Montverre, a sly trick of the brain.

After Carfax died, Léo saw him everywhere—walking down the
street, gesturing to a waiter in a restaurant, laughing outside the
scrapyard gates in a collarless shirt and flat cap. He learned not to
react, not to flinch or say Carfax's name or even stare too long. If
he had to see ghosts, at least he'd keep it to himself. That was years
ago, and it hadn't happened for a long time; but when he saw Magister Dryden that night in the corridor it was the same sick wel-
ter, the world lurching backward on its spin as though his mind was
betraying him again . . . If only someone else had mentioned it, if
only she hadn't told him herself. He winces at the recollection of
her expression—*pity,* how dare she—and the way he didn't have the
presence of mind to do anything but look at her. That face.

Even later, he didn't let himself examine his feelings too closely. But the next time he replied to Émile, he found himself writing:

> She is, of course, isolated and, one assumes, lonely. Her politics—as one might expect from a woman who has apparently never encountered real life in any of its manifestations—are liberal and soft, resisting change and clarity, based on a sort of kindly instinct that doesn't stand up to scrutiny. Surprising, given her abrasive manner, but I suppose this is merely an example of feminine contradictions! Of all the magisters, I'd guess that she is the most opposed to the Party, but perhaps more because of misplaced idealism than self-interest. Her influence is small, I suspect, but it might be enough to prove awkward if the Council were not wholeheartedly supportive of any new measures. I can't comment on her skills as a teacher—the scholars murmur about being taught by a female, and one can't exactly blame them, given her lack of formal education, but otherwise seem content enough to concede her authority. In fairness I should mention that she does have a certain charisma.

He set down his pen before he wrote another sentence that he'd have to cross out. His words were all true, so why did belittling her make him queasily triumphant, as if he'd squashed a mosquito? He folded the paper and shoved it into the envelope without bothering to sign off. His eyes went to the past papers on the desk, the mimeographed slip of essay questions on top. Time to get back to work. But all that afternoon he had a sense of someone at his shoulder, a censorious ghost that disappeared when he looked at it head on.

Was that the week that Émile sent the bottles of brandy? He can't remember. He let them gather dust in the corner of his bedroom, and spent hours tracing the motif of the *Four Seasons* in the light of the Broken Seam hypothesis. He didn't exactly promise himself not to mention the Magister Ludi again, but the next time he wrote his letter was taken up with a slight that had been related to him, indignantly, by the Magister Cartae, and a nasty incident with the Christian scholar—Charpentier, is it?—in the first year. He even went to the Magister's door, planning to thank her for the book she'd left in his pigeonhole; but he decided against it at the last moment. He despised himself for wanting to go crawling to her, to appease his own conscience. She'd look at him with a transparent surprise that he thought she'd care . . . When he woke at night (the *bloody* clock!) he could see her face and Carfax's, two faces that were somehow only one. Had Carfax ever mentioned her? What would he think now, seeing her and Léo together? But there were no answers, and that way madness lay. He made himself get up and study the Broken Seam hypothesis until he was too tired to see straight. The *grand jeu* was nothing if not a shield.

But he is leaving tomorrow for the vacation, and sudden life is prickling in his bones like pins and needles. He doesn't know what made him pick up one of the bottles of brandy; but he's standing in front of the Magister Ludi's door with it in his hand, the glass faintly slick against his palm. This time he doesn't give himself time to think before he knocks.

There's a pause before she says, "Come in," as if she knows who it is.

He opens the door. She's sitting at her desk, her face turned to him but her pen still poised above the page as if she's mid-thought. When she sees who it is, she slides a sheet of paper down over her work—although he could have sworn the page was blank.

"Yes?"

"Am I disturbing you?"

"You should have thought about that before you knocked."

"Yes, I suppose I should."

She sighs and screws the cap on to her pen. "How can I be of assistance, Mr. Martin?"

He has prepared himself for this, but all the same it stings. He isn't an importunate first-year, for goodness' sake. He puts the bottle he's holding on the corner of her desk. "I brought you this. To say thank you."

She blinks. All at once he wants to snatch up the inappropriate bottle, with its foreign label and red wax seal, and leave the room without a backward glance. Or dash it against the wall and leave her picking splinters of green glass off her white robe. But if politics has taught him anything, it's how to hide humiliation.

"How kind," she says at last.

"A friend of mine sent it. It's good. French. I thought perhaps . . ." If she had been her brother she—he—would reach out for it, scrutinize its provenance, and nod, trying not to show his pleasure. And then he'd glance at Léo, at his work, and finally with a reluctant grin he'd rock back on the legs of his chair, casting about for something to drink from.

But she doesn't. Of course she doesn't. Léo pushes his hands into his pockets. "Well, never mind. I thought you were allowed."

"I am *allowed*," she says.

"Good." A silence. "I'll leave you to your work." He turns to go.

"Thank you," she says a moment before he gets to the door. "I didn't expect . . . I haven't done anything for you, Mr. Martin. I dug out a few past papers. You don't have to give me expensive brandy."

"I know. Of course. But I . . . they were . . . I enjoyed working on them. You seemed to have spent a great deal of time finding interesting questions, suggesting further reading." It takes an effort to smile at her. "I'm grateful, that's all."

"I'm a teacher, Mr. Martin. I'd do the same for any scholar."

"And any scholar should be grateful." He tilts his head, in a half-ironic hint at a bow. Ah, this insistence that she has done nothing to be thanked for, that he is pathetic to see any hint of goodwill in her actions . . . He could hit her. The thought shocks him; he has never hit a woman in his life, and never wanted to before. "It's nothing. I apologize if it seems excessive. I can understand—well, living here, like this, as you do . . ." He gestures to the room, the dusty austerity, the snow outside, with casual disdain. "But honestly, it's a trifle. It's not even terribly good. If I gave a bottle of that stuff to my mistress she'd drop it off the balcony into the street."

Now it's easier to smile at her. He squashes a spark of self-contempt; it's *her*, making him like this. All he wanted was to be polite.

She draws a long silent breath through parted lips. Then, unexpectedly, she gives a quick snort of amusement, as if they're playing a game. "All right," she says. "I'm glad you liked the topics. I did look for questions that you'd enjoy."

"Did you? How did you know?" He laughs, too; then, abruptly and too late, he realizes that it wasn't a ploy, a flirtatious suggestion that she knows him inside out. She isn't Chryseïs. Her face has hardened again, and that momentary warmth is gone.

"It's what I give the first-years," she says. "Those questions sound very imposing, but ultimately they're rather facile."

He opens his mouth. But he can't bring himself to answer. He nods once, and reaches again for the door handle.

"No, that's not true," she says suddenly, and he hears her getting to her feet. "They were all finals questions, actually. I am glad you liked them. It's only that . . ."

Slowly he turns back to her. She is standing beside the window, staring out into the banked snow. From here he can only see the side of her face, her temple and cheek, the corner of her lips. She looks painfully like Carfax. It's funny how his features are different, transplanted into a female face. She has the same wide mouth and cheekbones, strong jaw, and narrow eyes, but where he was handsome, she is plain. She must be the same height as he was, or almost:

and again, where he was a good height for a man, she is gawky, for a woman. Where Carfax is dead, she's alive. It's like a parody, the universe's vicious joke.

For an instant he waits for her to finish her sentence. Will it be an apology of sorts? Then he realizes that she isn't going to. He wants to leave and slam the door on her silence. But then she shoots him a swift, jerky glance, as though she's been trying to resist the impulse. That's how he's been looking and not-looking at her these last few weeks.

"Well," he says, "you obviously know me better than you realize." For some reason that makes her bite her lip. "I can imagine the conclusions you've come to. 'Must try harder.' 'Generally inauthentic.' Or 'overly reliant on integral transitions.'"

"Not integral transitions," she says, frowning, "so much as text loops. You always—that is, it might help you to focus more on math and music. Science, even. You resist the abstract, and it weighs you down."

He stares at her. For a second, with the light behind her, she could be Carfax's ghost. "All right," he says, not knowing whether to laugh. "Fair enough. If I still played seriously, I'd take your advice. As it is . . ."

"What did you make of the last essay, by the way?"

He can remember the title word for word: "A *grand jeu* is a kind of web made of abstractions. It glitters, it seduces; but its beauty is essentially functional—indeed, predatory—and its aim is to draw down the divine into a human trap." But when he read it, he couldn't concentrate on the question. Instead he saw again the spider's web that was strung across the path, that first predawn morning when he'd walked up the mountain to Montverre. He remembered sweeping it aside, breaking the threads and bubbles of light, and Carfax's stifled protest. It was beautiful, but it was in the way, and he'd wanted to be first. He still wanted it.

She shifts her weight, and he realizes that he's been standing in silence for a long moment.

"It was interesting," he says. "Amadé de Courcy was one of your ancestors, I assume? I think I've heard of him . . . Perhaps he's right. Or perhaps it's the other way round, and the *grand jeu* is a divine trap in which to catch humanity. Like love."

Too late he anticipates her voice, pronouncing judgment on him: the clipped way she said *rather facile* a few moments ago. But she's looking at him with a crease between her brows, as if she's trying to put a name to a face. A strange shiver goes down his back.

Then she smiles. "Very neat," she says. "Do you really believe that? Or is it a gimmick?"

"Never mind."

"Games," she says very softly. "That's what you're good at, isn't it? And somehow you ended up trying to play the one game that— isn't."

"The *grand jeu*?"

She doesn't answer. Again—appallingly—he feels the itch to hit her. Who does she think she is, telling him about himself? The Delphic oracle? His game is one thing, but pronouncing on his whole life . . . She has the same taut authority that Carfax had—say what you like, but he was clever, he was observant—only in her it's arrogance. She's a woman, she doesn't know him, she has no *right* . . . He came in here to be charming, to thank her and leave again; and her spikes and prickles have snagged all his silky intentions into a hopeless knot. "Well," he says, "thank you again. And goodbye. I'm leaving tomorrow."

"Leaving?" Her voice is breathy—with relief or regret? No, he's flattering himself. Relief, without doubt. She must have thought he was staying here for the vacation.

"Yes. I know there are a few days left before the end of term, but I've been invited to address a local group of *grand jeu* amateurs in

Montverre-les-Bains, so . . ." He knows how it'll be, paunchy Party members frowning at him through a jovial alcoholic haze, while he tries to shoehorn games into official policy like mutilated feet into glass slippers. It'll be excruciating. His old colleague Pirène sent him tacit sympathy along with the invitation; they both knew he wasn't in a position to refuse. "It's easier to stay in a hotel there before I go home. To my mother's house, that is."

"I see."

"So . . . I hope you have a very happy New Year."

She nods. She goes on nodding. "Thank you," she says. "And you, too, Mr. Martin." She sounds distant, preoccupied.

"Goodbye, then." He realizes that he's waiting for her to dismiss him.

"I—wait," she says. "Léo—"

It's the first time she's used his first name. It makes him respond too soon, too eagerly. "Yes?"

"I want you to know that I—I wish—if things had been different, maybe I would have . . ." she says again, and tails off. Something is moving in her face. Ice on the edge of thawing. Fragility that seemed solid, a moment ago. "Never mind." She makes a quick, abortive gesture, as if she's going to offer her hand and then thinks better of it. "Goodbye."

Léo stares at her. She's worked so hard to make him believe that she despises him, but for a moment . . . He wonders what she would do if he took her hand without giving her the chance to back away. He says, "Goodbye, then. I'll see you next term."

"Next term?" There's a second of silence. Then the color in her cheeks deepens and spreads. "You're coming back? I thought you meant . . ."

"Yes, I'm coming back." Émile's last letter hinted that he might be able to leave Montverre at the end of the Vernal Term, if he was lucky. But even if Émile has kept his reputation alive, there's nothing for him in the Ministry of Culture. He'll have to start again from the bottom, or find something else—local government, perhaps, or a job in the scrapyard business. He's not sure anymore that he's looking forward to it.

"Oh. I see." She rubs her face with the inside of her wrist, as if she can wipe away the wash of pink. Belatedly he understands and wants to laugh. *That's* why she was almost kind: because she thought she was rid of him forever. Now she's regretting it.

The flush in her cheeks and forehead is like red light falling on her, like an untimely sunrise or sunset. Her eyes flicker to him and away. Something twists inside him, wringing tighter and tighter. He knows where he is, and when—of course, he's sane, he's sober—but he's twenty again, a scholar again, in the music room with Carfax, laughing at his own joke. The way Carfax raised his head, the smile that was like a crack in his armor, the bloom of color under his skin—exactly the same, subtle and unmissable, like a hoarfrost melting . . . A second ago, he wanted to reach out to her from sheer mischief: now it's something else, something much more dangerous. He blinks, trying to see the differences between her face and Carfax's to break the spell. The softness along her jawline, creases by her eyes, escaping wisps of long hair brushing the side of her neck. But it's like an optical illusion: no matter how hard he tries—how certain he is that the picture is a vase, not two faces—he can't make himself see her clearly. Carfax is there, on her face, like a mask. His stomach clenches.

"What is it?" she says. Her voice does what her face couldn't, wrenching him back to the present. "Are you all right?"

"Quite. Thank you."

She glances at her desk. "I'm afraid I must get back to work."

"Yes. Yes, I should go and pack my things." He shuffles toward the door again, but something prevents him going immediately. "How is the Midsummer Game coming along, by the way?"

She glances at him, sits down, and starts to unscrew the lid of her fountain pen. "Happy New Year, Mr. Martin."

"Happy New Year."

"Oh—and take this, please." She nods at the brandy. "It's generous of you, but I don't want it."

Their eyes meet, a level, intimate stare. It's not about the brandy—somehow he has no doubt that she'd drink it if it came from someone else—but about scoring a point. And she thinks *he's* the one who plays games? For an instant his irritation flares; then some other emotion takes hold of him. Slowly he reaches for it. "All right," he says, "if you insist. But on one condition."

"What's that?"

"That you let me bring you something else instead." He goes on speaking as she's about to answer. "Whatever you want. You must want *something*. Please. It would give me pleasure." He doesn't know himself how much of his pleading is real and how much a stratagem.

"What makes you think I care about your pleasure, Mr. Martin?"

"You found games you thought I'd like."

His heart is drumming in his fingers, around the neck of the bottle. It's as if the pulse is in the glass. He's pushed her; now she'll order him out and refuse to speak to him again.

Suddenly she grins. "A box of marrons glacés, then."

"Is that all?"

Her grin subsides into something more ironic, more guarded, and she doesn't answer. She bends over her notebook and waves him away; but she's still smiling as he bows himself out of the door, like a music-hall butler.

He stands in the corridor, and he realizes that he's grinning, too. It takes him a second to identify what he's feeling: and then—with a jolt of disbelief—he realizes that he was flirting with her. With Magister Dryden . . . As though she's a woman like any other, who can be bought with bonbons and jewels and pastel-colored Russian cigarettes. As though she's Chryseïs, who can be undressed only if she's been dressed first at Léo's expense, in something chic and silky and beautifully cut. An incongruous picture flashes through his mind's eye: Magister Dryden in Schiaparelli pink or a Mainbocher suit. It makes him laugh, but the picture has a rough edge to it that leaves a splinter under his skin. Beneath Magister Dryden's white gown, she *is* a woman. A woman to whom he's promised to bring a box of sweets. He'd have thought—if she asked for anything—it would have been books.

He wanted to please her. Why did he want to please her? To prove a point? Because she's so resistant to his charm? Because every smile won from her is a point scored, a concession made? Because he can't abide the thought that she might *win*?

No, it isn't that. Not only that. He sees himself setting down the little wooden box of marrons glacés on her desk, waiting for her thanks. It's not about pleasing her, or not really. It's an offering. As if the power of life and death is in her hands. As if he might—as if—if he does everything right—if he can somehow alight on the exact right move in the game—as if, yes, then she might look at him and not be herself anymore but Carfax—as if he could turn back time—

He wants forgiveness. The realization brings a taste of bile into his mouth, a surge of self-disgust. Stupid. Pathetic. Even if he deserved it, there's no way back.

He turns down the corridor, hurrying, but it's not fast enough to leave himself behind. He speeds up until sweat starts out on his forehead; then he breaks into a clumsy run, not caring if anyone sees him.

15

FIRST DAY OF WINTER VACATION

I'm at the station, writing this in the tearoom. I have almost an hour before my train comes. To sit here, I had to order some tea, but it's bright orange and tastes of grease and dirty dishcloth, so one mouthful was enough. But it was only so I could avoid the others. Émile and Jacob change here, too, but I saw them go into the gentleman's bar. It's a pity, I could murder a brandy, but I can't bear the prospect of having to talk. It was hard enough on the train from Montverre, everyone shouting and messing about, but now I don't think I could string together a coherent sentence. Not aloud, anyway. I'm so tired I've come out the other end of it, and everything is a bit too clear and bright, as if I'm seeing it through a diamond.

Yesterday we only had morning lessons—mainly magisters handing out the last of our vacation work. I can tell you already that next term is going to be oh so amusing, given that we've been told to meditate on trees in all their forms (!), research the ancient Greek and Roman rituals of communion with the divine, and familiarize ourselves with the *Bridges of Königsberg*. Not to mention tick off everything on Magister Holt's reading list, which is full of books that will definitely not be in our local library. Gah. I suppose they have to find some way to keep us out of mischief for two months, while the old place is snowed in . . . Anyway, after lunch we had the Quietus early, and then a few hours to pack before dinner. I flung everything into my trunk and then lay down on my bed, hoping to drift off to sleep, but I couldn't. I was too nervous. The marks for the joint game are always posted before dinner, the last day of term.

Finally the bell rang. It was as if everyone was waiting for that moment. I heard all the doors in our corridor open at once and a rush of footsteps. I got up as slowly as I could, splashed my face with water, smoothed my hair down where it was stuck in a stupid tuft, and then couldn't think of any other way to distract myself. I didn't want to be there at the same time as the rest of them, pushing and shoving to see the noticeboard, having to elbow people in order to stay at the front long enough to find my name . . . *our* names. But I felt worse than before an exam, and I wanted it to be over. So I went downstairs to look.

There was a muttering group of scholars in front of the noticeboard. Paul looked around and said to me, "They haven't put the marks up yet."

"What? Why?"

Paul shrugged. Freddie said, "Because they're cold-blooded bastards," with real venom. His father promised him a motorcar for New Year if he received more than fifty. Funny how it's always the hopeless cases who get offered bribes. Maybe that's why; if Dad had promised me the same, he'd have had to cough up last term.

"They're still debating," Émile said. "I walked past the Capitulum on my way here."

"Past the Capitulum? To get here? Where were you, the servants' quarters?"

I'd been joking, but Émile gave me a strange look. Someone (Jacob, I think) said, "Well, they'll have to put them up soon. Won't they? Before we go home?"

"Forget it," I said. "I'm going to dinner." I wasn't remotely hungry, but I wasn't going to stand there mithering like an aristocrat in the queue for the guillotine. So I stalked off. Some of the others came with me, and we all made a point of talking and laughing as if we couldn't care less.

It wasn't until halfway through dinner (I have no idea what I ate, or even if I ate anything) that Felix came rushing into the refectory and announced, "They're up!"

And then he caught my eye and said, "Well done."

Seventy.

Seventy. A *distinction*. The nearest mark to us was Émile and Paul, and that was sixty-two.

I can't remember what Felix said or getting to my feet or walking out. I was in front of the noticeboard, and our names were at the top of the page.

Aimé Carfax de Courcy and Léonard Martin, *Danse Macabre*, 70.

People were behind me. Someone swore, someone said, "Oh, come *on*, we deserved more than that!" and someone else said, "Phew, I was sure we'd completely messed it up." I let the current push me to one side and leaned against the wall, still reeling. Seventy. I can't remember anyone getting higher than sixty-five, not even Carfax.

After a while Émile came over and stood beside me, watching the huddle of people in front of the noticeboard slowly dwindle. "You must be pleased," he said. "Bet that's why they were late putting it up. Must've been contentious. A distinction for two second-years."

I didn't meet his eyes. "It's not bad."

He glanced at me. "What's the matter? Would you rather have got a bare pass, like Felix and Freddie?"

"No."

"You're not annoyed because you have to share it with Carfax? You've got a year and a half to beat him, Léo. Make the most of this, why don't you?"

I couldn't look at him. I was afraid that if I did, I'd start to laugh and not be able to stop. Or worse, start to cry. I'd been so scared of failing. Of having to face Carfax, thinking I'd let him down. I said, "Yes, you're right."

"How's he taking it? Insufferable, I suppose?"

"I don't know." I hadn't seen him. He wasn't at dinner and he wasn't here. And I thought I had self-control . . .

I reached past Pierre and Thomas, who were the last people left in front of the noticeboard, and ripped the paper off its drawing pin. By the time they reacted I was already running toward the stairs; I heard their protests fading behind me, and Émile laughing.

It took Carfax ages to answer his door. When he finally said I could come in, he was sitting on his trunk, his arms crossed, as if I was bothering him. "Martin," he said, "what is it? I'm packing."

I didn't point out that he'd clearly finished. I held up the piece of paper and said, "I thought you'd want to know."

I saw him resist the reflex to leap to his feet. He tipped his head back and said, "So?"

"I thought it was all right, our game," I said. "But I guess we misjudged it."

He stood up and plucked the page out of my hand. I waited for him to laugh. He sat down without saying anything, folding himself carefully into the chair as if he was afraid of breaking a bone. He rested his elbows on the desk and put his head in his hands.

"Carfax? I was joking."

He said in a muffled voice, "Piss off, will you?"

"I was only—"

"I know." He raised his head. His eyes were wet and red. I don't know why it felt so indecent; hadn't I been on the edge of crying myself? "It was hilarious, Martin. Now leave me alone."

I opened my mouth to argue. We'd got a *distinction,* for pity's sake, and he was behaving like I'd murdered his grandmother. What a family of lunatics. But then he hid his face again and I think he was trying not to cry.

I didn't know what to do. I thought about walking out. He'd told me to go, hadn't he? But it seemed inhuman. So I stood there, helpless. I tried to pat his shoulder, but he shook me off. Actually, I knew how he felt. All these weeks . . . Maybe that was why I stayed. Finally I sat down on the end of the bed, at arm's length.

Slowly he managed to get hold of himself; I couldn't see his expression, but his breathing grew steadier. He sat up straight and said, "You absolute weasel, Martin," but this time it was without rancor.

"I had no idea—it was only a joke."

"I'm exhausted, that's all." He blew out air, shaking his head. He peered at the piece of paper. "Seventy. Was it really *that* good?"

"Better."

He laughed. We both laughed. I think I was only an inch away from crying, too.

"I could do with a drink," I said. "They should've given us wine tonight, not the day we had to hand it in." I could've bitten my tongue as soon as I said it, remembering what had happened, but Carfax didn't blink.

"If only we knew where they kept it," he said.

"I can't believe you don't. How many generations of your family have come here? Surely by now it should be a family secret, handed down from father to son?"

He shook his head, with a crooked smile. "Nope. My father died before he could hand me anything."

"Right." After a second I added, "Sorry."

He didn't answer. It occurs to me now that he was taken aback; he must have expected me to say something snide. He picked up the page and ran his finger down the marks, but I don't think he was actually reading them. The clock struck nine; I hadn't realized it was so late.

"Well," Carfax said, "thanks for letting me know, anyway. About the marks."

"Sure." I got to my feet.

"Good night, Martin."

"Good night."

I went out into the corridor and shut the door behind me.

But I couldn't walk away. I don't know why. Seventy! I hated the thought of just going to bed, as if nothing had happened. I knew I wouldn't be able to sleep. What's the point of a triumph if you behave like it's nothing? Carfax was the only one who knew how I felt, who knew how hard we'd worked. So I went back into his room without knocking. He spun around—he was in his shirtsleeves, he must've been getting undressed—and dived for his gown. As he dragged it over his head, he said, "Martin, what do you think you're—"

"We've all seen you in your shirt, Carfax, remember?" He carried on grumbling, but I spoke over him. "Let's go somewhere. Let's go up to the Astronomy Tower. I want to be outside. Come on."

"Now?"

"I've got some cigarettes in my room. I've been saving them all term."

I thought he was going to refuse. We've been enemies for so long, I wouldn't have blamed him if he had. I wondered myself why I'd suggested it. After all, he's still the same person who made fun of my games in front of the whole class. He's still an arrogant bastard. And he probably thinks I'm still . . . well, whatever he's always thought of me. But he glanced back at his desk, at his trunk, at the empty room; then he nodded and pushed past, obviously expecting me to follow.

So we went up to the Astronomy Tower. As we were climbing the stairs, I thought it was a stupid idea. It was perishing cold and a long way up, and if we got caught we'd be in trouble. But then we came out on the top, and there was nothing around us but battlements and snow and the night sky.

We hunched down in the corner and smoked and talked about the *grand jeu* and made fun of the others, and agreed that we were the best players ever and he'd be Magister Ludi when I was Magister Scholarium, or the other way around. It was freezing; the air made me cough when it hit the back of my throat, especially when I laughed.

When we'd finished our cigarettes, he got to his feet and held out his hand to help me up. Bits of me had gone numb and I held on to him for longer than I meant to, steadying myself. I didn't care how cold I was; I would have said anything to stay there forever.

I didn't. Say anything. Nor did he. We went down the staircase in silence. But when I glanced back at him he was smiling.

I can't remember the last time I felt this happy.

16

THE RAT

She knows that the black ones are going to leave. For days before they go, the air of Montverre is disturbed, the silent spaces between bells muddied by noise and bustle. She stays in her nest during the day, knotted in her blankets, but even there the sounds of their footsteps and laughter lap at her like flotsam on a tide. These are the times that scare her the most, the beginnings and endings: this is when the world is most unpredictable. Is that a human way to think? Perhaps. Perhaps a rat would have no concept of time past or future, wouldn't feel the change in the air as the voices rise and recede. Perhaps she is already losing her grip on her rat-self. There are words in her head that should not be there: *Afraid. Sorry. Simon.* She endures them as if they're a contagion. Soon they will be gone, the way the black ones will be gone, and her mind will be quiet again. But they're heavy, like stones. When she moves her head, she can feel them thunking against her skull, hard enough to hurt. *Simon.* The only remedy is to lie still.

It's night. She is thirsty. Her jug is empty. She has been waiting for too long, hoping each day that she'd hear the grumble of the bus coming up and down the road, taking the black ones away in batches. It hasn't come. Tomorrow. But tomorrow is too far off, and she's thirsty.

A rat would not be afraid. (The word again: *afraid.*) A rat would get what it needed—careful, not afraid. Or would it? Isn't that what a human would do? A rat, above all, wouldn't need to *think* . . .

She uncurls herself. It's cold. As soon as the air hits her skin, she starts to shiver. She hesitates before she wraps herself in a blanket; it's worth it for the warmth, but it will slow her down, if she has to run. Then she creeps out onto the narrow staircase, down and through the cluttered storeroom—stiff-jointedly high-stepping over the moldering brooms and buckets—and out of the window, pushing the jug along the windowsill before she clambers out. Her hands almost slip as she inches along the sill and she lands clumsily, scraping her back down the wall as she falls into the next room, the jug cradled in the crook of her arm. Her defenses have never seemed so elaborate or so fragile. The blanket has caught on an uneven corner of stone and rips when she pulls it. She stops and listens, in case someone has heard her. Quiet.

She eases her way out into the corridor and along to the room where a row of man-size porcelain bowls gleam in the snow-and-moonlight. Each one has nubbed levers and pipes at the end; she knows—she has always known, although she doesn't remember how—that they spit water if she turns them. Risking the noise of the pipes, she drinks until she gasps, then fills her jug. The water is so cold it makes her teeth ache.

There's a noise in the corridor. She slides into a cubicle, but she has left the jug on the floor, in full view. If she leaves it behind she will have to steal another one, so she waits, hoping the footsteps will pass.

They come closer, echoing. She presses herself against the wall.

"Hello?"

A pause.

"Is someone . . . ? Hello?" He steps toward the cubicle. She could swing the door closed, but the latch is broken, and if he tried to batter it down, he could. And . . . is there a part of her, the human, word-burdened part of her, that doesn't want to hide? She stands still, wedged between the china hole-chair and the wall, while he tilts his head to see through the gap.

"Hello."

There is something about the angle of his face or his eyebrows that makes an unfamiliar impulse tug at her mouth. She has seen him only once before, but she would recognize him out of all the black ones with their interchangeable human faces. Why?

"It *is* you!" He smiles. "Remember me? Simon. Sorry if I scared you."

The words inside her head are suddenly outside her head. *Simon. Sorry.* It makes her blink, as if objects are materializing out of thin air. She thinks of bread and cheese and fruit, hopeful, but nothing happens.

"I couldn't sleep, I've been walking about. Last night they came to my cell and—anyway. I was outside, then I heard the tap running, and I thought . . ." Gently he pushes the door wider. "I was hoping I'd see you again." He gives a laugh, although not much of one. It nudges at her memory: a laugh-that-isn't-a-laugh, a twinge of misery. A woman saying don't take any notice of me, darling, I'm all right, only a bit silly . . . She bends her knees, ready to leap past him and out of reach.

"I'm going home tomorrow. Are you . . . ? I mean, you live here, do you? Are you a servant? You don't look . . . Sorry, listen to me, I'm talking too much. I'm not crazy. It's just that no one speaks to me anymore, not even the magisters . . . I feel like I'm invisible some-times." He tugs at his collar. "Is it this, do you think? I don't even know anymore. I feel like I'm not human. Like a ghost."

He takes a step toward her. The wall presses into her back. A trap, this is a trap. His voice. If only he'd stop talking, stop filling her at-tention with stupid human words.

"Are you all right? I don't mean to . . . Please don't look at me like that, we're not all bad. Wait." He fumbles in his gown. "Would you like this? It's my last bit, I was saving it."

He holds out his hand. There's a square, glinting morsel in it. His fingers are open, ready to catch at her if she reaches out to take it. She knows better. The nerves in her teeth tingle. The soft flesh above his collar is exposed. If she has to bite to get away . . .

He doesn't move. At last he exhales and steps back, still watching her, until he bumps into the edge of a man-size bowl. He looks around jerkily, as if it moved on its own. Then he puts the glinting square down on the lip. "I'll leave it here, shall I? It's fruit and nut."

Is it bait? What does he want? She stares at him until he bobs his head.

"I'd better get back. Early start tomorrow. Can't wait to get home. I have a sister about your age. I hope my family are . . ."

Silence. She stays very still. Maybe if she doesn't move, he'll forget she's there.

"Good night, then." He turns away, as if something has broken. "And, um . . . happy New Year."

She waits a long time before she moves. He has gone—she knows he's gone—but something lingers, a queasiness in her belly as though his questions have made her ill. Finally she picks up the thing he left for her and raises it to her nose. It has a skin of paper and metal, folded around at the top; when she unpeels it, the thing inside smells rich and creamy.

She bites it. For a second she is not a rat (a rat would be wary). But she is nothing else, either: only the taste of chocolate on her tongue, the little soft nub of a raisin and the harder crunch of a hazelnut. Another mouthful and another, and it's gone. She stands in the freezing silence, light-headed, disbelieving, her mouth full of fading sweetness. Why would someone give this away? It's incomprehensible. No one gives her anything. Not since before—food, comfort, a woman's voice singing her to sleep . . .

A trap. Of course it is a trap. That hand held out, that gentle voice, the expecting-her-to-be-human. A poison. She should have been careful. She should have known better.

She thrusts her hand into her mouth, gags and gags. At last the sweet stuff comes back up, thick and stringy and tinged with bile. She crouches, vomiting on the floor until she is sure it has all gone. Better. Then she scrubs the dark mess with her blanket until the stain is almost invisible. But her mind is not so easily purged: the words stay there—*Simon, sorry*—and the memory of his hand, offering. Those are a different kind of poison.

She gets up. She is careful as she goes out into the corridor, in case he is there; but the shadows are empty, the night silent. She tells herself that she is safe now, that she has averted whatever danger she saw in his eyes. But underneath she feels a perverse flicker of disappointment; and his voice echoes in her head, being kind, saying she's like his sister, wishing her a happy New Year.

Part Two

VERNAL TERM

17

LÉO

Léo sits back in his seat and takes a deep breath. He's alone in the carriage. The smell of steam and hot metal surrounds him, catching in his throat. The guard blows his whistle and the train judders and rattles, gathering speed. It's like being twenty again: here's the familiar sense of freedom, the faint guilt, the ache to stay on the train all the way to the terminal and stumble out into bustling streets and fleshpots . . . But he knows—as he always knew—that he won't. He'll change obediently for Montverre, without pausing to watch the train puff away to the capital. He stretches out his legs and crosses his ankles on the seat opposite; then he lights a cigarette and blows a plume at the ceiling. Mim hates to see him smoke. For the first few days at home she winced and coughed delicately when she came into his room, peering through the virtually nonexistent tinge of gray-blue as if she could hardly make him out. Finally he gave in and leaned out of the window or stood on the terrace, staring into the drab flower beds with their wintry hand-me-down air. It took the pleasure out of it, which was quite probably what Mim had in mind. She has a gift for that: for serving meals that are oddly savorless, no matter how much seasoning the cook has added; for pouring cocktails that seem to be mainly water; or for giving presents that clutch depressingly at the heart. At New Year he unwrapped a blotchy silver-paper packet that held a wilting tie the color of mold.

It's possible, of course, that he's being unkind. He's nearly forty—well, over thirty; he can't bear the wet-wool sensation of being a child again. The afternoons, airless and muffled, while he tried to read in his room or made desultory notes on Magister Dryden's essay questions. The evenings spent alone with Mim, or, worse, with her guests. The pretty but fatuous cousin in her high-necked blouse, asking earnest questions. The spinster of a certain age who acts as Mim's unofficial companion, who somehow gives the impression that she's wearing an unraveling cardigan even when she isn't. The pigeon-breasted local bureaucrats that Mim imagines fondly are the sort of people Léo was used to meeting when he was Minister for Culture . . . It should have been touching, at least, that she tried to entertain him like some visiting dignitary; but it only reminded him of the old days of being home from Montverre, when Dad would show him off to his friends. *Here is my son, a credit to me.* Léo would put on an act, affable and charming and a bit self-deprecating, to try to take the edge off Dad's bonhomie-filled resentment: and now, even though Dad is dead, he finds himself donning the same mask. This time he doesn't know whose resentment he's trying to defuse. His own, maybe.

But the nights he spent in town were worse. One evening he went to an enormous party at the Winter Palace. As soon as he crossed the threshold, he had to steel himself not to turn around and leave; the noise and the light were like a fever. He shoved his cloakroom ticket into his pocket and made his way to the main ballroom. He plucked two glasses of champagne from the nearest waiter, drank one down in a gulp, and slid it back onto the tray before the waiter had time to move away. He forced himself to sip the other as he navigated his way from group to group, smiling and nodding at acquaintances, pausing for a few minutes to swap pleasantries with businessmen or Party officials before moving on. He hadn't expected to see the Old Man or the Chancellor, of course, but he found himself scanning the crowds for Émile Fallon; he wasn't sure if he was pleased or disappointed not to see him.

At last he disentangled himself from a group of industrialists and ducked into a quiet carpeted alcove. He'd drawn aside a curtain and was wrestling with the catch on the window, desperate for a breath of cold air, when a voice behind him said, "Léo! Long time no see."

He turned. He knew her a little: Sarah Paget, was it, or Sara? She'd never been in the Ministry of Culture, fortunately, she was one of the Chancellor's underlings. Or was she at the Ministry of Justice these days? She was wearing a tuxedo and a monocle, her short hair slicked back. "How are you, old chap?" she said, slapping him on the shoulder. "Looks like the monastic life agrees with you, at least."

"Thanks. You look well, too."

She gave him a dry smile. "It's strange not to see your lady friend—no, wait, she isn't your lady friend anymore, is she? Never mind, you know what I mean—not to see her here. She did attract attention . . . I don't suppose you've heard anything?"

Léo shook his head. Chryseïs knew Sara and despised her; he remembered her saying contemptuously, "She'd rather be an honorary man than speak up for other women," rolling her eyes before adding, "and that hair is simply grotesque."

"Just as well, I expect. Better to keep your distance."

"What?"

"Oh—you hadn't heard?" She flipped open a cigarette case and offered it to him before she took one herself. "She walked out on Marco Boyer. Packed her bag, no sign of foul play. She hasn't been back to your flat, either. She's disappeared." She lit both cigarettes with a flourish; the flame drew Léo's gaze, while a part of him registered without surprise that the Party had been watching his flat.

He didn't answer. Clearly Chryseïs had found someone new, someone better.

"She got wind of the new Purity Laws, I imagine. I must say, you had a lucky escape, didn't you? There was gossip last year that you'd get engaged . . . Did you know she was on the Register?"

"She isn't."

"Oh, my dear, but she is! Didn't you guess? With a name like Christina . . ."

He stood up. "Don't be absurd," he said. "It's Chryseïs, not Christina. You're getting mixed up." He walked away. For goodness' sake, people were so ignorant: they heard *chrys* and thought it must mean Christian.

But he could hear Chryseïs's voice, that half-cracked drawl: "Jesus Christ, Léo." How many times had he told her not to say it? Because someone might think—because it was dangerous to sound like—

Could Christina be her real name? All right. Maybe she was baptized. Maybe, without Léo's knowing, she was actually on the Register. And she'd disappeared.

Noise spilled out of the doorway of the ballroom. Suddenly the whole thing was sickening: the open mouths, the sweaty faces, the self-important laughter.

He left. It was raining, but he didn't put his coat on; it was good to feel the icy water running down his back, soaking into his dress shirt, as if it could wash away the smell of the Party.

The next morning he went to see Dettler—who had stepped into his shoes as smoothly as a fox-trotting screen idol—and then Pirène. He didn't stay long in his old office; the busyness set his teeth on edge, and every smile and bright social answer from the secretaries rasped against his skin like sandpaper. As soon as he could, he climbed the stairs to Pirène's dark storeroom and wound his way between boxes of papers to the two chairs in front of the gas fire. Even the chairs had files on them. Pirène was in the kitchenette; as he shouldered the door open and came out again, holding a tray, he said, following Léo's gaze, "Oh, move them. Anywhere will do, honestly. I haven't seen my secretary for months, it's possible she's died." He set the tray down and began to pour. "How were the burgomasters of Montverre-les-Bains? Did you manage to impart much wisdom?"

"It was one of the most boring evenings of my life. Thanks for setting it up."

Pirène gave him a little smile. "Politics, my dear boy. One of them was the father-in-law of one of my superiors. Or is it the other way round? Anyway, it can't have done you any harm." He passed him a cup of coffee. Real coffee, not the watery chicory that even the magisters seemed to drink at Montverre. The bitter-roasted flavor flooded over his tongue: real, familiar, disappointing. All that time at Montverre he'd been dreaming of it. Along with martinis, foreign novels, brand-new bedsheets, smoky jazz clubs, brioches for break-fast, sex. There were still a few of those he hadn't gotten around to. Would they all be equally anticlimactic?

"By the way," he said, trying to be casual, knowing that Pirène wouldn't be fooled, "you haven't heard anything about Chryseïs, have you? My mistr—my ex-mistress. Apparently no one's seen her for a while, and some snide old virago from the Ministry of Justice told me she was on the Register."

Pirène reached for a box of chocolate fondants and held them out. "Oh, the blonde? No, afraid not. A lot of people are keeping to the shadows, these days."

"I see." Léo waved the box away. "But I'd know if she *was* on the Register?"

"Well, you could find out, I expect. Did you ever see her papers?"

"She would never have signed up. She's not stupid."

Pirène raised an eyebrow. "It depends," he said. "If her baptism was recorded and she renewed her passport in the last couple of years . . . Oh, come on, Léo, you know how these things work. It's getting impossible to dodge. The amount of money in that budget, honestly." He sighed and plucked a fondant from the tray, popping it into his mouth and chewing thoughtfully. "Wonder what the country would look like if the Old Man hadn't gone to a Catholic school?"

Léo shrugged. It hardly mattered. One way or another, the Register existed, the Culture and Integrity Act had been passed, and more Purity Laws were on their way. "Could you look into it for me? If she's in difficulties . . ."

Pirène swallowed and dabbed at his mouth. "The less said, the better, I'd say."

"If she were to get picked up—"

"Drop it." He shook his head. "I mean it, Léo."

"I'm worried."

"You can't do anything. No one can. If she's gone into hiding, it's best not to draw attention to her. If she's been picked up . . . well, you can't help. Trust me." He gave Léo a long look.

"Fine," Léo said, "I'll ask Émile Fallon."

"Don't be a bloody fool. Yes, I know you've been writing to him. Keep up the good work and you might get something out of it. There are rumors that you're worming your way back, that the Old Man might be softening—that's great—but only if you *stop rocking the boat*. Haven't you learned anything? Grow up, Léo." Pirène sat down, leaning back until his chair creaked. "You're on your second chance, and that's more than most people get. If you blow it, you might as well take out an expensive life insurance policy."

Léo put his coffee cup on the table beside him. The tiny, humid room was smoke-stained. He could practically smell the pleas and letters and decayed hopes that were pressed inside Pirène's files like flowers. "Thanks for the advice."

"Time was you wanted my advice."

He stood up. "I have to go."

Pirène scratched his head. A few flakes of dandruff fell to his shoulders. "Léo . . ."

"Yes, I understand. I have a train to catch, that's all." He wanted to get out, but he paused in the doorway. "This wretched place," he said, "I don't know how you stand it. It makes me glad I'm going back to Montverre. Getting away from all of this."

"A sanctuary, eh?" There was a strange note in Pirène's voice.

"What?"

"Don't count on it, that's all."

Léo stared at him. Pirène got to his feet and started to collect the coffee cups, keeping his head down. Then he disappeared into the kitchen without a word.

Léo trailed down the stairs, along the brown-and-cream corridor, past the bubble-glass windows that gave on to the typists' hall, and out into the street. The rain had stopped, but there was a chill mist that made him cough. He was carrying his case with him——Pirène had given it an amused look, as if he thought Léo was planning to move in——and he made his way to the station, grateful he didn't have to return to his hotel.

She was safe somewhere. Of course she was. She was Chryseïs, she was beautiful and clever and she could squeeze gold out of a stone. There was no need to worry. He *wasn't* worried. For a fraction of a second he imagined her wandering the streets, clutching a suitcase, a hat pulled low over her face: but no, she'd be on board a boat to America or Ireland, or already in an Italian city. Still in diamonds and furs, no doubt. She'd always been one to wear her fortune.

But he'd never felt so useless. There was a weight in the pit of his stomach: fear and guilt, and the dragging sense that he'd failed. All that time, she'd wanted his protection as well as his money, and he hadn't known. He sat in the bar beside the station waiting room and ordered a whisky; it was still early, but he didn't want to think. It helped a little—he managed to stop thinking about Chryseïs—but instead he found himself staring out into the station concourse, idly noticing how it had transformed since he first lived in the city. He'd visited with Dad a few times, but when he arrived alone, girding himself for his new life, armed with nothing but the address of the Party's Central Office, a stamped receipt from his new landlady (oh, that first flat above the milliner's shop!), and a valise of new clothes (recommended by Dad's tailor as "suitable for a politician" and turning out to be anything but), his heart had sunk at the grime and poverty, the papered-over windows and streaked glass ceiling, the rust and beggars and stink of indeterminate sewage. It had reinforced his resolve: be part of changing things.

And he was. Wasn't he? He'd been there, part of the Party, in those heady days when the Old Man marched the streets with the rest of them, and the grizzled old veterans looked at them with suspicion, and their soup kitchens were chaotic and full of roped-in sisters, idealistic young ladies who had never seen a rat dropping or a cockroach before. Back when there were brawls with the Communists that ended with everyone swabbing minor wounds in the lavatory of the same tavern, and the Party "uniform" was a green armband, and the leaflets left cheap ink on your hands, mirror-imaged words like *prosperity* and *hope*. When rooting out the Christians was only a bee in the Old Man's bonnet, easy to ignore, and you could *see* people's faces light up when the parades passed. It made Léo feel alive. Perhaps he threw himself into the fighting a little too hard, or wooed the soup-kitchen ladies a little too avidly and broke their hearts with too little compunction. But he was useful. He wrote propaganda with a better turn of phrase than anyone else; he knew how to charm the industrialists and donors, because they were like his dad; he could speak to a meeting, orating with nuances and gestures that wouldn't have disgraced the Magister Motuum himself. It didn't matter if he was lying, because he had faith in the greater good. And then the Party was elected, and the world was theirs. Whatever they'd achieved, he was part of it.

So the clean station, the shiny tiles, the way he could walk all the way to platform 12 without treading in anything that stank . . . The rubbish bins shaped like architectural features, their gold crests gleaming. And best of all, the people. Not that they were oil paintings, most of them—Chryseïs would have huddled deeper into her furs if they got too close, wrinkling her nose—but they looked a good deal more affluent than they would have ten years ago. They had coats and hats and gloves. They moved with more purpose. Fewer of them hacked and spat dark globs onto the railway tracks; fewer of the children had rickets. And no cigar sellers clawing at your sleeve, no gypsy kids threatening the evil eye if you didn't buy their lucky charms, no beggars. It was good, wasn't it? Not to have to brush people off or jump when a bluish human hand emerged from a grimy pile of rags. It was something to be proud of.

Except that the rumors . . . There was a faint chiming sound. Léo looked down. He was tapping his thumbnail unconsciously against the thick glass. Where did they go, all the beggars? In Dettler's office this morning a leaflet had been sitting beside the secretary's typewriter. *No more cadgers! No more tramps! Now you can feel safe on the streets.* It went on to quote glorious statistics about employment, the end of inflation, the Housing Projects. As if every vagrant had gone from blood-coughing despair to a new job and a new flat, to sunlight and fresh paint and full cupboards.

Nothing about policemen in vans. Nothing about where the vans might go once they were loaded up with reeking old men and coughing consumptive whores. Maybe it was only in Léo's imagination that they trundled off into the hinterland, with weak fists pounding the metal side panels. Even the rumors didn't go into detail. The streets were cleansed of riffraff, the way the educated professions were cleansed of Christians. No one asked where the rubbish had gone . . .

And Chryseïs? Would she be in the same vans if someone picked her up?

He stood and went to catch his train, even though he had twenty minutes before it left.

The next time he went back up to town, he didn't go to his club or to any of the Party haunts; nor did he go to the Ministry or to look up Pirène. He went to buy candied chestnuts.

Now they're in his case, wrapped in sapphire-and-gold paper. As the train rattles over points, he can imagine them bumping against his shoes, along with . . . Oh, god. He's glad he's alone in the carriage, because he knows he's grimacing involuntarily. He must have been mad that afternoon when he went up the spiral staircase at Maison Angelarde, tilting his head up to see the winter sunlight streaming through the Art Nouveau dome. He already had the box of marrons glacés under his arm; there was no need to buy anything else, and certainly no reason to go to the ladies' department, among the cabinets of perfume, the miniature pagoda roofs in ivory and pale green, the smells of jasmine and cold cream. He'd been here before with Chryseïs, trailing about after her in an agony of tedium, but this time it was different. He was a tourist, admiring this feminine world of silk and nail lacquer, filmy stockings and lace and little trifles. For a few minutes he could almost imagine being a woman: being entranced, frivolously absorbed in decisions of style and color, poring over the relative merits of ashes of rose and eau de nile.

Years ago, Carfax had argued with him about whether girls should be admitted to Montverre. He'd been passionate almost to the point of incoherence, insisting that these days, now that women were doctors and lawyers, it was sheer prejudice that kept them out. Léo remembered using the familiar counterargument that if the *grand jeu* was an act of worship, it was tantamount to letting them be high priests—and that it was foolish anyway, as everyone could *see* that there was no chance of the rules changing, not for another twenty or fifty years. They reached a stalemate when Léo sighed and said, "All right, find me a woman who can play the *grand jeu,*" and Carfax had rolled his eyes and said, "Because they're not allowed to study it! If my sister was here, she'd wipe the floor with you." Maybe that had been a sensible point, in a way; but seeing the women here, buying handkerchiefs and wax roses and gold compacts, Léo was reassured. He wouldn't let any of them near Montverre, and what's more they wouldn't want to be there anyway. The Magister Ludi was different—it made him smile, to think Carfax had been right—but she was an anomaly; she didn't disprove the rule. Maybe being a de Courcy trumped being female. Although she was both, wasn't she?

He paused by the scent counter. A girl with a brassy marcel wave—a little like Chryseïs, but not as beautiful—gave him a shy upward glance. "Can I help you?" And then . . .

Argh, what possessed him? He shakes his head with a wry smile, as if he's being observed. It's one of the skills he learned at the Ministry, dismissing his own embarrassment with panache; but this time there's no one here to absolve him, no one to charm or distract. The second blue-and-gold package is crammed into the corner of his suitcase, wrapped in a pair of socks. The only person who knows it's there is Léo himself; but he's the only one he can't deceive. What a fool. If he had any sense, he'd lean out of the window as the train winds along a ravine or over a viaduct and hurl it into unseen depths.

Then again, he can always keep it wrapped and hidden. No one will laugh at his stupidity except him.

The landscape slides past—fields, a windmill—familiar and unfamiliar, places that he's only ever seen from a moving train. How many times has he made this journey? Six times—no, seven times . . . Sometimes he liked the feeling of suspension, the in-between limbo before he arrived at Montverre; later, in his third year, he felt numb and taciturn, like a man on the way to the gallows. And now . . .

Now, he realizes, he's happy.

It's like the first glimpse of himself in a full-length mirror, the day he arrived at Mim's: he stuttered mid-step—no, actually walked backward—to get a proper view of himself, astounded at how much weight he'd lost. His clothes had been looser, of course, but he was amazed to see the clean shape of his jaw, the straight drop from chest to waistband. He hadn't realized he'd had that much to lose. And feeling happy is the same, somehow; it's alien, dislocating. He can't understand it. Is it merely relief at escaping Mim? No more tense dinners, grayish slabs of meat, painfully dilute cocktails. Or is it something else? The pleasure of serenity and sacrifice. Going back to a sanctuary from politics and the Purity Laws and his own guilt. The frisson of renouncing the temptations of the world and the flesh.

It's nothing, nothing at all to do with the little blue-and-gold package in his suitcase.

18

FIRST DAY OF VERNAL TERM

It's all so familiar. Slogging up the hill, the first sight of the towers through blinked-away sweat, the walk across the courtyard. Bright clouds scudding over the sky, so that the snow glared and dazzled and then died to dull gray. And when I looked up, it looked like the Great Hall was toppling. About to fall on me. *Tragedy as promising scholar crushed by collapsing building. Bereaved father campaigns for compensation.*

Carfax wasn't at dinner. I went and knocked on his door after the Quietus, but he didn't answer, and when I pushed it open a crack, the room was empty. Nothing there. His trunk wasn't at the foot of the bed. I suddenly thought of that time he received a telegram from home. What if something happened and he couldn't come back? Surely he wouldn't stash it now. But then, where is he?

SECOND DAY OF VERNAL TERM

Last night I couldn't sleep. Again. I got up to put on an extra shirt and a big woolen jersey and another pair of socks. Then I didn't feel like going back to bed. I'd given myself only a sketchy wash because of the cold, and I had an itchy, grimy crawling sensation on my skin from the train journey. I thought about going to the lavatory and running myself a bath, but at its best the water is tepid, and the idea of stripping off and getting in was worse than feeling dirty. I looked out the window, but there was no light anywhere. Everyone else was asleep. Remember that night when I saw Carfax's window casting a square of lamplight on the curtain of snow? It seems years ago.

Where *is* he? All over the vacation I kept thinking of things I wanted to say to him—jokes, ideas, fragments of *grand jeu* play, things that only he would understand—and now they're all stuck in my head. It never occurred to me that he might not be here. He has to come back. He has to.

I found myself going out into the passage. I didn't know where I was going, but I set off as if I did. I kept listening for other foot-steps, but it was as if I was the only person in the world. I don't think it's forbidden to wander around at night, but I'm pretty sure it'd be frowned upon. We've all got chamber pots, and the library's locked at midnight, so it's not like there's anywhere you can legit-imately go.

I made my way down to the Lesser Hall and crossed the empty space to stand for a while at the window at the far end. The clouds were still sailing across the sky, so that you'd swear the moon was moving. Then I went out into the lobby. I actually considered going out into the snow—it looked so *clean* out there, almost daylight bright—but instead I went over to a low, narrow door I'd never been through. This is another tacit rule: we're not allowed in the servants' corridors. I left the door ajar behind me, in case I got lost, but the light disappeared as I climbed the spiral staircase, and in a few moments I was in pitch-darkness. I had to feel my way along, and I was starting to think I should turn around and go back when I came out at the top. I think I must have been above the kitchens. I was right below the roof, with low windows on one side and doors on the other—not big arched oak doors like ours, but plain and set close together. Staff dormitories, I guess. The place smelled of stale sour soap. I swear I could hear the servants breathing behind those doors. It was like standing outside a kennel: half comforting, half alien.

Then I saw Émile coming down the corridor toward me.

Obviously, in the dark I couldn't tell who it was immediately. It took me by surprise. I froze, I think. All right, all right, I probably jumped and screamed. At any rate, Émile was laughing as he grabbed my elbow and dragged me back to the stairs. "Calm down, calm down."

"Émile—"

"Shut up!" He pushed me ahead of him. I stumbled down the stairs with his hands on my shoulders. I shouldn't have let him shove me like that, but I wasn't thinking properly. Finally we spilled out into the antechamber to the Lesser Hall and he let go of me. He was still giggling. "What were you doing up there, Martin?"

"Me? What about you?"

"Well, I know why I was there. But I'd be surprised if it was the same reason for you. Unless . . ." He squinted at me. "No."

"Why, what were—" Then I stopped. He smelled like sweat and something a bit more acrid, like soap—a kind of rank sweetness. I'd noticed it as he bundled me down the stairs, but I only then realized what it meant. I said, "Whoa-ho, Émile. Who? One of the *servants?*"

He grinned. There was just enough moonlight to glint on his teeth. "*Et in Arcadia ego,*" he said. "Sex, I mean, not death."

I'm shocked. Stupidly shocked. That Émile would risk it here. If anything qualified as bringing the school into disrepute, it would be that. We all talk about it, sure, but actually doing it . . .

I thought I was such a man of the world, with my fumbles in the dark corners of Dad's scrapyards, feeling superior because I could keep my own secrets. But this feels *wrong*. Playing the *grand jeu* in one room and fucking a servant in another . . . Sacrilege.

At the same time I can't get it out of my head. I don't mean Émile, specifically. But the specter of it, the possibility. The idea that Montverre isn't different, after all. That the whole fleshy, dangerous, messy business is within arm's reach, in spite of the rules. We're all as human here as anywhere else. If I wanted—if I dared . . .

Why should the *grand jeu* be separate from desire, anyway? It's not always sordid.

And a good *grand jeu* breaks the rules, doesn't it?

THIRD DAY OF VERNAL TERM

Carfax is back. I was on my way to do some piano practice and saw him coming out of Magister Holt's rooms. He's arrived here two days late, but he didn't look as if he'd been told off. He didn't see me; he walked away with a spring in his step and I didn't call out to him.

Bloody typical. He doesn't even turn up on the right day. But does he get hauled over the coals for it? No, he comes swaggering out of Magister Holt's office like we should all be grateful he's here. This whole vacation I've been remembering what he was like last term— that night when we ended up on the top of the Square Tower, for example—but no, it was all fake, wasn't it? We were only putting up with each other. Making the best of a bad job.

LATER

After dinner there was a knock on my door. It was Carfax. I suppose I guessed it would be.

"What do you want, Carfax?"

There was a split second when I swear I saw his face fall. As if he'd been expecting us to be friends again. As if he thought we *were* friends. But it was gone almost as soon as it came. "Just wondered if you picked up my Hondius last term," he said. "I thought I'd put it in my trunk, but I can't find it."

"I have one of my own, thanks." I picked it up and waved it at him.

"I didn't mean deliberately."

"I haven't got it."

"All right. Never mind." He paused, as if I might say something else. I didn't. He nodded and turned to go.

"You were late," I said. "I saw you come out of Magister Holt's room. Didn't look like he was worried. Let me guess: you don't have to follow the rules, because you're special."

"Don't be stupid. I had to go and explain . . ."

"What? What happened?"

He hesitated. "Nothing."

"Sure. Why *would* you turn up on the right day?"

He rolled his shoulders as if they were aching. "I . . . family business," he said at last. His eyes flickered to my face and away again.

"Really? Did someone get hold of a box of—"

"Please don't—" he said at the same time. We both stopped, watching each other. "Please," he said again in a strange low voice.

I didn't answer. The clock chimed—it was later than I'd thought—but he didn't give any sign of hearing it. He was still staring at me. I know I hadn't imagined his tone of voice: pleading, almost. Appealing to my better nature. No, that makes it sound too like Mim. As if for once he was opening himself up, like someone dropping their foil in the middle of a bout, spreading their arms and standing still. Letting me hurt him if I wanted to. Believing that I would.

And then the moment had gone and I hadn't hurt him, and with a silent jolt we were on solid ground.

I scrabbled around for something to say. I almost asked him if his family had been pleased about our seventy, but something stopped me; suddenly I didn't want him to think I was being snide. I really didn't want him to think that. In the end I came up with, "Well, since you're here . . . I was wondering what you made of the *Bridges of Königsberg*. I can't see why it's supposed to be so brilliant."

"I agree. It's bloody awful."

We both smiled at the same time. I looked down, flipping through my book without seeing it. There was a sharp, light feeling in my chest. "One of the third-years said we're going to be studying it all term. Imagine."

"Ugh." There was a different sort of pause: easier, like all those evenings we spent working in the library last term. Suddenly he yawned. "I'd better go to bed now, but maybe tomorrow . . . ? What are you doing after the Quietus? We can destroy the *Bridges of Königsberg* together. And there's something I wanted to run past you, an idea I was playing with. When you have time."

"Sure. Come and find me."

He didn't say goodbye, just touched his forehead in a sort of salute and shut the door behind him.

Maybe I am glad to be back, after all.

19

THE MAGISTER LUDI

Please don't. Please . . . She looks up from the page and she can hear her voice as she might have said it, as she would say it now if she wasn't biting her lip to stop herself. She shuts the diary with a snap, flattening Martin's words against one another. It's her own fault that he's inside her head: she is doing this to herself. If she had any sense she'd burn the ledger, along with the two copies of the *Danse Macabre* and the other papers she's stolen from the archive. If anyone found them . . . She tells herself that she is exaggerating the danger. She could explain. Yes. She is Magister Ludi, she has a right to borrow whatever she wants for private study, and so what if she sometimes forgets to let the archivist know what she's taken? And as for how personal papers found their way into the library at all—well, how would she know? Perhaps her brother might have had a hand in it. There's no need to destroy Martin's diary. It would be neurotic. But then, it's neurotic to pore over it like this, torturing herself. And it *would* be safer to get rid of everything . . .

You were late. What happened? She might as well not have closed the ledger, because she can still see the page in her mind's eye, as clear as a photograph. *Family business* . . . That last New Year, her brother was euphoric, scribbling and composing for whole days, singing into the night until she staggered wearily back to her own bedroom, too tired and resentful even to worry. At first she'd thought he was simply happy: when he'd first seen her he'd swung her around in a flamboyant embrace that became an impromptu polka, saying her name through joyful laughter. And for a little while the atmosphere was intoxicating, like a proper holiday, the sort that they had never had. They played pranks on each other and the housekeeper; when she wasn't there, they ran wild, alone in the crumbling château like the orphans they were. *I almost asked him if his family had been pleased about our seventy . . .* She bites her lip. If Martin *had* asked, what would the answer have been? The truth? She still remembers how the mere number *seventy* became a kind of joke between her and Aimé: they'd say it to each other at breakfast, at dinner, at random times during the day; they'd write it on scraps of paper, in chalk on a door, in gravy on a plate, as though it was a shared triumph; giggling, they'd shout it back and forth along the damp corridors until they hardly knew which of them had earned it. They played music together, drank musty antique wine, tried to pretend that the vacation would go on forever.

Then gradually he became . . . strange. Perhaps she did, too. Even now she winces at the thought of it. His energy and hers sparked and exploded; his nightmares seeped into hers. The old de Courcy rottenness . . . But it was Aimé who struggled, who shouted in his sleep and cried out as if he was drowning. Montverre would have been bad enough, full of scholars who thought the de Courcy blood was a joke, an easy target; but the shadow of lunacy must have seemed even darker at home, beneath the disintegrating roof of the château, where it had already stolen their parents. Both of them were afraid— had always, she thinks, been afraid—but it would have been the basest treachery to say it aloud. Even to think the word *madness* was to invite it in. No help. No doctors. Doctors took you to the insane asylum. So she watched him and perhaps he watched her, and she wouldn't have been surprised if he thought she was trying to poison him. What would Martin have said if he'd seen Aimé laughing so violently he gave himself a nosebleed? Or smashing a whole cupboard of cut glass "to see

the math on the floor"? Or, oh, god, white and silent at the thought of
the term ahead, watching her fold his shirts into the trunk? She told
herself that he was fine, really, that he'd calmed down, he was ready
for another term; but he was dreading it. And if she hadn't treated him
like a child, shamed him into saying that yes, of course he was all right,
he'd be fine . . . ? If she hadn't—

   She catches her breath. Stop it. It was years ago. It's gone, it's past
help. She shuts the door on her memories, ignoring the seep of red
over the sill. This is pure self-indulgent hysteria. She should be working on the Midsummer Game, not wasting time rereading Martin's
juvenile outpourings, narrowing her eyes at handwriting that's become more familiar than her own brother's. She only has months—
weeks—before she'll have to stand in the Great Hall to perform a
grand jeu, and so far she has nothing. This is no time to wallow in guilt
and self-pity and nostalgia. But she can't concentrate; there's a strange
gravity-levity inside her, like a ball of mercury expanding in a surge of
heat. Martin has been back at Montverre for nearly a week now, and
he hasn't spoken to her beyond a nod and smile when they've passed
in the corridor. She flinches from seeing him alone, but she wants to
get it over.

   She skims her fingers over the ink stain on the marbled cover. It
leaves a smudge of darkness in the whorls of her fingertips. It's been
a long vacation, but she's not ready for the term to begin. She is used
to the long winters here, the dead days of New Year, January, and
February, pillowed and muffled by the snow. The other magisters
leave from time to time, visiting their families or foreign academics,
celebrating New Year with more than a quarter of a liter of wine,
mingling with other important men in the capital—this year the
Magister Cartae boasted about how he'd been invited to advise the
Minister for Culture on national policy—but she has always stayed
here. She likes to be free, invisible, her own woman. She's never
wanted to stay with Aunt Frances or to go to Cambridge or Paris or

Wittenberg. She's never wanted to be reminded of the outside world: Montverre is everything, and more than everything, she needs.

Was. *Was* everything she needed. But not this year. There's a feeling in the corridors, as though the rock underneath Montverre has started to fall apart. She thought she was safe here—from the world, from desire; but Martin's presence has stripped a layer off her skin. It's as if she's becoming younger day by day, turning into one of the scholars. She can remember too clearly what it was to be their age: those heart-swelling sleepless nights, the terrible vulnerability of happiness. Her ten-years-younger self is too near, selfish and light-hearted, only now and then giving a thought to her brother's misery. Oh, she tried. She did her best. But she was caught up in her own life and didn't try hard enough; and Aimé died . . . She has learned the hard way to protect herself, never to give herself away. And yet she can't help it. This restlessness is foolish. No, it's dangerous. Irresistible as a drug, and yet, and yet . . . She's afraid of herself. Ever since she saw that black automobile roll into the courtyard . . . Or before that, before the beginning of term, when she felt someone in the shadows, watching her . . . She catches herself. Hysteria. Or—no—is this how it starts? How Aimé started—

No, of course not. No doubt it's much more prosaic: she'd like a change of scenery. To change the ideas, as the French would say. To get out of this place that has always been her home, but which feels more and more like a prison.

She knocks her temple with her knuckles, deliberately stopping her chain of thought. The *grand jeu* is her escape. No wonder she feels trapped; she needs to do some work. If she can't work on the Midsummer Game, she can write a test paper for her first-years or glance over her third-years' vacation essays. Anything to remind herself that she is Magister Ludi. She reaches for the nearest book—Jermyn's *Imaginary Spaces*—and flicks through it, looking for a quotation she can use as an essay question. *Mathematics is the first and the greatest discipline . . .*

There's a knock at the door. She leaps to her feet, drags the book sideways to hide Martin's diary, and stumbles toward the door. It opens before she reaches it—why did she leave it unlocked?—and for a moment she blinks at the figure in the pale light of the corridor. It's Martin. Of course it's Martin. For a moment they stare at each other. Too late, she is conscious of how she must look, tense and undignified in the middle of the room. She isn't wearing her cap and her plait is unraveling. "Mr. Martin," she says. "How can I help you?"

"It appears you have an admirer," he says.

"What?"

"There was someone lurking." He points behind him. "The Christian scholar, I think. I saw the cross on his gown. When I came along, he ran away."

"An admirer?" It must be Charpentier; the thought of him gives her a pang of guilt. She ought to do more for him. She, of all people, should know how hard it can be, when the scholars turn on someone; but she knows, too, how helpless the magisters are. Especially with the government—the whole country—on the side of the bullies.

Martin hesitates. He was smiling, but something in her tone has taken him aback. "I'm only joking," he says. "I suppose . . . no, perhaps you *don't* get much of that sort of thing."

It shouldn't sting, but it does. She doesn't want to be treated as female—in her experience, the less of that idiocy, the better. Nevertheless it's humiliating that he dismisses her so easily, and even more humiliating that she notices and cares. "What do you want?" she says, more brusquely than she means to.

He hesitates. He raises one hand and proffers a blue-and-gold-wrapped parcel. "Your marrons glacés," he says. When she doesn't answer immediately, he moves to her desk and puts the packet on top of her papers. She fights not to flinch: he's so close to his diary that if he merely moved the Jermyn to check the title, glanced down . . . but he doesn't. He turns back to look at her.

He expects thanks. She catches at the thought, almost too late. "Thank you," she says, but it comes out breathless, bewildered, and he frowns.

"You asked me for them. Last term. When I . . . You do like them?"

"Yes. Yes, I did. I do. Yes. Thank you."

"Good." He nods, fidgets with his tie. He's standing awkwardly, half twisted away from her; it's somehow childish, like a guilty boy who's hoping to get away with something. He clears his throat noisily. Then suddenly she realizes that he thinks *he's* at a disadvantage.

He must see the thought in her face—or something funny, anyway, because his mouth twitches; and as his expression broadens into a smile, she finds herself smiling back. Blast him. She crosses to the desk and leans past him, casually piling more papers on top of *Imaginary Spaces* so that even the narrow spine of his diary is hidden from view. "That's kind of you," she said. "I never thought . . . that is, I imagined you'd be far too busy—"

"I promised, didn't I?" His breath stirs the hair behind her ears.

"Oh? I forgot." She has misjudged the distance between them, and as she straightens, she brushes against his sleeve. He pulls back, but not as much as he should. "Perhaps I underestimated you," she says. It comes out more seriously than she intended.

"Impossible." He grins.

She turns away. What is it? The long, long vacation, the days of nothing but snow and books and silence, the years of *grand jeu* and—yes—loneliness, the flash of warmth that for once someone has brought her a gift, something sweet. Or is it mere morbid sentimentality, brought on by his diary? Whatever it is, she doesn't trust herself to look at him. "If you say so," she says. "Now, if you'll excuse me—"

He speaks over her. "Did you stay here all vacation?"

"Yes. Actually, I'm trying to write an exam paper, so—"

"I thought of you," he says, and the words cut her off like a gag. "I went into town a few times," he goes on, oblivious. "That's when I bought your sweets. But most of the holiday I was staying with my mother, up north. It was horribly dull. So I spent a lot of time working. That paper you lent me, the one comparing Philidor to Schoenberg—I wrestled with it for ages. Trying to understand why I didn't under-stand it." He gives her an amused grimace. "My faculty for critical thinking is pretty rusty. Then I realized why it didn't make sense."

"Oh yes?"

"Yes. Because it's nonsense."

"You thought so?" she says, tilting her head to one side. "That's . . . interesting."

"You *know* it's nonsense," he says. "You gave it to me deliberately. Admit it."

She hesitates. But it's too late. He laughs, and after a second she allows herself to join in. "I suppose it was a kind of test," she says.

And then he says, "You're so like your brother."

She stands very still. The air seems to crystallize around her, form-ing a layer of glass on her skin: the smallest movement might break it. Distantly—miraculously—her own voice says, "Yes?"

"He'd do something like that. Try to trip me up. Dare me to call his bluff. It was his way of getting me to tell the truth . . ." He swallows. "He taught me a lot."

"I'm not like him."

"Not in some ways, of course." He pauses, and she can almost see him counting the ways in which she's different: female, older, uptight, plain, inferior. Alive. "But in others . . . He was a genius, you know. Really. The way he could play the *grand jeu,* the way he taught me to play it. I didn't always understand—I was too young then, we both were—but . . . My word, he was talented. And . . . *sly.* Clever. He understood about games, I think. The way the whole of your life can be a game."

"I doubt that."

"All I'm saying . . ." He falters to a stop. Clearly he expected her to be flattered by the comparison. It hasn't occurred to him that her brother never made it into the third year at Montverre, and she is Magister Ludi. Then he raises his eyes and looks at her, and a trickle of fire runs down her backbone. Something has changed in his face. He says on an outrush of breath, "I did something terrible."

She doesn't answer.

"It's my fault he's dead. Did you know that?"

She shakes her head, although what exactly she's denying she isn't sure. It *is* Martin's fault. Almost as much as it's hers.

He says, "If I could go back . . . I miss him. I—"

He stops, as if she's interrupted him. But she hasn't.

He goes on slowly, picking his words as if they're footholds on a precipitous path. "I dream about him all the time. But the last time I dreamed about him, I think I was also dreaming . . . about you."

She tries to clear her throat. "I don't know what you mean."

"It was a good dream. You being here . . . my having met you . . . it feels . . ." He bites his lip. All the irony, the charm, the urbane glint in his eyes has gone: now he's simply telling the truth. She wants to reach out, take hold of him, and rest her forehead against his; and she wants to slap his face so hard he never opens his mouth again. Can't he *see*? "It's as if—"

"He's dead," she says. "You can't bring him back."

"I know that. Of course. I didn't mean—"

"I'm not him. You understand? I'm not Aimé."

He nods. His jaw is set, and there are red blotches deepening around his hairline, as though she's told him off. For god's sake, it's only the truth. But if it's the truth, why does it hurt to have said it aloud? There's a fierce ache stitching her throat and heart and gut together, tightening. And why is he looking at her like that, as if he can see how she feels?

"Please," she says, "please don't," and then she falls silent, thinking of the page she read in Martin's diary a moment ago. Is she standing like a duelist who has opened his arms, inviting a blow? Perhaps. Well, too bad if she is: if he steps inside her guard, she'll scratch out his eyes.

He holds her gaze for a long time. The clock chimes. A long way away a door slams, and two young voices come down the passage in a counterpoint of laughter, rising to a crescendo and fading again until another door shuts on them.

"I must get back to—"

"Well, I should let you work," he says at the same time, and they both wince and share an unconvincing smile, as though they've nearly collided at a blind corner. But it's Martin who carries on, assuming he has right of way. His manner is easy again, assured; the politician is back. "Let me warn you, though, that I'm going to pester you this term. I have an idea for a new game, and I'm too out of practice to compose it without help."

"I'm not sure that I can."

"You offered. You did offer."

"Yes, but—this term, Vernal Term is tricky."

"I won't be any trouble. I promise." He shrugs boyishly, and she can't be bothered to point out that he's just said he's going to pester her. She is perfectly capable of avoiding him later. She blocks out the treacherous whisper in her head that says she might not entirely want to.

"In the meantime," she says, and gestures at her desk.

"Yes, of course." He bows his head in ironic obedience. "Oh—one more thing." All this time—like an amateur magician concealing a card—he's kept one arm at his side, the hand hidden by the cloth of his trousers. Now he holds it out with a nearly casual flourish, offering her another little package. It's smaller than the marrons glacés, but wrapped in the same blue-and-gold paper. "I took the liberty of . . ."

"What's that?"

"I wondered if—I saw it and I thought—well, after all, you don't get to town much, and—" He stops. Again, her reaction has fallen

short of what he wanted. "It doesn't matter. It's nothing. It's stupid."
Now he sounds confused, accusatory. She thinks he's going to retract
his arm and storm out without a backward glance. Instead he puts the
second package on the desk next to the other. As he steps backward,
he trips against the chair and nearly falls over. Then before she can say
anything, he's gone.

She shuts the door after him and stays there, her head close to the
doorway, until his footsteps have died away. But when she finally
straightens, breathing more freely, the two gaudy parcels on top of her
books catch her eye, stubbornly refusing to disappear. Like a reproach?
A threat? Or something else . . . She picks up the smaller one, weighs
it in her hand, considers throwing it out of the window into the snow-
bank. But she's bluffing, of course. This is what Martin does to her:
she's reduced to performing, even when she's alone. She can't get rid
of his gaze. What is it he wants from her? What does she want from
him? Nothing. *Nothing.*

She takes off the paper, sliding her fingers beneath the folds to avoid
tearing it. Another game for her invisible audience, to show that she
isn't interested enough to rip it hastily.

A dark red box rippled with orange and saffron. Gold writing. *In-
censo Lagrime.*

The inside slides out, like a drawer. Like a matchbox. A bottle lies
on padded silk, gleaming. Even in the pale wintry light of her study, it
shines like a flame. She lifts it out, holds it up. The glass is stained scarlet, crimson, Indian yellow, imprisoning a bright swirl of gold sparks.
It spirals to an asymmetric point, so that when she twists her wrist it
seems to move, narrowing and flickering. She lifts the stopper.

Frankincense and smoke, amber, cardamom, harsh resin,
beeswax . . . She shuts her eyes and breathes in until her lungs
creak. She hears herself gasp, exhale, inhale again. It's rich, al-
luring, and complex; she begrudges having to breathe out. A line
of poetry runs through her head: *where blossomed many an incense-*

bearing tree . . . Something else, a line of terza rima, the *Inferno*. The phoenix, she thinks, feeds only on the tears of incense and spices. Dies and is reborn in flames. And all at once, dancing on the edge of her mind, she feels the heat and blaze of fire.

She catches her breath. Clumsily she shoves the stopper back into the bottle and sets it down.

The smell of burning. His gift is the smell of burning. She shakes her head, trying to laugh; but it stings like a whip on raw skin. An appropriate perfume for the granddaughter of the Lunatic of London Library. Another sly reminder that she is a de Courcy, and de Courcys go mad, de Courcys are dangerous. She thought all those jokes, the de Courcy jokes, had been left behind: but no, here is another one. If she closed her eyes, she'd see matches scattered everywhere. Or hear Léo's voice, malicious, as he gestured at a dying fire: *Hey, de Courcy, can't you find a couple of books to throw on that?* Except this time, as she's a woman, the joke is more elegant. An expensive present. Beautiful. Feminine. Only a hysteric would object. How dare he? For a moment, when Martin was talking about Aimé, she thought he was sincere. But this . . .

She slides the bottle back into its box. The scent has dampened her fingers and she resists the urge to lift her hand to her face. She puts the box in the back of a drawer, behind a pile of past papers, and slams the drawer shut.

Then she stands, locks her door, and goes back to work. But it takes her a long time to turn her attention to the essay questions she's trying to write, and the heady spice of smoke lingers all day, clinging to her skin. Later, when she teaches a lesson, she sees the scholars frown, sniff the air, and let their eyes linger on her speculatively: as though a mere waft of molecules is enough to bewitch her against her will, change her from a magister into a woman.

20

SECOND WEEK OF VERNAL TERM

The second week! That's gone quickly. I thought last term was hard work, but now . . . We've got, what, ten weeks till our games begin? The third-years have had the whole year to work on their games, but of course this is only a practice run for us, so we don't get half as long. (Although I bet if we called it that in front of a magister, we'd get bawled out. We're supposed to pretend every opportunity to play a *grand jeu* is sacred. Ha. It's not as if second-years ever have a real shot at the Gold Medal.) Carfax has already drawn up a plan for his, curse him.

It's as if the vac never happened. Almost as if we're still working on a joint game. Carfax and I are spending nearly every evening bouncing ideas off each other. First we walked over the *Bridges of Königsberg*—and when I say walked over, I think we've been back and forth over every one of them, I feel like I could draw a map of every single street in Königsberg and I STILL CAN'T WALK OVER EVERY BRIDGE ONLY ONCE—but then when we'd finally thrashed out exactly why we both hated it, I couldn't help asking his opinion about an article I read over the New Year. And then we didn't finish talking about it, so the next day . . . etc., etc.

Something's changed since last term. He's changed. He laughs more. Unless it's me. I suppose it could be me.

SIXTEENTH DAY, I THINK

Struggling to think of a theme for my game. Hate this feeling. Mentioned it to Carfax and I *saw* him start to say something pitying. Then he bit it back. I didn't know whether to cuff him round the head or kiss him.

For not saying it, I mean. Obviously.

SEVENTEENTH DAY (ASSUMING I WAS COUNTING RIGHT YESTERDAY)
Weird, brilliant Motuum class today. I think the Magister gets bored; every so often he does something odd, and I can never tell whether he's teaching or ragging us. We ended up going out in the snow to practice our forms—knee-deep, stumbling about like drunks— which was odd and funny and surprisingly useful.

We hurried in at the end of the lesson, dripping, and the Magister told us to go and get dry before Cartae. I was still breathless from laughing, scuffling with Jacob and Paul. Even Émile had got into the spirit of it. Then I heard someone say, "Dancing about in snow isn't my idea of the *grand jeu*," and someone else said, "What about water? Or fire? Hey, Carfax—"

"Yeah, Carfax, was that what your granddad was doing? Maybe he wasn't a raving loony, maybe he was poncing about on hot coals to practice."

I swung around. I didn't think. "Shut up," I said. "Leave him alone."

It was Felix and Freddie. They smirked and looked at each other. Felix said, "We were only asking Carfax about—"

I didn't trust myself. I grabbed Carfax's arm and dragged him up the stairs, leaving them behind. We'd come up the southwest tower, so we reached his cell first. I shoved him into it and followed him, shutting the door before the others went past. After a second he said, "Turn your back while I get changed." I sighed loudly (why would I care what he looks like anyway?), but I did. While I was still staring at the wall, he said, "Don't defend me."

"What? I only thought—"

"Don't. I don't need it. I never did."

"All right." I turned round.

"I can cope with them."

"I never said you couldn't."

There was a silence. He straightened his gown and pushed his damp hair off his face. But then, instead of opening the door to leave, he sat down at the desk and stared at the bare wood. "You know," he said, "I'd do anything to stop being a de Courcy. For a day, even."

I rolled my eyes. "Sure. Being descended from the most famous family of *grand jeu* players who ever lived must be such a burden."

He raised his head. "The mad de Courcys," he said. "You've heard of the Lunatic of London Library. And the Half-wit Poet, I expect. How about Lady Dulcamara de Courcy de Corombona? She lived back in the eighteenth century. She invented the Italian *quaintise* and poisoned a couple of lovers." He held my gaze, narrowing his eyes when I smiled. "Did you know my mother committed suicide? And she was only a de Courcy by marriage, it must be infectious . . . My aunt died in an asylum. My father drank himself to death. We play the *grand jeu,* and we burn out." He added, with a sort of mirthless hiccup, "Literally, sometimes."

I swallowed. "I didn't know. Not . . . that."

"That's why I don't find the jokes particularly amusing."

"Yes."

"You wait for it to show up. Every mood. Every nightmare. Every time you're happy. You think, is this it? Is this how it begins? Today I can't sleep for thinking about the *grand jeu,* tomorrow I'll be setting a library on fire. Slitting my wrists. I don't want to be a doomed genius."

I said, "You're not a genius."

He glared at me. He was right, the de Courcys do have a murderous streak. I gave him my most anodyne smile.

At last he said, deadpan, "Thanks."

"You're welcome."

Sometimes I feel like we understand each other, but this time

I didn't even know if he was being sarcastic. He's always holding something back. I wish I knew what he was thinking; it's like he's wearing a mask all the bloody time. I'd give anything to see him without it. For a second. Just long enough to . . .

I do it, too. But at least I know what I'm hiding.

I said, "I'll see you in Cartae," and went to change.

TWENTY-SECOND DAY (I THINK)

Starting to panic about my summer game now. Nine weeks.

It's fine. I can write a game in nine weeks.

Well, if I had an idea for it, I could.

Come on, inspiration. You're leaving it pretty late, aren't you?

It's so bloody stupid. They tell us the *grand jeu* is art. No, actually—worship. It's a mystical process of creating an abstract object that allows communion with the divine. A testament to the grace of God in the minds of men. The paraclete blowing where it listeth—if you'll excuse the Christian reference . . . That's right. Oh, and by the way, you have to produce games to order, when we say, on the dot, and we'll mark you out of a hundred.

No contradiction there, then.

I said something like that to Magister Holt today, but he only smiled.

TWENTY-THIRD DAY

Today in Historiae the Magister referred to adversarial games, which I'd never heard of. He mentioned them only in passing, and when I asked him to elaborate, he waved his hand as if he was striking through a measure and said, "I'm afraid we must move on." I didn't push it; he hasn't liked me since I lost my temper about politics last term. But it sounded interesting, so after the Quietus I went to the library to see what I could find. There wasn't much, though. Or at least, if there was, I didn't know where to look. The archivist on duty was useless. I spent ages looking through concordances, trying to track down some games to have a look at, but I didn't find any. Not even any articles.

I don't understand. How would it work? I can't even imagine it. Two players, standing opposite each other, all of it improvised, so no score for the audience . . . Not like our dead, rehearsed, perfected games. Something alive. Something actually *happening*.

TWENTY-FOURTH DAY

Argh. If we have one more lesson on the *Bridges of Königsberg*, I will kill someone. The Magister Cartae, ideally. (I wouldn't have to make much of an effort—he's teetering on the edge of the grave as it is.) At the beginning of the term he put this on the blackboard and made us copy it: *A few games well chosen, and well made use of, will be more profitable to thee than a great confused Alexandrian Library*. To which I would like to say, *Oh shut up, you old windbag*.

The worst thing, the positively worst thing, is that bloody tune. It keeps going around and around in my head. And yes, I realize that's the point, but it's driving me potty. Carfax thinks it's hilarious, of course. He's got into the habit of using the same rhythm when he knocks on my door.

Speak of the devil.

LATER

It's past two, but I can't sleep. I've been trying to scribble down some ideas, but I've got past the point where they make any sense. But the main thing is, I've got it. I've got something, anyway.

Thanks to Carfax.

It was him knocking, earlier. He'd come to show me something he was working on, and he sat down on my bed and watched me while I looked over his notes. It was his summer game—all meticulously planned, naturally—and it was all about storms and maelstroms and whirlpools, fluid dynamics and wave mathematics and Beethoven. I told him it was quite overwhelming and he bristled and said, "Yes, well, storms often are," but a second later he said, "All right then, smart aleck, so what should I do about it?" So we got into a discussion about that, and I told him I thought it was too abstract and too clever, and that he needed some narrative. (Narrative! Dear me! Whatever next?) I suggested he have a look at *The Tempest*, and he nodded with that noncommittal expression that means he thinks I'm talking drivel, and I threw a pencil at him. Anyway, we got onto my complete dearth of ideas, and he asked without conviction whether there wasn't some old draft I could resurrect, and I said no, and he said, well, why couldn't I find inspiration in the library, and I said without thinking that the library might as well have been burned to the ground for all the help it was. He shot me a glinty-eyed look, but he didn't say anything, so I couldn't tell if he was offended or not. In any case I was already babbling about how I'd tried to look up adversarial games and found literally *nothing*.

He said, "You went to look up adversarial games? Yes, of course you did," and laughed.

"What's that supposed to mean?"

"You are absolutely obsessed with *winning*, Martin, aren't you?"

"It's not that. No one's ever told us about adversarial games. I wondered what they were like. How they worked."

"You want to start with Wright and Percy. They were midsixteenth, I think. Or the Poets of Nishapur. Or have a look at Babbage and Klein—early nineteenth, they were probably the last to play *really* adversarial games. After that it all started to merge into joint games, which isn't exactly the same."

"How come you know so much about it?"

"I don't know. My—someone probably told me. Lots of the players were women, incidentally. Gransen and Gransen were sisters. And there were a lot of married couples. In an adversarial game, no one could pretend it had all been written by the husband."

"I don't get it. How can the *grand jeu* be competitive? I mean—was there a point system? How did they know how to score?" I reached over to make a note of the names. "I can't imagine what it would look like. Is it like an antiphon? Or harmony?"

"Go and read the books, Martin. I can't explain it to you."

I scowled at him, and he grinned.

"All right," he said. "Imagine you're playing the *Bridges of Königsberg*. No, bear with me," he added as I stifled a groan. "You're in the middle of the first movement, trundling, as it were, over the eternal bridges."

"Resisting the urge to throw myself into the Pregel."

"Yes, and you're pausing before the node where the historical motif comes in."

"Please, put me out of my misery!"

"Concentrate, Martin. Now, you've just completed that measure. But as it happens, you're not playing the *Bridges of Königsberg* as we know it, you're playing an adversarial game against, let's say, Felix. Who stands up with a gesture called the *assauture*—stop me if I'm patronizing you—which looks like this." He sketched an unfamiliar flourish. "And then, being Felix, he decides that the best way to proceed is to elaborate on the literal map of Königsberg, restate the original motif, introduce something only tenuously relevant, and then step back with the *conjuration,* inviting you to proceed." He paused in the middle of his impersonation and added, "Control yourself, please."

I was sniggering like a kid, but I couldn't help it. His mimicry was uncanny.

"Or perhaps your opponent is Émile, who will slip in sideways," he said, demonstrating a sort of wriggle, "and perform something so obscure it's impossible to say exactly what it is, and then go completely blank and look at you as if expecting more from him is only showing your ignorance."

"Stop it—"

"Or . . ." He was laughing by now, too, although not as much as I was. "Or Paul, who'd go straight for the math and sort of stamp it into a circle like a dog getting ready to lie down."

"I can't bear it, it's like they're in the room."

"Or if it was the Magister Cartae, he'd make sure you'd understood your own work by repeating it back to you, and then step back and glare without adding anything new, and you'd flounder like an idiot, because anything you did would get reflected straight back . . ." He tried to go on, but the giggles had caught up with him. It made me laugh even harder.

For a few seconds we couldn't speak. Then I took a deep breath. "Like the bridges in the water. Back and forth. The same, only another voice—the—" I stopped.

"What's up?"

I was suddenly sober. At least, I had that rising, queasy feeling in my gut, the quick heartbeat, the shivers. An idea. Like falling in love.

"Will you—I've had a thought. Go away. I need to write it down."

Anyone else would have argued. Carfax made an obeisance like a genie from the Arabian Nights, handed me the pencil I'd thrown at him, and disappeared.

Reflections. Left-handedness and right-handedness, symmetries, canon. Abstract, but with hints of imagery—the trembling of water, the sharp edges of a mirror, a modulated section on shadows.

Echoes. No narrative. Or if there is, only hints and fragments. The sense of a voice answering itself. Clear, clean, classical. Lucid, transparent. The opposite of the *Danse Macabre*.

I know Carfax didn't exactly give me the idea—I mean, not like a present, he wasn't deliberately handing inspiration to me like a parcel—but I feel so absurdly grateful I want to stand outside his room and serenade him. Maybe Magister Holt was right to make us work together. Maybe, after all, he knew what he was doing, the wily old crosser.

21

LÉO

He leans back, puts his hands behind his head, and watches sunlit drops of water flashing past the window. He's been working, but the falling gleams kept catching his eye, and now he can't bring himself to go back to his book. He's restless. It's not the end of winter, not by a long way, but on the end of every icicle there's a trembling bead of light; for the first time this year the air carries the scent of water and earth. This morning, when he crossed the court to the refectory, the sun struck his face with real warmth. Suddenly the short mountain days are opening like buds, heralding the spring. He knows that the weather can be treacherous, that it can plunge Montverre back into winter, refreeze the waterfalls, blanket the shabby snow with another layer . . . But all the same, his spirits rise. Soon—well, fairly soon—there will be wide green slopes instead of this endless monochrome. Wildflowers, the scent of herbs on the breeze, birdsong. And as the days lengthen, the magisters will look more and more harassed, tempers will run high, scholars will come to blows in the library over choice volumes. Spring will turn to summer; they'll hand in their games and take their exams. For years, Léo has paused in his work on hot summer days to look up at a cloudless sky and be glad he wasn't in the Lesser Hall, sweating over an exam paper that wrinkled and stuck to his hand as he tried to write; but this year he feels different. He's almost nostalgic. Almost.

He rolls his head from side to side against his linked hands and then stretches his arms over his head. His muscles creak. He's not in his twenties anymore, and the lack of exercise this winter has taken its toll. But he feels younger than he has for ages—since he left Montverre . . . no, since he won the Gold Medal, since the moment when the Magister Scholarium stood in front of them and said, "I'm afraid, gentlemen . . ." He has to swerve away from that memory, but it's easier than it used to be. He can turn his attention deliberately toward this afternoon, when he'll knock on Magister Dryden's door with a first draft of what might turn out to be a pretty decent article for *The Everyman's Game* or *The New Herald* or even, if he's lucky, *The Gambit*. He knows already what she's going to say—that in quest of populism he's sacrificed subtlety—but he's looking forward to it anyway.

These days he sees her often. They have evolved a routine, and he turns up at her door almost every other day—half supplicant, half peddler—offering articles, essays, plans for *grands jeux*. A few times they have ended up talking about the Midsummer Game, although she's refused to show him any of her work in progress. She's still, of course, as graceless and prickly as ever; but his perseverance is paying off. She has gone from hostile resignation to acceptance. Sometimes she forgets herself far enough to argue with him, leaning forward and pounding her fist on the desk, passionate about Philidor or Harnoncourt, and sometimes she even grins at something he's said—although that's a Pyrrhic victory, because she always dismisses him a few minutes later, claiming curtly that she has to return to work. And every so often, as though she doesn't realize she's doing it, she gives him a glancing, elusive look that could almost pass for tenderness. The thought takes him by surprise, and he straightens in his chair, pursing his lips. Tenderness? Really? But yes, he's not making it up, he's *definitely* seen something of the kind—and why wouldn't he? He can be charming when he tries; he built a whole career on it, for goodness' sake. And he's trying as hard as he can, because in spite of himself he wants her to like him. Those moments when she cracks a smile or gives him a look as though she knows him better than he realizes or . . . They kindle sparks inside him, sparks that sting a little and warm a little. She isn't Carfax, but gradually he's starting to forget that.

A moist breeze rattles the window, and a sudden spate of jewels streaks down from the eaves. He blinks away the vertical comet tails of darkness that linger on his retinas. She's never mentioned the perfume he bought her, but perhaps that's a good sign; she's not the sort of woman who'd be used to receiving gifts, who'd accept them as her due or coo meaningless thanks, like Chryseïs. Perhaps she was overwhelmed and still doesn't know what to say. He's imagined it over and over, her unwrapping the bottle, the flame colors shining in that austere room like a jewel. When she removed the stopper, the scent must have risen like smoke, exotic, bewitching. He should have gone back and looked through the keyhole. He wants to see her face off guard, open, wiped clean by beauty.

He gets up, shaking the circulation back into his fingers and toes. The sun may be swinging through the seasons, but it's still chilly. He turns back to his desk and picks up the book he was reading. It's an anonymous little octavo, a *Treatise on the Harmonical Form of Play* that he picked out of the farthest, darkest corner of the library. Recently, as well as the *grand jeu,* he's begun to play another sort of game: can he find an idea that Magister Dryden hasn't already encountered or make an argument she can't refute? So far he hasn't managed to score a single point. He can't tell whether she knows what he's trying to do and enjoys her victories, or whether it's a sort of childish solitaire, as though he's making faces at himself in the mirror. He despises himself a little for how much pleasure he takes from it, but it's an antidote to boredom, at least. And his knowledge of the obscure points of the *grand jeu* has come on by leaps and bounds; it might not outstrip Magister Dryden's, but every flicker of her eyebrows as she suppresses surprise gives him a tiny jolt of pleasure. In any case, he has high hopes for the anonymous *Treatise*. He flicks back a few pages, to a line he's drawn in the margin: *the claim that all the disciplines, so apparently discrete and separate, are merely facets of one ineluctable Truth, and may find their apogee in combination, is the same claim of religion, that every man shares a spark of the divine essence and his sense of individuality is a mere illusion.* But on second reading, it strikes him as commonplace: in other words, the *grand jeu* is an act of love. That goes without saying, doesn't it?

Underneath the little book is a half-finished letter to Émile. These days, with a belated circumspection, he keeps himself to the small comedy of magisters jostling for status, the hints of scandal among the scholars (nothing new there, as Émile himself will know), and the occasional conversations he has with the porters or librarians: a Christian first-year beaten up in the corridor, the mayor of the village taken away on a trumped-up charge, the perennial rumor of a ghost. Nothing significant. In return for his musings, Émile sends parcels of tobacco and chocolate and books, which are much more welcome than Mim's inept offerings; and more important, Léo sleeps well at night. He hasn't forgotten Pirène's warning.

But he can't be bothered with the rest of the letter right now. His restlessness won't let him stay still. He puts the book into his pocket and goes out into the corridor. He crosses the court and pauses for a moment to look up at the blue sky. The low hedges are still covered in snow, but he can smell soil and sap and the metallic tinge of meltwater. Icicles hang like clear tusks from the gutter, and a gargoyle has a jagged beard of glass. He walks through the doorway into the murk of the passageway. His heart is light again, as though cheerfulness is carried on the spring air.

Down this corridor are the music rooms. Someone is practicing scales and arpeggios. He pauses, listening to the clean clarity of the notes as they rise and fall, until a pang of not quite memory makes him turn away. His mind's eye catches at a crescent moon in a window, the deep blue of an evening sky. A face, a shiver on his skin . . .

And there's a voice. For a split second it's both past and present, a familiar inflection that tugs at him like a dream. He turns. Magister Dryden is coming down the corridor with a scholar, laughing.

Laughing. Why does that bother him? Because he wants to be there at her side, the way he would have been with Carfax; wants to be the one to make her laugh. He draws back into the doorway of the farthest music room to watch her approach. She's not like the other magisters; she wouldn't be, even if she were a man. She's different in other ways, in almost every way . . . She pauses, turning to the scholar, and he hears a fragment of speech: ". . . clever," she says, "but is it *true*?" The scholar grins and ducks his head, conceding.

It's a strange feeling, watching her like this. Léo's not exactly hidden, but at the same time he feels the shameful, irresistible rush of spying on her. He wishes he could have seen her at her viva voce. She must have been exceptional, even if she was elected only because the short list was mismanaged. But he'll see her play the Midsummer Game. He asked the Magister Scholarium if he could stay for it; he wasn't expecting to be refused, but neither was he expecting the Magister to offer him a seat on the front bench. "I understand that you were unable to attend the year you won the Gold Medal," the Magister said, "so perhaps you should consider yourself to have earned your place there." It was absurd how much that pleased him, even if he suspected that his Gold Medal wasn't the only reason for the privilege. He hasn't told her yet that he'll be there; he wants to surprise her.

The scholar says, "Yes, I will. Thank you, Magister," and scurries through the door into the main courtyard. A gust of cool air—chilly but scented—swirls down the corridor. The Magister stands looking after him, that amused, authoritative look still on her face.

He almost doesn't say anything. He's relishing the secret pleasure of observing her without her knowing. But there's something about her expression that stings him into stepping forward. "Magister Dryden," he says.

She smiles. There's no hesitation, no thought: she sees him, and her face lights up.

It hits him like a draft of water when he didn't realize he was thirsty, like the first drag of a cigarette or the first mouthful of a martini. He smiles back. For maybe half a second the world hangs immobile, the space between them singing. The niggle of jealousy—was it jealousy? how absurd—evaporates; there's nothing but her gaze meeting his, the sense that they are the only people in the world.

He laughs. He doesn't mean to, but he can't help it: a gulp of delight and mirth because he can't quite—and yet he does, he knows, it's crazy but he suddenly realizes that she's different not only from the other magisters but from everyone else in the world, except possibly Carfax. What's happening to him? But he knows. He wants to stand here and stare at her forever. There is nowhere else he'd rather be, no one else he'd rather look at. In spite of her plainness, her masculine jaw and straight brows, in spite of—no, because, because she's herself, she's lovely, and he never saw it. He hasn't felt this way since—

She blinks, as if conscious of what her face is doing. She fusses with a loop of hair that has fallen out of her cap, and when she looks up, her expression is deliberately impassive. Momentarily she was so like Carfax it was uncanny. Now she's herself again, keeping him at bay; but that instant of pleasure and complicity has given her away. She likes him. In spite of herself, perhaps. He feels it like sunlight reflecting off snow. It blots out everything else. He tips his head back, still smiling at her, and the scent of spring whistles damply through the cracks around the doors and windows.

"Mr. Martin," she says, striding toward him, "what are you doing here?"

"Waiting for you, Magister," he says.

22

FOURTH WEEK OF TERM

Haven't had time to write for ages. Composing a whole game in nine weeks . . .

I love it, though. On good days I'm sure it's a good idea. *Reflections,* I mean. I've got that nervous euphoric feeling. When I'm in lessons I'm constantly struggling to listen; I've started taking my rough notebook to every class, in case something comes to me and I have to write it down. I'm having real trouble sleeping because things start whirling around in my head. As soon as I get an idea I'm trying to hold on to it, clenching my mind around it in case it slips away. I'm all sewn up, but in a good way, I suppose. At least, I can't think of anywhere else I'd rather be.

FIFTH WEEK

Odd thing this evening with Carfax. We were both on edge anyway, I think. This afternoon we'd received our analysis from Magister Holt, and he'd scored sixty-three and I'd gotten only fifty-seven, so I was feeling irritable already. Also I think we're both tired, in an electric unrestful way that means we spark off each other, and we were having one of those conversations where no matter how reasonable I'm being, he's determined to take offense. (Well, it felt like that. On reflection, I suppose I might not have been all that reasonable.) I'd criticized the middle movement of his *Tempest,* and he'd put his head in his hands and said through gritted teeth, "You said it was too overwhelming, and now you're saying it's underwhelming. What do you advise, Martin?"

I said, "It's not my place to tell you what to do, I'm explaining what's wrong—"

"All right, all right!" He stood and paced to the window. Running his hands through his hair had made it stand on end. He looked like a lunatic. I didn't point it out—see how tactful I am these days?—but I suppose it made me grin, because he frowned at me. "What? It's not as if *your* game is flawless. What's so funny?" He picked up a book and threw it at me.

"Hey!"

"Well, help me! Don't just sit there *smirking*—" He threw another and another. I shielded my head with one arm and scrabbled for the nearest book. By that stage I was giggling. "You're infuriating. You're not even taking me seriously. Don't do that—" he said, and dodged as I shied it back at him.

"You started it," I said, and went on pitching them at him.

"Some of those are priceless—irreplaceable—"

"Oh, stow it," I said. I tossed the last one at his head. He ducked. It flew past him and flopped into the corner, pages splayed. Something had come out of it, a bit of folded paper, and I crawled half off the bed to pick it up. It was a letter.

"Give me that!"

He grabbed for it. I would have handed it over, but his tone was so intense I couldn't resist holding it at arm's length. "Why? Is it a love letter? Have you got a girl waiting for you at—"

He slapped me.

It hurt. Although possibly not as much as it would have if I hadn't been so bloody shocked. I never thought, out of everyone I know, *Carfax* would turn violent. It didn't even occur to me to hit him back. I offered the envelope and let him take it. He didn't say anything. I swung my legs off his bed and got up to leave.

"I'm sorry."

I waved away his concern. I've been in worse fights. That day at the scrapyard, when they were poking fun at Dad, I came home with two black eyes and a split lip. A smack on the cheek wasn't going to kill me.

He stepped between me and the door. "No," he said, "I really am sorry. I shouldn't have . . ."

"Didn't anyone ever tell you not to hit people who're taller than you?" It was meant to be a joke, but it made him flinch. "It doesn't matter, Carfax."

"The letter . . . it's important. Private. That's why I—I was afraid—I didn't want—"

"I didn't read it," I said. I was so tired I was swaying. "Don't flatter yourself. You're not that interesting."

"It—" He hesitated. "It's from my sister. She's . . . not well."

"Let me past, will you?"

"If anyone saw her letters . . . I think—"

"Even me?"

"Yes, even you. I don't—I can't . . ." He stared at me. He was still clutching the letter. Suddenly he shoved it toward me. "All right. Go on, why not? What does it matter. Read it."

His hand was shaking. He'd gone white. Maybe he'd shocked himself as much as me.

"No," I said. "I don't want to. Thanks."

A kind of spasm went over his face. He turned away and crossed to the window. He opened it, ripped the letter into tiny fragments, and scattered them into the dark. Then he sat down on the bed. "Do you have sisters, Martin?"

"No. I'm on my own."

"I shouldn't be here. Sh-she needs me at home. She writes me letters telling me how unhappy she is. Sometimes they don't even make sense. She's alone there, going mad, while I . . ." He drew in his breath. "I'm tired of lying, Martin."

"Lying to her? About what?"

He bowed his head and didn't answer. I imagined fragments of paper whirling into the melting snow, sticking in the trees, the ink running. Gingerly I reached out and placed my hand on his shoulder. I must have touched him before, but it was like the first time. And he went rigid. I felt it, like Midas: flesh turning to metal under my hand.

I bent my head to look at him, but he wouldn't meet my eyes. It was like a pause in the *grand jeu*—the rest between the resultance and the motif—those moments that Carfax holds almost too long when he plays, prolonging the silence until it's unbearable. I could feel the next move, suspended, breathless. All it needed was for him to glance up. But he stayed utterly still.

I don't know what he wanted or what he was scared of. Neither of us spoke. I waited and waited, in case he'd pull away or turn to me, either, anything to break the silence. I was so sure that one way or another he'd show me what he was thinking.

He sat like a statue until my fingers started to ache and I began to wonder if I'd imagined the tension in the room. Then it was too late. I let go and left him to it.

LATER
Lying? What is he lying about?

FIFTH WEEK, WEDNESDAY
He said he was sorry. I didn't know how to reply. I acted like I hadn't heard. I was at my desk, going over the bit he's still stuck on. It's funny, his games are normally so perfect, structurally. But this one's got a big disjunction in the middle section. I think that's why it's not working. No matter how much brilliant stuff he throws at it, there's something missing or something extra or . . . I don't know. He was

pacing about behind me and I couldn't concentrate. Then he said, "Sorry about hitting you."

There was a bit of a pause. I kept on staring at his notes. That bloody porridge of classical and Artemonian. Can't believe I've grown used to it. I said, "How about an English contrevure?"

"What?"

"For this movement. An English contrevure. Look it up."

I heard him grunt and flip through a book. "It's not in the Snary."

"Try the index of the Theoric. I've seen it somewhere recently."

He riffled more pages and whistled. "An English contrevure . . . Hmmm. Interesting. You might be onto something."

"No need to sound so surprised." I'd come up with something he hadn't heard of. Finally.

There was another silence. Eventually I looked around. He was standing right behind me. His hand was hovering over my shoulder. As I watched, his fingers curled into a fist and he lowered his arm. "There's the bell," he said. "Give me a second to write that down. I'll meet you downstairs."

So that was that. His apology.

SUNDAY

This morning—not early, thank goodness—I got press-ganged into a couple of bouts with Felix and Jacob. Felix stood in my doorway and refused to go away until I came down to the Lesser Hall. Actually, in the end I enjoyed myself. And won, although I'm woefully out of practice. Afterward we all sat around on the steps of the Lesser Hall, looking down into the valley. It was a lovely day, one of those early spring days when the snow is melting and a warm wind is blowing; every so often a spatter of freezing water would spray into our faces from the gutter overhead. It was me, Felix, Jacob, Paul, and Émile. There was the usual banter, jokes about the magisters and one another, teasing about our prowess at the *grand jeu,* sex, etc. When they were trying to get a rise out of me, Felix was laughing the loudest, but at lunchtime when we all stood to go he hung back a bit and asked me if I'd have a look at his game. "I'm too busy at the moment," I said. "What about Paul? What does he say?"

"I haven't asked him. I'm asking you. Come on, Martin, if I fail——"

"No one fails, Felix. You might get a third, but it's not the end of the world."

"Please," he said. "Have a heart."

"I'll see. Put a copy under my door." He grinned, and I added, "I'm not promising anything. I'm working like a navvy myself. I don't have time to help other people."

I'm not sure he was listening, because he slapped me on the back and galloped off. I was about to follow him when Émile took hold of my elbow. "Liar," he said.

"What?"

"You're helping Carfax, aren't you? Every spare moment, it sounds like."

I tried to shake him off. "*You're* not jealous as well, are you?"

He laughed. "Certainly not. I'm only pointing out that you're lying."

"What if I am? It'd be a waste of time helping Felix, you know that."

"Yes," he said. "That's definitely true." I went to move away, but he still had hold of my arm. "One more thing," he went on, tilting his head at me as if I'd said something stupid in a lesson. "Don't forget that time he parodied you in front of everyone. You do realize, don't you, that Carfax is a ruthless bastard? Why do you think he's suddenly friends with you? Because not only are you second in the class, you're also apparently prepared to spend every waking hour with him, working on his game. It's not because of your charm, you can bet."

"Leave me alone, Émile."

"He's using you. Look at yourself, you're all starry-eyed," he said, and released me, stepping back and spreading his arms. "Don't fall for it, that's all."

It's not true. We work on my game as much as Carfax's. Don't we?

SUNDAY AGAIN, SIXTH WEEK
Early morning. I can't sleep. I haven't written for days because I didn't want to think. I don't want to admit it. I don't want to write it down.

But: I *have* fallen for it, haven't I?

For him.

I didn't even notice it happening. Not really. Not till Émile looked at me that way, all knowing and slippery, as though he could see inside my head. I keep telling myself it's because he's got a mind like a sewer, and he can't imagine that Carfax and I could genuinely be friends. But I'm kidding myself.

Carfax, for pity's sake. A pathetic schoolboy crush on *Carfax*. What is wrong with me? This isn't an opportunistic "sure, why not?" like those other times in the scrapyard. Not a quick toss-off behind a pile of finials, while everyone else smokes a fag or goes for a brew. I *want* him. I'd risk expulsion for him. Would I? I think I would. If he had turned around that time I touched his shoulder and . . . Shut up. SHUT UP. But all these nights we've spent playing the *grand jeu,* all the jokes and the ideas and the rush, being as happy as I think I could ever be . . . It's all part of the same thing. The whole world falling into place. All of myself, cock and balls and heart as well as brain. We play the *grand jeu* with our bodies, too, don't we?

(Essay question: "*As with scatological, macabre, or trivial concerns, there is no place for the erotic in the grand jeu; it ranks among the lowest of human impulses, while the grand jeu celebrates the most elevated.*" *Discuss.* And hang it, I want to discuss it with Carfax.)

Don't fall for it. It's too fucking late. But Émile's right. I can see that. Carfax and I won't ever be anything but rivals. He wants to beat me, that's all. And the best way to do that is to reel me in. Fake a meeting of true minds when all he cares about is getting a higher mark than me. Of course he acts strange around me. Of course he's fed up of pretending.

It's making me sick, the thought that he's done it on purpose. That's what Émile meant, wasn't it? And if it's true . . . Surely he's not that cynical? He's not *that* much of a shit. But I can't trust him. I can't let myself relax. I've got to stay on my guard. Pull back. Keep away.

Or lean in. Play him at his own game.

LATER

I worked alone in the library for most of the day. Then I was all thick-headed and miserable, and it was another lovely evening, so I wandered outside for a little while, watching the sun drop behind the mountains. Then I got too cold and had to come in. I came back along the music corridor, jogging to warm myself up.

There was someone playing the cello in one of the practice rooms. The music was Bach, one of those restless mathematical preludes that hovers on the edge of melody. You can feel the beauty, the drive, but all the time the piece is containing it; there's a sort of iron discipline that lets it shine through but won't surrender to it. It made me stop in my tracks. Outside, above the courtyard, the sky was a perfect deep blue, the bluest blue you can imagine, right on the edge of dark. There was a new moon, and the evening star was absolutely blazing. The prelude stumbled and started again.

I must have stood there for ten minutes at least, listening to that prelude being played over and over. There's a moment about halfway through—a low E, is it?—when it opens up abruptly into something different, something deep—it's what you've been waiting for, without knowing . . . and every time it made the hairs on my arms stand up. Every time. I wanted it to go on forever.

It didn't, of course. Finally whoever it was must have been satisfied and went on to the allemande. I was walking past, but then the music broke off and I heard swearing.

I pushed open the door. Carfax was there, wrapped around his cello; I thought I'd recognized his voice. He looked around. The expression on his face made me stop in the doorway: as if he wanted me to come in but he didn't want to say so. I said, "It's you."

"As far as I know," he said.

I shut the door behind me. He gave me a long look and then started to play again. He's pretty good, much better than I am at the piano. But he started getting notes wrong, more and more of them, until finally he lowered his bow and said, "What do you want?"

"Nothing," I said. I didn't know why I was there, except that I couldn't avoid him forever.

"I'm practicing."

"That's all right."

He raised his bow, sighed, and lowered it again. "Go away, will you? You're putting me off."

"I was listening outside. It was good."

He frowned, but he started to play again. At the end of the suite he sat back, stretching his neck to one side and then the other. "Better men than you would pay for that," he said.

"It's got an amazing tone."

"I should hope so. It's a Stradivarius." He laughed, probably at me, and moved so that I could see the light falling on the cello. It was the color of maple leaves, with a warm lustrous gleam. "The Auburn

Mistress," he said. "It's famous. You see the red varnish? *Vernice rossa.* It's almost unique. No one's entirely sure what it's made of."

"Of course," I said. "Nothing but the best for the de Courcys."

"We don't have many heirlooms. I expect over the last century lots of things have been thrown against the wall. Or smashed. Or burned," he added, with a glimmer of a smile.

"If I said that, you'd hit me."

He gave me a sidelong glance and brushed the purfling with his knuckles very gently. "It's lovely, isn't it?"

"Yes. Why *mistress?*"

"I don't know. Maybe men love their mistresses more than their wives."

"If I owned that, I'm pretty sure I'd want to marry it." I leaned forward and touched the varnish. It was like oil. Utterly smooth. "I mean, wouldn't you want your violins to be legitimate?"

He laughed and gave one string an affectionate twang. Then he looked up and into my eyes, and the smile died. Or rather, it sort of retreated; the warmth was still there, but there was something else in his face. And then he flushed. It was remarkable, like a red light shining on him.

I stared at him. For a second he held my gaze. Then I think he realized that he was blushing, because he got to his feet and fumbled the cello back into its case. It seemed to take an age. He glanced over his shoulder, as if he could sense me watching him, but he didn't meet my eyes. I was just standing there, hands in my pockets. As jokes go, it wasn't exactly obscene; and he'd laughed, hadn't he? And yet even his ears were scarlet. Somehow I was afraid I'd given myself away. I said, "What's up, Carfax?"

"Nothing."

I opened my mouth to tease him, but something stopped me. He put the cello into its case and leaned it against the wall. "I'll see you later," he said. "Give me a knock after dinner."

I was standing in front of the door. He waited for me to move. I took a step back, but not enough, so he stepped toward me and still couldn't get past. We wavered in the doorway for a second, our faces close together, in a kind of absurd dance. And then . . . his gaze flickered. His look skimmed my face, my mouth, and came back to my eyes. It hardly took a fraction of a second, and then he barged past me, clipping me with his shoulder.

But it was enough. That *something else* in his expression . . . It was there. I'm certain of it.

I started to laugh when he'd gone. I didn't know what to do with myself. I had to bend over and put my hands on my knees, breathing hard, until finally I got myself under control.

What if I'm making it up? What if that look didn't mean anything, what if it was just his manner? Arrogance? Sheer irritation, because I wouldn't move out of his way? I've only now realized how I feel about him, so what if I'm seeing what I want to see? The more I think about it, the less sure I am. But I *was* sure. When it happened, I knew. And now if I shut my eyes and remember . . . Yes. I'm *not* mistaken. That blush, that long look, his clumsy hands when he tried to put away his cello. How he reacts when I touch him. He may not realize, mind you—any more than I did, till Émile said his piece—but it's there. It has to be. Which means . . .

No, we can't. It's too dangerous. Even if we were careful.

I can't sleep. My stomach is churning. What am I going to do?

And I can't help thinking: if it's true, if I'm right . . . then I've won, after all. Haven't I?

23

LÉO

Something has given him the squits. He's lucky that the nearest lavatory is a small single one, meant for the magisters, but all the same he
curses as he stumbles between toilet and bed, sweating. The clock,
which he'd almost grown used to, rings through his dreams, making
him dizzy. The servant who banks up his fire brings him water, too,
and asks if he wants anything to eat; but the thought of it makes him
curl up, knees to his chest, trying to quell the twinges in his gut.
Later, when he falls into an uneasy sleep, the same servant is there in
his dreams: only now she's transformed into the laundress who died
years ago, the one who threw herself off the Square Tower when he
was in his second year . . . Carfax is there, too, and Magister Dryden
and Dad and Émile and Mim and Chryseïs and Pirène and that friend
Léo made in the first year of the Party who turned out to be a leftist
and got killed in a brawl . . . All of them, as if everyone he's ever
known is crowding around his bed, sly and reproachful. He can't
bear it. He lights a lamp—striking four matches before he manages
to keep one burning—to keep the dark at bay. The mess in his room
wavers as the shadows bob and dip: books, dirty clothes on the floor,
parcels spilling their contents. There are chocolate bars, packets of
tea and cigarettes, shaving soap, some new razor blades . . . A pile of
cheap blue-backed novels, none of them in translation, none of them
worth reading. Those were from Émile, keeping him abreast of cul-

tural developments, with a malicious note telling him how much the Party's new imprint needs a better editor in chief. The place looks like a looter's headquarters. Sometimes he wonders whether he'll drown in it all, like something out of a cautionary tale. The walls will creep inward and the tide of luxuries will rise . . . No, that's the fever talking.

He drifts, empty and exhausted. The window blazes and dims, the sunlight jumps from one section of the floor to another like a flea, then crawls under the bed and dies. When his mind is clear again, the lamp is burning low and the sky outside is spread thickly with stars. He's lost track of time: has he been ill for one day or two? At least now he knows perfectly well who he is and where, and that he's alone. Alone and ravenous. Gingerly he climbs out of bed, wrinkling his nose at the sharp febrile scent of his sweat. He reaches for his watch, but of course he hasn't wound it. Is it evening or night? He might be in time for dinner, if he's lucky. Soup and a glass of wine. Bread and butter. His mouth fills with saliva. He drags on some trousers and a shirt and jumper. His legs feel spongy, but his stomach gripes have stopped and he's no longer giddy. He makes it to the door and out into the passage without having to lean against the wall.

But dinner is over. He isn't sure where to go. Perhaps the Magister Domus would be able to help; or perhaps—since the Magister Domus takes great pleasure in refusing Léo's requests—he should go to the kitchens and see if he can scrounge something up.

As he steps out into the courtyard, he tilts his face up to the stars. The Milky Way is like butter. He stands there breathing, trying not to think. The clock strikes; he isn't counting, but it goes on for longer than seems plausible. It must be midnight. The door of the library opens, and two figures come out. One of them is a gray-robed librarian, ushering out a slim figure in white. Magister Dryden. "I'm sorry, Magister," he's saying, "but the rules are quite straightforward, and I . . . Next time, if you let me know in advance—"

"There's no need to apologize," she says. Her voice is very clear in the still air.

"It's just that there must be at least two people in the building at all times."

"In case someone takes it into his head to burn it down. I know."

"Not that—"

"It's fine. Thank you." She turns away from him in a whirl of pale wool and catches sight of Léo. "Mr. Martin," she says. "Is something wrong?"

"No," he says, blinking away the lingering image of Carfax. "Should there be?"

"No," she says, "but it's customary to wear shoes outside."

He looks down. "Oh. I thought my feet were hurting."

She tilts her head to one side. "Are you drunk, Martin?"

"I'm a bit light-headed, that's all. I've been ill." Her presence—her attention—eases something inside him. He pushes his hands into his pockets, trying to appear casual. "And how are you, Magister? Working hard?"

A flash of a grimace crosses her face. He remembers that feeling: how long did he struggle before he got the idea for *Reflections*? He wants to put his arms around her and tell her it'll come, that she's an artist, that it always feels like this at first. But of course he won't, he's not an idiot. "If you want to go back to the library, I can chaperone you," he says. He's not sure if it would be allowed, but the idea of being alone in the library at night, with her, is strangely exciting.

"No, thanks," she says. "What I really want is a drink. I've got some brandy . . ." She stumbles on the word, and for a second he remembers standing in her room, a bottle in his hand, the sting of rejection. It was only *his* brandy she didn't want, then. She shoots him a look as if she's read his thoughts. "It was a gift from my English cousins. I haven't opened it, because . . ." There's a tiny pause. Perhaps she notices that she's on the verge of apologizing, because she looks away. "I don't suppose you want to join me?"

"For a drink?"

"No, you're right. You shouldn't, if you've been ill. And I have a class first thing tomorrow."

"I'd love to. I mean—I'd kill for a drink. Yes. Please." Has she already retracted the offer? He hunches his shoulders in a gesture that's meant to be boyish and charming. "That would be lovely, thank you. By the way, have you seen this month's *Gambit*? There was a contribution from Millicent Cairn that made me think of you."

"Because she's a woman."

"No, because she talks about the liberating effect of not having been to a school. I thought perhaps—"

"How can not getting an education be *liberating*?" But it doesn't matter what she's saying, because he's distracted her into setting off across the court toward the Magisters' Entrance, obviously expecting him to accompany her. "You think all female players are the same, don't you, Martin? And yet *male* players are varied, because they're not hampered by having to think about being a woman all the time. Is that right?"

"I don't know," he says.

"My word, I'm sick of it. *Home, husband, and happiness,* isn't that what your Party wants for us? As soon as we were starting to get concessions . . . Do you realize that thirty years ago a married woman couldn't have her own *library card* without her husband's permission?"

"At least you got the vote."

She narrows her eyes at him. "Yes, things were getting better. And then there was the Depression and your lot came along and . . ." She takes a deep breath. "Never mind. You want some brandy, or not?"

They go in through the massive oak door and turn toward her rooms. The corridor is quiet and cold, striped with starlight. He hovers in her doorway as she lights a lamp and beckons him to come in. "Oh—wait . . ." She collects up her papers from the desk and dumps them into a drawer.

"I'm not going to *plagiarize*," he says, stung.

"No—I didn't think you—of course not," she says, but she bundles the last notebook away as if she means the opposite. She crouches down to take the bottle of brandy out of a low cupboard. "Wait, let me get a glass from upstairs."

She disappears up the stairs. Part of him wants desperately to rifle through her desk and expose whatever she's hiding, but of course he won't. He contents himself with turning in a slow circle, looking at the austere shapes of desk and chair and window. What's it like to live here? To know that she's here forever? A life sentence. Can she possibly be happy?

"Here," she says from the foot of the stairs. "I'll have to drink from the bottle." She hands him a toothglass and pours some brandy into it. He raises it to her and drinks. It's good and fiery, with that dusty, papery scent that makes him think incongruously of old books. It leaves heat on his tongue and seems to fill his empty stomach. He takes another mouthful and another. She watches him, smiling. Then she bends her head and takes her cap off, flicking it onto the desk like a deflated puffball. Her hair is falling out of its chignon, and in this light—and, he has to admit, with the alcohol already softening his senses—she looks like Carfax at the end of term, when his hair had been uncut for twelve weeks. They always looked like scarecrows, all of them; there was a servant in the infirmary who'd cut your hair on Sundays, but even though people like Émile had valets at home it was de rigueur to pretend you were above asking a servant to touch you. The first thing Dad always said when Léo got home was "Well, I'll be blowed. For a moment there I thought you were a girl." Now, as the Magister raises the bottle in response and drinks from it, it's the other way around. She could be a young man, especially now that she's spluttering a little and wiping her mouth on the back of her hand. He stares at her.

"I'm sorry," she says.

"Don't be. Please."

"It's been quite a day. I'm so tired. I haven't slept for ages, thinking about this blasted game. Yes, the Midsummer Game," she adds when he raises his eyebrows. She leans against the desk and pushes the chair toward him. "Sit down, please."

"Thanks," he says. It feels strange to sit while she's standing.

She takes a deep breath, tapping her fingernails against the neck of the bottle. Then suddenly she says, "I haven't got anything. You understand? I have to perform the Midsummer Game in two months, and I have nothing. Not an idea. Not a title. A blank page. I'm terrified."

There's a silence. He bows his head, turns his glass between his hands, watching the lamplight roll through the liquid. "I see," he says, almost under his breath.

"I have to write it. But I—oh, if I—" Her voice cracks. He glances up, confused. She's staring at the window, at her own reflection, with an expression of . . . what is it? Longing, he thinks, but it doesn't make any sense.

He says, "Have you ever written a joint game?" Somehow he doesn't think she'd be a natural: she's too rigid, too prickly, too passionate. She'd be worse than Carfax. He takes a mouthful of brandy, so big that he has to concentrate to swallow. He doesn't want to think about Carfax. Certainly not now, when he's here with her. With the Magister. Ha. How absurd, that even in his head he calls her that. Surely by now he should be calling her by her name. Claire.

She raises the bottle to her lips, but she doesn't tilt it to drink. She breathes out, and the air rings hollowly across the glass. "No," she says. "No."

"It'll be all right," he says. "I mean . . . I could help. If you wanted."

"You?" The edge in her voice flicks him on the raw. Perhaps he is being vain to imagine that he has anything worth contributing, but she could at least pretend to be grateful.

"It would still be your game," he says. "I know that."

"How humble of you." She flicks him a glance. "Would it give you a thrill to know that there's a Midsummer Game that you'd partly written?"

He's about to demur, as if it's the sort of thing that might happen to him every day; then the words suddenly come into focus. A Midsummer Game that he'd partly written. He wouldn't be standing up himself, as Magister Ludi, but it would be the next best thing. He imagines sitting there, heart beating in his mouth and fingertips, and the joy of seeing his own ideas come into being. Feeling the silence and attention—a whole hall of the finest minds of the *grand jeu*—form a game out of the Magister's gestures, like hands in clay. Collective worship, centered on something he'd made. And at the center of it all, Claire.

He blows out his breath. There's no point pretending. "Yes," he says. "My god, yes."

She grins. He grins back. As if it's a joke, that he's being honest. That she's right. He wants to laugh. He laughs, and she joins in. He's been trying to forget the wave of desire that caught him off guard, weeks ago—he told himself it was nothing, a mere brainstorm—but now it's back, stronger than ever; not that he would ever do anything about it, but it sweeps through him, fierce and heady as the brandy. This is how it felt with Carfax, on the good days: as though they had made their own language. All the words in the world falling into place. It shouldn't take him by surprise; but it does, it still does.

"Let me help you," he says. "Please." He hadn't realized how long he has wanted to say it: but now the words are out, he knows that they've been brewing for weeks. About a month ago she took an old-fashioned partition out of its file in the archive, spreading the fragile paper out on a desk to show him the eighteenth-century notation, and they bent over it together, their heads hardly an inch apart. He can remember the brush of her gown against his sleeve and the soft wisp of hair clinging to a tiny scar below her ear. She was so close he couldn't concentrate on what she was explaining to him. It was only when she stood up straight and rolled her neck that he noticed how tired she looked and heard the pauses as she searched for the right words. At that moment he wanted to smooth out the line between her eyebrows with his thumb; he wanted to present her with her own Midsummer Game, neatly written out, just missing a few diacritics. Perfume was all very well, but he wanted to give her a miracle. He wants one back.

"I'm Magister Ludi. I have to write it myself."

"I know. I'm not suggesting . . . I only want to help." He knocks back the last of his brandy and holds out his glass. She smiles as she fills it again, but her eyes are still on his face, and still serious. "Trust me," he says. "I promise it'll be all right."

"I don't need a knight in shining armor."

"Of course. Of course not." He reaches out and takes hold of her wrist. She freezes. They both look down at his fingers on her skin. "Your brother," he says, suddenly breathless, "your brother would tell you to say yes. If he were you, he'd let me help."

She blinks twice. "Would he," she says, but it isn't a question. "I wish I could be so sure."

She looks calm, but her pulse is beating hard against his hand. He can't remember the last time he was so conscious of being made of flesh, of being nothing but a collection of chemicals and nerves and electricity.

He kisses her.

It's as though he has split into two men: one of them is surprised. One of them would advise caution if it weren't too late; one of them knows it's useless, messy, that it can lead only to trouble. One of them has known for weeks that he wants her and has ignored it—has shut down every dreamy night thought, every fantasy, smothering the heat. He's the one who, as he leans in, has the time to notice the complex agate-brown of her eyes, the short lashes, the fine freckles on the curve between her cheek and nose; whose throat tightens at her resemblance to Carfax, who is lifted on a tide of memory . . . But the other Léo is living too quickly to pay attention: he has jumped from one heartbeat to the next like a broken record. One moment he is holding her wrist, looking at her, and the next he is mouth to mouth, tasting alcoholic sweetness on their combined breaths.

And the next he is stumbling backward, his face blazing.

For a moment he is blinded, deafened by his own humiliation; he can't hear what she's saying or take in her expression. All he knows is that she thrust him away. What was he thinking? It's not as if she's a proper woman anyway, it's not as if he really *wanted* . . . Oh, but he did. He has, for a long time. It's too late to lie to himself. "I apologize," he says, "I don't know what—"

"Please go."

"The brandy—"

"Yes, you're drunk. Is that your excuse?" She rakes her hands through her hair until hanks of it stand out from her head. "You think, because I'm a woman, I must want you? Or because I should be grateful for the offer of help? Is that what you want, a gratitude fuck?"

"I never—"

"Get out." She has gone pale.

The jumping lamplight and his doubling vision make him feel queasy; he closes his eyes. Really, it was only the slightest, clumsiest brush of his lips. Anyone would think he'd shown her his cock. "I'm sorry," he says. "I misread—"

"Misread what? Me? For goodness' sake, you've never paid attention to anyone in your whole life! You didn't misread me, you've never *looked* at me. Not properly. If you had . . ." She stops. She's breathing hoarsely, as if his mouth on hers was his hands around her neck. "Now *get out*."

He nods. He makes his way into the corridor. His eyes are stinging; the lamp must have started to smoke. He's still holding her glass. He sets it down on the nearest windowsill. A few steps later it occurs to him that he could have thrown it against the wall.

He goes out into the courtyard. A damp breeze is blowing; clouds are building up on the horizon and creeping like mold over the stars. He fumbles in his pocket for cigarettes, but all he finds is a single match rattling in a bent matchbox. He strikes it, and the wind blows the flame out immediately, leaving a scratch of purple on his vision. He flicks the matchstick away.

What a fool. What a blind, reckless, stupid . . . He should have known better. He *did* know better. As if she would let him . . . But for a moment he thought . . . Perhaps he was imagining it, perhaps it was the brandy or her shock; there's no reason to suppose that there was a split second before she pushed him away, an instant when her mouth responded to his. Perhaps it's arrogance. Or . . . he shuts his eyes and tries to remember, and it makes something swell behind his breastbone, a crazy impulse of joy. And then she pushed him away.

He knows this feeling. All at once he's back in the scholars' corridor, ten years ago. He blinks hard, as if the memory is a smarting speck of dust, but the dark behind his eyelids is hardly distinguishable from the looming shadows of the courtyard. He can see it like a photograph—no, clearer even than a photograph, in full color— eyes open or closed: the corridor dim, distant voices and laughter in the courtyard, the blue sky paling in the windows as the summer sun climbed the far slopes of the mountains. Himself, dizzy with fatigue and dread, on his way to find Carfax. Hurrying as though he knew that it was too late. Passing his own cell and finding the door ajar.

There was black on the floor, footprints, a smear. He stepped over the puddle, his mind still lagging behind. Ink. It was ink. There was a broken inkwell on the floor, a spatter of drops in an arc across the wall next to the bed. Someone had knocked it flying. On the desk there was another wet tract of black, smeared at the edge, seeping into the grain of the wood. No papers or stained notes, which was something, although had he left his diary out?

He glanced up, and then he didn't know how he hadn't seen it the moment he came in.

BASTARD.

The letters started above his eyeline and extended down to the height of the desk. They were formed from four-fingered swipes of ink, dark at their beginnings and fading to gray. Black trickled down from the upright of the *B*, the stem of the *T*, the underbelly of the *D*. The word was too big to identify the handwriting. How long had it been there? He touched it, and his fingers came away stained. Still wet.

He never saw Carfax again. The next day, or the day after, the Magister Scholarium stood up in front of the school and said, "I'm afraid, gentlemen, I have some very bad news."

Ten years have passed since then. But right now—standing in the dark, with his eyes closed—he feels as if nothing's changed.

24

THE MAGISTER LUDI

It's her own fault. She should have known better; she's been playing with fire. She should never have spent so much time with Martin. All the hours she's devoted to helping him this term, laughing at his quips, refusing to let him get away with sloppy thinking—she should have known that they were dangerous. That he would read more into them than reluctant politeness; that he would be too vain to attribute her kindness to a sense of duty. Did she enjoy them too much? Has she, god forbid, let him notice that she looks forward to seeing him, that in spite of everything it's exhilarating to speak to an outsider? No. Be honest. To speak to *him*. He's charming, he's energetic. Having him here is like oxygen, a strong drink, an open door . . . In spite of everything, she has to admit that. But it's a long way from that to wanting him to touch her. Inviting him to her room for a drink, what foolishness! She's ashamed of her own stupidity. How could she forget that she's a woman and he'd treat her like one? From the moment she opened the bottle of brandy, it was inevitable that he'd humiliate them both, somehow. Loneliness was no excuse. For a few dreamlike minutes, when she came out of the library, exhausted, sick of herself, she'd imagined that they could be friends. She wanted . . . what *did* she want? Not this, anyway. Not to stand here staring at the door, with her hand over her mouth. Her palm is soft against her lips, her lips moist on her palm. For a strange, thoughtless moment, all her attention is on the place where they meet. She can't remember the last time she really *felt* her body. It makes her queasy. In another life . . . but this is her life, and no one else's.

It takes an effort to turn away. She goes to her desk. At least she put her papers away where he wouldn't see them. She's been careless, these last few weeks, but not that careless: she has made sure that he never sees anything she's written. She has restrained herself even from leaning across him to add diacritics—why can't he *learn,* for goodness' sake?—limiting herself to pointing at the absences with the end of her pen, prompting him to dot them in himself. And his diary . . . She slides out the drawer, as if it might have disappeared. The ledger is still there, of course. The pebbled marbling on the cover is like a landscape seen from above: in the unsteady lamplight the black blotch could be as deep as a well. She puts her finger in the middle of the stain and presses down, as if to reassure herself.

She can still feel the brush of his mouth against hers. How long was the kiss before she pushed him away? It took her a second to realize— well, to believe—what he was doing, and then another instant to—

To what?

She wipes the last trace of dampness from her lips. Her chignon has collapsed on to her neck, heavy and hot. She shuts her eyes.

What would have happened if she hadn't stopped him? She refuses to let herself imagine, but she doesn't have to imagine. She knows. If she had opened her mouth to his, he would have frozen, then pushed deeper with his tongue, bringing his hands up to clasp the back of her head. A second later, when they came up for breath, he'd have pulled back to look into her eyes. And then he'd begin to kiss her again, but she'd feel him smiling, his teeth bared against her lips, and he'd break off and bow his head, grinning at the floor. If she'd pressed her forehead into his shoulder she'd have felt him laughing softly, as incredulous as she was: until she cupped his jaw and resumed the kiss, harder now. She doesn't want to think about his hands sliding down her neck, down to the small of her back, or the unexpected tenderness in his touch, a softness—almost a timidity—that you couldn't have predicted from his usual manner. Now that he was getting what he wanted, he'd be gentle: it would make her want to dig her nails into the back of his neck, make him wince and tighten his own grip until they were nearly wrestling, contesting and matching their strength in a sort of game that wasn't a game.

And later—how much later?—he would bunch her gown in his hands, ready to pull it up and over her head. And *then*—

She even knows what it would be like, to push him away at that point. Not like it was, this time: he wouldn't stumble backward, crimson-faced. He'd blink, half smiling, half confused. He'd raise his hand toward her face, and his sleeve would fall back to show the solid bones of his wrist. The vein, like a trace of blue glaze on porcelain. Skin she'd want to lick.

And she'd say, "No. Not now. Not—no," running out of breath on every monosyllable.

And mean it.

That's the point. She'd *mean* it. She reaches for the bottle of brandy and takes a swig. Perhaps alcohol will numb the hollow, tight sensation in her belly or drown the incendiary crackle in her spine. She drinks again and again. She has to lower the bottle and gasp, but immediately she lifts it for another mouthful. Her head spins. Good.

She shoves the open desk drawer shut so roughly the whole desk shudders. Then she climbs the stairs, her shoulder bumping against the wall. She's still holding the bottle; it wasn't deliberate, but she takes advantage of its being in her hand by drinking some more. Maybe this is the first stage of alcoholism, and she'll die like her father, bruised and swollen, weeping at the stings of invisible insects. Well, he died; she supposes the details might not be exact. She remembers Aimé whispering, "He said there were ants inside his skull. He said they were eating his brain . . ." It was late at night, when both of them were hunched together on his four-poster, listening to Mama cry. Aimé must have been too young to remember Papa, too, but for years she thought his deathbed tales were unadorned truth. Now she isn't sure which are real. Papa died, anyway. And then Mama went, too, going away "on holiday" and never coming back, jumping alone from a moonlit hotel balcony. She wasn't a de Courcy, except by marriage: but that's what the de Courcys do, they spread the contagion to anyone who gets too close. At least Mama was dead before Aimé.

She has reached the top of the stairs. She puts the bottle on her washstand, bends over the basin, and splashes her face. It's too dark to see her reflection, although a slice of starry sky shimmers on the surface of the water. She's feeling sick. But at least the night's events seem to have receded—or, rather, grown less convincing, as if a half-open door has turned out to be trompe l'oeil. She's glad to be drunk. She drags her gown over her head, then stops. Undressing further is too much trouble. She sits on the bed, and the world bounces and re-settles. Gingerly she leans back, breathing deeply, and when she closes her eyes, oblivion floods up around her.

She wakes with a raging thirst. It's still nighttime; she couldn't swear to it, but she's pretty sure she's slept for only an hour or so. When she gets up and drinks—from the ewer, because for some reason, fumbling about in the dark, she can't find her toothglass—it satisfies her thirst, but she discovers that the alcoholic languor has passed and she's wide awake. Her brain is humming like a machine. The papers she was looking at this evening quiver in her mind's eye, sparkling with anxiety. How many corners of the library has she mined fruit-lessly for ideas? And she hasn't come up with anything. Pages and pages of her notes thrown away, crumpled, still half blank. The pros-pect of the Midsummer Game grows closer every night, every hour: what if she has nothing to perform? Would they sack her? *Could* they sack her? Maybe not; but then, no one has ever failed before. And the humiliation . . . She's a de Courcy. It might send her mad.

She tells herself she's failed before. She's been humiliated before. It's not reassuring.

She walks to the window, vaguely surprised by her inability to hold a straight line. The muscles of her scalp throb, as if they no longer quite fit the shape of her skull. She looks out and up, to the infinite, impersonal stars.

Could she run away? There's nowhere to go. She sold the Château d'Apre when she was elected as Magister Ludi; she was sure then that she'd live and die at Montverre, and the château was too full of memories of Aimé, too much of a reminder that the de Courcy line ended with her. She has never regretted it until now. At a pinch she might go back to live with Aunt Frances. But she can imagine her life there too clearly: the stagnant, stale Sundays, the long weeks of doing good works, the slow-growing claustrophobia. She wouldn't be Magister Dryden, she would be Claire, Miss Claire Dryden, forever. She has chosen her life, and it's here. It's the *grand jeu*. It's the path to God.

She closes her eyes, listening to the silence. The clock chimes.

Léo Martin wanted to help her. Wants to help her. It would be so easy to let him. Would he expect her to let him kiss her, afterward?

Something flickers in her head. A memory, a thought. A veil slipping. Her eyes fly open. The starlight tingles on her face like a gust of snow.

Her keys. Where are her keys? She stumbles back to her bed and rummages in the shadows, searches the pocket of her gown by touch. She pulls out the jangling ring and runs it through her hand like a rosary. Here is the big knobbly key to the Biblioteca Ludi. It's forbidden to be in the main library alone, but the Biblioteca Ludi is hers, and yes, her fingers find the smaller key, rusty with disuse, that opens the back door to the staircase. She has never used it—never been there at night—but there's nothing to stop her. Nothing, that is, except the dark and the fear that her hand might, in spite of itself, throw her lamp

to the floor in a splash of flame. Neurosis. Hysteria. She clenches her
hand on her keys and gets to her feet, refusing to let her mind race
ahead of her down the starlit corridors. She is not going to go mad
tonight; but just in case, she leaves the lamp behind.

She is still drunk. She must look like a puppet, shambling hurriedly
along. Doesn't matter. Who cares? Well. If Léo Martin is still awake. If
he sees her like this, looking like a scholar . . . An imitation of a man,
in her trousers and shirt. Hair sagging on her neck.

She unlatches a door, steps out into the cloister that runs along the
outside edge of the building and then through the little back door to
the Biblioteca. Here are the library stairs: opposite her is the locked
door to the library itself, and the Biblioteca Ludi is above her head. She
clings to the handrail as she makes her way up, in case the world starts
to tip again, but it stays steady. She opens the door to the Biblioteca
Ludi and stands still, smelling dust and spring dampness. The window
throws a fuzz of silver across the floor and the bookcases, the piles of
pamphlets and papers. As she goes to the far corner, her foot catches a
tower of magazines and she hears it slither over with a sigh.

She kneels down and pulls the metal trunk out from under the lowest shelf. It's lighter than normal because Martin's diary is in her desk.
She takes it over to the window, where the light is strong enough for
her to make out what's written on the papers. Exercises, exam papers, essays, old games: the *Potato*, the *Chartres Cathedral*, a pastiche
of the *Four Seasons*. They're all mixed up. She takes them out and
dumps them, first on the desk and then, when the pile grows too high,
on the floor. First- and second-year exam papers. None for the third
year, of course. The *Danse Macabre*. Two copies—the first labeled *Aimé
Carfax de Courcy*, the second *Léonard Martin*, both scrawled all over with
corrections. She bites her lip, staring down at them. If he knew she had
them—well, he suspects, doesn't he? But if he knew why . . . Was she
being overly careful, to take those for the sake of a few words and dia-

critics? It's too late now, anyway. If it hadn't been for Martin it would have gone unnoticed that she'd abstracted them from his file—but naturally the first name Martin looked up in the archive was his own. Why on earth can't she get him out of her head? She was fine before he came: she was untouched, untouchable, master of herself and the *grand jeu*.

She returns to the trunk of papers. She is letting herself get distracted. Somewhere in here . . . Come on. Where is it?

She draws out an exercise book. On the front is scrawled *A. Carfax de Courcy*, and underneath that, *Tempest*. She hasn't looked at it for years. She opens it at random: pages of notes in Artemonian; longhand comments. *Link back, prefigure, L says too overwhelming?* Next there's a page in classical notation and opposite it an annotated graph, analyzing the arc of the movement. The distant, sober part of her notices that it's a feinted septime, which is arcane for a second-year—but then, if you're a de Courcy, you learn *grand jeu* moves in the nursery. A is for *artemage*, B is for *botte secrète* . . . She and Aimé learned Artemonian at the same time as the alphabet, and spent days squabbling over who'd used the last of the colored pencils and gold ink decorating their "Gold Medal" games. When he was eleven, Aimé spent a whole month composing fugues, hunched over the jangling piano like a little old man. She begged and begged for a turn, but he refused to let her have even an hour at the keyboard; one day, after trying to drag him away, she barricaded the door so that he couldn't get out, crying with fury. Later, when they were both big enough to play on the Auburn Mistress, they argued about that, too, bickering like two rival lovers competing for favors. Small wonder, she thinks, that the de Courcys go mad.

She turns another page. There's a paragraph of dense writing; at the bottom, halfway through a sentence, the pen has left a long trail as if the writer's hand was knocked away from the paper. Underneath, Léo Martin's handwriting says, *I've had enough, going to bed, see you tomorrow.*

She flips forward again. It's familiar, of course, like a map of a country she's visited. The melodies intertwine in her head; her fingers twitch, picking out silent bars of Beethoven. And it's good. It would have received sixty-five, at least. If it had only been submitted . . .

She takes a deep breath. There's no point getting angry. Not now. The point is that it's promising. A game that no one here has seen—except Léo Martin, but he won't be here for the Midsummer Game. So if she were to use this . . . not as it is, obviously. But with eight weeks' work . . . Yes. She can imagine how it will go—the motifs she wants to emphasize, the subtle intricacies she can introduce, the movements that need to be pulled back from adolescent excess. She can transform it from a competent sixty-five to a Midsummer Game. She closes her eyes and imagines herself on the silver-outlined *terra* of the Great Hall, her arms raised. How long has she been dreading it? Before, she always loved that moment immediately after the *ouverture,* when you feel the weight of the audience's gaze, when you wear their attention like a cloak. She used to love the anticipation. She's missed it. But with this game . . . Relief leaps inside her. She breathes out, and her bones feel soft and light. She's been afraid so long, but now . . . She can do it. In two months she can present a Midsummer Game. There won't be anything to be ashamed of. She won't have failed.

She bends over the page, laughing softly. Why didn't she think of this before? All this time wasted on searching for ideas when what she needed was right here. She raises the book to her face and puts her lips against the cover. Can she smell ink and sweat? Perhaps. The passions of ten years ago, the hours spent in the library, the exhaustion and euphoria. The late nights, the sleepless nights, the white nights . . . Nights like this one. She tries not to think about Léo's mouth against hers, that moment before she pushed him away. A wave of gratitude crashes over her, and for a moment she doesn't care that Aimé's dead or that it was her fault. She says under her breath, "Thank you," and then, because she can, she says it again aloud.

25

LÉO

He dreams, not of Claire, but of Chryseïs. She is in front of him in a queue, in mourning—in the dream he isn't surprised, as if it has come back into fashion—her back turned to him, her hair hidden under an elegant little hat. They are in a hall that is both the Great Hall at Montverre and the Central Immigration Office, and they are waiting for something important. Final marks. There is a slick of blood on the floor, but people step decorously around it, without commenting. They have been waiting for a long time. But whenever the queue inches forward, there are more people in front of Léo, more people separating him from her, and somehow he is incapable of pushing forward. She is afraid. They are all afraid; and as well as the fear, Léo is full of a creeping sense of guilt. It's his fault that Chryseïs is here, and in black. If he could call out, he would.

She reaches the front of the queue, and the man behind the desk looks up. In that instant Léo sees that it's Carfax. He doesn't understand why he didn't notice before. If he had been more observant . . . But it doesn't matter. For a few flaring seconds he is full of joy, because it has all been a misunderstanding, and Carfax is somehow alive.

Then a bell rings, and it's too late. Out of nowhere there is a glass wall between Léo and the rest of the room. He knows that he is trapped, and something appalling is about to happen, and he will have to watch.

He wakes in a panic. He's been left behind, behind glass. He has done something terrible. Something stupid. He has to sit up and wipe the sweat off his face before he knows what's the dream and what's true. Carfax is dead, but Chryseïs has gone, and please let her be in hiding or on her way to safety. He draws a long breath. Only a nightmare, the remains of the fever combined with too much to drink.

He gets up a little shakily, dresses and shaves. He has been getting better at shaving without a mirror, but today he manages to nick himself and the blood stains his cuff before he can get it to stop. He pauses to stare at the drop of scarlet spreading into the weave of the fabric. Red as the *Red* game, red like—

He kissed the Magister Ludi.

The memory comes from nowhere, so vivid that for a moment he thinks he's dreamed that, too. But no, it's real, it really happened: his mouth against hers, hot breath and smooth skin, the moment where he thought she was going to kiss him back. Before she pushed him away. He grimaces.

He has to see her. He splashes his face, blinking and gasping, until the cut on his chin has stopped stinging. The water in the basin is pink. His face wavers in it, a ruddy ghost. He's glad to turn away from it; although as he leaves the room he imagines his reflection still there, staring up at the ceiling, waiting for him to come back.

It's late, long past breakfast. The corridors are mostly quiet, although here and there gray-clad servants are sweeping or dusting. They move aside silently to let him pass. As he turns into the magisters' corridor, there's the sound of an engine, and a khaki police van drives through the gatehouse into the courtyard. He stops to watch.

Surely it's an emergency, if it's been allowed into the courtyard itself? But the bell is silent, and no one hurries out to meet it. Instead the porter who has waved it through slouches back into the lodge, and a single policeman gets out with a weary groan. He has a sheet of paper in one hand, and he consults it. There's something in the gesture that reminds Léo of his dream. He leans closer to the window so that he can listen unobtrusively.

The clock strikes ten. As if on cue, a scholar hurries out of the far tower with a suitcase. He isn't wearing a gown, and he looks out of place and awkward, like a tourist. A cloth cross is tacked crookedly to his waistcoat. The policeman gets a pencil from behind his ear and says, "Charpentier or Throckmorton?"

"Throckmorton."

The policeman nods and makes a mark on the paper. He opens the door and gestures to Throckmorton to get in. Then he leans against the van and waits. After a few moments he lights a cigarette and passes the packet in through the window to his colleague.

Nothing is happening; the policemen smoke, and Throckmorton sits quietly on the bench in the dim space behind them, only his legs and suitcase visible. But Léo's unease grows, prickling up and down his spine. He has never seen the police at Montverre . . . No, that's not true. He has seen them once, after that servant fell from the Square Tower, not long after the news about Carfax; then they came to scrape up the body and certify the death as an accident. This is different.

What are they waiting for? One policeman mutters something to the other and laughs. Léo wants to turn away, but something keeps him at the window, watching. As if being a witness can prevent— whatever it is he's worried about . . . He remembers Sara Paget and Pirène talking about the new Purity Laws.

Footsteps echo at the far end of the corridor. He looks around. A figure in a shabby jumper and trousers is knocking at Magister

Dryden's door, a suitcase in the other hand and an armful of books
balanced in the crook of his elbow. Another scholar. This time Léo
recognizes him, vaguely: Charpentier, the other Christian. He has a
hangdog look that makes Léo want to shake him; and the brownish
clothes make him look even weedier, like grass that's been flattened
beneath a rock. He knocks again with a defeated air, as though he
already knows that Magister Dryden is elsewhere. At last he sags to
a crouch and piles the books next to the door. Then he picks up his
suitcase again and walks toward Léo, toward the exit to the courtyard.

"Hey!"

Charpentier flinches. "Sorry," he says reflexively.

Léo despises himself. He should let this pathetic young man go.
"There's a police van out there. Is it you they're waiting for?"

"Oh—yes. I'm going home."

"Home?"

"Yes, I was returning the Magister's books." He hunches, like an
animal making itself small.

"The police are taking you home?"

Charpentier jerks his head as though a wasp has flown at him. But
he's used to being spoken to roughly; he doesn't protest. "Yes," he
says. "We had a letter . . . They're updating the Register. Only for
a few days. We've been told to pack night things and our papers but
nothing else."

Léo looks at the suitcase. It's small and battered, with chipped
initials painted on the side: *SC.* It was expensive once; now it inspires
him with pity that's tinged with distaste. He glances out of the window to where the policeman is checking his watch. Smoke drifts on
the air. Throckmorton's feet haven't moved.

"Don't go," he says, and before he can stop himself, he has grabbed
Charpentier's arm and pulled him around and back down the corridor, toward Magister Dryden's door and the cairn of books.

Charpentier tries to pull away. "What? But I have to."

"Don't be a fool. They're not taking you home."

"We were told——"

"Yes, you said, but *I'm* telling you otherwise."

"What do *you* know about it?" Charpentier jerks his arm out of Léo's grip. Suddenly he's flushed, his eyes wide with his own daring. It's all very well, but why, for goodness' sake, why is he choosing to do it now, when someone is finally on his side? "We had an official letter. From the Ministry of Information. I'm only doing what it said."

"Don't be so naive!" He takes hold of Charpentier again, trying not to lose his temper. He doesn't want to think about how he knows—— *what* he knows or why or his own part in it; it's important only that Charpentier listens, that whatever happens, he doesn't get into that van. Léo tries not to think about Throckmorton, who is already beyond help. "You can't go. Look . . ." He hesitates. The urge to shake him is so strong he can feel the muscles in his forearms twitching. "All right, you don't trust me. Why should you? But think. Don't you read the newspa——no, of course not. But you know how things are out there. You must have heard. So please. *Please* don't let them take you away."

Charpentier stares at him, his mouth open. His eyes slide to the window and back to Léo's face. He looks frozen, stuck, like a rabbit watching a weasel dance. For a moment Léo thinks he's not going to listen. But then doubts flicker across his face; he seems to crumple. "But . . . where do I go? I can't stay here. What am I supposed to do?"

"Hide."

"What? Where?"

"Anywhere!" He manhandles Charpentier to the end of the corridor. On one side, there's a door to the scholars' tower; on the other, a narrow staircase leads down into the murk of the cellars. He shoves Charpentier toward the stairs. "Find somewhere out of sight. If they look for you, I'll say I saw you run off. I'll leave some food in my room and the door unlocked. Just go."

"But—"

"*Go.*"

Charpentier gives him one last look of appeal, as though he's hoping this was all a joke. Then—as Léo is raising his hand to give him another shove—he scuttles down the steps into the shadows. His suitcase bumps against his legs. There's the sound of his footsteps disappearing, and then nothing.

Léo is sweating. Outside, the policemen are waiting. Someone calls distantly, someone laughs. What has he done? Aided a fugitive from the state. If he's still being watched—if anyone gets wind of it . . . And he'll have to go on helping; now he's taken responsibility, the kid's life is in his hands. He's an idiot. And all on a hunch, he doesn't even *know* that the danger is real; maybe he's overreacting from months of exile . . .

No, he does know. He refuses to look again at the van and Throckmorton's shabby, patient feet. Instead he puts his hands in his pockets and whistles a few bars of a song. Magister Dryden isn't here; he'd do best to go to the library and try again later . . . But as he leaves, he can't stop himself turning back to stare at the dark archway and the steps beyond, and there's an odd quietness in the air, as though something has been swallowed alive.

26

THE RAT

The Rat knows that something has changed before she knows what it is. As if there are invisible strings that extend through the corridors and halls and empty spaces, and now they tremble, brushed by a distant, clumsy hand. She lifts her head halfway through a gulp of water, suddenly uneasy; she wakes for no reason, as if someone has called her name. Not that she has a name: she is the Rat.

Something has changed. There is something new now haunting the places that should be hers. Along with the scents of earth and pine, the elusive promises of spring, there is . . . something else. Perhaps her senses are sharper than she knows, and she sees the swirl of dust in a shaft of moonlight, hears a footstep, catches the vibration of air, all unconsciously. It may be simply that something deeper has shifted. She finds herself looking around as if her own shadow has detached itself from her heels and slipped away—become her enemy, her rival, her friend.

But as time goes on, there are clearer signs. A sink gleaming with moisture when all the others are dry. A trace of vapor on a windowpane, evaporating as she watches. She trails her hand along the sill and there's one place where the stone is warmer: someone sat here, his head against the glass, staring down into the courtyard. Someone who disappeared moments ago, just before she arrived. There is no more food missing from the storeroom, no blankets stolen from the

linen cupboard with the broken lock; nonetheless she is sure, almost
sure . . . It makes her uneasy. Someone else might betray her, alert
the servants: she has nightmares of gray-clad figures throwing open
doors, calling to one another, shining torches into dusty corners.
She has been free because she's invisible, but if the balance tips . . .
A cold, shivery feeling prickles in her toes and her scalp and between
her shoulder blades. If someone discovers her . . . She has been a rat
for so long that she can't imagine what would happen: only that it
would be bad. Not sharp teeth or trap or poison, but worse. Human
worse.

She will be careful. She will be even more careful than she normally is. But her unease makes her awkward, unratlike. Her feet
make more noise than they should. She runs out of breath faster.
She's slowed down by thoughts rattling around in her head. They
hurt. Like fragments of bone that have broken off, with sharp edges.
She has to stop and wrap her arms around herself, trying to remember what it feels like to be safe.

For three days she hides. She has gone without food for longer
than that, and this time she has some hoarded crusts and fruit. She
stays in her nest, curled on her blankets, only venturing out for water. For the first days and nights she isn't even hungry: her stomach
feels like a bunched drawstring bag. When she finally drops off to
sleep, she has vivid labyrinthine dreams. The last one sweeps her
sideways and down, like a current of water in a pipe. Then it spits
her onto the floor.

She sits up. She is wet with sweat; she can smell herself. Possibly
she has a fever. Certainly she's hot, on a cool night. If only there
was a draft sliding in under the slates . . . but the air is like glass.
She stands up, a little giddy, and goes to the door. She pauses at the
top of her narrow flight of stairs, breathing. Then she makes her
dazed way down, clambering through the broom cupboard and out
into the bigger corridor. The momentum of the dream is still with

her, so that she feels out of control, half cradled and half drowned. She doesn't know what she's looking for, but she comes out into the moonlight and drifts along the black and white of it, unafraid. She is still not hungry.

Then she sees him. For a second, seeing his pale shirt, she thinks he is one of the white-robed ones, and she checks herself mid-step, suddenly aware of her own danger. Then, with a jolt of relief, she recognizes him. Simon. How does she know that he is the one who has been hiding? Maybe it's only instinct or the way he's moving. He's stumbling from shadow to shadow, hasty and furtive. The sounds his shoes make (scuffle clickclickclick drag, pause) would be enough to make someone frown and turn around to look. Of course he has never had to hide before. She almost expects to see him close his eyes to try to make himself invisible. But she is not surprised: somehow she has always known he was prey, different from the other young ones, cowed and pecked bare long ago. There is a bleak animal logic in his being here now, hiding. She might have guessed as soon as she saw his breath on the window.

He sets off again. She follows. The clock strikes. He is carrying a bundle against his chest. At first she thinks he is going back to his cell, but he doesn't. He might be taking another roundabout route, as if he's trying to shake her off; but she is sure, too, that he doesn't know she's there. Once he freezes and scrabbles backward into the depth of a doorway, catching his breath. But the only sound is the clock winding up to strike. He sags and waits for the chimes to pass, like a squall, before he launches himself again. By now they're on the other side of the courtyard from the scholars' corridor. The Rat lets herself drift closer, nearly catching up with him: he won't look around. Although part of her—a sneaky human part—wishes he would. She has never been the hunter, instead of the hunted: it's unfamiliar, exhilarating.

They climb a flight of stairs, and another. He pauses, panting.

Then he goes on. Finally they come to a narrow slant-roofed passage, under a gaping mouth of missing slates. The far end of the passage is clogged with darkness. All she can see is the jagged field of stars above and Simon's ghostly shirt. There's the sound of a door scraping as he pushes it open, and he disappears into the blackness beyond.

Somehow she knows that the room beyond that door is tiny, with no other exits. It could be from the way the noise echoes as he drops to the floor, heavy on old floorboards; or because of the sloping roofs that join in a V above her, the looming chimney against the night sky. She hasn't been up here before. They're right at the top of Montverre. If she climbed out, she could stand and see for miles, down to the scattered lights in the valley. But why would she want to? All her attention is focused on Simon's breathing. It's the only thing that breaks the silence, apart from her own heart. She tells herself that as soon as he does or says anything human, she'll go. But he doesn't. He sets something down on the floor—the bundle—and a second later she hears him eating. It's over very quickly. Whatever he had, it wasn't enough. He breathes, and she can hear that he's still hungry.

She takes one step backward, and then another. She can't feel his hunger, can she? She can't. It must be her own. He is over there, and she is here: there's no way hunger can cross the gap. Hunger is inside you. Like sadness. It isn't catching. So: she is hungry. She knows what to do. Food. Simple. She is a Rat. Rats eat when they're hungry. But what she wants more than anything is to give him something. A memory of sweetness floods across her tongue.

"Who's there?"

She doesn't answer. She doesn't know how to, even if she wanted to. But she can't move. Abruptly there's the scratch of a match and a flame jumps into life. The Rat flinches and covers her face.

"It's you! Oh, thank goodness, I thought . . . Sorry, I . . ." But his voice is rusty. He begins to cough, and when he gets his breath back, he doesn't say anything else. The light doubles and halves again.

Gradually, blinking away the gold dazzle, she peels her fingers away from her eyes. He has lit a stub of candle. He is on his knees, staring at her. Yes, he is hungry. But it is a different thing, the hunger in his eyes, it wants something from her. Wants her to be human. To be kind. It calls to the treacherous thing inside her that wants to help him. But she isn't kind. She isn't kin. He is human; she is the Rat. No.

The candle flame reaches up, stretching. She looks away from it, from him. There's a crack in the wall over the bulge of the chimney. This room—

The realization snaps shut on her, like a trap. This room is—

Not hers. No. Not the Rat's. It was the room where she lived before, when she was human, when she had a name. This is the room she never wanted to come back to. This is the room where she lay on the floor and waited for her ma—for the woman who used to feed her and sing to her. Where the ceiling used to swell as if it was about to fall, and the dark scuttled and crept. Where suddenly the panic became too much, feeding on the memory of something too gentle in Mam's kiss, the extra food she'd left, *don't eat it all now, sweetheart, this is for tomorrow, too*, until in desperation she flung herself against the door and it swung open, easily, giving way as if nothing was solid anymore. She remembers that wash of terror, when she understood that she could leave; it was like acid, wiping her out. After that, she was no one. Not human, anyway.

And then . . . when was it? The memory—a memory that's been locked in this room, in the stale air, a dormant germ—of that morning, trying to look for Mam but knowing that she had to keep out of sight because Mam had always said, *You must not leave, no one can hear you, whatever you do, darling, you must not*—but bewildered, almost hoping that one of the gray ones would run into her—wandering the corridors with tears dripping off her chin but being good, keeping quiet—and then—

She crept from corridor to corridor, all of it unfamiliar, a labyrinth of stone. She had never been so far from her room. It was
still early. The emerging morning was gray, but her eyes stung from
being in the dark so long. Her lips were pressed together, one long
silent *M*; she was afraid that if she opened her mouth she'd cry out
and Mam would be angry. But the door had been unbolted, Mam had
never unbolted the door—

A bell was ringing. Not the clock striking. A tinny, angry bell,
like a metallic wasp. She went to the window, careful to look both
ways before she crossed the open space. A van drove into the courtyard, squat and mud-green. A cluster of people—some gray ones,
some white ones—was waiting for it; one of the white ones hurried to the van. The others split apart, conferring: and she saw what
they'd been huddled around. At the foot of the highest tower, spread
out on the flagstones. Gray and red—more red than gray—a thing,
a person-shaped-but-not thing, a person-but-not—an orange-gold
plait of hair, a foot, a little way away a shoe . . .

Perhaps it was then that she became not-a-person, too. It was like
the unlocked door, only worse, because she knew then that Mam
wouldn't come back.

She staggers to her feet. This room is a trap. A poison. She should
never have come back. It hurts too much. Memory like arsenic.
Burns out your insides. Dries you to a cinder. She'll gnaw off her
own paw rather than—

"Where are you going?"

She freezes.

"Please don't go. I'm so lonely. I'm going mad. I don't feel real.
Please—"

He's an enemy. What she's feeling now is his fault. She wants to
pick up the candle and put it out on his hand. He would yell and let
her go. She'd run. She'd be safe.

"Please stay. Please. I'm not angry. I won't hurt you."

But this is a trap. His reaching out to her—she knows that trap, the human hand, a hand that might stroke your hair or slap you but one day will not be anything but broken bits on stone—

He is still reaching. What does he want? For a second she's full of blind, unexpected terror. It's like being the child she was. Stay silent or bad things. Whatever you do you must not. The walls closing down. The ceiling.

She turns and runs. The room-trap gapes open behind her. He says something, but she is already too far away, under the star-spread hole in the roof. Then down the stairs, down more stairs, breathless, sweating. Get away. There has always been danger but never danger like this. Never something wrong inside her, like this.

She won't follow him again. This was a mistake. This was unrat-like. She crawls into her nest and draws her blankets up to her chin.

She tells herself that he will soon die. But when she closes her eyes she can see him in that little room, the same place where she waited for Mam to come back, and there is no comfort in the thought at all.

27

It's done. Mostly. Oof.

I finished the main theme this afternoon, in the library. I remember looking up and suddenly, *suddenly* being present. The last strains of the theme echoing in my head, but fading. My *grand jeu* in front of me, almost done. The symbol of *fermeture* at the bottom of the page. The window open and grass-scented air blowing in, the blue not quite dusk. Spring has sneaked up on us. The servant beginning to light the lamps at the far end of the room. And Carfax finishing his phrase, glancing up at me, then pedantically dotting in his diacritics before he put his pen down. "Finished?"

"The theme," I said, and then I had to stop. I took a deep breath and stared out of the window. Stupid to be so relieved. But until it's there, you don't believe it will happen at all. No matter how many games you write, you're always afraid.

"Congratulations," he said.

"Yes," I said. I couldn't think of anything to say. I went on smiling. He went on smiling back.

LATER
Thought I'd sleep like a baby but I woke up again. Not anxious, but utterly unsleepy. Got up and looked over what I'd done today. I didn't expect it to be as good as I remembered, but it's really

not bad. Not a work of genius, but that's all right, somehow. Next year.

Anyway, Carfax's won't be *that* much better.

That thing I wrote, a couple of weeks ago . . . I was wrong. I was imagining it, of course. I haven't seen any hint of it since. Just as well, considering.

SUNDAY, NINTH WEEK

Carfax knocked for me this morning, early. I stumbled out of bed, swearing, thinking it was a maid who'd forgotten it was Sunday. When I opened the door he blinked at the expression on my face. "Martin," he said, "I wondered if you wanted—"

"I'm taking the day off, Carfax."

"I guessed that. I wondered . . ." He stopped and shook his head. "No. Sorry I got you out of bed."

"What did you wonder?"

"If you wanted . . . I know you mostly go round with the others on Sundays. Émile and Felix and . . . But I thought—listen, it was only an idea, forget it."

"Spit it out."

"I wanted to show you something. Take you somewhere." He didn't give me time to answer. "Never mind."

"Wait," I said, "I'm not awake yet. All right. Give me a second to get dressed." I left him at the door and dragged on my clothes. When I came back, he'd turned his back, as usual. "Right, then. Lead on. Where are we going?"

He strode ahead of me. He had a canvas bag across his shoulder, and I caught the whiff of garlic and cheese and saw the shine of apples. It made me want to laugh, somehow. "You'll see," he said. But instead of going down the staircase into the courtyard, he led us along the corridor and up, turning at a half landing and then pushing open the door to a storeroom. He held aside a leaning broom and ushered me forward.

"What on earth . . . ?" I stumbled over a bucket. "What's all this about, Carfax?"

"This way." He slid around an old tallboy at the far end of the room, disappearing into the shadows. There was a thud, and I heard him swearing, then the creak of a door. I squeezed after him and into a low, dusty passage. For a second I wondered whether it was some kind of trap and they'd find my desiccated body there months later. Then Carfax held his hand up to stop me banging my forehead on a low lintel. "All right? Careful."

"This is—are you—"

But he'd already moved on. There was another flight of stairs—I think, I was finding it difficult to keep track—and another passage-way, with small grimy windows and dust in drifts like snow. It was much quieter, as if we'd left the scholars' wing completely, and nei-ther of us spoke. I found myself trying to walk as softly as possible. Once, at the intersection of two little tunnels under the eaves, I thought I heard a child crying. It was hard to tell which direction it was coming from. I paused, remembering Jacob last term, and his insistence that his room was haunted; but then Carfax caught my sleeve and beckoned me forward, and I was glad to leave the sound behind.

All this time, I thought he was taking me up to the roof. We inched through a stuffy triangular space that smelled of woodworm and hot wood, ducking to get past the bare joists, and I was sure of it. But then he stopped right in front of me and said, "Here."

He stepped aside. We were at the edge of a huge, dim space. The roof met in an angle above us, seamed with threads of sunlight. In the far corner a shaft of gold sliced down, so thick with dust it looked solid. There were fragments of blue above us, where slates were missing.

The floor dipped and rose in front of us, the curves meeting in a central spine. It was disconcerting, like standing on the hull of a stone ship. Carfax glanced at me. "What do you think?"

We were above the Great Hall, looking down on the vaulted ceiling. I laughed—I couldn't help it—and the echo seemed to skim over the ribs of the floor like a pebble. "It's amazing," I said. "How did you know . . . ?"

"Sometimes I come here when I can't sleep."

I looked around. In the daytime it was odd and impressive, but I didn't fancy being there at night. Clearly he's got stronger nerves than I have.

He followed the curves of stone toward the long spine. Then he sat down on the slope, slung his bag on to the floor next to him, and leaned back on his elbows. I followed him. My knees felt tingly and loose; I knew the floor wouldn't give way, but all the same I made myself tread carefully. If he hadn't been there, I might have turned around and gone back.

"Here." He passed me the bag. It wasn't lunchtime yet, but suddenly I was ravenous. For a while we ate sausage and cheese and fruit without speaking. I was conscious of the hall and the empty benches and the *terra* underneath us, as though silence was welling up between the silver lines, flooding the whole space until we were breathing it in.

He didn't say anything else, and neither did I. At first my head was full of the *grand jeu* and bits of my game; but by the time we'd finished eating, I was in a dream, watching the shimmer of the sunlight where it came through the gaps in the roof. No words came. It was the sort of interior peace they're always telling us to aspire to in the Quietus, but I've never felt it before. As if the world was enough. I closed my eyes and put my hands behind my head. I think maybe I dozed off.

When I opened my eyes again, the sun had moved and the air

was bluish and soft, all shadows. I could feel the warmth of Carfax's body next to me, although we weren't touching. He was breathing so lightly I thought he was asleep, but when I turned my head, I saw his eyes were open.

"Sometimes," he said, as though he was answering me, "when I come up here, I'm afraid that I'll fall asleep, and when I wake up, everyone else will have disappeared. Afraid . . . No, maybe that's not the right word. But I have this conviction that I'll go down to the scholars' corridor and every cell will be empty. And I'll look out of the window, and I'll see that Montverre is starting to fall into ruin. No smoke from the chimneys, no one in the courtyard . . . The walls already crumbling. Gargoyles smashed where they've fallen off. Rain stains and piles of moldering leaves. No lights, no voices, no clock bell. Nothing. As if I'm the last person left on the entire planet."

There was a silence. It's crazy, but there was something about his voice, as if he was casting a spell. As if we *were* the last people left.

"What would you do?"

"I'd go home," he said. "I'd get into an empty train and it would start to move, and I'd check the other carriages because I wouldn't quite believe what was happening. And there'd be no one, and I'd sit down and try not to panic. And maybe there'd be an old newspaper on the seat beside me, and I'd read that, and there'd be nothing that explained . . . And when the train stopped, I'd get out and I'd walk the long way up, past the vineyards. And there'd be no one at home, either. And I'd call out, for—for my sister, and she wouldn't be there, there'd be all the family portraits on the wall and not a single living thing in earshot. And then . . ." He stopped.

"And then?"

"And then," he said, smiling at the slope of slates above us, "what else? I'd go into the library and I'd start a *grand jeu*."

After a few seconds I began to laugh. "You're mad, you know that? Absolutely crackers."

"I know." He rolled over to look at me, leaning on one elbow. In the dimness it was hard to make out his expression. The edge of his sleeve brushed against mine and I swear I felt it all the way down my backbone. I thought: *now.* Neither of us moved.

"So," he said, "what do you have nightmares about?"

"Was that a nightmare? It sounded like a fantasy."

"Come on." He tilted his head back and squinted at me. "You must be scared of something. Is it getting a lower mark than me at the end of term?"

"Shut up." I could tell he was still waiting for an answer. I tried not to think about the heat of him, the soft air around us, the sense of being alone together, in a different world. "I suppose Montverre disappearing would be pretty bad. Or getting chucked out. That would be worse."

He kept staring at me, very intent. "What would you do?"

I looked up into the rafters, because I couldn't hold his gaze. And in spite of myself I thought about what my life would be like without Montverre. Going home to Mim and Dad, with my life mapped out for me. A job in the scrapyard. Or with one of Dad's acquaintances. An office. Exports or law or—if I fought for it—journalism. Like being shut in a stuffy little room, forever. Without the *grand jeu* . . .

I said, "I think I'd kill myself."

He shifted. I slid a glance at him. After a second he pulled himself up and sat with his hands around his knees, farther away than before. He looked at me and nodded, with the shadow of a smile, as if we'd been arguing over a motif and finally reached a resolution.

My heart sank. I scrambled to my knees. "I didn't mean that the way it—"

"No," he said, "you're right. Montverre, the *grand jeu* . . . that's what makes life worth living."

I swallowed. I didn't want to agree with him. I wanted him to think there were things worth risking Montverre for. But I left it too long to argue. He bent and collected the apple cores and slung the bag over his shoulder.

"Come on," he said, "we'd better get back. I've got an essay for tomorrow." He reached out to help me to my feet. I took his hand. We stared at each other for an instant. Then I gripped his wrist and hauled myself to my feet.

LATER

I couldn't concentrate this afternoon, so I did my Historiae notes and then went to the gatehouse to get the letter from Mim that's been waiting there for days. I've been looking at it and putting it back. How long has it been since I've written to her?

Émile was there, leaning against one of the uprights, idly peering into the other pigeonholes. "Had a nice time with Carfax, then?" Émile said. "Did he show you where he goes to howl at the moon?"

"Very funny."

"You be careful, now. What if he flips when you're alone with—" He stopped. I glanced around at him. He slid a piece of paper out of his pigeonhole and unfolded it. The muscles over his jaw flickered.

After a pause, I said, "What's up?"

"Nothing."

"News from home?" But it can't have been, it didn't have an envelope.

"No. Nothing important." He ripped it in half and then half again. He went to throw it into the rubbish and then checked himself, crumpled it into a ball and shoved it into his pocket.

"Love letter, then?"

"Shut up, Martin."

"You're blushing," I said. "It's not still your unsavory liaison with a belowstairs beauty?"

"Shut *up*, Martin," he said again, and pushed past me so hard I smacked my elbow on the corner of the shelving. "Oh, and talking about unsavory passions," he added without turning his head, "you know everyone's gossiping about you two?"

I caught his arm. "What are you talking about?"

He swung round and shoved me backward. He was so close I could smell his breath. "You breathe one word to anyone about that servant," he said, "and I will go straight to the Magister Scholarium and spill the beans about you and Carfax. You think because he's a de Courcy they'll turn a blind eye?" I was still gripping his elbow. I forced myself to let go. "*I* don't care what you get up to," he said. "Boys, girls, who cares a toss? But you can bet the magisters do. They'd overlook my little peccadillo—but not yours. So watch your mouth."

"I haven't laid a finger on Carfax," I said, "and I don't intend to."

He raised his eyebrows. I held his look.

"You're so naive," he said finally. "You really think it makes a difference?"

I feel sick. Who does he think he is?

But they're wrong. They're *wrong*. It isn't like that. Carfax and I aren't . . . We haven't broken a single rule. There is nothing, *nothing* we've done that brings the school into disrepute. Émile is being bloody-minded. All he wants is to stir up trouble. There's no danger.

SECOND DAY, TENTH WEEK

Sometimes I could strangle him. Honestly. Carfax, I mean.

I spent all the time between lessons and dinner trying to sort out my game. Writing the first draft of a *grand jeu* is like mining, chipping away for days and days, sometimes hitting a rich vein and sometimes a flat wall of adamant. Editing is more like staring at a bit of machinery and wondering why it won't work. Finally I collapsed forward onto the desk with a sort of groan.

Carfax said, "Want me to have a look?"

"No."

"I don't mind. I'm not working on anything important."

I raised my head. "Are you saying the *Tempest*'s not important? Could've fooled me. You were begging me to look at it the other day—"

"That's not what I'm working on."

"Don't tell me you're doing the essay for Magister Holt. It's not due in until . . ." But he shook his head. I grabbed his notebook and wrenched it away from him. "What, then?"

It was hard to read. Or hard to take in, anyway. I had to blink at it.

It was a game. A *grand jeu*. But . . . not. It was utterly sparse, utterly austere. Hardly anything on the page, only the one principal mark. Like a single slash across a canvas. *Red*.

He swallowed. "I'm just playing with it, really," he said, after a pause. "I want to know how much space I can leave. Can one move be a game? Can you compose a *grand jeu* without math or music or words?"

I said, keeping my voice very flat, "Well, clearly you know the answer to that."

He frowned, trying to work out whether I meant yes or no. But I didn't help him out.

"Writing one game to submit for the Gold Medal isn't enough for you," I said in that same expressionless voice. "You have to write an extra one. To show me how *easy* it all is. Right?"

"I won't submit this."

"Why are you writing it, then?"

He shook his head. "For fun. Don't be stupid. You know how it is, you get an idea and . . . anyway, what's wrong with that? I've finished the *Tempest*, more or less. That's the one I'm going to submit."

"You've *finished* it? For God's sake, Carfax." I stood up. All that time he'd been watching me sweat over my *Reflections*. He must have been giggling merrily to himself.

"What's the matter? It's no skin off your nose, is it?"

I pushed his notebook at him. I didn't mean to hit him, but he jerked away and put his hand over his eye. I should have apologized, but I didn't. "You make me sick," I said, and left him to it.

SIXTH DAY, TENTH WEEK

He didn't mention it again, and neither did I, and we've been mostly polite to each other since Tuesday. But over the last few days I couldn't stop thinking about it. So yesterday night I asked him if I could borrow his notebook. He said yes, but I could see from the way he hesitated first that he didn't quite trust me. So I said, "I won't take it out of your sight. Just let me have a look, okay?"

Later he brought it to my room. He lay on my bed and read a textbook while I studied the game. I don't know, *studied* isn't the right word, really. I contemplated it. It's like one of those religious icons: utterly simple in some ways, but you can stare and stare.

It's so good. It's gone beyond our competent, clever games. It's something else. It's as if everyone is writing symphonies and suddenly he's played a single note—one note that holds other notes inside it, like one strike of a standing bell. Echoes and resonances but astoundingly simple, a challenge to the whole question of what makes a *grand jeu*—and yet it's skillful, it isn't empty because he can't cope with complexity, it's technically dazzling, it's whole . . . One well-chosen move that alludes to the whole of perception and culture and humanity . . . I don't know whether

I admire him or resent him. Well, both. But I don't know which one is winning.

Red. I suppose in a way he's engaging with semeiology on the most fundamental level. No one can ever know that *red* is universal, that what I mean by it is the same as what you see. We take it on trust—that's what language does—but we can never *know* . . . Which is obvious when you're talking about a color, but in the context of the *grand jeu* it becomes a metaphor for communication, understanding, pain, love, worship—our attempt to express something, anything, and hope that it's common to all of us. His game is about redness, but there's nothing red on the page. It's all there in black and white. That contradiction: language means absence. The *grand jeu* is about God, but it means God isn't there, because otherwise there'd be no need for it . . . Red. One single move. It's crazy, but it's perfect. It makes me angry that it's so weirdly powerful. It ought to be facile, easily dismissible, some undergraduate joke. (Essay question: *What is courage?* Answer: *This is.*) But somehow he's got power into it. So much space, one move sitting in the middle of silence, and it sticks in your head. Like the Magister Musicae talking about the margins of music, about how sometimes the most interesting things happen in the rests or the gaps between notes.

After a while I pushed my chair back and linked my hands behind my head, staring at the ceiling. Carfax watched me. Finally he put his book down on his chest and said, "It's only an idea."

I took a deep breath. "It's brilliant."

He snorted. Then he sat up. "Seriously? Do you mean that?"

"I said so, didn't I?" I leaned back until I could see his face. "Oh, come on. You must have some idea how good it is."

"I wasn't sure."

"I've never seen anything like it. I bet the Magister Ludi hasn't, either. Wonder what they'd make of it."

"I was only playing around."

"Oh, shut up." I let the front legs of my chair thud back on to the floor. "You're a de Courcy, I should've known that you'd turn out to be a genius. It's nothing to be ashamed of."

He was silent for a moment. At last he said, "Thank you."

"You're welcome."

I couldn't think of anything else to say. I shut the book and passed it to him. He took it, started to say something, thought better of it, and left.

How do I feel? Am I jealous? Yes. Of course. Part of me wants to burn it. Or write something better. Find a way to beat him once and for all. Show him he's human.

But also . . . at least it's him.

FIRST DAY, ELEVENTH WEEK

Two weeks to go. *Reflections* is nearly done. This morning I caught myself wondering if I might actually manage to finish it before the day it has to be submitted. And it's good. I'm moderately pleased with it. Although, after seeing the *Red* game, some of the shine has gone off it, to be honest.

FIFTH DAY, ELEVENTH WEEK

We had a late one last night. Carfax was helping me with the last (last!) bit of tangled thinking in *Reflections*. Now it's as smooth as a mirror. As I was packing up my books—the clock had just struck two, I think—he said, "Thank you, Martin."

"What for? You've been helping me."

"I mean . . ." He gestured, a wide *ouverture*-like movement. "Not only tonight. All of it. I know I can be a bit . . . It means a lot. I never thought I could be so happy here."

"Don't be soppy."

"I'm not." He laughed. "All right, I am."

Things have been going around in my head. The *Red* game, Carfax, *Reflections*, the Gold Medal . . . But today in the Quietus it all stopped. Suddenly I was full of happiness. As if the real me was somewhere above, weightless, hanging in the shaft of light like the dust motes.

THIRD DAY, TWELFTH WEEK
Done. Early.

SEVENTH DAY, TWELFTH WEEK
Last night we stayed up late, talking. Sometimes it's like the ideas catch fire, and he gets up and paces, as if the room's filling up with smoke and heat. But yesterday it was easy, relaxed, the opposite of that. I've never felt so comfortable before, like it didn't matter if I said something stupid. Carfax was lying on his bed, his hands behind his head, smiling at the ceiling, while I leaned furtively out of the window to smoke the last cigarette from the packet that Émile gave me when he apologized for losing his temper, a couple of weeks ago. Somehow the conversation got on to the *Red* game. He said, "You know I got the idea from you?"

"No. Did you?"

"I was watching you once in Factorum. It was while we were working on our joint game last term. When you still hated me."

"I didn't—"

"You made this . . . picture. It was just a panel of red paint. It surprised me. It wasn't like you."

It was weirdly flattering, to think that he thought he knew what *was* like me. "Oh?"

He shrugged and slid a glance at me under his eyelashes.

"So I was your inspiration," I said.

"Well, not exactly *you*."

"You should dedicate it to me. *To Léo Martin, without whose scintillating intellect and visceral act of imagination . . .*"

He got up. I didn't realize what he was doing until he was at his desk. He leaned over the folder and wrote *For Léo* across the front.

I sort of laughed. He looked at me.

I licked my lips. For some reason my mouth had gone dry. "I wasn't serious," I said. "It's your game, I didn't—"

He passed it to me. I took it.

At last I said, "Thanks. That's . . . Thanks."

This morning, when I got up, Carfax wasn't at breakfast. Everyone else was there, clutching their games, waiting for the clock to strike. I asked if anyone had seen him, but no one had. I squashed a roll into my mouth and sprinted up to the scholars' corridor, nearly choking myself. When I knocked at his door I wasn't sure if he'd answered, so I pushed it open and peered in.

He was on the floor, sitting against the bed with his knees drawn up to his chest. He was paper-white, and when he looked up, he hardly seemed to register that I was there.

"What's the matter? Are you ill?" He shook his head, but I crouched beside him. He gave off a sweaty, metallic scent, like fever. "Come on, I'll take you to the infirmary."

"No! I'm fine." He knocked my hand away. "I—need to rest. Dodgy stomach. It'll go off."

"Are you sure? Do you want some water?"

"Yes, I'm sure." He exhaled through his teeth. "Something I ate. Leave me alone."

I stood up, feeling clumsy and helpless. "What about your game? It's nearly time."

"I'll come down in a little while."

"Do you want me to hand it in for you?"

He shut his eyes. "All right. Now go away, will you?" He gave a stiff, dry cough as if he was about to start retching.

"I'll see you later," I said, but he only nodded and pointed at the folder on his desk. I took it, paused on the threshold, and looked back, but he'd already crawled into bed, facing away from the door.

I didn't hand the *Tempest* in for him. I handed in the *Red* game, instead.

28

THE MAGISTER LUDI

The games are in. Now the first- and third-years have their exams. There's a nervous hush in the corridors, as well as raised voices in the library when scholars are after the same scarce volumes. The tension is familiar——it's the same every year, seasonal as the snow or spring thaw——but this year there is a discordant note. Something extra or something missing. She isn't sure whether it's her own unease or an atmosphere that drifts through the whole of Montverre like a gas. She sits with a pile of marking at the desk in the Biblioteca Ludi, unable to concentrate.

Yesterday it was the first-years' Theory paper, and she called out Charpentier's name when she took the register. By mistake, or was it? Perhaps she wanted to hear it echo, to see the scholars avoid one another's eyes, before she coughed and said, "No, of course . . . Connolly?" And then, walking back and forth while they sweated and scrawled, she had to stop and clench her fists to prevent herself snatching the nearest paper and ripping it up. How dare they sit there so calmly when Charpentier was gone? They'd bullied him, and now they all looked merely sheepish, as if he'd had some embarrassing disease, as if it was the *right thing* for him to have run away. They might as well have said it out loud: *his sort don't belong here.*

If he has run away. Her stomach flips when she remembers the Magister Scholarium saying, at the beginning of a Council session,

"Gentlemen, it appears that Mr. Charpentier absconded when the police came. Obviously, if any of you know of his whereabouts, it is your duty to let me know. Most regrettable."

There was a pause, and the Magister Motuum shuffled his papers. It's unlike him to make any superfluous movement; it was only later that she wondered if he was trying to cause a distraction, and even later when she remembered his glance in her direction. Did he— does he think that she has helped Charpentier evade the police? She wishes she had. Or did it mean something else? When she last saw Charpentier, he was blank-eyed and unkempt, barely clinging on. What if, she thinks, what if he didn't run away? What if he went out into the forest with a rope?

But she is being neurotic. No doubt he simply left to go home without telling anyone. She is tired, that's all. Term will be over soon, and things will be back to normal. She's counting the days until the scholars leave: three days till the end of exams, another week of marking and discussion, and then, a few days after their final marks are posted, they'll be streaming down the mountain like ants, while the baggage-laden bus trundles up and down along the same road, puffing acrid fumes. After that the school will be quiet, until the dignitaries begin to arrive for the Midsummer Game.

But what she's looking forward to most is Martin's leaving. He came to apologize once, and she turned him away with icy courtesy— but even though since then she has never been within a few meters of him, she can feel his proximity: as if the very stones of Montverre have nerves, and every step he takes rasps against them and sends an electric thrum through the corridors. Last night she lay awake, long-ing to go to his room, her clenched fists squeezing moisture out of the warm air; but she's strong enough to resist, to know that no good could come of it. It won't be long now until he goes, washed out on the tide of scholars. Will she ever see him again? No doubt he has a post lined up for him, some overpaid Ministry where he can continue the Party's studied, deliberate destruction of society . . . She doesn't care, as long as it's far away. Once he is gone she'll be able to forget these last few weeks. She'll be able to think about something other than him.

She breathes in, anticipating the long summer days, the heat and lethargy . . . Every August Aunt Frances sends a package of novels for her birthday, and she reads them guiltily, like a child gorging on sweets. Most of the magisters will be elsewhere, on holiday or visiting other schools, so she'll be almost alone, left to her own devices. There will be hours that stretch, empty and inviting. As much time as she wants: to spend with the Auburn Mistress, drunk on melody, or in the library or meditating in the Great Hall. She will be able to sleep whenever she pleases, or stay up all night, flat on her back on the roof of the Square Tower while the Perseids rain down. But even in her imagination there is something unsatisfactory about the prospect, a new absence that rubs at her like a hole in her stocking. She blames Martin for this restlessness, the sense that there is a bigger, more vivid world beyond Montverre. She's already struggling against her desire for him, but to make it worse it's all mixed up with a fierce yearning for excitement, pleasure, the last of her youth. Curse him. He carried it on his clothes and breath, like a virus. Once he's gone, she'll be able to recover, coddling herself gently into innocence again. But what if it's incurable?

She bends her head over the third-years' Practical Criticism papers, trying to decipher Andersen's left-handed scrawl. At least the *Tempest* is almost finished. She's almost sure that no one will see past her careful edits to a game written by a second-year—even a genius of a second-year—and that they will admire her careful mastery, the balance of storm and (as it were) teacup. It will be good enough, because it has to be. And no one could accuse her of not trying: she's forced herself to the work, like an ancient priestess preparing an annual rite. No, not *like*, that's what she *is*—as if Midsummer itself depends on her game, and without it, the world will stop on its axis, singeing under the heat of a stationary sun.

The clock strikes. Suddenly she realizes she's late for the final Council of the year, when the Gold Medal is decided. At least it won't be as painful as a normal Council, as there won't be anything else on the agenda. Every year since she's been here, the Gold Medal has hung on one vote; it's traditional for every magister to fight for his preferred candidate, but as soon as the final decision has been taken, they swap glances and smiles, as if the whole thing has been merely a game. She has often thought that Martin would revel in it. As Magister Ludi, she introduces the top three games to the rest of the magisters, refreshing their memories. "Like a judge's summing-up," the Magister Scholarium said to her in her first year, "don't underestimate the power you have." Before, she has always begun clearly, guiding the others toward an understanding of which game she is advocating; but this year—is it Martin's influence, somehow?—she is determined not to give them that advantage. She has prepared a cool, detached, logical analysis, which hides its judgments like broken glass in water: she knows how they'll vote, so she'll sway them subtly with a double bluff. She'll use *audacious* instead of *original, elaborate* instead of *complex,* and they'll assume she's trying to hide her distaste and vote in favor. She wonders how she took so long to understand how to get her own way.

She grabs her notes from the desk drawer and hurries to the Capitulum.

Or maybe it's easier than previous years because she doesn't care as much. That's the trick. Out of Andersen and Bernard, she favors Andersen; but it won't be the worst injustice in the world if Bernard wins . . . The word *injustice* conjures up an empty desk, Charpentier trudging out into the forest. Suddenly she's filled with incredulity at the magisters' earnest faces, at herself standing in front of them with her notes. Charpentier's body may be swinging from a tree, and they're assessing the weight of a transition here and the arc of a movement there, as if being human was about marks on a page. She takes a breath, forcing herself to concentrate. She can see that the magisters are nonplussed. When she has finished—at last—they shuffle and turn pages, reluctant to speak first. Then the Magister Cartae heaves a sigh and says, "Well, the choice seems clear. I propose that the Gold Medal goes to Andersen."

"I agree," the Magister Historiae says. A ripple of nods goes around the table. In the silence, they all look from side to side, uneasy at the lack of contention: then, as one man, they look at her.

"Yes," she says. "I suppose . . . perhaps that's for the best, after all." The hint of regret in her voice is enough, she thinks, to prevent the Magister Cartae changing his mind.

"Well, then, gentlemen," the Magister Scholarium says. "It seems that we have reached a unanimous decision." He scratches his head. "Er . . . thank you."

No one moves; she's the first to get up. But once she's on her feet, it's as though she's snapped the threads that were holding them all in place. They stand up raggedly, passing remarks about the weather and the exams. She overhears the Magister Corporeum murmur, "I don't believe it. Last year that took *hours*."

She is collecting her papers when the Magister Cartae says, "May I have a quick word, Magister?" and waves at her.

She clenches her jaw; she was so close to getting away. "Yes?"

"I invigilated one of your exams this week, and I couldn't help noticing that some of the questions were . . . inappropriate. I took the liberty of warning the scholars, but perhaps, in future . . ." Next to him, the Magister Historiae coughs into his fist.

"I beg your pardon?"

"You quoted Lawrence O'Reilly, I believe. *Cardinal* Lawrence O'Reilly."

"There is absolutely no reason why a quotation from a Christian should be inappropriate. The *grand jeu* evolved from the liturgy. It can coexist with older forms of worship, you know. It isn't in conflict."

A few other magisters look around: she has spoken too loudly, too clearly. The only person who doesn't look uncomfortable is the Magister Cartae. Belatedly she realizes that he expected her to react exactly as she did. "An interesting viewpoint . . . But you must have read the guidelines." He gives her a lipless smile. "The guidelines, Magister? They were issued some weeks ago. No? Perhaps you should check your pigeonhole more often. I drafted them myself— after some consultation with our friends in the Ministry of Culture, of course."

She stares at him. His smile stretches like a wire, thinner and thinner. She wonders what it would take to snap it.

He turns to the Magister Historiae. ". . . over three days," he says, as if the interruption came from her. "A triptych of commissions. Short, of course, to appeal to the uneducated audience. Liberty, Prosperity, Victory. I have hopes that the Prime Minister himself will be there." He glances up as if he's surprised she's still standing there. "Such a pity you turned it down, my dear. A festival like this does so much for national pride. Wonderful to get the *grand jeu* to a wider audience. It may well influence Ministry of Culture thinking in the longer term."

She doesn't trust herself. If she says anything, she won't be able to stop. Outside in the corridor the air is cooler, and a breeze is blowing in through an open window at the far end. It smells of pine and earth, with an acrid edge. She doesn't pause to breathe it in; she wants to get away from the others as quickly as possible. Forget it. It's done. That was her last duty as Magister Ludi. Now she's free for two weeks. She's not even expected to attend dinner in the refectory; her meals will be brought to her on a tray. She's on retreat, preparing herself for the Midsummer Game, like an acolyte fasting before a rite.

Martin is standing at the far end of the passage, looking out at the high pasture. He has his hands in his pockets, his hair over his face: for a moment he could be ten years younger. There's nowhere to go; she'll have to walk past him. But she stops. Why is he here? To eavesdrop outside the Capitulum, the way he did ten years ago? Before he—but her mind skirts away from the thought, because it ends with Aimé's death. A sharp pain jabs into her skull, above her eye socket. She kneads it away and walks toward him.

"Magister," he says, turning away from the window. "That was quick."

"What are you doing here?" But she already knows: he was waiting for her. Was expecting to wait much longer . . . His eyes go to the hand at her forehead and she drops it with an effort.

"I wanted to say—before you go into purdah—"

She starts walking again. He takes it as an invitation to accompany her. She speeds up until he's bobbing in her wake.

"How did it go?" he says, with a cocktail-party brightness.

"Fine. Thank you."

"Good. The right person won, then? I know it isn't always—" He stops, swallows, pushes his hair off his face.

"It isn't always the case," she says. "No. Sometimes the wrong person wins."

There's a silence. He bites his lip. There's no need for her to say anymore. But she can't stop herself. He's one of *them*; he'll betray Montverre, the *grand jeu,* and her, without thinking twice. He already has. The *Red* game. Everything else. She says, "I know what you did to my brother."

There's a split second—a heartbeat—and then he looks up at her. "You mean . . . How do you know about that?" He tries to hold her gaze, but his eyes flicker. "Did he—he can't have told you?"

Such outrage in his voice—and something else, not quite shame. It makes her want to—what? Slap him? Touch him, anyway. But if she touches him, who knows what will happen? She doesn't trust herself. If she lets slip that she has his diary—or anything else, anything worse, she is afraid of what she might say . . . It's dangerous, this urge to dance on the edge. Almost irresistible.

"Don't pretend—" Her voice breaks. Stupid, treacherous voice. "Don't pretend it was because you thought—that it was for his benefit. You wanted to win, didn't you? You would have done anything to win. And then . . ."

She wants him to defend himself. But he squints at the floor, as though he's admitting that even his diary is slippery and blurred, full of half-truths and self-deception. After a second he repeats, without raising his head, "And then . . . ?"

"Then . . ." But her throat closes. She can't say it. She doesn't know what to say.

She hesitates. Then she strides away. She turns the corner at the end of the corridor. On her left, the windows look out on the courtyard. As she walks past them, a movement catches her eye and she stops.

There's a motorcar in the center of the black-and-white tiles. For a second, time has looped over on itself and she's back at the beginning of Serotine Term, full of disbelief at Martin's arrival; then she jolts back into the present moment. He's not down there, he's in the corridor behind her. If this is a repeating melody, it's in a different key, or with a single note silenced. Instead, the man poking his legs out of the shining Rolls-Royce is corpulent and dark-suited. A gray-robed servant steps forward to help him up, obscuring her view, and two others busy themselves with a leather-strapped trunk. Then they retreat—struggling under the weight of the trunk as they lug it to the Magisters' Entrance—and the car's engine starts with a cough before it turns in a wide U and crawls toward the gatehouse.

Two men are left, one a spotty youth looking up at the towers with amiable disinterest, the fat one with his head bowed. On the other side of the courtyard, the Magister Historiae and the Magister Cartae emerge from a doorway. They hurry over to the men in suits and shake their hands. A welcoming murmur drifts upward.

She leans forward. Her breath mists the glass and evaporates almost instantly. Are they guests, arriving for the Midsummer Game two weeks early? The school will be full of outsiders—*grand jeu* masters, government officials, well-known amateurs, reporters from the *grand jeu* magazines—but the festival lasts for only a day, long enough for the Midsummer Game and lunch but short enough for them to catch the evening train back to the capital. Why are these men here now? She dislikes them already, and not only because of their loud voices and the smell of petrol fumes creeping through the cracks in the window frame. She draws back, turns to leave, and almost stumbles into Léo Martin. He's been looking over her shoulder; now he ducks sideways to let her past, grimacing briefly, before his gaze goes back to the men in the courtyard. He says, "Is that . . . ? Surely not."

"What? Who?" She looks down. The magisters have moved away; now she has a clear view of the men in suits.

"That's Émile Fallon," he says.

Émile Fallon. She feels her stomach lurch. For a moment she can't think clearly: would she recognize his name if she had never read Martin's diary? Has she ever seen a photo of him? The easiest thing is to stare down at him and keep her expression blank. He seems older than Martin, with a bulging belly and a double chin, although his hair is still dark and slicked close to his skull. He glances up at the window and nods to them like an actor acknowledging his audience. He has a sly, close-mouthed smile. Instinctively she turns her back. It's to hide her face, not to look at Martin, but he seems to take it as a question.

"He was in my year, when I was a scholar," he says. "He works for the Ministry for Information, these days. You wouldn't know him, he's not . . . it's all pretty hush-hush. He must have been invited to the Midsummer Game. Why has he turned up so early?"

She doesn't respond. The thought of Émile here, again . . . She focuses on her face, keeping the muscles still. She has already revealed too much of herself. Remember, she's never heard of him. She isn't meant to know who he is.

Martin raises his hand. In spite of herself she glances over her shoulder. Émile is waving with a languid motion, like seaweed in a tide. Then he reaches into his jacket and takes out a gold cigarette case. He lights a black-and-gold Sobranie, still smiling up at the window. He flicks the match away. She can feel his attention on them both, like a cobweb clinging to her cheeks.

"I suppose he's come to settle in . . ." Martin trails off. He was friends with Émile, years ago. Perhaps they're still friends. Why not? Swapping intelligence between their ministries. Having lunch on the taxpayer. Evidence of the old-boy network flourishing, the way it was always meant to. And yet he doesn't look exactly pleased.

"I must go," Magister Dryden says.

"Yes," he says, and his eyes narrow. "Listen—I wanted to say, I know you're angry with me, but please listen."

"No need."

"Yes, there is. I've been trying to find you. You've been avoiding me, haven't you?"

"I've been busy."

"What happened—I was drunk, I didn't mean to insult you."

"It doesn't matter," she says.

"It does to me. Is it because of your brother, that you—" He stops, as though she's interrupted him. But she hasn't; at least, not aloud. "I'm sorry," he says. "For everything. I've already said I'm sorry. Can't we go back?"

"No," she says. "Goodbye, Mr. Martin." She refuses to make space as she slides past him; her robe brushes his jacket and he's the one to step sideways.

She walks away, expecting every moment to hear his voice. But it doesn't come, and when she throws one last look behind her, he's gone. It ought to give her some satisfaction, to have dismissed him so easily.

Émile is still in the courtyard, alone now. As she watches, he blows out smoke through rounded lips. An O floats up, dissipates. Then he throws the cigarette butt away. He doesn't bother to stub it out before he drifts toward the Magisters' Entrance. It sits like an insect on a white tile, a narrow black-and-gold hornet, smoking.

She looks around for a gray-clad servant to hurry across the court and pick it up. But no one comes. The fag end sits there. The thread of smoke unreels and unreels, as if it'll go on forever.

29

SEVENTH DAY, THIRTEENTH WEEK FIRST DAY, FOURTEENTH WEEK

It's late. My head's going round and round like I'm drunk. But I have to get this down as exactly as possible. I don't want to forget a single detail.

They were meant to announce the marks this evening, before dinner. But they didn't. They put a notice up that said, *Due to unforeseen circumstances, the Gold Medal and other marks will be announced early tomorrow morning.*

I didn't wait around after that. I didn't go to dinner, either. The idea of food made my stomach turn—let alone having to listen to the others while they complained and speculated. I couldn't stop thinking about the magisters; it was like I could hear them still arguing, on the edge of audibility, in high, scratchy voices like a bad recording. I couldn't decide whether it was a good sign that it was taking so long. I always knew *Red* would be controversial—it takes everyone a while to come round to genius, after all—but they should have decided by now. I kept thinking, surely if they were going for Berger's latest offering it would have been a quick decision? Or not. Maybe not. Giving the Medal to a second-year would be pretty contentious—especially for *Red,* which will be contentious anyway—but maybe too contentious, maybe it was stupid to hope . . . I was so restless I couldn't even sit down. The only thing I wanted to do less than stay still was run into Carfax; I was so wound up I'd give myself away. So I paced around my room for ages, tidied my papers, etc., etc. (I buried the *Tempest* right at the bottom just in case, don't want Carfax to turn up and see it hadn't been handed in, it'd spoil the surprise.) I heard a group of the others come back from dinner—Felix shouted, "I can't bear the suspense!" and I had to bite my tongue to stop myself yelling back, "You'll have got something between forty-one and forty-five, now relax"—but when it all went quiet again I still couldn't settle down. There was no breeze and it was hot in my room. I was only in shirtsleeves but I was drenched in sweat.

When I left my room, I was thinking that I'd go out for a breath of fresh air. But when I passed the archway onto the courtyard I could see the lights still burning in the Capitulum, so I knew they were still at it. And somehow I found myself walking down the Factorum corridor, past the music rooms and the magisters' quarters, and then turning right into the Old Wing. I could have paused at any of the windows to breathe the air coming off the mountain, but I didn't. I carried on walking until I was in the gallery that leads to the Capitulum staircase.

I hovered in the doorway, looking up, but all I could see was the curve of the stairs, disappearing into darkness. I couldn't hear anything, either. Once I think I heard someone raise his voice and thought it might have been Magister Holt, but then it was quiet again.

I sat down on a windowsill and shut my eyes. My stomach was churning. The clock chimed.

It must have been about half an hour later when I heard voices. I leaped up, but there wasn't anywhere to go, so I stood near a window with my hands in my pockets, ready to pretend I was mid-step. There's no rule against taking an evening constitutional in the corridors. And I couldn't bring myself not to listen. At first I heard the Magister Historiae say something indistinct, and then ". . . pity, we expected better things of him, especially considering—"

"Arrogance," another Magister said. "He must have thought he was a dead cert. I personally don't feel sorry for him. It's unusual, but I think we've made the right decision."

"After five hours, I should hope so!" someone else said, and there was laughter. It was funny to hear the magisters laughing together, like they were scholars. I was in luck: when they emerged from the tower they turned left, without seeing me.

I was tingling with excitement. They must have been talking about Berger. And they thought he was arrogant, did they?

Then Magister Holt came through the doorway and said, over his shoulder, ". . . not sure it was the right . . ."

"What else could we do?" The Magister Scholarium paused next to him, sighing. "Let's look on the bright side," he added in a weary sort of way. "We have a most worthy winner. And such promise! What can we expect from him next year?"

Behind them, the Magister Cartae was hobbling down the last few stairs, breathing heavily. They moved aside to let him pass, and then the others came down after him, hurrying or yawning or muttering darkly about having missed dinner. But Magister Holt didn't move, and neither did the Magister Scholarium.

"Edward," the Magister Scholarium said finally, "I understand how you feel. But it is an enormous accolade that under your tutelage a second-year has achieved this much."

"That's kind of you. I merely wish—"

They stopped, staring at me. I must have made a noise. I cleared my throat. "I was only," I said, and then I couldn't finish the sentence. I gestured at the far doorway. "I'll . . ."

"The results will be on the noticeboard tomorrow morning," Magister Holt said. His voice was icy.

"Yes. I—sorry—I didn't mean to earwig."

"Whatever you overheard," the Magister Scholarium said, "it would be an offense punishable by expulsion if you disclosed it to anyone before the official announcement. Now make yourself scarce, young man."

I nodded. "Yes, Magister."

I walked away. Then, when I got out of sight, I broke into a run.

Carfax was in his cell, I could hear him moving about. I knocked on the door. At first he said, "Go away," but I carried on. Finally he wrenched the door open so violently I nearly fell into his arms. "What do you want? Martin?"

"Who else would it be?" When he didn't invite me in, I shoved him gently to one side. I would've sat on the bed, but there were shirts piled on it. His trunk was open and half full, and the Auburn Mistress was leaning against the head of his bed in her case. "What are you doing?"

"I have to go," he said. "I don't think I'll be back until next term."

"What? Now?"

"If I'm quick I can catch the last train from Montverre, and then I can get the sleeper home. I won't take all this," he added, following my gaze. "I'm getting it ready for them to send on."

"Yes," I said, "but *now*? Term ends in three days. Why on earth would you—"

"I have to." He didn't meet my eyes. "Move, will you? You're in my way."

"You're mad. Hey, Carfax, the marks are out tomorrow!"

"I *know*." He didn't shout it, exactly, but it made me stop arguing.

"What's happened?" I said. He glanced at the desk, and I followed his gaze. There was a curl of flimsy blue paper on top of his note-book. A telegram. He saw me see it and stepped across to block my view. "Is it your sister, again?"

He bit his lip. "Yes," he said at last. "She . . . I have to go home. She's not well."

I had to take a deep breath. "You can go tomorrow, can't you? She's probably exaggerating. You know what women are like." I shouldn't have said that: I saw his eyes narrow. "I don't mean it like that. Only that one night won't make a difference—please."

"You don't understand." He crossed to the desk, looked down at the telegram for a few seconds, and then crumpled it into a ball. "I have to go."

"You can't. Carfax, you *can't*." I sounded like a kid. "You have to stay for the marks tomorrow."

"It's not important. They can send me a letter." He gave me a crooked smile. "If you've done better than me, you'll have to wait and gloat next term. It won't kill you."

I exhaled through my teeth. I didn't know until that moment that I was going to tell him. I perched on his desk, deliberately getting in his way, and crossed my arms. "And what if I haven't?" I said. "What if I came here because I overheard the magisters talking after the meeting, and I happen to know for a fact that you've done rather well? *So* well, in fact," I went on, watching his face, "that you're the first second-year ever to win the Gold Medal?"

He stared at me. I started to laugh.

"It's true," I said. "I did. And you have."

"That isn't funny, Martin," he said.

"I'm not joking."

"That's not . . . I can't have done. My game wasn't *that* good."

I could have told him then that I'd submitted *Red*; but I was enjoying myself too much. And I wanted him to see it on the noticeboard when they put the marks up. I shrugged. "Guess it's better than you think."

"But that's mad—they *can't* have." He shook his head. Then suddenly he put his hands on my shoulders. I could feel him quivering. "You promise? If you're pulling my leg . . ."

"I swear. Cross my heart," I said.

There was a tiny moment when he was absolutely still, looking into my eyes. Then he swung away from me, collapsing forward with a rush of air as if he'd been punched in the gut.

"Are you all right?" I said. "Hey, sit down, put your head between your knees."

He sank onto the bed and put his hands over his face. He stayed like that silently, until I started to wonder if he'd had some kind of seizure. Then he raised his head. His face was wet and blotched, his eyes shining. He looked . . . undone. New. When he smiled, it was as if I'd never seen him before. "You're *sure*?"

"Sure and certain." I wanted to tell him then. I felt as proud as if I'd won a Gold Medal myself and dropped it into his hands like a gift. That expression on his face—*I* did it. I felt like a god.

There was a pause. "What about you?"

"What about me?"

"What did you get?"

"I don't know." It's crazy, I hadn't even wondered about mine.

He looked away. His forehead and mouth were damp. I think he must have been crying, because a single drop of moisture slid down the side of his neck and soaked into his collar. "So," he said, "do you hate me?"

"What?"

"I wouldn't blame you. I don't deserve the Gold Medal. Your game was better than mine. I'm not being humble," he said, cutting me off. "I mean it."

I swallowed. It took everything I had not to tell him; but I was looking forward to the moment when he'd see it for himself. When he'd realize and turn to me . . . "No," I said. "I don't hate you."

"Good." There was another silence. He got to his feet. He seemed to be looking out of the window at the trees and the first stars. But when he turned back to me he had the frown he gets when he's considering a particularly knotty *grand jeu* problem. "Why not?" he said.

He meant it. He was genuinely asking me why I didn't hate him.

I don't know how it happened.

We were standing face-to-face. Close to each other, less than arm's length.

I kissed him.

I need to write it down before I forget. Come on.

So. I kissed him. It wasn't really—all I did was put my mouth against his, not even . . . As if I could somehow show him that I didn't hate him. The moment I did it I thought better of it, a rush of embarrassment and second thoughts and fear that after all I was deluded, that Carfax would be disgusted, horrified, he'd tell the others and I'd get expelled—but then he grabbed hold of me and it honestly took me a second to understand that he was kissing me back, not pushing me away, and—I couldn't believe it, it was surreal—I stopped to look into his eyes, to check, and then we started kissing again properly, and I had to break off for a second to laugh, I remember looking down at his floor, the faint fuzz of dust, a gray plume clinging to the corner of the bedstead, I can still see it—and I put my hands in his hair, I was almost scared, somehow, it was so different from kissing anyone else—and then I think I was too gentle because he took over, pushing me, *daring* me . . . He dug his nails into the back of my neck and it felt like the most erotic thing anyone's ever done.

And then later, don't know how much later, I went to take off his gown, and he pushed me away.

Stupid. Stupid stupid stupid. What was I thinking? Carfax, he must be a virgin, he's as straitlaced as a corset. Even though we were kissing, I should've known better than to . . . It can't have been the first time he's *kissed* anyone, could it? Oh, shit. Maybe it could. And I can see how it would come as a shock, if out of the blue you found yourself kissing another man, if you hadn't had time to get used to the idea . . . Anyone would panic. But how was I supposed to know? I was in shirt and trousers, I thought he'd—and he must've known that I was—I had—oh, this is ridiculous, I can't even write about it. Maybe he wasn't turned on at all—I couldn't feel that he was, but the way he was touching me—I thought it was the way he was standing or something, that—and he was still wearing his bloody *gown*.

He said, "Not now."

I think I said, "What? Why?"

He was breathless. That's a good sign, isn't it? He was resisting himself, not me. Right? He said, "Not—no."

"Did I do something wrong?"

He shook his head. He was very flushed.

"It's all right, it doesn't mean that you're . . . just because—I've kissed girls, too, you shouldn't worry that . . ." I couldn't form a whole sentence.

For some reason that made him laugh, but quickly, and then he was serious again. "Oh, Léo, I wish . . ."

"You're scared," I said. "So am I. But I promise I won't tell. I promise."

There was a pause. He bit his lip, staring at me, and there was something in his face I couldn't name: not quite hope or fear or shame, all or none of them. I thought then that he might take hold of my wrists and pull me back to him. But he didn't, and all of a sudden I knew that if I pushed him it would be over.

"Right, okay," I said, trying to keep my voice steady. "But you have to promise you'll stay until tomorrow. Long enough to see yourself on the noticeboard with *Gold Medalist* next to your name. All right?" He didn't answer. "If you run away tonight, I'll kill you. Twelve hours, Carfax. Please."

He hesitated. "All right."

"Thank you." I meant to leave, but I couldn't stop myself pulling up in the doorway. I said, "There's something I should tell you."

He said, "I love you, Léo."

I knew it. I *knew* it.

It's half past three. I've been writing for hours. But I know already I'm not going to be able to sleep. I'm going to go and sit in the Great Hall and watch the sun come up.

30

LÉO

She knows, curse her. Somehow Claire knows about that last night with Carfax—and about the *Red* game, how does she know that he submitted it? But the *Red* game is public, of course, it would be in the archive if it hadn't been lost, perhaps she saw it before it disappeared . . . He can't think straight. It doesn't matter how. She knows. That he kissed Carfax. That Carfax's death was his fault—whether it was the *Red* game—he sees *BASTARD* on the cell wall—or the kiss—if it was that, the shame in Carfax's eyes as they drew apart, realization, fear, a truth that he couldn't handle . . . She knew all the time. But how? The police report said there was no note, and he'd never thought to question it. But perhaps there was. Or did Carfax tell her before he died—and if he did, does that mean it was the kiss? Or both. *BASTARD*. The one, then the other, when he could have survived either . . . Léo clenches his jaw. She knows, that's all. As though he has been walking around naked for months. And when he kissed her, she must have thought—what *did* she think? No wonder she's angry with him. The thought of her anger makes his skin prickle with shame and resentment. She has no right.

He's in the library, at his desk in the archive, trying to analyze Harnoncourt's Third Rule. But he can't stop thinking about her. *You would have done anything to win.* It wasn't that. It *wasn't*. He can't bear the thought of her judging him. All this time he's been trying to speak to her, he thought he'd go mad. He was haunted by the memory of her body against his, mixing with his dreams until he wasn't sure what was real, what was her and what was Carfax, years ago. It hurt to think about her and yet he couldn't resist. Her eyes, her mouth. *You never looked at me* . . . It's driving him mad. That exchange, in the corridor . . . It would have been better not to see her at all. If only they had been somewhere private. If only he could tell her . . . what? There's nothing, no magic word. No winning move. Even if he told her that he loved—

Carfax, Léo thinks. That he loved Carfax.

Then he thinks: her.

He stares at the wall, his heart thudding. Mad. Of course he doesn't love her. Not *love*. Desire, yes, although she's prickly, plain, rebarbative. Desire because he's lonely and frustrated, because she makes him laugh and think and work for her approval, desire because he was drunk and because she looked so much like Carfax in a certain light . . . But that's all. Nothing more. Nothing more than a lightening of the heart when she smiles at him, a fierce raw happiness that she exists, that they're under the same roof, that for a few seconds she didn't push him away. A sense that whatever game they're playing, it's at the center of the universe. Is that love?

It isn't only that she's like Carfax; it's the differences, too, the lines under her eyes, the fact that she's Magister Ludi, the softness she tries to hide. If he closes his eyes, it's her face, not Carfax's, that surfaces. Until it ripples, like a reflection, and for a moment he can see them both, superimposed; and then his guilt floods back and the moment has passed. What is he thinking? It's his fault Carfax is dead—she thinks so, too—and this is self-indulgent, pathetic. He has no right. And it's not only ridiculous, it's hopeless. She despises him. That's clear from how she spoke to him. And even if she didn't . . . Magisters are celibate, nominally at least; perhaps a few of them bend the rule discreetly, but she couldn't risk it. Too many people would be pleased to see her dismissed. If he loves her . . . He grimaces. It was different, when he kissed her, thinking that was all he wanted. Now he's struck by the enormity of it; and the impossibility. Love.

Can't we go back? he'd said, and she said, *No.*

The dinner bell rings. He clutches at the distraction. Hurriedly he tidies his desk and straightens his tie. Then he runs down the stairs to the main library and stops dead.

Émile.

It takes him by surprise, so he almost trips up. His head has been so full of Claire and Carfax that he'd almost forgotten that Émile had arrived. He catches himself on the banister. Émile turns and smiles. "Léo," he says. He's holding a book, flicking through the pages. "Good to see you."

"Émile." He regains his balance. "Thanks for keeping in touch."

"Not at all. My pleasure."

"And for sending . . ."—he gestures—"the parcels."

"You're welcome." Émile inclines his head. "My dear chap, it wasn't charity. You earned them."

The letters. When Émile was miles away, it was easier to rationalize them; now, face-to-face, he feels the humiliation of it. He's been so obedient, so useful. A servant. Frightened into compliance. He says, "I didn't realize you were coming."

"I must say it brings back memories, doesn't it?" Émile puts down the book he's holding and turns to take in the bookshelves and the empty desks. Of course, the Gold Medal was announced today: no one is studying tonight. He inhales theatrically. "Ah, the smell of youth and scholarship!" He slides a hand neatly into his pocket and gets out his cigarette case.

The bell stops ringing. "Well then," Léo says, "shall we . . . ?" He starts to move toward the door.

"Drop in on me later, won't you?" Émile says, "They've been very kind and found me a small suite above the Lesser Hall. Do come. I have some excellent brandy."

"I don't think—"

"No, I insist." He puts a cigarette between his lips and gets a box of matches out of his pocket. He lights his cigarette and flicks the match sideways without checking that it's extinguished. It lands under one of the desks. He takes a long drag and blows smoke into the air.

Léo stifles the urge to crouch down to check it's gone out. For a second he's reminded, unpleasantly, of himself when he first got here, flicking matches in the magisters' courtyard. Now he understands how Claire felt. "You can't smoke in here." He says it loudly, but the librarian at the far end of the room stays hunched over his ledger, studiously not noticing.

Émile laughs. "Well, I won't tell anyone if you don't."

"The books . . ."

"Relax. The most valuable ones have been taken off the shelves, I believe."

"What? Why?"

An expression slides on and off Émile's face like water, too quick to read. Then he blows a smoke ring toward the ceiling and says, "Come to my rooms later. I mean it."

"I have an article to write."

"You'll regret it if you don't." He smiles, as though it softens the words. Then he turns and walks away—not toward the refectory, but the other direction—before Léo has time to answer.

He leaves it as late as he can, but he's too restless to resist. It's either Émile or staying alone in his room thinking about Claire; and right now a bit of Party gossip might be a relief. He tries to ignore the mosquito sting of his vanity when he knocks at Émile's door like a scholar who's been summoned by a magister.

"Martin," Émile calls out, "come in. Have a drink."

The room is larger than Léo's. It's bright and warm with the honeyed breath of candles; light gleams on a white tablecloth and the bulbs of wineglasses, and one wall is covered with a dusty-looking hanging. There's no bed, but then Émile said *rooms*, plural, didn't he? So much for the Magister Domus insisting that Léo's room under the clock was the only one available for guests.

Émile waves him to a chair. "Sit down, sit down. How was dinner? Brandy?"

"Thank you." He takes it and sits, pushing aside a dirty plate with a napkin crumpled in its center. Several people have had their dinner around this table. He remembers noticing that two of the magisters weren't in the refectory. So Émile is playing host, now, is he? Is that why he's here, to ingratiate himself? "You asked me to come here. What did you want?"

Émile's eyebrow goes up. "Manners, dear boy. You're not Magister Scholarium yet, you know."

He doesn't pay attention to that. He reaches for the box of cigarettes across the table; when he takes one, Émile strikes a match and leans forward to light it for him. Reluctantly he says, "Thanks."

"You're welcome. It's good to see you, you know." There's a pause. Émile smiles. "By the way, I've left the Ministry for Information. Did you hear? I'm in your old department now."

"I see." The news squeezes his gut like a fist. Is Émile in his old office? Do the secretaries giggle and bat their eyelashes at him, or the aides straighten their ties when he walks into the room? "Congratulations."

"There may be some more changes there soon. Dettler has never been up to the job. You were a hard act to follow."

"Thanks."

Émile leans back in his chair. "What's the matter, Léo?"

"Nothing." The tastes of tobacco and brandy scald his tongue. He taps his cigarette on the rim of an abandoned wineglass, although it's hardly burnt down. "You said I'd regret not coming to see you. So what's up?"

"Oh, Léo." Émile laughs, but it doesn't take away the mockery. "I didn't mean it like that. Honestly, did you imagine . . . ? I wanted to catch up, that's all. Get your impressions of Montverre face-to-face." He looks away, brushing a bit of ash from his trouser leg. "I feel for you, Léo, getting shoved back into this bloody place."

"It hasn't been so bad," Léo says, but he isn't sure Émile hears him.

"Personally I'd go mad." There's a pause. Émile takes a gulp of brandy, throwing his head back with uncharacteristic abandon. He's staring out of the window at the dark outline of the Square Tower against the bowl of the night sky, visible behind the reflected candles. It's never occurred to Léo before that Émile had any strong feelings about Montverre, let alone this deep hatred; and perhaps, after all, he's mistaken, because Émile turns smoothly and refills both their glasses. "It takes one back to the days of one's youth, doesn't it? Worse for you, I imagine. Had you met our Magister Ludi before you came here?"

"What?" The blood rushes to his face and his heart at once. He doesn't want to talk about Claire. He'll betray himself. "No. When would I have met her?"

"Oh, I wondered if . . . You were Carfax's friend. Close."

Léo shakes his head. He must have been the only person in the world not to know that she was Carfax's sister and a de Courcy; but then, he spent all those years trying not to think about Montverre, turning the page of the newspaper whenever he saw it mentioned.

"Ah well, I hadn't either. I'll have to get to know her better after the Midsummer Game." He sips his brandy daintily, as if it was his first glass. "She gave me quite a turn when I saw her at the window.

Nothing like her photo in *The Gambit*, but then I suppose they were trying to make her look pretty. Uncanny, isn't it?"

There's something about Émile's tone that sets his teeth on edge. "What is?"

"Don't be disingenuous, Léo." Émile runs a finger through a candle flame; tiny flares of smoke curl upward like diacritics. "How are you two getting on, by the way? You haven't said much about her in your more recent letters. Has your dislike mellowed?"

"Somewhat."

"As I remember, your dislike of Carfax mellowed significantly."

Léo's thighs twitch, telling him to get to his feet; but that might give him away. He drinks and drinks again, dipping his nose into the glass. The brandy makes his lips tingle. He's lost his tolerance for alcohol. "Tell me more about your new job," he says.

"Oh, it's planning, mainly. Strategy, implications, all that sort of thing. Not much actual culture, but that suits me . . . I have a finger in a few different pies." Émile pushes the brandy bottle toward him, sliding it across the tablecloth. "Consulting."

"About this place?"

"Well—partly. The Chancellor is wondering how we can make the *grand jeu* pay its way." There's a pause, a change in Émile's voice. "We'll see. It depends. If I can make some progress while I'm here . . ." He smiles, a complicit sly smile that seems to include Léo in the joke: but there's no joke that Léo knows of, only this odd sudden silence. Abruptly he's aware of the empty wine bottles and dripping candles, grease on the stained tablecloth. The alcoholic bonhomie drains away, leaving a gritty tidemark around the inside of his skull.

He hears himself say, "What *are* you doing here, Émile? You're early for the Midsummer Game."

"My goodness. I'm sensing that you'd rather I was somewhere else."

He doesn't answer. He watches Émile's smile waver and reset.

"Well, dear boy, I wanted to get a sense of the school in its natural state. Be a fly on the wall, as it were. Not that your letters haven't been extremely useful."

"My letters? That was all . . . gossip and parish notices."

"Don't be so modest. Some of them were very articulate. Tomorrow you must tell me more about the Magister Ludi. Did she really say that the Party were . . . I can't remember the exact phrase. Parasites? Thugs?"

"No."

"Oh. Then am I mistaken?"

"For goodness' sake, Émile! What does it matter? She's only a teacher. It's only a school. You don't understand. You don't belong here."

"And you do?"

He gets to his feet. The room rocks a little before it settles. "I'm going to bed. I'm drunk."

"Yes, you do seem to be." There's a pause. Léo makes his way to the door, floating a little as if he's walking through water. As he reaches for the handle, Émile shifts in his chair. "Just one thing, Léo," he says. "You are still to be relied upon, aren't you?"

"What?"

"I understand that this must have been hard for you. It must have seemed like exile. And of course you *did* put the Old Man's nose out of joint, there's no denying that. But now you've done your time, and if you play your cards right, it may not be entirely wasted."

"What?"

"We might have something in mind . . . as long as you cooperate."

Léo leans one shoulder against the wall and makes a sort of vertical rolling movement so that he's facing back into the room. A candle collapses into darkness and the room seems smaller. "Oh, certainly," he says. "After a year of nothing but studying the *grand jeu* masters I'll waltz back into government. If you expect me to believe that . . ."

Émile's face puckers into a weary half-smile. "Humor me. I'd like to be sure that you're still . . . one of us."

"Of course I am." The word catches in his throat. He doesn't know if it's true. He thinks of Claire and her contempt for the Party. A second later he thinks of the food he's been leaving for Charpentier, the lies he's told for him. Poor Charpentier, who's hardly crossed his mind, except as an irritation; and yet if someone found out Léo had been helping him . . . Sweat tingles on his palms and hairline.

Émile stares, his pudgy face blurring and slipping into two fleshy, shadowy masks. Léo blinks until his eyes focus again. At last Émile nods and leans back, scratching a scab of wax from the tablecloth. "Good," he says. "You haven't changed, then. I'm glad to hear that."

31

THE RAT

There is something wrong. Her head is full of things that aren't there. She raises her head to listen when there's nothing to hear; she flinches when all that lurks at the far end of a corridor is a shadow. Since that night—when was it? but a rat wouldn't remember, wouldn't try to count days—she hasn't seen Simon again. Perhaps he has fallen victim to hunger or fever or an accident. But still she finds herself mouthing the two syllables of his name, trying out the shapes they make on her tongue. *Si-mon. Si-mon.* Every time it makes his face rise in her mind's eye like a mirage, wavering. He is dangerous. He is a trap, a particularly insidious human trap, and she should swerve aside. But she doesn't. She wants to see him again, without understanding the wanting. She thinks of him in that room, and something blurs inside her. She thinks of his hunger and she is hungry, too.

No rat would go looking for trouble. No rat would creep toward a box of poison, knowing that one lick would make her tongue start to fizz and her stomach dissolve. But somehow tonight—wrong wrong wrong—she has come back from the kitchens a different way. What is she doing here? She looks up. It's only now that she can name *here* as the place under *there. There* is where he is. That room. She hates that place—she can feel it above her head, like a boulder waiting to fall—and yet she came. A rat would have taken the shortest path from the kitchens to its nest. A rat wouldn't have paused, wondering, drawn by an elusive waft of something, a not-scent that made the not-hunger flare . . . A rat wouldn't run the risk. A rat would be safe and eating now, gnawing at salty sausage, unthinking.

She wants to turn aside. She wants to take the safe path. But she wants to go up the little staircase and the next until she can push open the door and see him again. She wants him to say, *Oh, it's you,* in the way he did. And she wants to hold out the bundle of food in her hand, and . . . what? The rival desires knot around her like threads until she can't move at all. A rat would despise her for her helplessness.

Someone is coming. It isn't Simon. The footsteps are clipped, like hooves, but slow. She doesn't like the sound of them. They stride. They wander. They pause until she thinks it might be safe to move, and then come closer the instant she steps out of the shadows. She freezes. There is a figure at the end of the corridor. If she takes another step, he'll see her. She is trying to breathe silently, but it's getting harder and harder; fear is rising like water, up to her shoulders, her chin, her nose. How has she let herself get cornered like this? She could run. Is it better to run or to stay still? A rat would know, but she doesn't. When did this hesitant human voice take over, instead of her clever unthinking instincts?

She crouches, hunkering down like a gargoyle. She doesn't know why, except that perhaps this way she'll be out of his eyeline. In the shadows. Or maybe it's because her knees have gone soft, like rotten fruit. There is something about the sound of him, the smell . . . A faint bitterness on the air. Smoke. Something else. The hairs on her skin stand up.

He walks past her. He doesn't seem to see her, but there is something slippery about him, something that makes her unwilling to trust her senses. There is a narrow window at the far end of the corridor, beyond the stairs, and he stands by it. Now—in the thin strip of moonlight—she can see him better. He is overfed but still nimble. He has thick curling hair, slicked to his head, and a line of shadow along his top lip. He slides a hand into his jacket and brings out something shiny and flat. It opens like a shell and inside there are dark-and-gold cylinders; it's only when he puts one between his lips and produces a flame that she understands it's a cigarette. She has seen those before, although she doesn't understand what they're for. Is it some kind of medicine? He inhales and exhales. The smoke billows across the edge of moonlight, white and dark.

He turns, back to the window, and blows a plume of it into the corridor. The exhalation goes on and on. As if his lungs contain enough smoke to fill every passage and room and crevice. Whenever she breathes, he'll be there.

His face. Tightness in his mouth, narrow eyes. It creates a space around him, as if even the air doesn't want to get too close. She trembles, unable to run. Predator. Predator who would break your neck and leave your corpse where it is, without eating. He looks around at the blank walls, and through some sickening magic she sees what he sees: termite mound, wasp ball, rat's nest. Kick it apart and stand back.

He turns his head. The moonlight slides across his cheek, narrowing it. There is something in the plane of it, the shape. There is sharp grit in her throat. Her heart is her enemy, threatening to give her away. He crushes out the cigarette on the windowsill as though there is skin underneath it, and suddenly she knows him.

She shuts her eyes. For a moment she feels Mam's hands dragging her shirt over her head: *skin a rabbit, sweetheart*—and then Mam jumps to her feet, whirling to hiss at her—be *quiet*—and back to the door, eyes wide. The Rat (although she is too small and young to be a rat, she doesn't yet know what she is, only that she is Mam's) trembles. There was comfort, and now it's gone. Mam bends her head, listening, and the room takes advantage to creep inward, the way it always does when Mam isn't looking. She cracks the door open, holds her finger to her lips, and slides out into the passage. The Rat knows she is meant to stay where she is. *Make no noise, stay where you are, whatever you do, darling, you must not . . .* But Mam inches along the passage, under the shreds of sunset sky between the rafters. Then she disappears. She has gone down the stairs. For once, distracted, she has left the door open.

The Rat (not-yet-Rat) slides her body into the gap. She takes a few steps and nothing happens—the floor doesn't collapse, nor does the sky explode. She can smell fresh air blowing through the gaps in the roof.

She goes down the stairs. She's holding out her hand, wanting Mam to take it. But Mam is out of reach, standing by a little round window with a black one, a human-headed crow. He laughs, and immediately she dislikes him, wants to run forward and drag Mam away.

". . . mustn't come up here, not in daylight—you gave me a shock."

"I was curious. You didn't go back to your room."

"You mustn't follow me!" But she sighs, and the Rat can hear the beginning of a laugh in her voice, like the onset of a cold.

"I can't resist your animal magnetism."

"I'm not an animal. I'm a woman."

"You can say that again . . ." He leans forward. "I could do it here, right now. Just *looking* at you . . ."

"No!"

He laughs again and grabs her. They reel. The Rat shivers, wanting to rip him off, somehow knowing that Mam would be angry. The two of them are crushed together as if they're trying to step into each other's clothes. He grunts. He nuzzles into her neck as though he's going to bite her.

Then he stops. He looks up, over Mam's shoulder. At the Rat.

"Where did *that* come from?"

Mam whirls around. Her mouth opens. "Get *back!*"

"Is it *yours?*" He tilts his head, looking at the Rat as if he's calculating how much meat is on her bones. "I didn't realize . . . She looks like you, doesn't she?"

"You mustn't tell. No one knows—they'd throw me out."

"Of course I won't," he says. But he's smiling, his eyes still narrowed, and his gaze hasn't wavered. "A bastard in the attic. I shouldn't be surprised, should I? When you're such a hot little whore . . ."

A silence. Mam's face is flushed. Those words were bad words, you could hear it in his voice, but she is smiling. Smiling as though she hasn't heard. The Rat—the bastard, whatever that means—takes a step down, toward them both.

"Get back to the room! I told you before. *Now.*"

She hesitates. She opens her mouth.

"*Now!*"

She stares at them. The black-robed man's smile widens. He raises his hand and gestures, twirling a finger in the air: *go on then, run away.* Then he pulls Mam back into his arms. He puts his mouth on hers, but his eyes flick to the Rat with a pleased glint, enjoying his victory.

The Rat turned and went up the stairs. All the way up she was waiting for Mam to run after her and take her hand. But she didn't. The Rat got to the room and lay down on her back, with the door open a crack. The sunset light went redder and smaller and then it was dark and Mam still didn't come. She stayed awake for as long as she could, waiting and waiting for Mam to say good night, but she didn't come that night, and the way it feels now, it's like Mam never came back at all, ever, after that; even though she did.

Watching the man breathe out the last lungful of smoke, the-fat-and-old-but-same man, she remembers the empty ache in her chest, the sobs building, because Mam had never—she always—she *loved*, before that the Rat had always known that whatever happened she *loved*—

It is the same feeling as the not-hunger she feels now, thinking of Simon. And fear. Fear like now, too. She puts her hands over her mouth, very quietly, and bites into the soft part of her palm.

The man puts his hands in his pockets and walks forward, toward the foot of the stairs. He cranes to peer upward. Then he ascends, step by deliberate step. The banister wobbles and he shakes it harder, pausing to enjoy the faint crackle of breaking wood. Then he disappears into the darkness at the top.

She relaxes. Her insides are shivery, but now he's gone. She can run. The predator-shadow has passed over her. His attention is elsewhere.

His attention . . . He must be at the foot of the other staircase now, the one that leads up to her little room—Simon's room.

Simon. Simon is hiding, too. He mustn't be found. It's important. *Whatever you do, you must not* . . . Not by this man, especially not by this man.

She scampers up the stairs. She has made the decision too quickly to be afraid, too quickly to see how unratlike it is or to care. She makes noise, deliberately. And then they are facing each other, at the foot of the second flight: as they were ten years ago (a lifetime ago) only reversed, with him on the lowest step, her below. He jumps and blinks at her. His teeth are bared.

He says, "My word."

She lets him see her. She stands in his gaze, even though it burns. A rat would run. She *should* run.

And now she does. She spins and swerves, takes the gray ones' corridor and flies along the length of it, nearly silent on her bare feet. She pauses at the end, where she could go either way: and she looks back over her shoulder. He's following, intent, treading lightly. He is a hunter. A wave of terror goes through her; but there's something else there, too, a fierce pleasure, because (this time at least) she'll escape, and she has led him away from Simon.

32

LÉO

It's Midsummer Eve. The air is still, like glass. The valley holds the night like a bowl, frothy with stars. The silence is as thick as deafness. Léo sits in the magisters' courtyard, lighting match after match and flicking them away. He could be the only person left in the world. A few nights ago—after he'd been drinking with Émile and two of the magisters—he went past Claire's door and stood there listening, aching to knock. But she was on retreat, and he couldn't face the thought of her anger. *Can't we go back? No* . . . Now, when it's too late, he wishes he'd been braver. Tomorrow he'll be sitting with the other Gold Medalists, another face in the audience. She doesn't even know he's going to be there.

Everyone else is asleep. The guests that arrived yesterday are asleep in the scholars' cells, and for once, although it's not midnight yet, there's no light in Émile's window. Léo stares up at it; he wouldn't put it past Émile to be standing in the dark watching him. He has felt Émile's gaze on him for days, sly and constant. Even when Léo is alone, there's an itch at the back of his neck, a sense that he's no longer safe. If he ever was. It's almost better when he's in Émile's rooms, drinking and politicking, ignoring the others' jokes about female magisters: at least then he *knows* he's under scrutiny, and he can perform as though he were back at Party headquarters. At least then he knows it isn't paranoia.

But he has no right to complain. For months, he's been the spy. Those fucking letters. Details of who was a Party supporter, who'd said something subversive, who had a weakness and might be bribed . . . How could he have thought that gossip was innocuous? He sees his own treachery in the way Émile smiles at him. Another thing he wants to confess to Claire and be forgiven for, somehow.

And he's not just a traitor—he's a coward. He should have done more to help Charpentier than leave food out for him in an unlocked room: half-eaten bread and sausage and fruit piled on a plate, easily deniable. It's not enough, but now that Émile is watching him he daren't do anything else. He's hesitated about writing a note—leaving cash, or the contact details for an official who owes Léo a favor—but if Charpentier can get into his room, so could Émile. His skin crawls at the prospect of Émile's finding incriminating evidence. So the food is all he can do—food, and an occasional sheepish prayer. Sometimes he hopes that Charpentier has absconded, but then the next day's leftovers will disappear, and Léo guesses with a sinking heart that he's still in hiding, slowly starving. If only Léo knew what to do—or if only he had never tried to help in the first place . . .

Match after match dies until the box is empty. He closes his eyes. He's so tired he's light-headed. He aches to see Claire. Tomorrow he will. He wants to see the Midsummer Game. But does he want her game to be brilliant or only good? Or does he—the question wafts into the back of his mind like a fetid smell—does he want the Magister Ludi to fail conspicuously? No, of course not. He loves her, he wants her to silence all her critics forever. The way he wanted Carfax to triumph with the *Red* game. He swallows the taste of guilt. Somehow Claire knows about that; and she thinks he betrayed Carfax. She thinks he did it on purpose, that he'd known that the magisters would despise the *Red* game for its daring, its newness, its sheer audacious genius—that he'd known that Carfax would fail . . . *You wanted to win, didn't you? You would have done anything to win.* But that wasn't why he did it. It wasn't. He was shocked, wasn't he, when he saw the marks?

He can remember it now, joy—all that sleepless night he'd sat in the Great Hall, full of a dazzling rush of happiness—evaporating into numb disbelief as he saw his own name and slid his gaze down the page: *Léonard Martin, Gold Medalist,* Reflections—and then nothing. It was only as he scanned the rest of the page—*First Class,* mostly third-years, *Upper Second Class,* a few second-years, Paul and Émile, but most of them in the *Lower Second Class*—that he'd begun to feel giddy and unreal, as if an odorless gas was seeping into his bloodstream. Someone jostled him, said, "Get out of the way, will you, you're blocking everyone else," but the voice was muffled, distant. Where was Carfax? Surely . . . not in *Third Class,* and the only name under *Pass* was Felix. He splayed his fingers against the burlap-covered board, skimming the list again. He must have missed—

"Bernard will be fed up. Is Martin that cocky second-year? Oh, right." A suppressed giggle. "Oops, didn't see him there . . ."

"Wow," someone said with a chuckle. "Never seen anyone *fail* before."

"Specially not a de Courcy."

"Yeah, the Lunatic of London Library'll be turning in his grave."

He shut his eyes and opened them again. At the bottom of the sheet, there was a single line, easy to miss, above Magister Holt's signature.

Unsuccessful candidates: Aimé Carfax de Courcy, *Red*

No. He'd thought—he hadn't imagined—yes, he'd submitted the wrong game, but . . . And then he was pelting up the stairs, desperate to explain, to protest that all he'd meant was—he hadn't—not for a moment had he meant to . . . . But it had been too late. He sees again the scrawled ink on the wall of his room: *BASTARD*. And when he got to Carfax's room, Carfax was already gone.

He'd written a letter. It took him most of the next day, while people knocked on his door to congratulate him and speculate about how de Courcy could possibly have messed up so badly . . . He smiled at them and accepted their compliments and resisted the urge to drive his pen into their eye sockets. When they left, he went straight back to his scrawled draft. He'd wiped the wall down as best he could, but while he scraped about for the right words, he found himself staring at the smear of gray, and the shape of the word seemed to linger. *BASTARD*. Yes, he was. A bastard, and an idiot. *Please believe me, I never meant to lie to you. I thought . . .* But what had he thought? What if deep down he'd known, he'd wanted . . . ? What if, after all . . . ? He squashed the thought. Carfax would forgive him once he'd explained. *I'll go to Magister Holt and fess up, and give them the* Tempest *instead. They can't fail you for a game you didn't even submit . . . I'm sorry. Honestly, I thought . . .* but he was back to the same sentence, the one he didn't trust himself to finish.

He started a new paragraph. *Last night—I mean, the night before results day. I . . .* The memory made his insides ache with shame and desire and pleasure; but it was a kind of talisman, too, because Carfax had said . . . Well, that thing Carfax had said—he wouldn't have said it unless he meant it. And if he'd meant it, then he'd forgive Léo for being an idiot and a bastard and a Gold Medalist . . .

He scratched out that line. It was better to leave it at *I'm sorry*. After all, once Carfax had forgiven him, they could talk about— well, anything. Anything they wanted. He copied the letter out, so it looked as though he'd written it all in one go, straightforward and eloquent, and sealed it up ready to put in the post the next day. He didn't even know Carfax's address, he had to ask in the office. *Château d'Apre, nr. Montravail* . . . But the next morning all the scholars were called to the Great Hall.

I'm afraid, gentlemen, I have some very bad news . . .

He can't remember much about that day or the one after. Fragments. Felix giving him a sheepish smirk of sympathy and then flushing scarlet; Freddie, uncharacteristically subdued; the magisters elusive and somber. A deadened feeling, as if all the floors were carpeted with felt. Even Émile, whom Léo might have expected to be philosophical or sardonic, was dead silent and white-faced. Perhaps it was even the same day that some servant fell from a window. It hardly seemed to matter by then; it was part of the nightmare, the same motif played in counterpoint. She was taken away before most of the scholars saw her body, but the rumor spread, and there were black jokes about the time of year and the corrupting influence of the *grand jeu*. Someone suggested that she and Carfax had been having an affair; she'd been pregnant, they said, and that was why . . . It was a neat story: Carfax driven to suicide by a bad mark, and his trollop driven to suicide by being abandoned . . . Léo turned away, too sick to correct them. He was the only one who knew exactly why Carfax had died; and he didn't say anything because it was his fault. He took his library books back and packed his belongings, ready to go home. His diary had gone. He was dully unsurprised at that; he imagined Carfax pounding on his door after he saw the marks, going inside, skimming the last few pages, and then squeezing his fingers into the inkwell to write *BASTARD* on the wall. He didn't know why Carfax would have taken it with him—but now he was dead, what did it matter? Léo would have burned it, if he could.

Felix knocked on his door while he was slinging books into his trunk and came in before Léo answered. He frowned. "I thought . . . what are you doing?"

"What does it look like?"

"But the Midsummer Game isn't for two weeks."

"I'm not staying."

"You're not staying for the *Midsummer Game*? You're the Gold Medalist!"

"Leave me alone, Felix," Léo said. There was a pause. He threw Hondius on top of the other books without looking up, and heard the door close.

He didn't have the guts to tell Magister Holt. He wrote a letter. It was easier than the one he wrote to Carfax; it was much shorter, for a start. *Although I'm honored to have been awarded the Gold Medal, I regret that, due to personal circumstances, I'm unable to attend.* He knew he wouldn't regret it, not ever. It would have made him sick to sit in the space that should have been Carfax's. All he wanted was to go home. Maybe he should have told Magister Holt the truth—if anyone would understand, it would be him—and the night before he left, he actually got up and tried to write something that wasn't a lie. But he couldn't do it. And then he was on the train and the landscape slid past the dingy glass, and the first thing he saw on the station platform was Dad, striding forward to congratulate him.

Excuse me, sir?" One of the servants pushes a program into Léo's hand. "The seats reserved for Party members are here, to your right."

"I'm a Gold Medalist," Léo snaps. He is unwashed and unshaven, and his eyes are gritty. The summoning bell is still ringing, but he is one of the last people to sit down; he could kick himself for oversleeping.

"Oh, I see." The servant hesitates and ushers him to the front bench. Léo lowers himself down next to the Magister Historiae. The magisters and gold medalists are clearly expected to sit on a bare wooden bench without complaint, but on his right, the Party members are sitting on bottle-green cushions with tassels. Most of the guests had arrived by yesterday evening, but he can see Dettler, Vouter, and Taglioni, who must have been brought up this morning in the black automobiles in the courtyard. Dettler is sitting next to Émile; they seem to sense his gaze, and Émile smiles and raises a languid hand. Léo gives them a nod. Later he'll have to talk to them; the thought is like a splinter under his thumbnail.

The bell's note dies away, and nothing comes to fill its place. It's clever, this part of the ritual: you get so used to the incessant peal that when it falls silent, it's as if some fundamental part of the world has changed.

His heart is still beating uncomfortably hard—harder than ever. He hasn't been to the Quietus since he's been back at Montverre; he's swerved away from the prospect of being stuck with his thoughts, unable to run away. Now he can feel his muscles tensing. He tilts his head back and stares up at the vaulted ceiling, trying to distract himself; but abruptly he remembers the morning when Carfax took him up to the attic above, the soft heat and the shadows. *I think I'd kill myself.* Oh, what a fool he was to say that—and less than two months later, Carfax was dead . . . He shuts his eyes. The audience is still murmuring and chuckling. He wants to get up and throttle them all, one by one.

Don't they know they're supposed to shut up? Magister Dryden will be getting ready, composing herself in an anteroom.

On the other side, to his left, is the bank of benches where the visiting professors and masters are sitting. They've come from all over Europe, arriving by dribs and drabs in the last week. Now they at least are attentive, a few waiting with folded hands, a few flicking back and forth in the program to examine a move. Léo's own program lies in his lap, but he doesn't open it. He wants to see Magister Dryden's *grand jeu* unfold in front of him, without preconceptions. He wants to see her interpret every move; otherwise he might as well go home and read it later in the special edition of *The Gambit*.

He closes his eyes. Behind him, the Magister Cartae murmurs something to his neighbor, and laughs under his breath.

Then, like a draft of cool air, silence spreads across the room, deepening until you can hear a sigh or the twitch of a toe. Even the Party members have gone quiet. He sits up straight, blinking, and his heart hesitates and catches up with itself.

He'd meant to watch the doorway for her entrance, but she's here already; she must have entered quietly, soft-footed on stone, so it's only the power of her presence that shut up the muttering audience. She's performing without notes, so her hands are empty, hanging by her sides with a sort of neutral grace. Is he imagining the scent of incense and smoke in the air? He bites his lip: perhaps she's wearing his perfume, perhaps not, but it doesn't mean anything. In her white robe and cap, with the light slanting down from the high windows, she looks taller and slimmer than ever; her face is smooth and serene, and he thinks suddenly of the old war memorial outside the Town Hall at home, a young soldier in pale marble. You can say what you want, but she has the knack of commanding a space. She looks every inch the Magister Ludi—well, she *is* Magister Ludi—and even the people who want to despise her are leaning forward, attentive in spite of themselves . . . She steps up to the line of the *terra*. But before she crosses it, she looks around, taking in the audience, her head held up.

And flinches.

She was looking directly at him. A moment, a flicker, and her eyes moved on after that missed heartbeat, so that for a moment he thinks he's imagined it—but there's a tinge of rose along her cheekbones, and a second later it's as if red light floods across her skin, her cheeks and forehead crimson. She bows to her left, to the guests, to her right, the Party members—a shallower obeisance, on that side— and finally to the Magister Scholarium; when she straightens he can see a sheen of sweat on her temples that wasn't there before. Then she steps into the *terra* and lowers her head, taking the traditional moment for private contemplation. The folds of her gown quiver: she's trembling. He swallows, and his mouth is so dry it makes a faint clicking noise. She didn't know he was going to be here . . . But why would his presence put her off? Why would he make her more nervous than, say, Dettler or Émile? He looks down at the fabric of his trousers and counts to five, to give her time to recover. Maybe women players are simply more fragile, more sensitive . . . Or maybe it's because, out of everyone, she cares most what *he* thinks of her game. And she's wearing the scent he bought her. He tries not to feel a pulse of pleasure.

But when he looks up, she's composed herself. The color is fading from her cheeks, like the last rays of a sunset. She looks straight ahead, the resolute serenity back on her face; and then she moves into the gesture of *ouverture* as though she's opening a door to a kingdom.

She begins.

He can't remember the last time he watched a *grand jeu*. Once or twice in the last few years he's shown his face at a gala or a charity event, but he only ever sat through one movement at the most before slipping out into the bar for a drink with other Party members; his secretary knew to book him the seat next to the aisle. For the few minutes that he *was* in the crowded hall he'd hardly pay attention to the player—he saw Philidor's last performance and can't remember a single gesture—because he'd be subtly scanning faces, calculating who would be a useful person to know, who should be avoided if possible, and which fat old industrialist should be the recipient of Chryseïs's charm that night. He thought of the *grand jeu* the way he'd think of a gramophone or a wireless: background, a mere irritant. So now—watching Magister Dryden, trying to concentrate . . . it's a strange feeling, like taking up a book after years of refusing to read. He knows he's missing nuances in her delivery that ten years ago he would have absorbed effortlessly. And his understanding and attention span are rusty, so that when he loses the thread of the first transition he spends the next few minutes trying to make sense of it, missing more and more, a vague panic rising. He has to bite the inside of his cheek to bring himself back into the present moment. But after that first slippery lapse, he relaxes. Magister Dryden is easy to watch; there's an authority about her, a knowledge of her own strength, that won't let anyone look away. Her performance is precise, but it has the fluency of passion; as she moves from a quiet, simple opening into something deeper, more complex, he can almost see the ideas hanging in the air. Around him there's the rustle of paper as the others turn the page, more or less in synchrony.

And now she brings in the motif. He has always loved this moment, especially in the great classical games: when the elegance of the resultance, an exercise in restraint and seduction, gives way to something deeper, more human. He takes in a long breath, slow and silent, and around him he senses the audience sharing his anticipation. And she does it justice—holding a rest a beat longer than she ought to, conceding to them in silent complicity, before she makes the move. It's clean and melodic, with a kind of *rightness,* a sort of familiarity, setting off echoes and resonances like a song that he's forgotten but once knew well. The musical element is Beethoven, "The Tempest"; and the math is lovely, too, letting order form out of disorder, underlined by fragments of poetry. Yes, it's beautiful. *She's* beautiful. But that sense of recognition rises, stronger now, and with it a sour, greasy taste. *Nothing of him that doth fade . . .*

He tries to sit still. But as she winds her way further into the maze of abstraction—with such clarity that he can almost see the thread of her thoughts—a scum of nausea washes into the back of his throat. He knows where this game is going; and it's not because he knows Magister Dryden. It's changed—sea-changed—but it can't be coincidence. He remembers leaning over to Carfax and saying, "It's overwhelming. You need to pull it back," and Carfax retorting, "Yes, well, storms often are." She's edited it, but it's the same *grand jeu*.

She's stolen it.

He opens his program. He's clumsy, and Andersen shoots him a dirty look as the pages flap. Other people turn to look as he flips forward—it's bad form, but he doesn't care—to the middle movement, then, fumbling, to the dénouement and the conclusure. He has to blink to focus. He wants to be wrong. But he isn't. It's been transformed, but the bones of the *grand jeu* are the same, even down to his own suggestions. *Those are pearls that were his eyes . . . I'll drown my book . . .* He shuts the program harder than he means to, and the sound is as loud as a single clap. Magister Dryden doesn't falter, but she heard. Another flush creeps over her face, like the sun shining through a single red window. Her gaze slides toward him and away, without settling. No wonder she didn't want him here. The one person who might realize that she's cheated.

How dare she? It should be Carfax standing here, performing that game. She has no right . . .

He swallows. He can't do this. He digs his nails into the back of his neck, but he can't make the pain last; it burns and fades, and even when he adjusts his grip and tries again, it blurs into a single hot ache. He must look like a madman, clutching his own vertebrae as if he's afraid his head will fall off. He lowers his hand and knots his fingers in his lap. Magister Dryden glides into a graceful transition. Behind her, in his line of vision, even Dettler is sitting up straighter. She has them hanging on her every gesture: even if they still don't think a woman should be Magister Ludi, they can't look away. She'll triumph. With Carfax's game.

Breathe. He shuts his eyes and tries to think of something else.

He shoves images into his mind's eye like magic lantern slides: his old flat in town, Chryseïs asleep in pale sheets, Mim's garden, the railway station, the top of the Square Tower under winter stars . . . But they flicker, insubstantial. If things had been different, it would have been Carfax in the *terra*. Unless it was Léo himself. In that other life, one of them would be Magister Ludi, one Magister Scholarium: which way round wouldn't have mattered. They might have written the games together. One of them would be standing there, in command of the space.

Instead, Magister Dryden has taken—*plagiarized* . . . How dare she? It's more Léo's game than hers: all right, she's edited it, but he was there when Carfax wrote it, he affected the direction it took, if it hadn't been for him—

If it hadn't been for him, the *Tempest* would have been handed in ten years ago and she couldn't have used it, and Carfax would still be—

There's a murmur. He doesn't remember standing up, but he's on his feet, his heart pounding so hard he can hardly see. He opens his mouth.

Magister Dryden has frozen. Slowly she lowers her arm.

He can't speak. Everything above his heart feels like stone. It's appalling, suddenly, that no one else in the hall understands: he shouldn't have to say it aloud. But his silence can't go on forever. They'll think he's a lunatic, or that he's been taken ill. In the corner of his eye he catches a gray-clad servant already scuttling toward him to catch him, waving frantically to a colleague. He clears his throat and he's horrified by how it's the only sound in the room.

Magister Dryden is still staring at him. Of course she is, he's interrupted the Midsummer Game. But her expression is unreadable; if she's shocked, she's hiding it well. The high color is still in her cheeks, but her eyes are very steady.

He steps forward, once and then again. His shoes are on the brink of the silver edge of the *terra*, but he can't cross it. He hesitates. Magister Dryden tilts her head, very slightly. It's as if she's giving him permission to speak; but that's absurd, if she knew what he wanted to say . . .

And then she makes the gesture of *conjuration*, inviting him into the space.

For an instant the air seems to thicken. She straightens and there's a gleam in her eye, a tension at the corner of her mouth. Daring him. Is she serious? He can't believe it; an incredulous part of him wants to laugh. What would happen if he took the challenge? When was the last time anyone here even *saw* an adversarial game? And yet somehow he knows that it would work, that he could trust her to spin and deflect and mirror his own moves back to him, like a dance, like a duel, that between them they would play a dazzling, brilliant Midsummer Game.

All he has to do is perform the *assauture*. He feels the possibility of it singing in his backbone and in his shoulder blades. And if he did . . .

She reaches out: it's not a *grand jeu* gesture, but a human one. She sees him glance from her hand back to her face. There's something naked about her expression, as if they're alone. Is she pleading with him not to expose her? No, it isn't that. It's level, intense, the look of an equal, but . . . what is it? He blinks. He can't stand still forever, but something is making him feel unsteady, eroding the ground under his feet . . . She looks so like Carfax—she *is* so like Carfax—that he's afraid he won't be able to speak after all. Coward. Now is the moment to shame her, if he wants to.

She's so like Carfax. She even plays the *grand jeu* the way Carfax did. What wouldn't he give to see Carfax standing there, with the same steady eyes, the same elegance, the same hand beckoning?

He catches his breath. A sickening note sings in his ears: the whole world has turned hollow, is going to break. He staggers. Distantly a servant murmurs, "Sir? May I . . . ?" but he jerks his arm away, unable to take his gaze away from her face. That pale bony face, the gray-green eyes, the curl of hair that's escaped from her cap, the tiny scar below her ear. Unmistakably a woman's face—but . . . It's so familiar. The face he's dreamed about for years. Seen in his nightmares, underlined by the great gory grin of a cut throat. No. It's crazy. He's crazy. His sleepless night is catching up with him.

But that *conjuration* . . . that invitation. No, he isn't crazy.

He says, choking a little, "Aimé?"

Silence. He doesn't look away from her, but somehow he knows that the audience's attention has reverted from him to her, as if it's her turn to move.

She holds his gaze for what seems like a lifetime. Her mouth is a little open, her cheeks slapped red.

Then she swings around and strides out of the Great Hall, crossing the line of the *terra* without ceremony, as if it's a mere crack in the stones.

33

THE MAGISTER LUDI

She walks blindly, empty of any thought except the need to get away. She can't think about what has happened; all she cares about is putting distance between her and Martin and the other open mouths, the hungry eyes. Suddenly black clouds boil up around her knees and sweep toward her from the far corners of the corridor. She has to stop and bow her head. A moment ago she was calm, but now she is breathing hard and drenched in sweat. Will they send someone after her? She glances over her shoulder—blinking away the billowing blackness—and sees movement in the doorway of the Great Hall. She sets off again, breaking into an ungainly, panicky run; behind her there are footsteps. A man's voice calls, "Wait! Magister!"

She reaches the end of the corridor. On her left a spiral staircase leads up to the Capitulum; on her right, a door leads out into the courtyard. She feels years older than this morning, when she crossed the monochrome pattern, sick with stage fright: but when she goes out into the sunlit heat it's clear that hardly an hour has passed. She hurries across the court to the library.

Inside it's dim and cool, full of the scent of old paper and beeswax. All the attendants and archivists are in the Great Hall, of course, so it's silent and still, as though it has been abandoned for centuries. She realizes with a jolt that she is breaking the rules by being here alone. If she wanted to set a fire, there'd be no one here to stop her. She laughs aloud. It has a high, hysterical note, and she covers her mouth. If anyone heard her . . . Her cuff smells of frankincense and amber, and she lowers her hand again, in case she gags. This morning she dabbed scent on her wrists, behind her ears and in the notch of her collarbone—like a silly girl, not a Magister Ludi. But she thought it was harmless. She'd imagined Léo Martin in the capital—thinking of her, perhaps, as he sipped coffee at a rickety table on a pavement and caught sight of the date in the newspaper; she never dreamed that he would have been asked to stay. Another surge of sweat prickles as she remembers seeing him on the front row, next to the Gold Medalists. Did she falter? Did anyone see? Not that it matters, now, after . . . She scrubs her wrist on her gown until the skin burns, but the perfume lingers.

She has reached the staircase. She climbs it two steps at a time, breathing hard, and unlocks the door to the Biblioteca Ludi. Dust swirls and settles. It's a relief to shut the door behind her, but the room is stuffy and airless, and somehow the old comfort of possession has lost its power. If this is hers, this chaos of overcrowded bookshelves and forgotten jetsam, what does that say about being Magister Ludi? And what sort of Magister Ludi walks out of a Midsummer Game? Her guts wring themselves tighter. It was unforgivable. The Magister Cartae will say that she is weak, spineless, neurotic—and he'll be right. She goes to the desk and leans on it. She knows it's her own body that's trembling, but as the judders run up her arms, she has the sensation that Montverre itself is trying to shake her off. She has never doubted her right to be here until now. There's a glass paperweight, gritty with dust, next to her papers, and she picks it up and squeezes it. Solid glass against her solid bones, enough ache to keep the tears at bay . . .

There's a spate of footsteps, running up the stairs—she scarcely has time to hear them, to turn—and then Léo is there, flinging the door open with such violence that it slams into the wall and lets loose a trickle of plaster. He says, "Aimé."

"How dare you?" she says, and he flinches—stupidly, as if he didn't expect her to be angry. "Do you have any idea what you've done, you—" She starts to say *bastard*; but suddenly she sees the word scrawled on a wall in black ink, and it dies on her tongue. "Get out," she says, like ice.

"I'm not going until you talk to me."

"What else do you want from me, Martin? You've destroyed my career. How *dare* you stand up in the middle of a Midsummer Game, *my* Midsummer Game, you stupid, self-absorbed, arrogant—"

"I only—I thought—your game—"

She swings her arm. Glass shatters against the wall beside his head, with a crash. A second later, in the silence, she realizes what she's done. He glances at the round-backed fragments around his feet, the rough demi-semispheres still glinting with trapped bubbles, and swallows. A foot to the left, and the paperweight would have hit him. Was it too close for comfort or did she miss? They stare at each other. Her breath is unsteady; trying not to cry is like trying not to be sick.

She's never seen him like this: pale, blundering, his eyes fixed on her as if she's the only steady point against a rocking horizon. In the pause she can hear ten years' worth of reproaches.

He says again, "Aimé?"

"Aimé's dead."

He shakes his head, but slowly. "You're a woman. You always were. Yes? I mean, you're not a man—pretending to be a woman?"

She laughs, incredulous. "Why would a man pretend to be a woman *here?*" He blinks, and an aftershock of fury goes through her: that casual blindness, that stupidity in the face of anything that doesn't affect him personally. "It was the only way I could come here. Females aren't allowed to be scholars, remember?"

She shouldn't have said it. She should have denied it. But it's too late, and the admission is like a pane of glass evaporating. Suddenly they are in the same room for the first time. He says, "Yes. I see," and the tone of his voice is oddly humble. Maybe if he thinks about it, he *does* see.

She draws in a long breath. "You didn't imagine I'd fake my own death and then dress up as a woman? Why? To seduce *you*?"

"Well, no," he says. "Hardly a foolproof tactic." And then he glances at her with a brief glint of amusement, and it comes back to her in a stinging rush, what it was like to be Aimé—especially, to be Aimé with Léo. The sparks that were never quite friendly, the hostility that was never quite disagreeable. The heat of it building until that final night—good god, why would she remind herself of that?

She turns away. She has buried those memories for so long that they surge up like undigested fragments, tasting of bile. Another life. Another person. In one sense she was Aimé, yes, but not now, no longer, never again.

"But your brother . . . Aimé did exist." He says it slowly, as if he's talking through a tricky quaintise. "You had a brother. Who would have come here if you hadn't taken his place. And he really did kill himself. I mean, you *didn't* fake—"

"Of course I didn't!" How can he be so obtuse? "Aimé's gone." A breath later she adds, "I loved him."

"Yes. Of course. Forgive me," he says, each word like a weight. "I'm still taking it in. I'm sure you did, he was very . . ." He trails off: she can almost see the effort it takes him to remember that the Aimé he knew isn't the one they're talking about now. "I should have known," he says. "Part of me did know. Why didn't I see it before?"

"Because," she says, "you never actually looked at me, did you?"

She doesn't have to be watching him to know that he starts to speak. But he can't protest, after all; he thinks better of it. She tries not to like him more for that. "You look like him," he says. "I mean—I thought it was a family resemblance . . . You've changed so much. And . . ." He pauses, as if he's expecting her to answer; but she's not going to make it easier for him. "How did you *do* it?" he says. "All that time, no one noticed. I suppose we all thought you were strange, but we never dreamed—it must have been difficult."

"Not that difficult." Why should she tell him what it was like, to know she could never be herself, never undress—never even take off her gown, in case someone saw the bandages under her shirt? To push her voice deeper than was comfortable, to dread the days she menstruated, to have to sneak her bloodied rags into the servants' waste buckets and claim fever or diarrhea when her cramps were so bad they blanked out everything else in her head? Once, when Léo saw a stray blot of blood on her floor, she had to nick her jaw deliberately with a razor to explain it; she still has the scar, under her ear. But worst of all was the constant fear that somehow she would give herself away—not because of biology but something else, some violation of their mysterious untaught code. She cultivated arrogance, the most masculine mask she could think of, but at times it felt so flimsy she almost broke out in hysterical laughter, dreading the moment when someone would squint at her and say, "Hey, wait . . ." He wouldn't understand, not even if she tried to explain: two years of bleak, fragile, lonely happiness, until he got under her skin.

"No," he says, "well, you got away with it, didn't you? You must've thought we were all idiots. Especially me." He pauses. "Were you laughing up your sleeve at us all that time? Sniggering. Poor pathetic Martin, can't see what's in front of him. Doesn't even realize he's being beaten by a girl."

"Is *that* why you care?"

He doesn't seem to hear her. "I should've known—I should've . . . Émile always said you were using me. All that time. Lying about who you were. Was any of it true? Did you ever say anything you meant?"

"Of course. Don't be stupid."

"Letting us think you were someone you weren't—inventing a whole life for yourself."

"That's not the point," she says. "Why was it any of your business? Why does it matter? If I hadn't lied, I wouldn't have been able to—"

"I thought you were *dead*!" His voice cracks. He blinks, shocked, as if it was someone else who said it, not him; and then, with a strange slow exhalation, his knees fold and he subsides to the floor. He crouches there like an animal, his head bent. She stands still, frozen, uncomprehending; until he gives a sudden gasp, scrubbing at his face with his sleeve, and she realizes he's crying.

"Aimé died," she says. It sounds hollow. "My brother died. I never lied about that."

He says, forcing the words out, "I thought *you* were dead. I thought it was my fault. You let me think that . . ."

"It was," she says. "It *was* your fault." It's like finally being sick, after hours of rising nausea: a disgusting relief. She'd rather feel anger than shame.

He raises his head. His face is blotchy.

"He sent a telegram," she says. "The night the marks were meant to go up. He asked me to come home. He said he didn't feel safe on his own. So I packed. I was going to catch the sleeper. I would have been with him by the next morning. But—" She turns away from him. He looks obscene, unmanned and raw-skinned. "You came to find me," she goes on, staring unseeing at the sunlit slope outside the window, the road down to the village. "You told me I'd won the Gold Medal. You made me promise to stay. So I stayed. And when I got home, it was too late."

"I didn't know. How could I have known?"

"You lied to me!"

"No, I didn't lie, I got it wrong, I truly thought—"

"You lied to me. Don't pretend it was a mistake—you submitted the wrong game, you made them fail me! And then you kissed me." She tries to control her voice, but it's rising and rising. "What did you want? To humiliate me every way you could?"

He's on his feet. "It wasn't like that. You know it wasn't."

She swings around to face him, drawing breath. He meets her eyes. With his shaggy, unoiled hair and the weight he's lost, he looks young again. His eyelashes are still wet.

And suddenly, when she most needs it, her anger is gone, sinking away to ash. "Yes," she says, and her throat aches. "Yes, I know." Confusion flickers across his face. She shuts her eyes. What if she admits to herself that he wasn't the enemy? She's been so angry with him for so long: that he submitted the wrong game without asking her, that he told her she'd won when she hadn't, that he kissed her. Even his diary didn't absolve him, because he was only lying to himself. Self-indulgent, self-absorbed. Hadn't he said he wanted to *find a way to beat her*? And he'd done it. *Once and for all* . . . He fooled himself, but he didn't fool her. She'd seen through it. Labeling it *love*—she shrinks from the memory of the kiss, of reading about the kiss later—*love* just meant he hadn't had to think about *her*; he could tell himself it wasn't sabotage, it was a mistake. It was the best of excuses, an unassailable move.

And yet, what if . . . ? The sight of his face has caught her off-balance, as though all this time she's been the naive one. She has blamed him for so long that now she's lost. If it *wasn't* his fault, then . . . ? The question is an abyss at her feet: she's tried so hard not to look at it directly. But now it's there, undeniable, and she knows what the answer is. It wasn't Léo's fault, it was hers. Wholly hers. She'd read the telegram and he hadn't; she knew Aimé and he didn't. If it hadn't been for her own sentiment and pride and (yes) desire . . .

She sits down at the desk. How many times has she run the memory of that morning in her head? She climbed the stairs at home, under the crumbling plaster and dingy scrolling paint, calling Aimé's name. It was nearly midday, already warm, and in the silence she could hear a fly throwing itself against a window, the buzz-crunch of more impacts than a person could stand. "Aimé," she'd said. "Aimé!"—that name which was his and hers, the name she'd stolen—and then she pushed open the bathroom door and saw. If only it had been a moving picture she could have reversed it, so that as she walked backward down the overgrown drive the blood would trickle upward, defying gravity, sucked back by the wound in his throat and gathering force until the last drops were enough to knit his skin back together. And she would step, heel-first, into the train, and let it take her back to Montverre, all the way to the time before she saw her name, his name, on the noticeboard and knew Léo had lied to her.

Aimé gave her so much, and she'd let him down. If it hadn't been for him . . . She can see him now, that night when he'd got the summons for his entrance viva: he'd been sitting at the piano, hands crossed behind his head, staring at the damp patches on the ceiling. "What a drag," he said, as if they were in the middle of a conversation. "Montverre sounds like a prison anyway. I'd much rather stay here and read."

"You're lucky you get the choice," she said, turning a page, refusing to be drawn in. It was an old sore point—the subject of endless childhood taunts—that Montverre didn't accept women.

"They can't teach me anything. It's a waste of time." He grinned at her. When she didn't answer, he jabbed at the top C, plinking until she rolled her eyes. "I'm a de Courcy. I've been playing the *grand jeu* since I could read. I don't need three years in a monastery."

"Don't be so big-headed."

"And yet . . . if I don't go, I'll be letting down the family name."

"We'd survive." She went back to her book while he went back to twiddling on C-sharp. But a second later she lowered it again. "You don't mean it, Aimé?"

"What if I do?" He hunched his shoulders as if her stare was a jet of freezing water. Suddenly his voice was flat, with the weight of certainty behind it; that casual spontaneity had been fake. "I don't want to go. I've made up my mind, actually. I'm not going. So there's no reason to do a viva, is there?"

"What? You can't not go to Montverre!" He grimaced, looking mulish. She sat up straight and slammed her book down on the table next to her. "So why did you apply? I helped you with that game for *days*."

"You could go in my place."

"Don't be stupid. Aimé, of course you'll go."

"Did you hear what I said? I'm serious." He leaped up and bounced from foot to foot. "You could viva my game with your eyes closed. It's half yours, after all."

"Except they might notice the fact that I'm female." She sat back, crossing her arms.

"Oh, come on. You're tall and scrawny enough. Cut your hair, wear my clothes—maybe squash *those* down a bit," he added, waving at her chest, "but it's not like you're very womanly to start with. And your voice—you can pass for a tenor, easily."

She gave him a sour look; but the longer he held her gaze and didn't burst into giggles, the harder it was to keep that expression on her face. "You think I could?"

"Why not?"

"Because . . ." She inhaled through her teeth: it was like trying to explain the concept of a locked door. "You know it's not that simple."

"Worth a try, though, isn't it?" He paced toward the window and stopped, distracted, to scratch at a new patch of mold on the Chinese wallpaper. "I'm going to stay here and write my own games. I'm on the verge of a breakthrough, something really big; I don't want to end up like those idiots in *The Gambit*. And I'll be able to work all night and sleep all day."

"You'd be alone practically all the time. It wouldn't be good for you. I *can't*, Aimé," she said, "so stop harping on it. You should go to Montverre, and I'll go to stay with Aunt Frances, like we agreed."

"Is that what you want?"

Silence. A rat scuttled somewhere. She shut her eyes. For a moment she imagined packing her trunk—Aimé's trunk—and setting off. The train, the village, the mountain road—and then the buildings of Montverre, not in the intricate grays of an etching, but vivid against a real blue sky. Aimé might disdain the lessons, but she ached for them: math, music, words, notation, history. A library ten times bigger than the moldering, haphazard, pawnshop-decimated one here— the greatest *grand jeu* archive in the world. It was like being hungry and dreaming of food. "You know what I want," she said, her stomach twisting.

When she opened her eyes, he was standing over her. He took hold of her, pulled her out of her chair, and bowed. He was smiling; from that angle he looked like Papa. "You must be Aimé Carfax de Courcy," he said. "Pleased to meet you." And then, with a flourish, he made the gesture of *ouverture.*

That's how she wants to remember him: not how he was later, when the de Courcy strain started to eat away at him. That moment: his grin as he spun away and reached for the wine he was drinking straight out of the bottle, the way her heart nearly exploded as she understood what he was offering her. Or how he was later—after she and Léo got seventy in their joint game, the second year, when the word *seventy* became a war cry and he sang it to her, chalked it on the terrace, scrawled it on her mirror in soap. *My clever sister,* he'd said. Or sometimes, *clever Aimé, clever me.* Had he ever been jealous? If he was, he hid it. They celebrated like children, that New Year, running amok in the château, playing drunken hide-and-seek.

But then he began to slide. It started with little things. He'd forget to wash or eat, or talk to himself in long incessant monologues, or rip pages out of books because he couldn't find what he was looking for. Then he began to stay up all night to play the piano, to scrawl incoherent *grands jeux* on the wall with burnt sticks and shout at her when she tried to stagger to bed at four in the morning. But instead of helping him—what could she have done? If only she'd known what to do—she'd packed her trunk and the cello and spent the last days watching the clock, desperate to get away. And oh, that last night, two days after she should have gone back to Montverre, when he begged her not to leave . . . She clenches her jaw. She'd have stayed if she could have helped. But she was lost, worn thin by shame and helplessness; and she didn't think he was in danger, not really. The housekeeper would come in every day to cook, wash the sheets, tell him to eat . . . She crept away the next morning without saying goodbye.

Later she'd written to him, a breezy, cheery letter that pretended to assume he was fine. He didn't answer. When his telegram came—so naked, so direct—she should have known that he needed her. No. She *had* known. And she'd chosen to stay at Montverre, seduced by the glory of seeing her name—*his* name—on the top of the mark sheet. And by Léo. When Léo kissed her, she'd wanted more. More and more, until she was shocked by the heat building between her legs, the sweet shameless vertigo. The euphoria of having everything she wanted, all at once. When he went to take off her gown, it took all the strength she had to push him away. And then that stupid thing she'd said. *I love you, Léo . . .*

It doesn't matter now. Aimé is dead, long ago.

"Oh no," Léo says. "Please, shh. Stop it. Don't—please don't."

But it's too late. She can't help it. And there's a kind of luxury in letting herself go. There's no reason to pretend anymore: for the first time, someone else knows exactly why she's crying. She rests her forehead on her arms, and sobs judder through her like an earthquake.

"Hush," he says, "it's all right, shh . . ." It isn't all right, and it never will be; he knows that as well as she does. He crosses the room to her, and she senses him hesitating at arm's length. Then he murmurs, "Shh, shh," and pats her head. It's such a maladroit gesture that she could almost laugh. She raises her face to look at him, blinking away tears.

"I'm sorry," she says, and then she can't say anything more, because the grief rises again—this time at what she's done to him, because ten years ago he could have become anyone, he could have been Magister Ludi, and now here he is, old and exiled and helpless, not even a politician.

"Don't cry," he says. "Please, Aimé—Magister—Claire . . ."

And then he puts his arms around her.

She stiffens. Even now her instincts cry out against letting him touch her, in case she gives herself away: but there's nothing left. What will he discover? That she's a woman? That she's Aimé? She's stripped of all her secrets already. She doesn't have the force to push him away. He leans into her, warm against her shoulder, and his hand strokes her backbone—slowly, firmly—steadying her, comforting her. He goes on murmuring, the syllables blurring into one another, meaningless. Gradually her sobs grow smaller. It's ridiculous, that he should be comforting her, when she's the one who lied to him: and that she should let him, when only a few minutes ago he capsized her Midsummer Game. But in the solid heat of his body against hers, those things seem distant. She can't remember the last time she was held.

Finally she can stop crying. But even when she pulls away, the space between them is softer, elastic, as though it would be the easiest thing in the world to fall back into his arms. She wipes her eyes on her gown, sniffing wetly. He makes a tiny sound of amusement, but when she looks at him, he isn't smiling. He says, "I love you."

"*What?*"

He has the grace to grin, but he holds her gaze; and with a twist of her gut, she realizes that he means it. Or thinks he does. He says again, "I love you. I always did."

She laughs. It doesn't feel very different from crying.

"It's true."

"Is it? And what do you want me to do about it?" She is still laughing as she says it. It's as though he's made an outrageous, barely legal move in an adversarial game: she can't take it seriously.

"I don't know. That is——" He hesitates and glances away.

"Oh," she says. "That."

"Well, yes, *that*," he says, "obviously. But not only that."

"So what else do you want?"

"Everything." He pauses, and looks back at her with a smile that's somehow deadly serious. "Anything. What will you give me?"

She wipes her face, taking more time than she needs to. The salt is sticky on her palms. She shouldn't believe him, but she does. Her heart feels swollen and thin-membraned, like a bubble: the lightest touch and it might pop, but for now it's quivering, iridescent, drifting. She bites the inside of her cheek, trying to bring herself back to earth. He loves her. He wants everything, anything, whatever she's prepared to give. With a jolt she realizes she wants the same from him. "You may have noticed," she says, fighting to keep her voice cool, "that magisters have to take a vow of celibacy."

"I know. I know."

"And a vow of lifelong service. I'll be here forever."

"Well, yes, I wasn't——" He stops and glances away, as if there's an answer he doesn't want to give her. "But what if . . ." he says, "what if——"

"I'll always be Magister Ludi." She says it loudly, announcing it to the whole of the Biblioteca Ludi, to all the books with their backs turned, all the ghosts of former magisters. She may have walked out of her own Midsummer Game, but she is still Magister Ludi. A magister is magister for life: there is no *what-if*.

"All right," he says, although he's still avoiding her eyes. "I mean . . . of course. But that doesn't mean we can't find a way."

"To break my vows? You're assuming I want to find a way. What makes you think that I would do that?"

He cuts her off. "You loved me." A tiny pause. "Didn't you? You said you did."

"More than ten years ago."

"Was it true?"

She exhales. What difference does it make now? "Yes," she says.

He leans forward. She catches the scent of cologne, and underneath it the salty male note of his skin. "Imagine the games we could play," he says. "I'll never be as good as you, but I can give you a run for your money. Right? Remember when we got seventy for the *Danse Macabre?*" He gives her a flickering smile. "I know it sounds crazy. But we could make it work. Please . . ."

"It's too late."

"No, it isn't. It's a second chance." He rubs the desk with his thumb, back and forth, as if he's erasing a stain. "Wouldn't you go back, if you could?"

She looks past him out of the window. The quivery feeling of tears or laughter surges again, and she focuses on the breeze swaying the pines, the shadows sweeping back and forth over the flower-studded grass. Would she go back? Of course. She was happier as Aimé than she has ever been since. If she could, she would . . . But what's more, she can imagine the life she might have with Léo: long days spent arguing and joking and studying—that joyous ongoing duel that left them both breathless and nights that fanned the flame . . . She's missed that, more than anything. No one has ever been her equal, the way he was. She turns back to him, and perhaps he can see what she's thinking, because his eyes search her face as if he's going to kiss her.

But he doesn't. He stays very still, waiting. As if something has changed, and it's her responsibility, not his, to make the first move. For the first time in years she remembers what it's like to be a man, and it goes straight to her heart like a drug. She pauses for as long as she can bear to, savoring the rush of power in her veins.

"You're alive," he says. "I can't believe it. You're alive."

34

Dear Léo, I

You'll hear that I'm dead, but I'm not. Aimé Carfax de
Courcy is—but he's not who you think he is. I'm not who you
think I am.

Today it was my brother Aimé's funeral. It was this
afternoon. He was buried in the de Courcy vault with our
parents. It was hot, the air was like glass, the clouds were
building up over the hills. There weren't many people
there, only the family lawyer and the mayor and a few
others from the village. My aunt is on her way to collect
me, because young women shouldn't be left on their own
after a bereavement, but the boat-train was canceled because
of strikes and she telegraphed to say that she wouldn't
arrive till tomorrow. I stood there in my black dress and
high-heeled shoes and veiled hat and I felt them looking
at me, pitying me. No one mentioned my hair; perhaps
they thought I'd hacked at it myself as a sign of grief. I
didn't feel grief-stricken. I felt unreal and furious. Not
with Aimé, because he'd been ill, and he wasn't to blame.
With you. I was waiting to see you come through the gate
of the cemetery—late, sweating—and hurry over to us,
interrupting the service. I wanted to see your swollen eyes
and two-day beard, and the creases in your suit from the

train. I wanted to see you stumble to a stop and stare at the
entrance to the vault and wilt. I wanted to see you cry.

And then, when the service was over, and the mayor had
shaken my hand and wandered away, I knew you would
approach me. You'd introduce yourself. I'd hesitate before
I said my name, but then—in spite of hating you, right
then—I'd insist that you came back to the château to drink
to my brother. I wouldn't let you refuse. And you'd be too
addled by the journey and the heat to do anything but follow
me, lugging your overnight case, and we'd take the shortcut
through the olive trees, climbing the unkempt terraces up
to the back of the garden. There'd be bread and saucisson
and salad, left out for me by the old woman who comes in
to cook, and I'd go down to the cellar and bring up some
of the oldest, dustiest wine. Nothing but the best for Aimé.
I would pour you a glass and propose a toast, and as you
raised your glass you'd meet my eyes for the first time.
And suddenly you would realize who I was. You'd blink in
disbelief, and blink again as your eyes filled, and then you'd
put down your glass, overcome, and I'd watch you cry,
despising you a little, because after all my brother would
still be dead.

You don't understand, do you? You'd understand if you'd
come. But you didn't, did you? You didn't even come to
Aimé's funeral. Was it too much bother? Too long a journey?
Or were you too excited about staying at Montverre for
the Midsummer Game, basking in the glory of being Gold
Medalist? Do you even care that Aimé killed himself?

Because what you would have seen, looking into my
eyes . . .

It was me. The man you know as Aimé Carfax de

Courcy—the man you hated and cheated and kissed—is me.
Claire. His sister.

Don't tell anyone. You mustn't tell anyone, ever.

I was such a fool. Such a weak, credulous idiot. I'd never
been kissed before, you see. I thought it meant something
big. Important. But it can't have done. I spent that last night
thinking about you, wondering if I could tell you somehow,
swear you to secrecy, sure that you'd never betray me. I
lay on my bed, feeling your mouth on mine. Such a cliché,
but it's true. And all that time Aimé was waiting for me.
Pacing, maybe. Struggling every second to hold on until I
got to him. Thinking I was on my way to him, when I was
lying there, dreaming of you . . . I'll never forgive myself.
Or you.

My fingers are still black from writing on your wall. It's
just as well I had to wear gloves for the funeral. I wish I could
have seen your face. *BASTARD*. You deserved it. You deserved
worse.

It's over. I can never go back to Montverre. Aimé's death
was in the papers; now I'm stuck with being Claire. He killed
me, too, in a way. I thought, if you were there . . . at least
I'd know it was real, all that. Not some kind of de Courcy
hallucination. What if it was really him, and I've been at home
for the last two years, practicing the piano and reading? I don't
know who I am. Help me.

If they find out what I did . . . I'll be disqualified from
playing the *grand jeu* ever again. It'll be a scandal. They'll

call me a hussy and a whore. They'll say the other scholars must have known. How did she keep them quiet? I hear her brother killed himself from the shame . . . And if you decided to fuel the fires . . . Do I trust you? You've always been jealous, prickly—if you wanted to ruin my reputation, forever . . . It would be one way to make sure I never beat you again.

If someone else had found Aimé before I got off the train . . . Or if I hadn't come home at all . . . I was lucky. The blood, his body. The nightmares. Lucky.

No one can ever know.

For one night, I thought I was the Gold Medalist, and I thought you loved me. It's like a fairy tale: a girl who gets everything she wants and then loses it all because she had to lie to get it. Jewels that turn out to be glass, ground into white dust.

I didn't sleep, after you left me. I made myself wait until the clock struck six, and then I went down to see if they'd put up the marks. I thought that was enough time for the office to have typed up the list, and I was right.

You know what it said. I won't tell you how it felt. I won't give you the satisfaction.

I've taken your diary. It was on your desk, when I came to find you. First I looked at it to see whether you'd really submitted the wrong game. I thought maybe it was a mistake. But you did it deliberately. As though it was a favor. I didn't understand. I thought if I read all of it, your whole life, it would make sense. But it still doesn't. It's here now. Your handwriting makes me feel sick.

I think you never stopped hating me.

Dear Léo, I'm not dead.

Dear Léo, I'm dead.

I'm sorry.

I hate you.

Write. Write to me, to Claire. Send me a letter telling me how sorry you are, how much you loved Aimé. Then I'll reply. That's all you need to do. One letter, and I'll come back from the dead.

35

THE MAGISTER LUDI

This is the *grand jeu*. This—yes—is her Midsummer Game: not in front of the guests in the Great Hall but here and now, alone with Léo, the moment she has been waiting for. The pause, the absolute stillness before she leans toward him, the silently indrawn breath and the blood humming in her ears. This is not the *ouverture* but the main theme, the perfect move that floods a room with energy. It gives her the same pure clarity of mind, the same certainty. The audience, the *terra*, the rest of Montverre—none of that matters. They're irrelevant, left behind. Like her objections. The *grand jeu* is now, her heartbeat, his eyes on hers. It's all she needs.

That pause. If she could stay there forever, caught in that moment like a fly in a bead of amber, she would. But it's over almost before she has time to think; and then she's kissing him, and then it isn't a *grand jeu,* nothing like it, it's a kiss, imprecise and urgent and perfectly itself. She has never felt so human. It's like kissing him ten years ago, but it's different, too, of course: he is cleverer, gentler, humbler. At least he is at first, letting her take control; but as she goes on kissing him—hungry, thirsty, helpless with desire and euphoria—he shifts his position and catches his hands in her hair, pulling until it's on the edge of pain. Yes, she remembers this. Equals, opponents, rivals, lovers. This is how it was, this is the only way it could be. This is how she has always wanted it. And when he hesitates, drawing back to look at her face, she can see him seeing her. Finally she is visible—herself, her himself, the boy she was and the woman she is now, both and neither and whole. And as Léo sees her she sees him, and it's like a light on his face, and she has never encountered anything so beautiful.

"What is it?"

"I can't . . . I don't know. I give up." What has she become, to be so unmanned by a kiss and a look? A few moments ago she was torn between laughing and crying; now she feels sober and still and joyous, trembling on the brink of something she doesn't understand. "I'm mad. We're mad."

"Obviously."

"I must be. I walked out of my own Midsummer Game."

"Ssh." For a split second she bridles; then he shakes his head at her and gestures toward the door. A knock. They wait, frozen.

"Magister? Are you there?"

She doesn't answer. Of course they've sent a servant to find her. Léo watches her. She holds her finger to her lips.

Finally she hears footsteps retreating. She breathes silently, once, twice, before she relaxes.

"They're looking for you," Léo says. He's drawn back from her. "Don't you want to go?"

"No."

"You can't hide forever."

"I know that."

He nods. That knock has changed the feeling in the air; he looks older, sadder, as if he's about to tell her to leave. He says, "I'm sorry about your game. I shouldn't have—"

She takes hold of his arms and kisses him again. She takes pleasure in cutting him off, in biting his tongue when he tries to go on speaking. He winces and she pushes closer, feeling his bones against hers. She takes hold of his shirt and drags it out of his trousers. Her palms meet the skin of his back. The warmth of it makes her shiver.

He catches his breath. But he doesn't move to take off her gown; perhaps he's remembering when she pushed him away, ten years ago. She pulls away long enough to tug it over her head. Then, as if she's given him permission, he tears at her shirt, suddenly urgent.

She's read about all this. She's never done it. He pauses, as if he's overheard her thought.

"Are we mad enough to do this?"

"Yes," she says. "Yes."

36

LÉO

The door closes. On the other side of it he hears her footsteps clicking on the stone staircase, growing fainter. He puts his forearm over his eyes to block out the sun. He must look like a madman, flat on his back on the floor, his arm across his face. He can smell the perfume he bought her, the ghost of a burning incense tree on his skin.

Before she left, she told him to wait half an hour before he followed so that no one would see them emerging together from the library. He didn't reply, only smiled and checked his watch in an obedient gesture. She nodded—the Magister Ludi back in charge—and left him to it. Now that he comes to think of it, it's funny she didn't insist that he leave first, instead of leaving him alone in the Biblioteca Ludi. Perhaps she trusts him. The thought brings another bubble of happiness into his throat. How absurd this all is. Someone he loved has come back from the dead. It's crazy. Everything he thought he knew has turned out to be a practical joke; the world has exploded with sparks and stars and fleshy exuberant flowers as though it's been touched by a god. Later he'll be furious with her for her deception—he can feel it already, a cloud gathering on the horizon—but for now it's all sunshine and springtime, sheer disbelief shot through with gold threads of happiness. Absolution. Ten years of guilt, gone. Now he can begin again. Forget politics, he'll go back to the *grand jeu*.

He sits up and starts to fasten his clothes. Twenty minutes to go. He's lost a cuff link and has to kneel and peer under the desk for a glint of gold. Red-gold with tiny rubies: one of Chryseïs's rare gifts, presented with such nonchalance he wondered if she'd stolen them from another man's bedside table. He hooks it out with a ruler, cocooned in a roll of dust. When he gets to his feet his head spins, not unpleasantly; it's as though he's had a couple of cocktails. What wouldn't he give for a martini and a cigarette? But the craving isn't unpleasant: it would make this moment perfect, that's all. He shoves his hands into his pockets and sits on the desk, letting his gaze wander around the room. You could spend a fortnight here, reading continuously, and hardly scratch the surface. Right now he can't imagine anything better. It's as if the *grand jeu*—it was practically his birthright, his first love—has come back to him at the same time as Carfax. He wants to write a game about resurrection. The phoenix. Fire. The ideas are flooding into his head. It makes him reach for the nearest sheet of paper and a pencil.

He pauses. The paper he's picked up is scrawled with notes. He recognizes the theme—an elaboration of the *Tempest*'s first motif—and the handwriting. It's been ten years since he last saw that writing, but he'd know it anywhere. It gives him a jolt of wordless pain followed by sudden euphoria, as his brain says, *dead, not dead*. Carfax's, Claire's. Has he really never seen her writing before? It seems crazy, when she's been helping him for months, but it's true. As he racks his brains, he realizes how careful she must have been not to let him see her own work, to let him make his own corrections. She wouldn't even fill in his diacritics for him. And suddenly he realizes why she took all those files from the archive. The handwriting, *her* handwriting—even on Léo's own fair copy, because she wrote in his diacritics for him, didn't she? She must have stolen them in case someone saw them and started to wonder . . . Surely she could have bluffed it out? But for a few seconds he has an inkling of what it must have been like for her, trying to erase every trace, constantly on guard. No wonder she wasn't pleased to see him.

But it's her own fault, isn't it? Why is he pitying her? It's not as if she cared that he thought Carfax was dead or that he blamed himself. She must have realized that he'd be devastated, but she never bothered to disillusion him. She even *blamed* him. Ten years of thinking he'd killed someone he loved! And she didn't even care . . .

He wants to shout at her. He wants to spend the rest of his life shouting at her. He wants to spend every moment marveling at how she's alive and can shout back at him. He wants them to argue until they kiss, embrace until they draw blood. He wants their bodies to get used to each other. What they did . . . It makes him tingle at the memory, but it was awkward, full of false starts and laughter, crossing back and forth between hesitation and desire. He wants to do it again, better. Again and again, better and better. He wants to lie beside her, letting the sweat cool on his skin, hearing her breathe. He can imagine her in his apartment: flicking a finger along the spines of his books, raising an eyebrow at the dust on the piano, narrowing her eyes at the voluptuous nude over the dinner table. In his mind's eye, she's wearing boyish clothes, her hair cut short and curling on the back of her neck—but *gamine,* not masculine, the slight curves of her body made even more enticing by her direct gaze, her assumption of equality. He grins at a sudden memory: he'd said, *You don't have friends, only enemies and inferiors,* and she'd retorted, dry as a bone, *At least we're not enemies, then.*

She could stay Magister Ludi and be his lover in the holidays. Surely the other magisters had mistresses. A few months a year wasn't enough, but it was better than nothing. Or . . . could he stay here? What if, after all, he *does* want to devote the rest of his life to the *grand jeu*? He doesn't care about anything else. He could be happy here, writing games and scholarly articles, planning research trips in the vacations that could take them anywhere in the world . . . Oh, yes, he'd be happy. Montverre is the only place he can be happy now. The word is ridiculous, unfamiliar.

The clock strikes. He's left it longer than he needed to.

He goes out into the corridor, adjusting his tie as he goes. He's whistling as he goes down the stairs, through the library, and along the passage to the magisters' corridor, taking the long way around to avoid the crowd still milling outside the Great Hall. When he steps into the little cloister under the clock tower, warmth hits him, full of the scent of earth and box. He tilts his face up to the sky, closing his eyes against the light. Dark circles spin in the orange glow behind his eyelids. Summer. He hasn't felt like this for years. He breaks into a little shuffle step, and for the first time he hears the melody he's whistling. It's the *Bridges of Königsberg*—but scumbled and jazzed up. The repetitive tune has broken free of its foundations, like the bridges themselves rearing up off their arches and lumbering into a better position; so that now, perhaps, you could cross them all, and end up where you want to be.

37

THE MAGISTER LUDI

She rinses her face. For a while, after she got to her room, she couldn't stop laughing: now she bends over the basin, breathing deeply, and washes the crusts of salt from under her eyes. Her skin is tight, and she doesn't need a mirror to know that her lips and eyelids are swollen. She rinses her mouth out. She waits until the water is still again and leans close. Would she see a difference if her reflection were clearer? She feels different: raw and tender and afraid. There's a heaviness inside her like menstrual cramps, but she doesn't resent it. A deeper ache pulses in the same place, when she thinks about Léo. "I'm reliably informed that the first time generally leaves something to be desired," he said afterward, "not that I'm making excuses"; and she said, smiling, "I hope there'll always be something left to be desired."

She splashes her forehead, undoes her hair, and runs wet hands through it. She wants to cut it all off. Maybe she could. Why not? If Léo didn't recognize her, then why would anyone else? He was the closest to her, after all; maybe she's been too careful all along. Maybe she can turn into Carfax again, under their very noses, and no one will ever realize, because that would mean admitting they were blind or stupid. She feels freer than she's ever been. Is this what happens when you finally tell someone the truth? Or when you're in love? She sweeps her arm through the air, scattering droplets in the sunlight like glass beads. It takes her by surprise and she does it again, wondering if she could use the movement in a *grand jeu*: what would that sense of abandon bring to a swell of melody or a main theme? She could spend hours playing on her own, experimenting with the new feeling in her body, this shell-cracked-open intensity. Happiness.

But she doesn't have time. She replaits her hair and pins it up again. It smells of Léo and the leather-salt scent of skin. She strips, wipes herself with a damp cloth, finds a clean shirt, and dresses again. No matter how she feels, she has to look respectable. Although . . . not *too* respectable. She moistens her collar and trickles some water down the front of her gown. With her flushed cheeks—and her hands, which are still trembling—she can convince them that she was taken ill. Temporarily, and not seriously.

She shuts her eyes. Her mind is whirling. She counts her heartbeats, trying to calm herself as if she's about to begin a *grand jeu*. She has to stop thinking about Léo, at least for a little while. She is Magister Ludi, and she has walked out of her first Midsummer Game; right now she needs to concentrate. She has lied for years, but it's never been as important as this.

Ninety-nine, a hundred. Her pulse is still much faster than it should be, but she doesn't have time to wait until it slows. She dabs a last handful of water along her hairline, lets it run down her temples, and goes out into the corridor. Outside in the courtyard, men are in scattered, uncertain groups, some smoking and chatting, others silent; she hurries past the windows, head down, her cheeks prickling with renewed heat. She came the long way from the Biblioteca Ludi to her room, through the servants' corridors and empty classrooms; there's no alternative route to the Magister Scholarium's office, but no one looks around, and as far as she knows, none of the visitors have noticed her. A servant passes, clutching a note, and in spite of herself she imagines the chaos in the kitchens, the Magister Domus shouting as the cooks struggle to get lunch ready two hours earlier than planned. Her fault. She's already walking fast, but she speeds up, almost running.

When she knocks, there's a pause before the Magister Scholarium says, "Who is it?"

She straightens her shoulders and raises her chin. Then she pushes the door open.

He's not alone. She stumbles, as though the shock of it is a solid block under her feet. She has to catch herself on the back of a chair, and then they're all staring at her, the Magister Scholarium and Émile and another man, thin and mustached and faintly familiar. Was he in the audience earlier?

The Magister Scholarium says, "Magister Dryden," and she can't decide if it's a warning or a question.

She says, "May I speak to you alone, Magister?"

"I'm afraid that Mr. Dettler, Mr. Fallon, and I are occupied."

"It won't take a moment. I have to explain."

"No need," Émile says. He is leaning back in his chair, his hands crossed on his belly. There's a pause. The Magister takes off his glasses and starts to clean them on his sleeve, while Dettler—is it?—coughs dryly into his handkerchief.

She hesitates, taken aback. Of course she needs to explain. They ought to be insisting on it. "I was taken ill."

"I do hope you're recovered," Émile says, "but we're having a rather important meeting."

"But—"

The Magister Scholarium sighs. "It doesn't matter, Claire."

She stares at him. He's still rubbing his glasses on his sleeve, without meeting her gaze.

"Perhaps, since Miss Dryden is here, it might be as well to . . . er . . ." Dettler gestures at the desk. There are papers piled there, a newspaper, letters. She catches a glimpse of familiar handwriting: Léo's. "As it happens, we were discussing today's unfortunate incident. In the context of . . . wider issues."

"I beg your pardon?" She hardly notices that he's called her *Miss* Dryden.

"Well. Er."

"It shouldn't come as a surprise," Émile says, "that the Ministry of Culture has concerns about the education of our finest minds. Today's fiasco has merely confirmed that they were justified. We simply cannot have the school brought into disrepute." His voice is smooth. She can remember how he played the *grand jeu*: slippery, somehow unctuous and perfunctory at the same time. She remembers imitating it for Léo until he cried with laughter; now she can't imagine laughing.

She says, "Are you speaking for the school or the Ministry?"

"I'm speaking for the Prime Minister," he says, and smiles at her.

The Magister Scholarium puts his glasses on, finally. "Magister Dryden," he says, "I'm afraid Mr. Dettler has been explaining the government's position. That is . . ."

Another silence. Her scalp is prickling. "I don't understand," she says. "The *government's* position?"

"The *grand jeu*," Dettler says, "is our national game. We should be proud of it. We should make sure that it thrives, under our oversight. We can't allow it to be stifled. Difficult decisions have to be made."

She looks at the Magister, waiting for a translation; then, when he doesn't answer, she looks at Émile. "The point is," Émile says easily, "that Montverre is in an extremely fragile position. Its future is very uncertain. We don't want to destroy the legacy of centuries of tradition, but we have to face facts. The school needs to be sustainable, to pull its weight economically, and to work together with the government to achieve our mutual goals."

"The school's only goal is the *grand jeu*."

"Well, you see, that's exactly the sort of unhelpful approach we need to reassess." He smiles at the far wall as if it's an old master.

She says, "What's going on? Magister?"

The Magister Scholarium coughs dryly and shuffles the papers on his desk, but he doesn't say anything. Émile's eyes slide back to her, and the smile is gone, as though she imagined it. "We have explained to the Magister Scholarium," he says, "that if the school expects the government's continued support, it must be prepared to work with, not against, us. That it must be prepared to make significant changes."

"Changes?"

The Magister Scholarium glances up at her and then away; his fingers are twitching. "We have to ask you to leave, Claire."

"For how long? Where to?"

Émile sighs. "No. To resign."

She waits for the world to become real again. Outside the window there are birds singing and the whisper of a breeze. Sunshine glints off the cap of the Magister's fountain pen, off Émile's rings, Dettler's tie-pin. Her robe hangs heavy on her; a drop of sweat trickles between her breasts. She was expecting to be chastised—humiliated, even—but not this. This is impossible.

"Claire, this is terribly difficult." The Magister Scholarium shifts in his seat and then gets to his feet, wincing a little. "You know that I've always supported you. But you can't deny that it hasn't been easy for anyone. And now this . . . Perhaps it would be for the best."

"Magisters are elected for life," she says. She can't get enough breath into her lungs. "I can't *resign*."

"You're right, that was the wrong word," Émile says. "But there were irregularities with your appointment, I believe. Outside interference. Under the circumstances, the Capitulum will agree that it should be annulled."

"I'm Magister Ludi." For the first time in her life, she hears the foreignness of the words.

"I'm afraid not. As it turns out, you won't ever have been."

She opens her mouth, but her throat has tightened so that she can't answer.

"I'm sorry, Claire." The Magister Scholarium's hand twitches, as though he wants to reach out to her. "I have no choice. For the good of Montverre . . . for the scholars . . . the game . . ." She stares at him. He has the grace to stammer, but he goes on. "It's desperately unfortunate, but if this is the sacrifice we must make . . ."

"You're sacrificing me," she says. "And in return you get . . . ?"

The Magister rubs his forehead, leaving red traces on the papery skin. Then he takes a step closer to her, turning his back on the other two men. "Claire," he says, and his voice is soft, as though they're alone. "You know they want to shut Montverre down. They've been trying for months, looking for an excuse. But they're being reasonable. They've agreed that if you go, we can stay here. That we can retain our exemptions. Otherwise . . . it's finished."

Dettler coughs.

"And why *me*?" But the answers to that are easy: because she's a woman, because it's easy, because walking out of her Midsummer Game has made it even easier. Because the Party membership will rub its hands and gloat. And because they can replace her with another Magister Ludi, one that the government will choose. It'll still be the end of Montverre; but a slower death. She says, "And what if I refuse?"

"You can't refuse," Dettler says abruptly, as though he's lost patience. "It's not your decision. We're not asking you, we're telling you." He adds to Émile, "I still think a completely fresh start in the capital—"

Émile raises a hand, and Dettler falls silent. "It will be to your advantage if you leave quietly," Émile says. "I want this done with the minimum of fuss. Please," he goes on, forestalling her, "this isn't a fight you can win. Even without today's display, we would have ample justification for your removal."

"What?"

"Seditious comments, professed hostility to our democratically elected government, evidence that you tried to corrupt the scholars under your care—"

"*Corrupt* them? What on earth?"

"A moment." He reaches toward the desk and pulls the pile of papers toward him. "You think the Party is made up of 'thugs and parasites,' is that correct? Not to mention suggesting that our esteemed Prime Minister is—ahem—a 'bigoted, bitter old man'? And I believe that you have consistently insisted on teaching Christian values. For example, did you—where was it? oh yes—ask your class to assess the influence of Palestrina on the development of the *grand jeu*?" He gives her a glintingly unsympathetic smile. "Men have faced imprisonment for less, you know."

"I have every right to—"

"Not when you are charged with educating impressionable young men. Not since the Unity Bill. Didn't you have a memorandum about that? And I won't even ask about aiding an undesirable to evade the police, which is a capital crime." She only just has time to realize he's talking about Simon Charpentier before he goes on. "Perhaps it would be best to bow out gracefully, my dear. Or things could become . . . complicated."

"You can't. This isn't—" But she stops. *Fair. Allowed. Right.* None of those words is an argument, any longer. "How did you . . . ? How *dare* you?"

Émile ruffles the papers, flicking each corner with his thumbnail. "Oh, well, you know," he says. "We have friends everywhere." He lowers his hands a little, tilting the pages so that she can see.

Léo's handwriting. *Dear Émile.*

She reaches out to take the letters; but when she has them in her hand, the words blur. If she is shocked, she doesn't feel it. It is inevitable, so obvious she should have known it all along. All these months Léo has been spying on her, in spite of his denials. This was only to be expected. He has always been a liar and an opportunist. She has always been a fool.

She passes the pages back to Émile. Her hand is entirely steady. She says, "I see. Thank you." Then she turns and walks out, determined to be out of sight before she feels anything.

38

LÉO

He can't stay still. There's too much blood in his veins, too much electricity in the connections of his brain. He hears the clock strike above him. Surely explaining herself to the Magister Scholarium can't take this long; surely she'll come soon? Unless she doesn't *want* to see him. The possibility makes him cringe inside. If, after all, he said something wrong, if she's having second thoughts . . . But he only has to close his eyes to see her face, dazed and radiant, as open as a clear sky: she loves him, she's always loved him. It gives him a shiver of happiness and disbelief. He was so arrogant ten years ago to take it as his due, to think it was a game that he'd won. Now he feels incredulous. She loves him.

But where is she? He wants to go and look for her, but he's afraid that they'll miss each other. It's absurd to agonize like this, he'll see her soon, but he can't wait. He paces from the window to the wall and back again.

Footsteps come up the stairs. He leaps toward the door and opens it. "At last," he says, "I've been waiting."

It's Émile. He smiles widely and steps inside. "Have you?" he says, with a smoothness that doesn't give anything away. "How clever of you."

"Émile." His heart sinks.

Émile shuts the door. "I hope you're recovered," he says. "After your . . . what was it? A brainstorm? Bilious attack? The runs?"

"It wasn't serious."

"No," Émile says, "I didn't imagine that it was." That smile is still on his face, as if they're sharing a joke. He saunters over to Léo's desk and leans against it, surveying the piles of books, cigarettes, and chocolates. "I must congratulate you. I never considered such a direct form of sabotage."

"It wasn't sabotage." He tries to summon the memory of that giddy moment when he found himself on his feet. Had he meant to stop her? Well, yes, but only because he thought she'd plagiarized Carfax's game, not for any other reason. Certainly not to please Émile, and yet Émile is looking at him as if that's exactly what he thinks. "Look," Léo says, "you've got the wrong end of the stick. I felt ill, that's all."

Émile laughs. For once, it sounds as if he's genuinely amused. "Really?" he says. "Not sabotage? The way you substituted Carfax's game by mistake, I suppose."

He blinks. How does Émile know that? Did he piece it together from overheard snippets at the time, or from something Carfax said, or from Léo himself? Or is it simply that these days it's Émile's business to know things? It doesn't matter. "Yes," he says, "that was a mistake, too," and there's hardly a hitch in his voice. "I have every respect for the Magister Ludi. I would never try to undermine her. It was a . . . misunderstanding."

Émile narrows his eyes, his smile fading. "I don't follow," he says. "You must know it's precisely what we needed."

"That's not . . ." He fumbles for a cigarette packet and pulls one out. Where is Claire? Why hasn't she come? He doesn't want to think about the moment when she turned away and left the Great Hall. Something in Émile's expression makes him remember a row of men on the back bench, balancing programs and notebooks, scribbling furiously; when he ran past them, they were craning to look, their eyes gleeful. "It's nothing. She was taken ill. Or rather—it's my fault."

"What are you talking about?" Émile holds out his lighter but he doesn't let go of it, so Léo has to twist it out of his grip.

He lights his cigarette, more deliberately than he needs to. He has to stop talking; nothing he can say will make a difference. He humiliated Claire, and it doesn't matter why. Oh, if only he'd known, if only he hadn't . . . "Never mind," he says. "What do you want?"

"I came to give you some good news."

He doesn't want to ask. He turns to the window and stares out without taking in what he's seeing. For a second he thinks he hears footsteps—is it Claire? Surely this time—but as he turns his head Émile starts to speak again.

"I know you're sentimental about this place," Émile says. "You'll be pleased to hear that it's staying as it is. Dettler had grand plans—a school in the capital, a whole new institution—but I always thought it was more trouble than it was worth. Far better to keep it here, with its august traditions and so on. There'll be a few minor changes to the financial structures, perhaps. A bit more quid pro quo . . . But the Old Man doesn't want to see Montverre dismantled."

Léo stares at him. *A school in the capital.* Was that what Pirène was hinting at, at New Year? The thought makes him shudder. If he'd only known . . . At last he says, "You're leaving us alone?"

Émile raises his eyebrows at the word *us*, but he only nods.

Léo laughs. He turns away, because he doesn't want Émile to see his expression. Relief pools in his knees, his gut. He hadn't realized the damage he might have done. Of course Montverre is strong enough to weather a storm. A tempest. It isn't made of glass, after all. He forces himself to speak. "That is good news."

"I thought you'd like to hear it," Émile says, but he has a sly smile, as if he hasn't quite finished.

"I'm surprised. I thought you hated the place."

"Who says I don't? I'm happy for it to stay here, that's all."

"I see. Good." A silence. Léo steps round Émile, toward the door, to listen. No footsteps. He must have been imagining it. All the same, he wants to get rid of Émile; she'll come soon . . . "Well," he says, "thanks, but if that's all—"

"One other thing," Émile says. His smile widens. "We're appointing you Magister Ludi."

He must have misheard. *Assistant to,* perhaps—or magister of something else, maybe they're creating a post for him, who knows why? He swallows. "What?"

Émile laughs softly. "You're the new Magister Ludi. Congratulations."

"But there's . . . Claire—Magister Dryden."

"There were irregularities with her appointment. You may remember that the short list was badly managed. The school will issue a full apology, of course, to everyone involved."

"You're getting rid of her?"

"I don't think anyone will protest, after this morning's embarrassment. It came at the perfect moment to demonstrate her inadequacy. Couldn't have fallen better." Émile adds with a glint, "*Not* that it was sabotage on your part, of course." Silence. He turns his hand over in a graceful gesture, almost a contrevure. "I should hope you're pleased."

Léo remembers Pirène's advice before an important session in the House: keep breathing. "What will happen to her?"

"She has agreed not to make a fuss. For the sake of the greater good."

There's a sharp, hot pain in Léo's fingers. He's let his cigarette burn right down. He flicks it aside, shaking the sting from his knuckles. "And I'll replace her. Does she know that?"

"Not yet."

"Why? Why me? There must be others."

"Don't be so modest. You've proved yourself over the last few months. First your letters, then this morning . . . I've spoken to the

Old Man, and he's prepared to overlook your previous aberration. It's worth a lot to us to have someone here we can rely on. Help us implement the changes." A pause. "Aren't you going to say thank you?"

"What makes you think you can trust me?"

"Léo, we're making you Magister Ludi. The least you can do is accept with some fucking grace."

As if he doesn't have a choice. He inhales slowly. He says, "Magister Ludi," not meaning anything, simply putting the words into the air as if he's never heard them before. The room is so still that every sound is clear: outside, a bird takes to flight with a clatter of wings, a breeze rattles the window, footsteps scrape suddenly on stone, fade to nothing down the stairs. He can't think straight. Magister Ludi.

After everything, he could be Magister Ludi. He stares ahead of him, past Émile, as if his younger self is standing in the corner of the room. His pulse thuds uncomfortably in his temples. It was what he dreamed of for two whole years. The life he thought he'd have—that he should have had. Not a politician; a *grand jeu* player. Finally living up to his early promise. The youngest ever Gold Medalist.

He remembers abruptly the moment when he knew he'd won the Gold Medal. His name on the noticeboard. *Léonard Martin, Gold Medalist,* Reflections. He'd always told himself that he didn't care, that he didn't even pause, only scanned the rest of the names for Carfax's, but that wasn't true, was it? It would have been inhuman not to feel his heart leap. For a split second he was the happiest he'd ever been, full of fierce delight and triumph. He'd done it. And when his gaze slid down the list, did he care, would he have swapped his success for Carfax's? No. Yes. He didn't *want* Carfax to fail, of course he didn't, he genuinely submitted *Red* because it was brilliant . . . but was there a pulse of satisfaction, even a tiny one, when he saw?

If there was, does it matter? He would have given his Gold Medal up like a shot. If he'd had the choice. But he didn't. He hadn't done it deliberately, but he couldn't stop himself *wanting* to win the Gold Medal.

And he wants to be Magister Ludi. He does. He shuts his eyes, and for a moment he's in the Great Hall, standing in the middle of the *terra*, and the tense avid silence is for him.

It could happen. He doesn't even have to do anything.

He opens his eyes.

"No," he says.

Émile opens his mouth and hesitates. "Why not?" he says at last.

"Because you have no right to offer it to me."

Émile makes a fussy little gesture, as if he's plucking invisible strings. "Really, my dear chap," he says, "why so squeamish? You've done it before, after all. Pushed a de Courcy aside to get ahead. I don't—oh, I *see*." He chuckles. "That's it, is it? It wasn't your fault, Léo. He did himself in because he was weak. If he couldn't handle failure, he shouldn't have been here." He shakes his head. "It's a game, Léo. Some people win, some people lose. Don't let guilt stand in your way."

"It isn't guilt. The Magister Ludi—"

"Do you remember when a servant threw herself off the Square Tower?" he asks, cutting Léo off. "In our second year. It must have been about the time Carfax cut his throat, as I recall."

"What has that got to do with this?"

"I knew her a little. Actually quite well. We had a few nice times together. Then she told me she was pregnant. Obviously it wasn't my problem, and frankly I doubt I was the only one, but—well. At the time, I felt to blame. But the point is, she would have done it anyway. It wasn't my responsibility. I could have let it ruin my life. But I didn't. That's our way, isn't it? We have to be strong enough not to be dragged down."

Léo clenches his jaw. Émile is so matter-of-fact: as if this is something they have in common, having driven someone to suicide. With a sudden incredulous relief he remembers that Carfax didn't die—or rather, that it wasn't *his* Carfax and not his fault. For a fraction of a second he almost tells Émile the truth. "That's not why," he says instead. "It's got nothing to do with Carfax."

"Then why are you being so . . ." Émile stops. "Oh," he says, rolling his eyes, "please tell me it isn't *that*."

"What?"

"Claire Dryden? Really? My dear boy, I thought your taste had improved since Carfax. But I suppose . . . each to their own. Does the de Courcy blood hold some particular attraction?"

Léo wants to hit him. "I don't want to fuck the Magister Ludi," he says, "and I don't want to *be* the Magister Ludi, either. Now will you go, please?"

There's a pause. A veil of smoke hangs in the dead air. Faint voices rise from somewhere below, laughing as though it's a normal day. Émile stands up straight and brushes a speck of dust from his sleeve. "You're doing yourself an enormous disservice."

Léo doesn't answer. It's true, of course.

"If you don't want to be Magister Ludi, someone else will."

He shrugs.

"You idiot," Émile says. "You're throwing away the greatest opportunity of your life for nothing."

"Not for nothing."

"You want to commit political suicide? I can't help you if you do."

"I'm not asking you to."

"Stop being such a prig, Léo." Émile steps toward him. His cheeks are blotchy, and his hands in his pockets are pulling the fabric taut. "You'll do the fucking job and be grateful."

"Why do you care so much?" But as soon as he says it, he knows the answer. Because Émile has told everyone in the Ministry—and the Chancellor, the Old Man, and everyone else—that he's the one who can manage Léo. He thinks Léo will be tractable and naive—or that he's already so unscrupulous that he'd sabotage Claire's game without a second thought, out of self-interest. Émile thinks that this arrangement will give him control of Montverre. The *grand jeu* itself. How long has he been machinating for this? And perhaps it never even occurred to him that Léo might refuse. "No," Léo says before Émile can answer. "I'm not doing it."

"Yes, you are."

"You can't make me," he says, and almost wants to laugh. They're two grown men, for pity's sake.

Émile takes a deep breath; it seems to last forever. Then he crosses to the window. The color in his face has spread to his chin and his jowls, but when he speaks, his voice is softer. "Simon Charpentier," he says. "Someone helped him evade the police. It doesn't matter," he continues, raising his hand. "I don't care whether you helped him or not. If I say it was you, it was you. Your girlfriend was a Christian, wasn't she?"

"Émile—"

"Hasn't being here taught you anything at all? I can destroy you. You wouldn't even face trial unless I wanted you to. If I give the word, you'll disappear. An accident, a suicide, a brief illness. No one will care."

He feels his head spin. It's like looking down and seeing cracks spread out under his feet, branching farther and farther until nothing is solid.

"And there's your mother, of course. I'd hate for her to be put under any . . . pressure." Émile taps gently on the window, as if he's testing its strength. "Or perhaps . . . it would be a shame if Magister Dryden's temperament turned out to be as fragile as her brother's."

"Fuck you," Léo says. It's like a sudden draft of oxygen, to be angry: it gives him a rush of energy, leaving no room in his body for fear. "I don't care what you do."

"Really?"

"If being here *has* taught me anything, it's that I don't care anymore. The Party can fuck itself. The Old Man can go and fuck himself, too." He's running out of breath, but the words keep coming. "I've had enough of them. And you. I'm not your creature. I'm not doing what you want. So do your worst."

Émile looks at him, his eyes very level. They're enemies now; with a distant sense of shock, Léo wonders if they always were. "Oh, I will," he says. "By all means. And with pleasure."

Léo walks to the door and opens it. He holds Émile's gaze and waits.

Émile nods. He moves to the door, passing closer to Léo than he needs to. He pauses, his face a hand's breadth from Léo's. "Goodbye, traitor," he says, and smiles.

39

THE RAT

After the black ones leave, the corridors should be quiet. But this year there are people, new people, chattering and rustling like termites, spilling into the courtyards and wandering at night. They aren't black .or gray or white ones, they are brown and green and stone-colored. They murmur. They get lost; once, catching sight of her at the far end of a narrow gallery, one called out to ask her where the lavatories were. He had glasses that glinted moonlight; when she froze, he took them off and peered at her. She ran away and he didn't follow, but that feeling of visibility stuck to her skin like grime. He thought she was human. She's not human.

She doesn't know what to do. A rat would eat when it was hungry, rest when it was tired, shit and scratch and yawn without thinking. But the world has changed. She can't stop wondering about Simon, and whether he's still alive and huddled in the room under the eaves; and about the dark-headed dangerous one, the one she recognized. They lurk at opposite ends of her mind, so whichever way she looks, she is afraid. She tells herself that soon they will be gone and it will be quiet again: the long, quiet, lonely summer, when the gray ones lock doors and cover furniture in white sheets. When the building is empty, her head will be, too.

Then there is a morning when the bell rings on and on. It isn't an alarm. Although it's daylight she creeps out to look. More men than she's ever seen are crowded in the courtyard; slowly they clump and ooze through the doorway to the Great Hall, until there are hardly any left. Black shiny vehicles arrive purring and spit out some more. These new ones are fatter and smoother. They bray and gesticulate as they follow the others. Finally a single straggler hurries across the black-and-white and disappears after them. Not long afterward the bell stops chiming. She imagines them in rows on the benches, surrounding that silver-edged panel of stone. But there is no way of knowing why or what they are trying to achieve. She waits, hunched in the warmth of a windowsill, but the door is closed. Whatever arcane human mystery takes place in that hall, she is shut out. Dust swirls in the courtyard. Nothing else moves.

She goes back to her nest. Sometime later there is a stormy feeling in the air, sounds of confusion and men's voices, things having gone out of joint. She lets them wash into her ears and away again like a tide. Later still she emerges, turning her head from side to side as if she can hear someone calling. No one is calling. Nevertheless she finds herself creeping out into the open. She has food and water in her nest—the kitchens were well stocked, so she took as much as she could, enough to be able to hide for days—but she can't stay there. It is too like being small again, watching the roof inch down toward her open eyes. Is that how Simon feels? It gives her a strange, seasick feeling to wonder what he's thinking, as if she's spilling out of her body. Like poison.

A rat wouldn't take the risk. But she keeps moving. And although she takes a roundabout route, she gets closer and closer to the room under the eaves. Her mind is blank; she doesn't have a plan or even an intention. She wants to see Simon, that's all.

And then she rounds a corner and the fat dark-haired man is standing there. She turns to stone, except for her heart. She is safe in the bars of light and shadow, camouflaged by a cage of moonlight. In a moment he will look away and she will run.

Then he speaks. He says, "Simon Charpentier. Yes?"

A split second. A wave of vertigo goes through her as though he might be addressing her. No. But for the first time she feels the absence of her own name. She isn't Simon, but who is she? Her mother's voice: *darling, sweetheart*. But those aren't names. She has time to feel a kind of human, unfamiliar panic. What injury is this, that she hasn't noticed before?

Another voice answers.

"I—yes. Who are you?"

Simon. He's there, at the far end of the passage. His voice is thin and hoarse, as though his windpipe has begun to corrode. He steps into a patch of light. He is shaking and pale; his shirt is spattered with bile-colored flecks. What is he doing here? He should be hidden. She wants to call out to him, to warn him: the only clever thing is to run. But he won't.

"You know people thought you'd got lost in the mountains?" The man leans his elbow on the banister and looks at him sideways. "Where have you been lurking? I suppose someone's been helping you. Bringing you food and so on."

"I've been . . . I found some. Enough."

"Ah, I thought Léo Martin was taking an interest. Or was it Magister Dryden?"

"No." His croak barely reaches the Rat's ears. Run, she wants to say, *run*.

The man smiles. "In any case," he says, "I'm glad I've finally tracked you down. How about we get you to the infirmary? No offense, but you don't look like you're in tip-top condition."

"What?"

"You can't go on like this, Simon, can you? Now don't worry, I'm not going to get the police involved. They're thugs. I understand why you wanted to avoid them." He chuckles, and the Rat's lips curl away from her teeth. "Let's get you checked over, and then we'll see what we can do to get you home."

"I can't."

"Ah yes, your papers. That's all sorted out." He laughs, extends his hand to Simon, white fingers like maggots in the moonlight. The Rat wants to bite them off. Surely Simon won't be foolish enough to trust him? "Come on, old chap. It's all right now. Think of me as a Good Samaritan."

Simon's eyes are wide. He shifts from foot to foot. He looks like a child.

An ache sweeps from the Rat's feet to her gut and into her throat. This is her fault. She should have helped him. If she had done more, he wouldn't be standing there, hovering on the edge of danger. The fat man with yellow teeth is going to eat him alive. She should have given in sooner to the silent call in her head. *Should have. Her fault.* No rat would think like this, but she can't stop herself.

"Come on, then." The man clicks his fingers. "So when did Léo Martin spot you? Bit of a coldhearted bastard, isn't he, to let you struggle like this?" Somewhere—beyond human hearing—the Rat hears the faint soft sound of a trap being set.

"He promised to help. He said he'd get me some more papers," Simon says. "He was the one who told me not to go with the police."

"Oh?" The man grins. "It was Martin, then. Splendid." The invisible trap snicks shut. Then he reaches out. His plump pale fingers are alert, thirsty.

She doesn't mean to move. A rat wouldn't move. But it's as though the floor collapses under her feet, and the only way not to fall is to throw herself forward. She stands between Simon and the fat man, breathless, exposed.

There's a silence. She has her back to Simon, but she can feel him staring. She wills him to take the opportunity to run away, but he doesn't.

"My word," the man says, and he laughs. It's a bubbling spasm of laughter, full of bravado. "I *thought* I saw you . . . You survived this long, did you?"

She doesn't move. She doesn't want him to touch her with those maggoty fingers, but she won't get out of the way. She lets him look at her, even though every rat-instinct is screeching in her ears.

"Ha!" He wipes his mouth on his sleeve. When he speaks again it has a grating, jocular note. "I must say, if you had a bit more flesh on your bones you'd be the spitting image of your mother. And a bony thing like you won't have to worry about taking precautions . . . If someone gave you a going-over with a scrubbing brush, I wouldn't say no."

She hears Simon draw in his breath. She's glad. It's the sound of him realizing that he's in danger.

"Get out of my way," the man says. "Get . . . *out* . . . of . . . the . . . way."

She swings around. She grabs at Simon—whiff of vomit and empty-stomach-sour breath—and pushes him ahead of her. He gasps and staggers and she slams her hands into his back, driving him onward. At the bottom of the stairs he starts to stumble upward, but that leads to his lair and a dead end. It's not safe anymore. She grabs the back of his clothes in her fists and drags him back down and along. He makes a sound of protest, but she ignores it. Why is he so stupid? He's saying something now, but she doesn't stop to listen. Behind them the fat man is laughing.

It's hard to keep them both moving. She shoves Simon sideways and through an archway. She isn't thinking clearly. Panic flares, exploding in bright colors as she fights for breath, catching at her heels. A rat would know where to go, but she has left her rat self in the fat man's hands and now she is cloudy-headed and helpless. They climb a winding staircase, up and up and up, and the bright blood-flowers in her vision are blinding her. Another step, another breath. The man is gaining on them. She swerves to one side, through a little door and a dusty felt curtain, and beside her—she can't keep him in front— Simon trips and fumbles in the dark. Her arms ache as she steers him past her. Another staircase, a stone spiral that leads up and up with no exit. A trap. She should have known better. There is nothing to do but keep going and hope.

They pass a narrow window. At their backs, there's heavy breathing and the clip of leather soles on stone. And then, abruptly, they come out into the open air. The flat roof is bare, surrounded by low battlemented walls. Simon bends over, puts his hands on his knees, and stares at her, panting.

"What are we doing here?"

She stares back. And then the fat man appears in the doorway. His cheeks are shiny with sweat. The sly good humor has left his face; now his eyes are like needles.

"You little wretches," the man says, breathless. "Charpentier, come with me now. And as for *you* . . ."

"No." Simon's voice is faint. "Leave me alone. I'm not hurting anybody."

"Conspiracy to conceal a registered dissident, procurement of false papers, obstruction of police duty. Do you want to go to prison for that? Or shall we put Léo Martin there instead? Your choice."

Simon shakes his head. He glances at the Rat and away again, a tiny movement. It's an appeal for help. But what can she do? She feels the burn of failure in her lungs and eyes.

"You'd rather go yourself? You'll change your mind. Be a good chap now and do what you're told."

Simon clenches his fists. A gust of wind catches his shirt and presses it against him, showing his bones. She knows he is trying to be brave. He knows he's in danger, but he is trying to be good. *Whatever you do, darling, you must not.* Then she looks at the fat man and she can see how he was, when Mam—when—before . . . Avid. Malicious. There are too many things in her mind now, too many things that aren't real, aren't here. She rubs her eyes.

The man sighs. Simon takes a step back, into the wall. There is nowhere left for him to go.

"My goodness, you are pathetic," he says. "The sooner we get rid of you, the better. You lot—you're like *rats*."

He reaches for Simon's arm. His hand opens like a jaw.

She puts her head down and charges at him. Her whole weight is in the impact. His body is warm and solid. He spits bitter air into her face. His arms flail and grab at her shoulders. She pushes, ramming her shoulder into his ribs. He is a door, a wall, a prison. A trap. It is his fault Mam is dead and now he wants to hurt Simon, too. He drags at her hair, trying to wrestle her away. Her scalp burns.

She punches him. He staggers, stumbles against the low part of the battlement, clutches too late at the stone, and falls.

It's very quick. One moment he's there, with chaotic hands, loud breath, a not-yet-a-scream; then he's gone. The silence swallows him with a gulp.

Simon is staring at her. A rat would stare back, but suddenly she can't hold his gaze. She turns away. Her heart is beating too hard. She feels sick.

She's killed someone. Not for food. Not even because she was in danger. Because of a feeling, because of how she felt when she looked at Simon and imagined him hurt, because of what the man did to Mam all that time ago. She is a murderer. It is a funny word, a word she has never used. Rats can't be murderers. This must make her human. She looks down in spite of herself. A body. Blood on the tiles. Broken arms like wings.

"Did you . . . ?" Simon's voice wobbles. He is clinging to the wall, hands flat against it as though he wants to get as far away from her as possible. He swallows, hesitates. Then he says, "Thank you."

She can't bear it. Something closes dull teeth around her larynx. She runs away from him. All the way back to her nest she feels the way he looked at her, like a wound.

40

THE MAGISTER LUDI

The sunrise is glorious and bloody. It blazes across the sky, streaks and streamers of cloud in shades of scarlet and crimson, although the sun itself is still hidden behind the mountain. The Magister is awake to see it, standing by the window, her eyes stinging. She is in her classroom, staring out of the single window opposite the Magister's dais. From here you can see across the valley; the village is hidden by the slope, but she can catch a glimpse of the railway line, the metal reflecting the red sky like a thread of fire. Soon she will be on the train. On the train, and then . . . but her mind is a blank, as though the world simply stops beyond Montverre village. Where will she go? To Aunt Frances? But overseas travel is tricky; it will take weeks to get a permit. Thank goodness she has enough money to live on. That's something.

She turns to face her desk. No, not her desk. The Magister's desk. Soon to be Léo's desk.

She doesn't want to imagine him in her place. But it's so easy. He'll be confident, casual; he'll make the scholars laugh, they'll respect him. They'll talk in undertones about his political career and the sacrifices he made for the *grand jeu*. She takes a deep breath. She has been crying all night; she's tired. She doesn't want another wave of fury or loss to catch her by the throat. She doesn't want to think about what Léo's done.

Did he know, when he called her *my love*? Did he know that the letters he'd written would be used to get her out of the way? He must have: he knew he'd written them, he knew what they said. He was a spy, all along. So when he held her, when he said *Carfax* and corrected himself, when he offered her the rest of his life, laughing and tender and avid all at once . . . When she let him fuck her on the floor of the Biblioteca Ludi. He knew. Everything he's done has been to get the better of her. The humiliation is so strong she feels nauseous.

Ten years ago she stood at the front of this room and parodied Léo's game style. She can remember the heady, fierce pleasure of it, seasoned with a piquant pinch of shame. Is that how he felt today, when Émile told him he could be Magister Ludi? He's won on every count. Again.

There's a noise outside. It's an alarm, but not the clanging handbells that warn of fire. It's more like the cacophonous electric bell of a police car. She goes to the door and hesitates. She must be a mess: swollen eyes, sticky cheeks, straggling hair that's half in and half out of its plait. She hasn't washed or brushed her teeth. Part of her wants to show herself as she is, but they'd think it was shame, not defiance. So she rinses her face and neatens her hair before she steps into the corridor and goes to the window.

From here she can see out over the courtyard. There are porters and gray-clad servants grouped around something in the far corner, at the foot of the Square Tower. Someone hurries toward them in shirt and trousers, and with a shock she sees it's the Magister Domus, without his robe, unshaven, his hair uncombed. Another servant is trailing in his wake. He calls out something and the porter nods, replies, and shoos some of the servants away.

A police van drives into the courtyard. The bell stops as the policemen get out. The group spread out, leaving space for the police to get through, and at last she sees what it is they were staring at.

A body. Black and white and red. Like a joke, she thinks. In fact, there is something clownish about it: the fat man with his skewed legs, his intact face looking up in surprise. It's Émile. Or rather, it was.

She stares at the open eyes and sagging jowls, feeling nothing. She pulls back from the window as a policeman looks around, his hands on his hips. By the time she peers out again, the body has been covered up and the other policeman is talking to the Magister Domus, their heads close together. More and more people are stepping out into the court; a few seconds later the Magister Domus turns, his eyes wide, distracted by the growing crowd. A man in a greenish suit pushes a graying academician out of his way and strides across. He says something to the policeman, and all at once the police are chivvying everyone away, barking out orders. She recognizes him as he turns: it's Dettler. He looks wan and panicky, but no one questions his authority, not even the Magister Domus. Hardly any time seems to pass before it's only the policemen, the porters, and Dettler left by the body, while the Magister hovers by the police van, reluctant to admit he's been dismissed. There seems to be some kind of argument going on, but when the policeman takes a camera out of the van, Dettler stoops to help flick the sheet aside from the body, brisk and relieved. There are four or five flashes, just bright enough to make a difference in the growing morning light. Then the two policemen put the body on a stretcher and load it into the van.

They pause for a few final words with Dettler. Then the van drives out of the courtyard, leaving nothing but petrol fumes dispersing quickly in the clear morning air. There is a smear on the tiles where Émile lay; it looks brownish, dirty. Dettler is staring at it. He jerks his head away as if he's trying to break his train of thought and says something to the Magister. Or perhaps it's intended for the porters, who swap a glance and hurry away. A few moments later Dettler and the Magister move across the court, toward the Magisters' Entrance, and out of sight.

She's at a loss: even the smallest decision of whether to sit down or stay on her feet seems beyond her. Last night she wanted Émile dead. When she went to confront Léo yesterday—after she'd sat in the courtyard, trying to gather her thoughts—she heard Émile's voice, and it stopped her in her tracks. Until he said, *We're making you Magister Ludi* . . . and she couldn't bear to listen anymore. When she stumbled down the stairs again, she would have killed him with a click of her fingers, if she could have. She should have been pleased to see him spread out on the tiles, bleeding. But now it's real, and he's *dead* . . . And now there will be police asking questions. When Aimé died, there was an inspector who looked at her sidelong and asked questions about where she'd been. She was lucky that it was so clear what had happened, that people had seen her arrive at the railway station—and lucky, too, that Aimé's telegram had been addressed to *DE COURCY*, with no forename. She'd changed into a dress on the train—a little crumpled from being hidden under her mattress all term—and no one guessed that she hadn't been with Aunt Frances, no one checked her ticket. Otherwise it might have been awkward. She was too tired and numb to be frightened; it was only later that she had nightmares about imprisonment and nooses and being naked in front of a mob. This time . . . She doesn't have an alibi for last night. She couldn't bear to be in her room or in the Biblioteca Ludi; she was here all night, where Léo wouldn't find her.

She has to get away. Run. Catch a train today. There's nothing to stay for. No job, no *grand jeu,* no friends among the magisters. Simon Charpentier probably left long ago.

She hurries down the stairs and along the passage toward the magisters' corridor. She turns the corner and Léo is outside her room, on the floor, his knees up. He sees her and scrambles to his feet.

They look at each other. There is nothing to say.

She steps around him and opens the door. He follows her in, but she ignores him and goes up the stairs. She fills a haversack with trousers and shirts, pajamas, underwear, her washing gear. When she looks up, Léo is sitting on the bed, almost within touching distance.

"Were you going to say goodbye?" he says.

She swings around to stare at him. He looks back at her as though she's the one in the wrong.

"I don't owe you anything," she says.

"Not even a goodbye? Tell me I won't hear about your death in a couple of days, at least." It's a joke, and not a joke. Unbelievably, after everything he's done, he sounds *hurt.*

She wants to pick up her bag and fling it at him. Instead she looks around. She could take a few of her books, but which ones? To go from whole libraries full, to two or three . . . Better not to take any. As she turns, Léo catches hold of her wrist.

"I heard they're sacking you," he says. "It's not fair. But don't blame me."

She jerks away from him. "*What?*"

"I could come with you. Wherever you're going. They're bastards, but now you're free, and . . . I was serious about . . . Please, Claire. Let's leave now, together."

Of everything he could have said . . . She presses her fingers against her eyelids. She doesn't know where to start. If only she weren't so tired. "You're crazy."

"Possibly. Yes. Does it matter?"

She drops her hands and opens her eyes. "You really think I'd go anywhere with you?"

He frowns. "Why not?"

"Because . . ." How can he ask? Why should she even bother to answer? "Leave me alone, Léo. I mean it. Leave." He doesn't move. She has to resist the urge to kick his legs out of the way. She wants to see him flinch.

"Why are you so angry with me?"

She doesn't know where to start. What does he want? A list of all the ways in which he's destroyed her life? The cheek of it, to turn up and demand that *she* explain . . . But when she looks at him, there is a flicker of something in his face that—for a second, a split second—makes her certainty waver. He really doesn't know that she knows.

It would be something—the only victory left to her—if at least he understood. She wants to see his self-love shaken to the foundations; his conviction that he is a reasonable, upstanding human being shattered. If only—for once—he could see himself through her eyes.

She says, "I thought you'd changed since we were scholars. Yesterday I thought . . . I'm a fool, to fall for the same thing again. I thought you were sorry, that you understood, that you loved me. But you've done exactly the same thing, haven't you? You betrayed me without even thinking twice. You'll always be that person, Léo. The one who only cares about winning and doesn't care how he does it. What's it to you, if you lie or cheat, as long as you get what you want?"

He catches his breath. "I didn't—"

"All this time you were spying on me. Writing to Émile about me, about my politics, stupid things I said that weren't meant to be repeated."

"Yes, I wrote him letters, but they weren't—I didn't mean—"

"And then you interrupt my Midsummer Game. Oh, you weren't *trying* to sabotage it. The way you submitted the *Red* game—that wasn't sabotage, either. Right? And then—" Her voice wobbles, threatening to let her down. "Then you sleep with me. *Then* I find out that I'm not Magister Ludi anymore—the only thing I've ever done, ever wanted." She stops, closing her mouth before she says something she can't call back. Or starts to cry again. She's had enough of that.

"I only heard yesterday—after you did. I promise."

"Don't," she says, and something in her voice shuts him up. "Don't promise. Please." There's a silence. Is he beginning to understand? At least he's paying attention. At least he can *see* her.

He's staring at his hands. Without looking up, he says, "The *Red* game was brilliant. I submitted it because it was better than anything I'd ever seen. I was sure you'd win the Gold Medal."

"Really?" She waits for him to meet her eyes, but he doesn't. He looks like a scholar, with hunched shoulders and bowed head. Not a magister; not even a grown-up. "Well," she says, "now you can award the Gold Medal to whomever you please. I expect the Capitulum will listen to *you*."

His chin jerks up. "What?"

"I overheard, yesterday. I came to find you, after they'd told me . . . But Émile was there. I *heard* him, Léo. You're the next Magister Ludi. My replacement. Finally you don't have to pretend. You've beaten me. Again. Congratulations."

"You heard?"

"Yes."

"Then . . ." He frowns.

"There's nothing left to say, Léo. I'm going. You're staying. I never want to see you again." She slings her rucksack on to one shoulder. Then she realizes she's still wearing her gown. She dumps the rucksack and pulls the heavy white cloth over her head. When she drops it in a heap at her feet she feels lighter, colder, naked. She picks up her bag again. It's time to say goodbye, but the word won't come.

"I said no." Léo reaches out, although he doesn't touch her. It isn't a *grand jeu* gesture, and yet it could be: an urgent transition, deliberately awkward, his fingers splayed. "I said no, Claire. I told Émile I wasn't doing it. I'm not going to be Magister Ludi. Didn't you hear that part?"

She looks at his fingers, stretching toward her, and the space between his skin and hers feels heavy, like before a storm.

"Did you hear what I said? I'm not replacing you. I turned him down. I told him he could find someone else." He follows her gaze and drops his hand. "He wasn't too happy. Suffice to say, I think I've ruined my chances of getting an Order of the Empire in the next year's Honors."

She doesn't move. She doesn't believe him. Yes, she does.

"I swear to you. Claire, I *said no.*"

Silence. She can hear him breathing.

At last she says, "Why? Don't you want to be Magister Ludi?"

She sees him wonder whether to lie. Then he takes a deep breath. "Of course I do," he says. "Of course. I've wanted it all my life. But there are other things I want more."

She nods slowly. "And now," she says, "you expect me to be grateful."

"No, that isn't . . . I never said that."

"It doesn't change anything. They sacked me because they could. And they *could* because of your letters. Émile threatened me, too. With evidence that you'd given him."

"I was naive—I never meant for those letters to be used like that. At all. I wasn't thinking when I wrote them."

"It doesn't matter, Léo. That's what I'm saying." She leans against the wall, so weary suddenly that she isn't sure her knees will hold her up. "You did one honorable thing and you think that makes everything all right. Love conquers all. But it doesn't. I've lost everything. Why should I care whether you've made a noble sacrifice?"

"I thought . . ." He has gone white. Whatever he says, he *did* think it would make everything all right; he thought that she would forgive him and they'd go off into the sunset, hand in hand. A quick, saccharine *fermeture,* a resolution on the major chord.

"You turned down something you wanted. What do you expect, a medal?"

"I did it for you."

"Then I'm sorry it was wasted."

He mutters, "You're very hard."

"I don't have any reason to be kind to you, Léo. That's what you think women should do, isn't it? Make you feel better. Help you live with your mistakes. Drop a veil over the mirror. Well, too bad. I don't have anything left to lose, so I can tell the truth."

"I thought the truth was that you loved me."

"The truth is that it's too late." She wasn't sure, before she said it, whether it *was* the truth; but the act of saying it seems to make it so. It sends a shiver of pain down her spine: dulled by fatigue, but unmistakable. It's also true that she loves him.

Léo says slowly, "I was afraid, so I gave Émile what he wanted. It was cowardly. But I didn't realize he'd use them to hurt you. Don't you believe me?"

In a way it's a relief that she doesn't have to decide, that it doesn't make a difference. "I'm leaving now," she says. "Goodbye, Léo."

She doesn't assume he will fight for her—doesn't want him to—but all the same it registers like a bruise when all he says is "Where are you going?"

"I'm not sure. The capital, probably. A hotel somewhere."

"Not back to your château to start a *grand jeu*?" For a second she doesn't know what he means, and then she remembers: a summer day, the cavernous space above the Great Hall, a moment when they might have touched. Her old fantasy terror, of Montverre in ruins—and her old arrogance, to think that, whatever happened, the *grand jeu* would be enough.

"I'm not twenty anymore," she says. "Neither of us is," and he winces. "And I sold the château."

"I see."

"Maybe I'll see you again."

"Maybe . . ." he says, and she doesn't know if he's agreeing or merely echoing what she's said. Now he looks old. He glances at her and perhaps he sees something in her face, because all of a sudden he straightens his shoulders and the spark comes back into his eyes. He says, faintly self-mocking, "I don't know what to do if I can't come with you."

She holds his gaze, determined not to speak. It isn't her problem to solve; it isn't fair to ask her to imagine how much it will hurt, later, to know that he might have been at her side.

"I'm still afraid," he says. After a moment he gives her a wry smile.

"I can't go back to politics, and even if I wanted to run my dad's old scrapyard business, someone else is looking after that now. It's going to be very empty . . . But not just that. After what I said to Émile, he's got it in for me. He threatened me and I told him to do his worst. I'll be lucky if I don't have to leave the country."

Doesn't he know? But perhaps he's been here all night, waiting, and the sound of the police bells didn't reach this corridor. "Émile's dead."

"What?"

"It looks as though he fell. They found his body this morning. The police came."

Léo's expression doesn't change, but she has the impression of things moving behind his eyes, like a whirlwind beyond a stone wall. "Are you sure?"

She doesn't bother to answer that. "Did you say those things to anyone else?"

"No," he says.

"So you haven't burnt your bridges," she says, and abruptly the theme of the *Bridges of Königsberg* asserts itself in her head, jaunty and smug and insoluble. She can remember how they laughed at it together, united in their dislike; how she used it to mimic the other scholars, and Léo begged her to stop, holding his sides. It brings a sudden ache into her throat, piercing and sharp-edged. After everything he's done, he's still the only person who's seen her like that.

She catches her breath. "Goodbye, then."

"Goodbye." He gets to his feet, stumbling slightly as though the floor isn't where he thought it would be. He leans toward her. But if she kisses him, she will never be able to leave. She steps back. It's not enough, though: she can't not look at him.

He holds her gaze. There is nothing on his face, no mask. If he can carry all of himself into a *grand jeu,* this is what it will look like. It takes her breath away.

He says, "I'm sorry."

"It doesn't matter."

"No. Listen." He raises his hand to cut her off, a quick short movement like a reversed stramazon. That sense of the *grand jeu* comes and goes at the edge of her mind, like the sound of the sea. He bites his lower lip and steps toward the window. "You're right. I was always jealous of you. Even when we were friends, I wanted to be better than you. I wanted to be more intelligent. I wanted the Gold Medal. When I submitted the *Red* game . . ." He draws in a breath. "It was brilliant. But I knew they might hate it. If you'd won, then I would have been glad. Honestly. But . . . I took the risk, knowing that it might go wrong. I never admitted it to myself, that part of me wanted to beat you. Wanted to see you fail. Because I did love you. I still love you. But I can't—get rid of . . ." He clenches his fist over his breastbone, as if he's dragging something out of his chest. "I'm sorry. I wanted to be the best. I did."

There's a silence. She wishes she didn't understand, but she does. This is the game they have always played, full of desire and hostility, reflections and shadows. At least now he's being honest.

"I never even met your brother," he says at last. "I'm sorry for your sake that he died. But to know you're alive, *you* . . . Even if you leave like this, even if I never see you again. It wasn't you that came back to life, it was me."

He smiles at her. She smiles back. She can feel the walls of regret and loss closing in: but for now they're in the space between them, still with room to breathe.

She says, "Be Magister Ludi."

"But—Claire."

"I'd rather it was you than anyone else," she says. "You'll be good at it. Better than me. And who knows? Maybe one day you'll be a better *grand jeu* player, too. As long as you stop trying to be so bloody clever."

"Thanks."

"I mean it, Léo. Stay here. Be a thorn in their sides. Write *grands jeux* that make people think you're a lunatic. Have the life you should have had."

"The life I should have had has you in it."

She reaches out for him and he comes to her arms so quickly it makes her stagger. He kisses her forehead and then without moving—so that she feels his voice vibrate in her skull—he says, "You don't have to leave."

She shakes her head. And he doesn't insist; when he bends to kiss her mouth she can tell that he understands, even if he doesn't want to. Of course she can't stay here, now she's been sacked. Even if she wanted to. There isn't room for both of them and the *grand jeu*; maybe there never was. Maybe there never will be.

She doesn't know how long they stay like that. The clock chimes. She pulls away, and he lets her go. "All right," he says.

"Yes." She reaches into her pocket for the keys to the Biblioteca Ludi and drops them on to the bed. "You'd better have these." She hesitates. "There are some things in there that belong to you already. Some games from the archive. Your diary. A letter I wrote you and never sent. You'll find them."

Slowly he bends and picks up the keys. She nods and swings her bag onto her shoulder. He follows her down the stairs into her study, but when she walks out into the corridor, his footsteps stop. She looks over her shoulder. He touches his forehead and his heart. It's a gesture that's half familiar and half strange, but she doesn't stop to think about what it means. It's only when she's hurried unseen along the passageways, through a servant's door and out onto the road, into the cover of the trees, that she gives herself time to pause; and then she wonders whether she's seen that move before somewhere, in a diagram or an old-fashioned illustration. It might be the *rendry*, the old gesture of surrender in an adversarial game, when one player concedes untimely defeat and truncates a game that might have gone on forever.

41

LÉO

He can't stay in the doorway, staring after her as though she's left some trace of herself behind. His head is spinning, full of Émile's death and Magister Ludi and Claire, her mouth and body and eyes. Claire, most of all. She loves him. She didn't say so, but that's what it meant: *be Magister Ludi.* Somehow she knows what he did and she loves him anyway; even though she's left him here, he's forgiven. But she's gone. He let her go. He doesn't know how he feels, except shaky and exhausted and adrenaline-drunk. He goes out into the corridor.

He cups her keys in his hand, feeling their weight. The Biblioteca Ludi. The thought of it is tinged with gold. He can still see her in the sunlight, eyes narrowed against the glare, her hair shining; he can still smell the scent of books and dust and their mingled sweat. At the moment the memory is half pleasure and half pain: the further away it gets, the more the balance will tilt.

Outside the window, servants are going to and fro. In the far corner of the courtyard, under the Square Tower, one of them is swabbing the tiles, spraying bright droplets of water as he swings the mophead out of the bucket. The Magister Domus hurries across the court, accosted by other gray-clad figures as he goes. Through the glass Léo can hear, not words, but the tone of his voice as he tries to wave them away: harried and impatient, with an undertone of resignation. There is too much

busyness, too much confusion; things are out of joint. After yesterday, the whole school is steeped in uncertainty. A broken Midsummer
Game and then Émile's death. There have been deaths here before—
Montverre is hundreds of years old—nonetheless he has the sense of
something unraveling. Émile, dead. He can't quite believe it. How did
it happen? *It looks as though he fell . . .* It doesn't matter, dead is dead.
But what happens now? Something is happening, but it's hard to tell
what. The servants come and go, crossing from shadow to shadow.
A few visiting academics are loitering in the doorway of the scholars'
tower, their heads together like pecking birds. Dettler emerges from
the refectory, flanked by Vouter and Guez. They light cigarettes.

Dettler looks around and raises his hand. Belatedly Léo realizes
that he's beckoning. His heart sinks; he's hardly slept, he can't concentrate, he doesn't want to speak to anyone but Claire. But he was a
politician for too long to snub a colleague lightly. He shoulders open
the door and crosses the court, wrapping his fingers tightly around
the keys in his pocket. "Good morning," he says, and nods to Vouter
and Guez.

"Bad business," Dettler says, jerking his thumb at the wet mopped
patch on the tiles. "You heard?"

"About Émile? Yes. Was it—" Belatedly he realizes what Dettler
means, and what it was that the servant must have been cleaning up.
So Émile fell from the Square Tower. It makes an uneasy spark leap
in his head as Émile's voice comes back to him: *at the time I felt to
blame . . .* It's a strange coincidence. A coincidence, because anything
else is absurd: Émile wasn't the type to be overtaken by remorse. He
says, "How did it happen?"

"No one really knows. A servant found his body this morning."
There's a slight movement from Vouter—just a sideways glance,
quickly quashed, but enough to make Dettler clear his throat and
add, "The police have been and gone, but there's no sign of foul play."

In spite of himself, Léo says, "Émile would hardly have—"

Dettler says, "This place is a deathtrap. Old buildings, not properly maintained, no decent lighting. If anything I'm amazed there haven't been *more* accidents."

Vouter's eyes slide to Léo and away again.

"It merely goes to show what I've always said," Dettler goes on more loudly. "We need a fresh start. Not some outdated monastery of a school, but a bright new future."

"But . . ." Léo looks up to the top of the Square Tower. The battlements aren't low enough to stumble over. Are they? "Do they think Émile was drunk?"

"The police were entirely in agreement that it was an accident." Dettler gives him a long look. "Best not to dwell on it. Which is not to say it's not a tragedy for us all."

Vouter coughs and Guez flicks a spent match onto the tiles. Nobody is looking at anybody else. And abruptly Léo understands. Dettler wants it hushed up as quickly as possible. No awkward questions. Which means . . . was it convenient or even deliberate? Léo's been afraid of a shove in the dark, a poisoned fruit, a greased step, but perhaps after all it's Émile who made too many enemies.

Tension grows between his shoulder blades. "Of course," he says. "It's a great loss for the Party." The shiny patch of damp on the tiles is beginning to evaporate. In another life, Émile would already be on the telephone to his office, with a few well-chosen words about Léo's future or summoning the police to conduct a thorough search for Charpentier. Instead, Léo can stand here with the others, and no one heard him say *fuck the Party*. Two lives saved, then. But mixed with the relief there's a tiny, treacherous hint of regret.

"Actually, Martin," Dettler says, "there's something I want to speak to you about." He holds out his arm to usher Léo away from the others. "The Old Man has always had a soft spot for you, you know, even though there was that hiccup last summer . . . What are your plans for the next few years?"

"I hadn't thought that far ahead," Léo says.

"How would you feel about being our new Magister Ludi? We're thinking an interim contract to start with—all these automatic jobs for life are a farce—but maybe longer, if it went well."

Here it is, his second chance; and now he has permission from Claire, he isn't betraying her. Léo looks up. Above the Square Tower, a ragged cloud is being blown across the sky. It creates the illusion that the building is tipping over. Wisps peel away from the bulging white underbelly and dissolve. "That's very unexpected. I've never considered . . ."

"Fallon suggested you. Said you'd be ideal. New school, new blood, new start. We'll be taking over the Cathedral buildings on the North Bank. Lovely place."

A beat. "I thought—that is, isn't Montverre staying—"

Dettler waves a dismissive hand. "I think after this we can make a very good case for new premises. Not to mention a new approach. There's been some debate, but I think this will sway any dissenters. They've agreed a temporary closure to let things calm down . . . Anyway, think about it. It would be good to have you back on board."

He imagines himself in a cannibalized church on the side of the river. Montverre, transplanted alongside the new polytechnics that line the boulevard: Geography, Engineering, Science, *Grand Jeu*. Scholars in smart suits with slicked-back hair, magisters in short gowns and trousers. But Magister Ludi, after all. Maybe that would be enough. "I'll certainly think about it," he says.

"Let's meet up in town, tomorrow or the day after."

"Of course." A movement—above, to the left—catches Léo's eye. There's an archivist leaning out of one of the tall library windows, reaching for the shutter. He swings it shut and latches it. A few moments later he moves to the next window. One by one he closes the shutters. Inside, the library must be growing darker as the sunlight is cut off. But then, there won't be anyone at the desks; no scholars, no visiting professors. Even the archivists will have shelved their ledgers and catalogues, packed the unsorted bequests away, and emptied their inkwells. All that's left for them to do is the final housekeeping: dust sheets, locking up the valuables, storm shutters. If Charpentier is still here, what will happen to him? A *temporary closure,* Dettler said. But no one will be fooled; Montverre has never been closed, not even during the influenza epidemic.

"Well . . . good," Dettler says; and then, with a little shrug, he moves away.

Léo watches until the last window is shuttered. He has always assumed that the biggest danger to Montverre was fire. Someone splashing oil everywhere and setting it alight, cackling, like Carfax's mad grandfather. One individual, one moment of crazy destruction. But it won't be like that at all. Its breath will stop when the last person leaves; after that, it'll be a slow death, so gradual that the moment of no return will come and go, unremarked and unobserved. A death by mold and mice and the passage of time. Not dramatic. There won't be a story to tell at the end of it, except of bureaucracy and inertia. And the battle somehow is lost, when Léo barely knew it had started.

He looks up. The tower is still tilting. A high note rings in his ears.

"Are you all right, Martin?" Guez is at his elbow.

He nods. The Magister Domus crosses the courtyard again, a piece of paper flapping in his hand, a servant gesticulating at his elbow. There's the sound of the old bus coughing up the hill; it'll come and go all day to collect the visitors. How long will it take, for the school to empty itself? He doesn't want to be here to see it.

He turns and strides toward the library. Guez says something, but he doesn't look back. The great oak door is still open, and he makes his way down the central aisle, past two librarians talking in low voices. There is enough light coming through the slats of the shutters for him to grope his way up the staircase and along the landing to the

Biblioteca Ludi, but when he opens the door the room is dazzling, like noon after dusk.

On Claire's desk—is it his desk, now?—there's a ledger, patterned like a riverbed, with an ink stain across its front. His old diary. So she had it all this time. He flips it open. As he skims the page he can remember the feel of the pen, the ache in his neck from long hours of study, the burn of sleepless nights. What it was like to be young.

A page falls out. *Dear Léo.* His heart thuds; but the paper is old, yellowing, the ink faded.

Dear Léo, I'm dead. Dear Léo, I'm not dead . . .
I think you never stopped hating me.

He stands at the window. It's blurred at the edges of the panes by cobwebs and dirt, but the sunlight makes the grime blaze like silver.

Soon Montverre will be closed. He shuts his eyes and tries to imagine it without magisters and librarians, archivists, visitors, servants. It gives him a sick feeling in the pit of his stomach. Even when he hated the thought of Montverre and Carfax and the *grand jeu,* he would never have wanted it to end like this. So much stone, so much hollow space, standing empty. There's so much of the school he's never seen, kitchens and broom cupboards and pantries, the rarely visited alcoves in the archive. And all of it will crumble slowly. With a jolt he thinks again of Charpentier. *Is* he still here in hiding? What can Léo do if he is?

In his mind's eye Léo sees all the Christians, the Communists and undesirables, the beggars and invalids: a long line, stretching into the distance, the last few turning to stare over their shoulders at him as they're ushered away. Please let Chryseïs not be among them; please let Charpentier not. But that doesn't mean that the others aren't real. He can do something for Charpentier, even if it's only leaving cash in his room and hoping that it'll be found—but there are too many to help, too many to fight for.

He clenches his fists. Nothing is safe. Montverre isn't a sanctuary anymore; maybe it never was. Even the *grand jeu* itself . . . More than anything he wants to feel the joy of it, the exhilaration of making something from nothing. But with those gray faces watching him, with the walls of Montverre crumbling and the Party looking over his shoulder . . .

He *wants* to be Magister Ludi, but here, not in the city. He wants to stand in the Great Hall with the ranks of watchers around him, playing his own Midsummer Game. He wants Claire to be there. He wants to pace the anteroom with her before he goes in, rehearsing the transitions, trying not to betray that he's nervous. He wants to feel the moment of complete attention—like the stillness at the height of a parabola, the instant between up and down—when the game takes off and everything is miraculous, needle-sharp and effortless.

But the Great Hall may never witness another game. And Claire has gone. If he plays a Midsummer Game, it will be in front of the stripped altar of the converted Cathedral, and swollen ranks of Party members who don't know the first thing about the *grand jeu*. Watched by betrayed stained-glass saints and the ghosts of the people who used to worship there. Complicit.

He's a politician. Has learned to be a politician. The scruples are unfamiliar, like a stone in his shoe. He wants to shake them away. He could do some good as Magister Ludi. What did Claire say? *Be a thorn in their sides.* She gave him permission. She wouldn't judge him for compromising. It's only human.

But. But, but, but.

He remembers Carfax asking: "Shouldn't the *grand jeu* make us better people?" and then how he answered his own question. Her own question. *Yes.* What would it mean, to play a *grand jeu* with an atrocity at the heart of it?

He glances down at the desk. Her letter is lying in the sun. Already the words are well known, like a text he's planning to use for a motif. *Write to me, to Claire. Send me a letter telling me how sorry you are, how much you loved Aimé. Then I'll reply. That's all you need to do. One letter, and I'll come back from the dead.* He thought it was all over, then; but if he had sent that letter . . .

He doesn't make a conscious decision. It's his body that takes over, swinging him into the middle of the room as though there is a tiny *terra* between the overloaded bookcases. He turns to face the sky. Then he lifts his arms, pauses, and then dips them into a wide movement, the motion of farewell and welcome that forms the *fermeture*. And as if in response, the cloud that has dipped across the sun slides sideways and the light floods his eyes. It's over. In a moment he'll go to his room and collect overnight things; he'll make his way down the road to the village and the station. And Claire. If she's still there, if an earlier train hasn't swept her away, if . . . But some deep, irrational conviction tells him that he'll find her, one way or another.

He reaches out to the cobweb that's clinging to the windowpane, idly testing its elasticity. The threads are silver, trembling a little in the draft. Instinctively he starts to swipe it away, to get a clearer view of the trees and the slope below; but something makes him pause. It's beautiful. His heart is beating as though he's climbed a mountain.

He turns on his heel and goes out into the dim passage and down the stairs, leaving behind the sun and the web and the *fermeture*.

42

THE RAT

She isn't sick. She knows what sickness is like, and it isn't this. Sickness is waiting, drifting, blank as a gray sea, having nothing to do but surrender. Sickness is vivid pictures in her head, thirst, drenched blankets, a bitter smell. This is different. This is like shedding a skin, feeling the old world stretch and split around her, sore as a burn. She curls around her elbows and knees, conscious of her bones, and tries to breathe slowly. If she closes her eyes, she sees a man falling, over and over. Sometimes the picture blurs and it's a woman with a plait of hair. Then there is a red smash, and the Rat jerks upright, blinking until she is back, seeing only what's visible. It takes a long time before she lies down again, shivering.

The noise comes and goes. If she had been paying attention, she might realize that there is something wrong. In the summer the school subsides to an easy murmur, a long exhalation of relief as the servants' workload eases; but not now, not this year. Now there is more noise than usual, thumping and dragging of trunks, emptying of cupboards, a frantic and mutinous muttering. The bus roars and recedes, back and forth, for days. And then, slowly, a silence descends that isn't the contented quiet of high summer but something thicker, unseasonal. But she isn't listening.

Until one day she wakes and there is no sound at all from anywhere. She sits up, and the shuffle of her limbs reassures her for a moment that she hasn't gone deaf. She gets to her feet. She is shaky; patterns swirl in the dim corners of the room as she walks past. She steps out into the passage and it's like being underwater. She ventures farther out, looking around, until there seems not to be any reason to be afraid. Just this muffled, dead quietness. Rats do not notice the passage of time: but some wary part of her knows it has been longer than an hour since the clock struck. The clock has always been there, the same way her pulse has always been there.

The main corridor is dark. She steps out into the middle of it and looks around, the back of her neck crawling. The windows are shuttered. Thin slats of silver daylight show between the louvers. The corridor is a long stone tunnel, the entrance to a labyrinth. She can't make out the stairs at the far end, only a doorway and more darkness. Carefully she makes her way toward them. Silence. Such silence, not a footstep or voice or the scrape of a broom. She could be the last moving thing left on the face of the Earth. She goes down the staircase.

The door at the foot of the staircase is closed. It is never closed in the day. Her heart jolts into panic, her mouth opening to gasp for air—a trap, a trap—but a second later her fingers are scrabbling at the latch and it yields. She throws the door open. The sky is flat and as pale as a pearl. She breathes deeply; but when she steps into the courtyard, the terror is still there, only dulled. Closed doors, shuttered windows, silence. Solitude. A punishment. *Whatever you do, darling, you must not.* But it's too late. She looks across to the part of the courtyard where the man was splashed on the tiles in the moonlight. Where Mam . . . But nothing is there, not even a shadow. The tiles are jet and nacre under this fish-belly sky.

She crosses the court, keeping close to the walls. In spite of the blinded windows she feels watched. The smooth cloud above her is like a pupilless eye. She unlatches the far door and slips through it into another dark corridor. In front of her is an archway: and beyond it is the Great Hall, full of daylight from the high windows. Another observer might wonder why the servants left these windows unshuttered—laziness, rebellion, or some strange instinct of reverence?—but the Rat only moves forward, searching for something she can't name. The floor, the benches, the walls, everything is in shades of gray and trompe l'oeil. There is no game board. The silver line demarcating the *terra* is dormant. Invisible.

Something crunches underfoot—underpaw—underfoot. A scatter of sharp bits digs into the Rat's soles. Yesterday she would have stiffened at the sound and darted for safety; but now she only blinks and breathes, taking up more space. If this is a trap, she is lost. She sits on a bench. She is the only audience now.

What is on the floor is ash, blown from the chimney, out of the hearth and across the stone by yesterday's wind; no one has swept it up. Tiny fragments of soot and charred wood glint like dark dice. She can feel the fine dust of it on her feet and one gritty piece of charcoal between her toes. Here, under the bench, the ash is thick enough for a footprint to show, just. She twists her heel back and forth until there's a bare arc. A rat would never leave a mark deliberately: but it leaves less of a mark than a man's body on the ground. She stares at the smear, wondering what it means.

"Oh, Jesus, I didn't—thank god, I—what's going on? Where is everyone?"

Simon. His voice echoes in her skull.

She looks up. There's a pain in her gut, as if meeting his eyes is a kind of poison. She wants to be a rat again. She wants him to be only another stomach, or sometimes a warm thing in the cold. She wants not to care that he saw her push a man from a tower. She wants to scratch her human body until it peels away and leaves a little, mindless, scuttling thing. Something that doesn't mind being alone. She has been so good at not being human, and now it has deserted her, when she needs it most.

"Has everyone gone? The library's locked. I don't know . . ." He trails off. He sits on the bench opposite her. "I found some money," he says after a long time. "Maybe we could . . ."

She stares at him.

"Well, a lot of money. Maybe there's a way to get you some papers." He draws his arms into his sides and shivers. "I don't know what's happening. It's creepy."

She spreads her toes and presses. The floor is always cold, even at Midsummer. Cold stone, cold bone.

"You can't stay here. There's no one left. We could . . ." He trails off again.

No one left. It's true. Only the two of them. Two unpeople. Somehow they are here together. She can see a skewed red-hemmed body at the bottom of the Square Tower, a plait of red-gold hair. She can see Simon's hand holding out chocolate, and although they are different pictures they are part of the same thing, the same mysterious ache. That which makes her human. In spite of herself she knows the word for it.

"I'm sorry," he says, stumbling on the words as if he's the one who hasn't spoken for years.

She raises her eyes to his face.

"You saved my life. Thank you."

He waits. He doesn't understand that she is a trap, that she is poison. He holds out his hand, and even though he is too far away to touch she can feel the warmth of his skin, the not-being-alone of his reaching. She has killed someone, and he is thanking her. He is wrong. He is stupid. A rat wouldn't . . . but neither of them is a rat. Not anymore. She opens her mouth, and she can feel more words nudging at her tongue and the back of her palate. *Whatever you do, darling, you must not.* She wants to reach back. She doesn't know how.

"What's your name?" he says.

She gets up. He shifts, but she's not trying to leave. She lines up her toes with the runnel of silver between the flagstones. Then she steps into the *terra*. At the far corner of the space a single feather curls upward, white tinged with gray. Somewhere at her feet is a smudge of blood, so worn and ingrained that no one would know it was there.

She swallows. There is a lump like clay in her throat. She says, "I don't know."

He makes a sudden, repressed movement. His eyes are wide; now he is staring at her as if he has never seen her before. It makes her want to scratch his cheeks and leave red tracks like tears.

"You don't know?"

A pause.

"You spoke! I didn't know you could speak."

She laughs. It bubbles up, alien, her body betraying her. It makes her eyes run wet and her breath rasp. It's like a scab coming away too soon; it hurts and hurts and hurts.

"We can—will you—"

He stops, because she has turned away. She has turned back to the empty hall, and the bare benches. She is hungry and light-headed. *Tomorrow,* she thinks, and the word is so human it makes her eardrums tighten. Tomorrow she will go with him, or not. There will be time later to wonder what she is and what he is. Rats don't think about the future, but people do. There is plenty of time. She feels the rest of her life stretching out, bare and wide as the mountain.

She drops to her knees. Behind her, he draws in his breath. He doesn't come to her. He stays outside the silver line, and that is as it should be. The space is hers now.

She leans forward until her forehead touches the ground. Then she draws an arc in the ash with her arm, twisting farther and farther so that when she gets to her feet again, she is standing in a circle. Her hand and knees are dark with soot.

"What are you doing?"

Then he falls silent. His silence fills the whole hall, as though he is giving her a gift. He nods once. At her feet, the crooked makeshift circle is nothing and everything, a mess and a perfect *grand jeu*. One move. Enough.

They stare at each other. Tomorrow there will be time for other things; but now there is only a circle in ash on the floor, two people, an unmade *fermeture*. The circle holds the *grand jeu* like a shallow cup. It trembles on the brim, incomplete, on the edge of spilling over.

AUTHOR'S NOTE

As many readers will already have guessed, *The Betrayals* was in part inspired by Hermann Hesse's brilliant novel *The Glass Bead Game* (also known as *Magister Ludi*). What I call the *grand jeu* has a lot in common with the Glass Bead Game as Hesse conceived it: an elusive game that combines math, music, and ideas in an atmosphere of meditation, and is overseen by the Magister Ludi (Hesse's pun on the Latin for "schoolmaster"). *The Betrayals* is set in a very different world—and is a very different kind of book—but nonetheless it owes a huge debt to Hesse's masterpiece.

ACKNOWLEDGMENTS

The Betrayals is my second book for adults, and I wrote it in a very different frame of mind from my first: I was at once exhilarated and slightly terrified by the amazing work that was being done to publish and promote *The Binding*, and I sometimes struggled with the pressure of feeling that this as-yet-unwritten book had to measure up. So the first person I want to thank is Sarah Ballard, my brilliant agent and the dedicatee of *The Betrayals*, who kept me sane, grounded, and clear-headed (well, relatively) throughout the process, as well as helping me to nudge the novel toward what it wanted to be. Dedicating a book can seem a bit meretricious if you do it retrospectively, but as I wrote *The Betrayals* I was inspired by knowing that she would be my first reader.

Equally, my editor at The Borough Press, Suzie Dooré, was—as always—fantastic, combining incisive feedback and razor-sharp editorial talent with tact, humor, and across-the-board excellence, and I also owe enormous thanks to Jessica Williams at William Morrow. Between them, they transformed *The Betrayals*. It's never easy to admit that sixty thousand words of your precious second draft won't be missed, but I have to concede that they were right.

There are so many other people who have contributed to *The Betrayals* at The Borough Press, William Morrow, and HarperCollins (on both sides of the Atlantic) that if I tried to thank them all individually I'd run out not only of space but of adjectives. It's a delight and a privilege to be surrounded by people who are so talented, generous, and passionate—thank you all. Massive thanks are also due to everyone at United Agents, and Eleanor Jackson at Dunow, Carlson & Lerner.

And, of course, I should mention my lovely friends and family, who supported, indulged, and motivated me. Again, there are too many of you to list (although Nick should get an honorable mention for having to put up with me *all the time*). *The Betrayals* is in part a book about the joy we find in our playmates, in moments of shared humour or creativity, in seeing and being seen; I'm grateful to (and for) everyone who has helped me encounter that, whether they knew it or not. Thank you.

P.S.

Insights,
Interviews
& More...

Meet Bridget Collins

Symon Hamer

BRIDGET COLLINS is the author of the #1 international bestseller *The Binding*. She has also written seven acclaimed books for young adults and has had two plays produced, one at the Edinburgh Festival Fringe. She trained as an actor at the London Academy of Music and Dramatic Art after reading English at King's College, Cambridge. She currently lives in Kent, United Kingdom. ∾

An Interview with Bridget Collins

A version of this interview was first published by TheNerdDaily.com on May 14, 2021.

Q: What book sparked your love of reading? And if it's different, what book made you want to become an author yourself?

A: Gosh—I've loved reading for longer than I can remember, so it's tricky to know. But I guess the first proper book I remember reading, and loving, was R. L. Stevenson's *The Black Arrow.* It was a very weird choice for a six-year-old— I think I might have heard my dad talking about it, and decided I'd try it . . . ? Anyway, it's Victorian historical fiction, so it's full of Ye Olde English, and I doubt I understood more than three words in ten—but in some ways that set me up for life, because I didn't *mind* that I didn't understand.

I think the book that inspired me to start writing novels (although I've always written poems and short stories, as most kids do, I think) was *Going for Stone,* by Philip Gross. He's mainly known as a poet and you can tell, because it's a ▶

beautifully written, incredibly evocative YA thriller about a kid learning to be a "living statue." There are overtones of a cult as well as drama school, and it's incredibly gripping—but at the same time it has this wonderful metaphor at its heart. It made me feel that I wanted to write a coming-of-age story with the same visceral power. Hmm, you've reminded me to reread it!

Q: *The first line in the description for* The Betrayals *inspires all sorts of intrigue, so naturally, we've got to know . . . "If your life was based on a lie, would you risk it all to tell the truth?" Why or why not?*

A: Um . . . I want to wimp out and say, depends on the lie, depends on the truth! I suppose as a Quaker I ought to say yes, because I do profoundly believe that the truth matters—but I'm not the bravest person ever, and if your entire life was resting on a lie that wasn't that important, would it be worth it? Let's just say that if I were friends with the character in the novel, I'd probably advise them to keep shtum.

Q: The Betrayals *is chock-full of secrets and the arcane arts. Can you tell us a bit about your writing and research process? Or how exactly you keep all the details straight in such an intricately crafted world?*

A: When I'm writing, I try to write as if I'm reading, feeling the excitement as the plot develops, so I do as little planning as I can get away with; bearing in mind, of course, that a lot of the story has already germinated in my head before I start. It's sort of the "stepping stones" model—I know there are some plot points I have to hit for the whole thing to make sense, but I want to enjoy discovering it as I go. Then, once the first draft is complete, I know what the book is meant to be about, and I can go back for a major edit. (And I mean *major*—I added and then subtracted a third of the book in the second and third drafts of *The Betrayals*.) Mostly I can keep track of everything in my head, because if it all makes sense it's easy to remember, but the details have to be written down—and because *The Betrayals* has an ambitious structure and lots of interlinking points of view, I had to ▶

An Interview with Bridget Collins
(continued)

create an Excel spreadsheet to make sure I knew what was happening when! I think my editor was much, much more excited about seeing that than the manuscript itself. . . .

Q: If you could only describe The Betrayals *in five words or less, what would they be?*

A: A game. Not a game.

Q: What's next for you? Any hints you can give readers about what you're working on now?

A: I'm currently writing my next book, which has a working title of *The Silence Factory.* It's about a factory in Victorian England which spins spider silk to produce a fabric that creates silence on one side and crazy-making echoes on the other— it's about silence, obviously, but also about seduction, moral ambiguity, grief, and courage. ∽

Questions for Discussion

1. Consider the chapters from the Rat's point of view. What do you make of this character, and why do you think the story begins and ends with her?

2. How do you interpret the *grand jeu*? What do you think the game entails, and what is its significance?

3. What parallels did you note between the Party and real history? How does Collins portray the gradual rise of oppression and the people who perpetuate it?

4. What was your initial impression of Léo, and how did it evolve as the novel progressed? Did the alternating timelines affect your understanding of him?

5. Consider the attitudes toward gender in this world. How do the female characters in this novel view their womanhood, and how do they treat other women?

6. Léo says of Carfax, "You know, what I hate most about him is the person he makes me into." In what ways do these characters influence and change each other? ▸

Questions for Discussion *(continued)*

7. When Claire and Léo meet in the beginning of the novel, they have just reached the highest and lowest points of their careers, respectively. How do their paths and the sacrifices they have made along the way mirror or foil each other?

8. How does ambition push the characters to their best or worst moments? Do you think competition is a positive or negative motivator?

9. Did you anticipate Claire's secret? How did this revelation alter your understanding of her character?

10. What do you make of the title of this novel? Which betrayals do you think it refers to? ∽

More by Bridget Collins

THE BINDING

Imagine you could erase grief.
Imagine you could remove pain.
Imagine you could hide the darkest,
most horrifying secret.
Forever.

Young Emmett Farmer is working in the fields when a strange letter arrives summoning him away from his family. He is to begin an apprenticeship as a bookbinder—a vocation that arouses fear, superstition, and prejudice among their small community, but one neither he nor his parents can afford to refuse.

For as long as he can recall, Emmett has been drawn to books, even though they are strictly forbidden. Bookbinding is a sacred calling, Seredith informs her new apprentice, and he is a binder born. Under the old woman's watchful eye, Emmett learns to handcraft the elegant leather-bound volumes. Within each one they will capture something unique and extraordinary: a memory. If there's something you want to forget, a binder can help. If there's something you need to erase, they can assist. Within the pages of the books they create, secrets are concealed and the past is locked away. In a vault under his mentor's ▶

More by Bridget Collins (continued)

workshop rows upon rows of books are meticulously stored.

But while Seredith is an artisan, there are others of their kind, avaricious and amoral tradesmen who use their talents for dark ends—and just as Emmett begins to settle into his new circumstances, he makes an astonishing discovery: one of the books has his name on it. Soon, everything he thought he understood about his life will be dramatically rewritten.

An unforgettable novel of enchantment, mystery, memory, and forbidden love, *The Binding* is a beautiful homage to the allure and life-changing power of books—and a reminder to us all that knowledge can be its own kind of magic.

"*The Binding* succeeds in creating
the magic it proposes."
—*New York Times Book Review*,
Editors' Choice

"A true epic in every sense of the word."
—*Cosmopolitan*

"A rich, gothic entertainment that
explores what books have trapped
inside them and reminds us of the
power of storytelling. Spellbinding."
—Tracy Chevalier

Discover great authors, exclusive offers, and more at hc.com.